Aphrodite Unbound

An Olympus Inc. Romance

Kate Healey

Contents

Content Description

While this book is primarily a romantic comedy with a guaranteed happy ending, there is some content you should be aware of. *Aphrodite Unbound* contains examples and discussion of ableism, racism, internalized ableism, violent stalking, violence, and sexual harassment in the workplace.

Chapter One

Aphrodite Urania wondered if someone could die from being asked enough boring questions.

To be fair, if that were true, she'd have been dead a long time ago, what with the endless repetitions of "What's your exercise routine?" and "What's your diet?" and "Do you *really* eat fries?" You could only hear "Who are you wearing?" so many times before your brain threatened to dribble out your ears.

It was tempting to make things up, just to add a little excitement to the world, and she'd done that a few times when she was younger. But Aphrodite was coming up on ten years of modeling, which practically made her a veteran, and she was supposed to be beyond all those impulsive tricks now.

She was sitting at a long, red-cloth covered table, three seats down from the people the reporters *should* have been focusing on. Dana Sellen and Marjorie Qu were the actual stars of *A Light in Dark Places*, the movie the press conference was promoting. Aphrodite herself had only been in three scenes—barely more than a cameo.

"I have a question for Aphrodite," the next reporter began, and she flicked him a smile. "Do you wish the role of Doctor Greenblade had given you more exciting costumes, like your recent Met Gala look?"

"No," Aphrodite said, and waited just long enough to see the panic rise in his eyes before she relented. "I was playing a scientist, and that meant practical shoes and a lab coat. But the role was already exciting, because I got to support these women kicking ass!" She gestured at Dana and Marjorie.

"Didn't you want to play a superhero yourself?" the reporter pressed.

"I think I was really lucky to get any role in this movie," Aphrodite said, with total honesty. She wasn't an actor. The camera loved her, obviously, and she could hit a mark and hold a pose like nobody's business, but they'd really had to work with her to get the lines to come out right, and Marjorie and Dana had been so patient through all the takes, nice to her every single time she'd screwed it up. "A female-focused superhero film is so rare. It was an honor to be included at all."

The next question was for Marjorie ("How was this movie different from shooting an ordinary martial arts film?"), and the question after that was for Juan Lopez ("What was it like being the only major male role?") and Aphrodite relaxed a little, her shoulders settling against the chair back. She was only at this conference because she had a shoot in LA scheduled for tomorrow, and her film agent had arranged her coming out a day early, to the delight of the film's press team. The real actors had to do a lot more press, traveling to Europe and Asia to answer questions there. Aphrodite's only job after this was turning up at the premiere in three weeks, wearing a fabulous dress.

Now that was a job she could do.

"This is for Aphrodite," the next reporter said.

Aphrodite sucked back a sigh and looked attentive.

"Do you have any comment on Harmonia Amazon?" asked a reporter in a purple blazer, with a really unfortunate tie.

Aphrodite blinked. She knew Harmonia a little—they'd walked some of the same Milan and Paris shows last year. Nice girl, good runway walk. "What kind of comment?"

The reporter's smile sharpened, and Aphrodite braced for it, whatever it was. "Any comment on her relationship with Ares Irontosser?"

Oh, it was about her ex. Of course. "Why would I have a comment?" Aphrodite said, widening her eyes. "Whatever—or whoever—Ares does isn't my business." Damn, she hadn't meant that to sound like a crack at Harmonia. "We've been over for six months," she continued. "When are you guys going to stop asking me about him?"

The press stirred, and Aphrodite replayed what she'd just said, hearing the genuine annoyance leaking into her voice. Oh, no. You couldn't be honest with the press. They sensed weakness and tore you apart.

"You haven't been seen with anyone else in that six months," the reporter said, which wasn't even a *question*, it was just a statement about her love life which, however true, was completely unwarranted, and Aphrodite was about one second away from losing her shit.

Dana leaned forward and said, "Let's move on," and Aphrodite just loved her *so much*. Purple Blazer subsided and started tapping at his phone.

They got more questions about the movie, thank goodness, and then a blonde with a perky ponytail at the back of the room said, "I have a follow-up for Aphrodite," and Aphrodite fixed a smile on her face and thought *I bet you do.*

"Harmonia is the seventh model or actress Ares has been linked with since you two last broke up," the reporter said, trying for the sympathetic angle, all big eyes and soothing voice. "Are you worried he's moved on forever?"

"*Wow*," Marjorie said, her tone deeply unimpressed, and Juan was saying something about needing to end the conference early, but Aphrodite heard a roaring like a rising wave as her blood pounded in her ears, and she leaned forward, tossing her red-gold hair back in the way she'd perfected ten years ago, the new girl on the block and already booking covers. She curled her mouth into her wide, generous smile, the one that promised *everything*, and every reporter in the room was looking at her, paying attention to her, and they would *listen* to what she said next.

"One, *we* didn't break up. *I* dumped *him*," she said sweetly, lifting a perfect finger with a perfect French-tipped nail. She raised another finger. "Two, I sincerely *hope* Ares has moved on forever, because I definitely have. And third—" shit, shit, she needed a third "—third, actually, I *am* seeing someone, and have been for a while."

The flashbulbs went off. Aphrodite didn't blink. She held her smile and turned slightly to the right, faking a shy retreat and flashing them one of her famous dimples in the process. The reporters were shouting questions over top of each other, a cacophonous chorus in which the only recognizable words were her name and "Who?"

Aphrodite held up one hand and waited for silence.

When she got it, she called on the reporter who was currently annoying her the least. "Selene."

"Who are you seeing?" Selene asked.

Aphrodite smiled coyly. "That would be telling."

More flashbulbs; more shouting. Dana was clearly caught between amusement and frustration at how quickly the room's attention had shifted from the film.

"Is it Juan?" someone shouted.

Juan cleared his throat and spoke into his microphone. "I wish," he drawled, and there was an appreciative burst of laughter.

Aphrodite laughed along with them. "I mean, no lie, Juan is a babe, but it's no one from work," she said. "The person I've been dating has a real life. They're not part of all this." She swept her hand around the room, summing up the film stars and paparazzi. "That's why we've been keeping it quiet. It's really different when, you know, you're not dating a string of people to keep your name in the news." There, that was a good reason for nobody to know, and also, fuck Ares. "Now, I think that's enough questions about my love life, don't you?"

The reporters, predictably, did not agree, but Aphrodite let herself look increasingly annoyed and said, "Let's move on from that," a few times, until they gave up and finally went back to asking Dana about whether it had been hard to be both an actor and a director.

When the conference was over, Aphrodite wandered over to Dana in the green room. "Hey, so, sorry about the distraction," she said.

Dana smiled at her. "I should be thanking you," she said. "The extra publicity certainly won't hurt."

"But it wasn't supposed to be about me. I'm just lucky I got to be in the movie."

Dana gratefully took a bottle of water from her assistant and downed half of it, then shook her head. "Aphrodite, you're an amazing PR pull. *We're* lucky to have you *in* the movie. And now the press are going to be writing about this mystery person you're seeing, so that's even more free publicity." She sighed. "We could definitely use it. The studio has reneged on a lot of the marketing budget."

"Really?"

"Yes," Dana said. "Assholes." She said it without rancor, just an annoying fact of life, as if it wasn't even worth getting mad about.

"But it's a really fun movie!"

"Well, I agree," Dana said. "But it's also a nearly all-female cast, and the main characters are middle-aged female superheroes who kiss in the final shot. We're lucky it got made at all, and the studio still thinks majority-female casts are a risk. Which is hilarious, because how on earth are they ever going to know unless they put the same amount of money into marketing as they do for their majority-male casts?" She shook her head. "Sorry. Old rant. But yes, you did us a favor today." She smiled at Aphrodite. "And I'm glad you've found something real. Worth holding onto, in this business."

"Oh, sure," Aphrodite said awkwardly.

"It's a shame you can't bring them to the premiere," Dana continued. "Now, *that* would be a publicity coup."

"What if I could?" Aphrodite said.

Dana sat up straight.

"I'd have to talk about it with them first," Aphrodite said quickly. "But if they're okay with going public, would that be good for the movie?"

"Yes," Dana said immediately. "We could spin that. Aphrodite, that would be really, *really* helpful." She blew out a breath. "But only if they're okay with it, of course. That kind of attention is a lot to deal with."

Aphrodite, who had been dealing with *that kind of attention* since she was sixteen, smiled widely. "I'll talk to them," she promised, and left a grateful Dana as she headed out the venue back door and directly to the car pulled up for her outside. Lina, her driver, held the door open.

There were a few enterprising photographers haunting the door, but Aphrodite waved and walked through them without breaking her stride.

Aphrodite's manager was sitting in the back seat. Thea was short, round, and dark, and looked like she'd be comfortable with a kid on one hip and a mixing bowl full of something sweet on the other. In fact, she was a sharp-eyed shark in an expensive suit, and Aphrodite loved her a lot.

Thea looked up from her phone as Aphrodite slid into the seat beside her and grinned. "Nice work, kid," she said.

Aphrodite preened. "Who are you calling a kid?"

"I'll stop when you catch up to me," Thea said. "You've got a couple decades to go. So, amazing news: you're trending everywhere. A lot of people want to find this mystery man."

"I didn't say it was a man," Aphrodite protested.

"No, and there's a sizable contingent pointing that out," Thea assured her. "So it's not a man?"

Aphrodite blinked at her. "What?"

"This person you've been seeing. Lady? Themfriend?"

Wow, she must have been *good* in there, if even Thea had believed her. Maybe she was more of an actor than she thought. Lina was making eye contact with her in the back mirror. She, of course, knew that she hadn't been driving Aphrodite to any dates lately.

"I made it up," Aphrodite said.

Thea put her phone down. "You made it up."

"Sure," Aphrodite said. "I'm sick of people asking. I thought that might shut them up."

"Okay," Thea said, and took a deep breath. "Well, okay, so in a few weeks you let slip that it didn't work out and you wish them all the best, and the press drive themselves nuts trying to figure it out in one last extinction burst, and then it's not a thing anymore. That works. No problem."

"Oh, no, I have to find someone now," Aphrodite explained. "I told Dana I'd bring them to the premiere, for the publicity."

"Of course you did," Thea said, taking another deep breath. "Hm. Actually, that's not dumb."

"Thank you."

Thea picked up her phone. "I've got a friend who sometimes arranges 'girlfriends' for her male clients who don't want to be out yet. I'll see if she can put something together for you."

Aphrodite frowned. "Aren't those people in it for the fame?"

"Usually there's money involved too, but yeah, they're C- or D-listers at the same agency who need the exposure."

"Then that won't work. It has to be someone with a real job. I told the press it was a real person."

Thea rubbed the spot between her eyes. "Aphrodite, I love you like an adopted kid sister, but you are stressing me the fuck out right now. Do you even *know* anyone with a real job?"

"Sure," Aphrodite said. She knew lots of people who worked for a living, but that wasn't what Thea meant. No one connected with her modeling career, so no photographers, stylists, make-up artists, designers, no one involved in film or TV, no people famous-for-being-famous, no one in an entourage, and absolutely, definitely no celebrity sportspeople.

Hm. When she thought about it, that really was most of the people she knew. But it wasn't *all* of them.

"I know two people," she said triumphantly. "I know an artist and a lawyer. And we're doing lunch on Sunday. They'll help me out."

Thea muttered something to herself, but Aphrodite relaxed back against the smooth leather. Persephone and Hecate would help her find a good, normal person to take to the premiere, she'd get a lot of publicity for Dana's movie, and, bonus, Ares would be totally fucking furious.

Problem solved.

***

Heph Smith hesitated before he got out of the car.

"You okay, man?" his taxi driver asked.

"I'm fine," Heph said. "Just bracing myself. Mothers' Day."

The driver laughed. "My mom lives down south. I sent flowers."

"Smart man," Heph said, and opened his door. He maneuvered his crutches out with minimal effort, and held onto them with one hand, then hoisted himself out of the car. His leg twinged, but it wasn't too bad.

"Need a hand?" the driver asked.

"No, I've got it," Heph said. "Have a good day."

"You too, man." The taxi pulled away from the curb, and Heph made a mental note to remember the company he'd booked through. The driver had asked instead of assuming, and then taken him at his word. That was unfortunately rare enough to be worth remembering.

The garden gate had been left open for him. He made his way up the gently sloping path around the side of the house.

Nomi and Thetis Smith-Waters had bought the sprawling ranch-style house a few months after Heph's adoption. He didn't have any memories of the earlier two-story house, but his sisters did. Once, when he was

9

fifteen and in the throes of teenage resentment and misplaced guilt, he'd accused his mothers of abandoning his sisters' childhood home just to accommodate his disability.

Thetis had blinked at him. "Well, that contributed," she'd said. "But it was also the bathrooms."

"And the neighbors," Nomi added. "They were incredible snobs."

"Remember when that woman from the Homeowner's Association came round with a ruler to measure the grass?"

"Was she the same one who called in a noise complaint because Heph was crying?"

"No, that was the one who couldn't work out which one of us she should ask to bake for the park beautification fundraiser."

"Oh, and you told her we weren't the baking kind of lesbians!" Nomi smiled fondly at her wife. "What a terrible lie."

"Well, *I'm* not the baking kind of lesbian," Thetis said, undeterred. "So *we* weren't, plural." She'd kissed Nomi on the nose, and Heph had gotten out of there before they could get any more affectionate, muttering to himself as he went.

It had often been hard to maintain surliness in the face of his mothers' tendency to turn complaints into another celebration of how much they loved each other and their children, but as a teenager, Heph had given it the old college try.

Now a grown man, even if no one else in his family seemed ready to believe it, he walked past the bold ranks of tulips, followed the turn of the path around the house, and instantly received the undivided attention of every other member of the Smith-Waters clan.

Gathered around the patio table, they didn't look like many people's conception of a family. Thetis was white, little and fierce, her grey hair cut in a pixie cut and her eyes huge behind her round glasses. The political cartoonists liked to make her look even more owlish, but they didn't need to exaggerate much. Nomi's racial background was lost in the tangled, secretive bureaucracy that had been her own blind adoption, but her features hinted at Black, Asian and probably European ancestry. She was also short, but generously proportioned, with wide hips and a full stomach.

Sitting next to them—and towering over them—was Heph's oldest sister, Mellie, tall, thin and pale, with long, dark hair, high cheekbones, and huge, dark eyes that scanned Heph from his crutch tips to the hair he abruptly realized he hadn't cut in a while. Mellie had once been a model, and she could say a lot with a look.

Opposite Mellie was Narnie, the middle sister, dark-skinned, sturdy, and energetic. She was sporting athleisure wear and a buzz cut, and sitting beside her was his youngest sister Aoide, deceptively waif-like in her floating linen dress, her dyed-blonde hair drifting around her tanned brown face.

"Hi," Heph said, and joined them at the table. The head and foot had been left clear, in case it was a chair day for him, but he lowered himself into the empty spot beside Aoide and leaned his crutches against the end instead. "Happy Mothers' Day."

"And to you!" Nomi said, and put a plate of food in front of him. Heph addressed himself to it. Only a fool would do anything but give Nomi's cooking his undivided attention.

Besides, no one could ask him questions if he kept his mouth full. It was what came after lunch that posed the danger.

The Smith-Waters kids automatically fell into their chore roles in the kitchen. Mellie washed. Narnie and Aoide dried and put away. Heph got the tasks he could do sitting at the kitchen island; portioning out the leftovers into Nomi's huge collection of containers for one of the others to throw in the fridge, and on special occasions like today, polishing and sorting the silverware back into its velvet-lined carrying case.

Which meant, as his sisters finished their jobs, stopped flying around the kitchen, and prepared for their actual kitchen task, "interrogating Heph about his life," he was still trapped at the island, rubbing industriously at cake forks.

Mellie took down her practical ponytail and snapped the hairband back onto her wrist, shaking her hair out in a move Heph recognized as a declaration of war. "So," she said. "How's work going?" Mellie always started with work.

"Fine," Heph said, rubbing at a tarnish spot on a butter knife.

Mellie's eyebrows signaled polite disbelief. "Really. No problems with your most important client?"

Heph's most important client was Olympus Inc, his first and only real employer before he'd gone into business for himself. He'd restructured a lot of their network before he left, and had also coded most of the security measures. When Olympus needed a contractor, Vulcan Consulting was the obvious choice.

The problem was that recent events had complicated the obviousness of that choice. Zeus Kronion, the CEO of Olympus Inc, had assaulted an intern—and his brother's girlfriend—in his office to try to keep secret the evidence of a child he'd had with a mistress. Not coincidentally, he was also currently going through a bitter and very expensive divorce. His brother Hades, who was also the CFO and head of the Finance department, had responded to Zeus's misdeeds by pointedly taking an immediate leave of absence.

As a result, Zeus Kronion wasn't exactly on top of his game at work. In fact, for the first time since he'd taken over Olympus, the business was running at a loss.

"There might be a few issues with the boss," Heph conceded.

Heph had played a small part in Zeus's self-inflicted downfall. He'd actually witnessed the final moments of the horror show in Zeus's office, and had zero regrets about his actions before and afterwards. But he thought it was safe to assume that when he finished his current Olympus Inc. contract, that might be the last one for a long time, perhaps ever.

It helped that the Olympus IT department didn't care about what part he'd played in Zeus's professional and personal difficulties. They wanted Heph to stay on call, with an urgency that was as touching as it was concerning. But hiring Heph for another quarter would require the approval of a man who was both generally vindictive and personally pissed at him.

It wasn't going to happen.

And the smaller clients he currently scheduled *around* his work for Olympus weren't going to be able to fill the gaps.

He thought about all this in barely a second of real time, but that was more than enough space for Mellie to seize the opportunity.

"You know," she said conversationally. "I do events for some pretty big organizations. I could put a few feelers out. See who could find some work for my genius baby brother."

"I'm okay," Heph said automatically.

Narnie put the last wineglass in the cabinet, dropped into the stool beside him, and poked his shoulder.

"Ow," Heph said, for form's sake.

"Let your family help you," Narnie told him.

"I already said work was fine," Heph said, and recognized his error immediately.

"Good," Narnie said, white teeth gleaming in her dark face. "Then you have time to date. There's this lovely new technician at the lab, just moved to the city, doesn't know anyone, could really use a local guide."

Heph grunted, and sought for distraction. "How's the wedding planning going, Aoide?" he asked.

"Oh, nearly done," his youngest sister said cheerfully, from where she was nesting serving bowls. "Mellie's dealing with the vendors, and Narnie's doing the seating chart."

"See?" Mellie said. "Aoide lets us help, and she gets a beautiful wedding at a great price."

"There's one problem with this seating chart," Narnie said. "It's got an empty space next to your name."

"Leave him alone," Aoide said, but not very firmly. She joined them at the kitchen island, sitting on Heph's other side. "Heph's trying to be a self-made man."

"No such thing," Mellie said, snorting. "Aoide, does your fiancée's workplace need an IT consultant?"

"No one's an island," Narnie agreed. "Heph, I'll tell Deborah you'll text her?"

"I'm going to go *live* on an island," Heph said, and finished polishing the last spoon. He slotted it into its place with much more force than the task required. "A quiet, wind-wracked island, where I can pursue my life in *total solitude* without my *nosy, interfering sisters*."

A silence fell over the kitchen, unusual enough that he looked up to catch Mellie and Narnie exchanging significant looks, and Aoide glaring at both of them.

"I'm sorry, Heph," Mellie said.

"I'm sorry," Narnie echoed. "You know we love you, right?"

Heph sighed. "Yes," he said. "I love you too."

"But still," Aoide said, and laid her hand gently on his arm. "We worry about you."

He blinked at her, blindsided by the flanking maneuver. Aoide was the gentle one, the baby of the family until Heph had turned up. By the time he was old enough to have memories, Mellie had already been out of the house, pursuing her glamorous first career, so that for a while he'd seen more of her on magazine covers and in fashion news highlights than he had in person. Living with Narnie he mostly remembered as being lovingly ushered out of her room so that she could study for her many AP courses or listen to death metal undisturbed by her fast-crawling little brother.

But Aoide was only seven years older than he was, and she'd been delighted to have a baby brother to play with and sing to. One of his earliest memories was of Aiode singing him to sleep in her soft, lilting alto. In the memory, his leg hurt, but Aoide's voice soothed the pain away, until he could rest. It had felt like a miracle.

Adult Heph knew the miracle had more likely been the baby-safe painkillers he would have been given with dessert, but his child's memory was firm that Aoide's song had done the trick.

"Okay," he said, and braced his hands on the edge of the breakfast island. His spine was complaining about staying sitting too long in one place. He twisted to the left, to the point where there was a pleasant tug on the muscle, and stayed there for a moment before returning to base. "I get that you want to help me. I know that you want me to succeed in business and in romance, and I share those goals." He nodded at Mellie and Narnie in turn. "I know that you love me and want me to be happy. What can I do to assure you that I'm fine? And also, and this is the important part, convince you that I can handle it myself?"

Mellie and Narnie exchanged significant glances again, and then looked to Aoide.

"Bring a date to my wedding," she said promptly. "Or secure a new big contract. And we promise we won't say anything about anything, until next Mother's Day."

Heph suspected collusion. It stung more than he'd expected.

"I accept those terms," he said, a little more sharply than he meant to, and then had a brainwave. "And if I do *both*, you'll concede that I am an adult in control of my own life, and not offer help or advice unless I ask for it, ever again."

Mellie opened her mouth. Heph raised a finger. "I mean it," he said. "I'm the youngest, but I'm also twenty-five, and this is getting old. That's my half of the bargain."

"That's fair," Aoide said, and glared at her older sisters until Mellie nodded.

"All right," Narnie said. "A wedding date *and* a substantial new contract, in four weeks. If you can do both, I'll butt out forever."

"Excellent," Heph said, and held his hand out for a four-way handshake that rapidly got complicated. He sighed. "You realize that this is deeply weird, right? I don't think normal siblings shake on this stuff."

"Oh, it's totally weird," Mellie said. "It's probably our abandonment trauma."

"Speak for yourself," Narnie said, and the Committee to Interfere with Heph dissolved into the familiar discussion about adoptee trauma and how much it was exacerbated by trans-racial adoption, and whose therapist had said the most insightful thing recently.

Nomi came in for the last five minutes of the discussion, to contribute some thoughts from her own therapist and also to make sure that no one had put anything away in the wrong place. As she and Mellie entered into perhaps their dozenth argument about whether it was better to store wineglasses stem up or stem down, Aoide tapped Heph's shoulder.

"Sorry," she said, her voice pitched perfectly to reach his ears, and his alone.

"Did you talk them down from something worse?" Heph asked, and gave an exaggerated shudder when she nodded. "Then don't worry about it."

"Besides, it's going to be worth it when you can remind Mellie she can't butt in anymore," Aoide said encouragingly.

Heph blinked at her. Did she actually think he was going to pull this off?

She beamed at him, her face shining with the force of her faith in him.

"Sure," Heph said weakly. "It's all going to be worth it."

***

"Stop laughing," Aphrodite said, pouting winsomely.

The pout didn't work. Hecate kept cackling, her laughter only increasing when Aphrodite fished a strawberry out of her champagne and tossed it at her.

Persephone looked sympathetic, because Persephone was a nice person. Hecate was laughing because she was a bitch, but she was a good bitch, so Aphrodite knew she'd help.

"You have to help me," Aphrodite said. "You're my only normal friends."

Hecate stopped laughing long enough to roll her eyes. "Wow, thanks."

"You know what I mean! You're a lawyer and Persephone's a designer. You're both, like, real people."

Hecate squinted at her. "So all your celebrity friends are fake people?"

"Yes?" Aphrodite said. "Obviously? I mean they're probably real people too, but only underneath the fake part."

Hecate and Persephone exchanged glances.

"Do you think of yourself as a fake person?" Persephone asked hesitantly.

"Sure. Not literally—my tits are real—but my, like, you know, the way I am with people."

"The persona?" Hecate asked.

Aphrodite snapped her fingers. "That guy. The Aphrodite persona is fake. She has to be, because no one real could take all the attention."

"Um," Persephone said. "I'm not a mental health professional, but talking about yourself like this might be one of those things to bring up with your therapist."

Aphrodite rolled her eyes. "She's brought it up."

"And?"

"And I told her that we can work on it when I stop modelling. Right now, it's a useful coping mechanism." She beamed at them. "So! You guys need to find me a real person who's willing to fake it with me."

"Wow, when you put it like that, who could resist?" Hecate said.

Aphrodite sat back and pouted some more. She was, in fact, hard to resist, and she knew it, but it was beginning to occur to her that this might not be as easy as she'd thought.

"I could ask Don," Persephone said hesitantly.

Aphrodite perked up. "Don Kronion? Sure, that guy's hot. Shoulders for days."

"You slept with his brother," Hecate pointed out.

"Oh, like that'd be the first time I've slept with brothers," Aphrodite said, and then reconsidered. Zeus Kronion, she knew from bitter experience, was very bad news. Persephone was crazy in love with his older brother Hades, who looked like he'd been born with a stick up his ass, but was secretly a total sweetie. Don might be another good guy, or he could fall closer to the Zeus side of the spectrum, and Aphrodite wasn't going to burn herself on that particular fire again.

"I don't mean that I would ask Don if he wanted to be your fake boyfriend," Persephone said, her cheeks flushing. "I meant that he knows a lot of people, and might know someone who would want to fake-date Aphrodite."

"I've got to think that anyone would want to be Aphrodite's fake partner," Hecate pointed.

Aphrodite preened, and then looked at Hecate with dawning hope. "Wait, would you—"

For a moment, Hecate looked tempted, then she shook her head. "No, I'm seeing someone."

"What?" Persephone demanded. "Who?"

"I'm not really *seeing* them, it's more of a friends-with-benefits arrangement."

"I repeat, who?"

"I think we need to focus on Aphrodite's problem right now," Hecate said smoothly. "Which is that finding willing candidates won't be an issue. The problem will be finding people who won't want to go further than Aphrodite does, who are willing to keep up a lie *and* can keep their mouths shut afterwards."

"I'm willing to go pretty far," Aphrodite said, mostly to make Persephone blush again, but also because it *had* been six months.

"That'll help," Hecate conceded. "But other than that... Essentially, you want to invite the press into the private life of some ordinary person, which is going to be absolute hell, and then, of course, you're going to publicly dump them."

"They can dump me," Aphrodite said, then frowned. That would make Ares way too happy. "Or we can have a mutual break up. A conscious uncoupling."

Hecate was shaking her head. "No one will believe that, Aphrodite."

"Well, some people might," Persephone said, more diplomatically. "But Aphrodite, the publicity part is a big deal. It's not just the press. The social media attention can be a lot if you're not used to it."

Aphrodite looked at her doubtfully. Persephone had spent some time in the public eye—she wasn't exactly a socialite, but her horrible mom was rich and did a lot of charity events, so she'd showed up on the socials every now and then. Persephone's biggest brush with outright fame had been connected with Aphrodite herself, during that last explosive break-up with Ares.

Aphrodite shuddered, remembering. Ares had been bitching about the food and she'd gone off to eat everything on Persephone's tray, just to show him. And then he'd followed her, and they'd fought, like they always did, only this time Persephone had stepped between them and tried to calm the situation down.

And Ares had shoved her out of the way.

Aphrodite remembered every second of it. The hurt shock on Persephone's face as she fell, the sound of her heavy glass platter cracking into shards. She was a good person who'd tried to do a good thing, and Ares had hurt her. Not exactly on purpose, but he'd done it.

The worst part was that he just hadn't cared. Persephone had been in his way, so he'd moved her, with neither malice nor regret. Aphrodite had seen it in his face. She'd thought, with startling clarity, *This is not a good man*.

And then she'd broken up with him, loudly and irrevocably, while the phone cameras flashed and everyone at the party gossiped about the latest Aphrodite/Ares break up, none of them believing what Aphrodite had known: It was the latest and the last.

No wonder Persephone thought being in her orbit would be hell. Her own experience of it had been.

Honestly, Persephone and Hecate were very cool about coming over to Aphrodite's place, or inviting her to theirs whenever they hung out. They'd tried cafes a couple of times, but if the press didn't find them, Aphrodite's fans inevitably did. If she shoved her hair into a ball cap and wore jeans and big sunglasses, she was relatively anonymous moving around the city, but she couldn't sit anywhere longer than twenty minutes before *someone* noticed.

So they were having their "Bad Moms Mother's Day" lunch at Aphrodite's place.

Aphrodite hadn't really wanted to buy a penthouse at first, but she'd come around. When she was a kid, she'd wanted to live in the Plaza Hotel, like Eloise, but that was way too many strangers. An apartment building with a 24-hour concierge was a close second. If she wanted one roast beef bone, one raisin, and seven spoons right now, she'd get them.

Of course, she wouldn't ask for them, because what was charming in a precocious fictional six-year-old was diva behavior in a 26-year-old real life supermodel, but she liked knowing she could *get* them. She could afford anything she wanted, now. She owned this apartment and no one could take it from her.

Not this time.

"Hey," she said, reminded of things she could afford. She poked Persephone with her bare toe. "When are you going to paint me a mural?"

"I'm actually booked out," Persephone admitted. "After I finished Hera's wall, she threw a look-at-my-new-mural party and I got twelve commissions on the spot. I have a waiting list."

"Ooh," Hecate said. "Career change?"

"No," Persephone said. "I still want to do design. Besides, this mural thing is a trend, that's all. It'll die down, and then there goes my market. I'm going to finish my internship after my deferment."

Aphrodite easily translated that as "After Zeus is out of Olympus." She didn't want to talk about Zeus Kronion, or his soon-to-be ex-wife, who she had complicated feelings about. "Put me on the waiting list," she said.

"Sure!" Persephone said, and pulled out her ever-present sketchbook. "Any ideas of what you want?"

"Pink roses," Aphrodite said. "I'm basic."

"You're *classic*," Persephone said loyally.

"Sure," Aphrodite said. "Hey, you girls want to make this a sleepover? Pancakes and mimosas in the morning?"

"I have work tomorrow," Hecate said primly. "And a prior engagement tonight."

"With this person you're seeing?" Persephone said, sitting upright.

"Maybe," Hecate said, shooting Aphrodite a panicked look.

Aphrodite took pity on her. "What about you, babe?" she asked Persephone.

Persephone shook her head. "Hades is expecting me," she said, and grinned. "We're moving in together."

"*What*?" Aphrodite demanded.

Hecate, who'd clearly heard the news already, smiled too. "Tell her how you're doing it."

"Well, I was worried, because obviously Hades earns a lot more than me, and I didn't want to contribute unequally, or end up in a position where he owned the house and I didn't," Persephone said. "I mean, I think we're it for each other, but lots of people have thought that, and then broken up, you know?"

Once again, the specter of Hera and Zeus's dramatic parting hovered over the party. "So what's the plan?" Aphrodite asked, in an effort to exorcise it.

"We're buying together, with me contributing a smaller percentage of the initial deposit," Persephone said. "And then I'm going to pay proportionally more of the mortgage, until we both have a fifty percent interest in the house. But even if we broke up the day after we closed the sale, I'd still have a financial interest in the home, and the security that comes with it." She smiled, proud of herself and her choices. "I mean, I couldn't afford a big mortgage, so it's a small place, and it's a bit run down, and the commute to Olympus is a lot longer, but Hades said he won't mind that."

Aphrodite was privately of the opinion that if Persephone had asked Hades to move to a cave in the middle of a desert, he wouldn't have minded that, either. "Well, let me know if you ever need cash," she said. "If you need anything over a hundred thousand it'll only take a couple of weeks to free up some investments."

Persephone and Aphrodite were staring at her.

"What?" Aphrodite said. "I'm bad with words, not numbers. My portfolio's solid."

"No, it's the part where you'd just *give* it to me," Persephone said. "That's just...you're so generous, Aphrodite."

Aphrodite shrugged uncomfortably. "I make a lot of money for looking pretty," she said. "I don't mind sharing it with people I like."

"I'll be your fake lover for a hundred grand," Hecate said. Unfortunately, she still clearly didn't mean it, but the joke did remind Persephone that Hecate had a real lover she wasn't telling them about, and she pounced immediately.

Aphrodite watched them wrangle and sipped her champagne, and when they said it was time to go, she didn't plead for them both to stay as they went out into the city to meet their special someones, leaving her alone in her apartment. That wouldn't be fair, and she was trying to be fair.

It wasn't fair to expect them to solve the problem of finding a normal person who'd be her fake sweetheart, either.

She was going to have to do that herself.

Chapter Two

"I've been asked by my employer to thank you for your assistance today," Ms. Eule said.

Heph nodded awkwardly. Minerva Eule was Hera Kronion's lawyer. She was brutally efficient, frighteningly intelligent, and a little bit younger than his moms, which didn't stop Heph from having a mild crush on her. He had a lot of respect for competence, which was what had got him to Eule and Spindle first thing in the morning.

Heph had some work to do at Olympus after this, and the delay meant he'd be arriving at the same time as everyone else, with all the added difficulty that meant for his mobility. But being able to impress—or at least not disappoint—Minerva Eule meant that it was worth the inconvenience.

"Now, can we go over your actions of the morning in question? Hades Kronion requested your assistance in checking the provenance of some emails sent to Ms. Aphrodite Urania, is that correct?"

"Yes."

"And what happened after that?" Ms. Eule asked.

"I told him that I wouldn't do that until I could confirm the recipient had consented," Heph said.

"Very sensible," Ms. Eule said, and led Heph through a minutely detailed account of the rest of that bizarre morning that had led him to Zeus's office, and then back down to his own, safe den. And there, a bruised and shaken Hades and Persephone had learned the final truth about Zeus Kronion—that he'd impersonated his wife and threatened his ex-mistresses in her name. The emails were one of the ugliest things Heph had seen, and his career had led him to some fairly disgusting corners of the internet. It wasn't so much the content of the emails, although they were bad, but the absolute betrayal they signified.

"Can you confirm that Zeus Kronion wrote them?" Ms. Eule asked, and Heph grimaced.

"No," he said. "I can confirm that they were sent from the network station in his office, and that someone signed in to that station with his credentials. I can't guarantee that he was the one doing the typing."

"In your professional opinion, what is the likelihood of anyone else writing those emails?"

"It's not very likely at all," Heph said.

Ms. Eule made a note on her tablet and clicked the recorder off. "Thank you for your time, Mr. Smith," she said, and got to her feet. "Would you be amenable to a further interview, if it should prove necessary?"

Heph felt as if a very busy raccoon had rummaged around in his brain, picking out the tidbits it wanted, and rearranging everything else. He couldn't think of what else she might need from him. "Sure," he said, and backed his chair away from the table. Ms. Eule opened the door for him and he wheeled into the small anteroom outside her office.

There were two women chatting out there. A small, pale woman in a black dress, and Aphrodite Urania. Heph didn't stop in his tracks, but only because the chair already had momentum. As it was, it took him a second to tighten his grip on the rims and control his motion.

"Ah, Hecate," Ms. Eule said to the woman in black. "Is that the report? Excellent. Would you mind waiting just a moment, Ms. Urania?"

"No worries," Aphrodite assured her, as the woman in black got up. "See you later, babe."

"Babe" was apparently the woman in black, who grinned at Aphrodite and then smoothed her face out to follow her boss into her office.

"Hey!" Aphrodite said, and smiled at Heph. "Nice to see you again, under different circumstances."

Heph's face must have done something, because she said, "We kind of met at the Olympus party in December. I had a fight with my ex and I didn't look where I was going, like a total dumbass, and I fell right into you. Remember?"

"Yes, I remember," Heph said.

He would never, ever be able to forget, and not just because the added weight had compromised the already faulty padding on his chair. His tailbone had momentarily hit the metal beneath, and the pain had been searingly bright, so sharp and intense that he hadn't even been able to scream.

And then he'd realized, as her weight shifted and the pain ebbed, that he was holding Aphrodite in his arms. Her long, red-gold hair had fallen around them, a shimmering curtain between them and the outside world. She'd looked right at him, her eyes startled and bright with tears, and he'd stared back, unable to speak or move.

And then she'd stammered an apology, lifted herself off him, and run.

He'd had to leave the party after that, firstly because he was in the kind of pain that needed strong opioids, and secondly because he wasn't quite sure what had happened. Logically, he knew that most men and a lot of women would have been just as stunned if Aphrodite Urania had literally fallen into their laps, but he couldn't shake the whisper at the back of his head that said it was more than just an accident.

"Did you get the fruit basket? I figured if you were on the guest list, the Events team would know where to find you."

"I did," Heph said, and because it seemed like something else was required, added, "Thank you." It came out surly, and he winced. He could never be charming, but at least he could be polite. The fruit basket had been lavish. He'd given most of it to the Olympus IT department, saying it was a gift, and letting them assume it was from a client.

He'd kept the card.

"So what are you doing here?" Aphrodite asked, and then her eyes tracked over his shoulder to Minerva's office. "Wait, are you here as part of the divorce stuff?"

"Um, yes," Heph said. "I, um, I forensically examined your emails."

"Oh, hey!" Aphrodite said. "You're the IT guy who needed to talk to me!"

"Yes," Heph said.

She beamed at him. "Thanks for checking with me that it was okay."

"Sure," Heph said. He wanted to say something cogent and impressive about privacy and how it was important and also how he thought she'd been brave to let a total stranger read those disgusting emails but before he could think about any way to phrase it that also didn't make him sound like a condescending dick, Aphrodite's smile got even brighter, and he felt actually breathless.

"So now I owe you two favors!" she said. "One for crashing into you, and one for the IT stuff."

The card had said "SORRY I OWE YOU ONE LUV APHRODITE." It had been written in marker, in wobbly capital letters with no punctuation. He would have thought it was the gift basket company, but when he'd handled it, he'd caught the scent of her perfume.

"You don't owe me anything for doing my job," he said brusquely, but an idea was percolating at the back of his head. "I think you know my sister. She used to be a model. Mellie Smith."

"Oh, Mellie! Yeah, I know Mellie!" She shook her head, her gold chandelier earrings tinkling slightly. "She helped me out on one of my first big jobs. She was super nice about it."

"Super nice" was not a phrase Heph would use to describe his sister, but Aphrodite seemed to mean it. "How's she doing?" she continued.

"She's great. Runs an event planning business now. Got married four years ago."

"You must be the genius little brother she bragged about. Didn't you graduate MIT at sixteen or something?"

"Eighteen," Heph corrected, momentarily touched that Mellie had bragged about him. The conversation had wandered away from where he wanted to point it, but Aphrodite unknowingly walked it back again.

"And Aoide Waters the singer is your sister, too, right? And I think Mellie talked about a third sister?"

"Yes. Narnie is a researcher at a biological lab. She's working on an experimental artificial womb."

"That's amazing!" She smiled at him. "I've got to confess, I'm a huge fan of Aoide's work."

Heph blinked. He wouldn't have imagined Aphrodite Urania as someone into country-folk music. But he shouldn't stereotype; he wouldn't have thought her the kind of person to handwrite an apology note, either. "Yes. Well, she's getting married in four weeks."

Aphrodite's smile flickered for just a moment, then renewed. "That's awesome."

"Yes," Heph said, and nerved himself up. She had said she owed him a favor, and she did know Mellie. This wasn't creepy, just awkward. "She's very happy. I don't have a date for the wedding."

"She's happy you don't have a date for the wedding?" Aphrodite wondered, and then her glorious eyes widened. "Wait, are you asking me to go with you?"

"I—" Heph said, and then found that his courage could carry him that far and no further. "No. Sorry."

"Because normally I'd say yes, but, well, you saw the press conference."

Heph, still stumbling over "normally I'd say yes," said, "What press conference?"

Aphrodite laughed. He'd seen her laugh in a few social media videos that he might or might not have looked up, a shimmering, tinkling thing, like a wind chime in a gentle breeze. This wasn't that laugh. This was a delighted bark, abrupt and a little rough.

Heph stiffened, but she wasn't laughing at him.

"Duh, of course you have better things to do than watch entertainment news," she said, her eyes alight with amusement at her own misstep. "I did this press conference on Friday where I mentioned I was seeing someone new. Someone who was outside the industry, someone with a real job."

"Oh," Heph said, ruthlessly stifling a whisper of envy for the lucky person. "That's nice. Congratulations."

Aphrodite sat very still for a moment, and then leaned forward. The gold top she was wearing had a cowl neck, and it swung low. Heph kept his eyes on her face. "You work in IT," she said. "That's a real job."

"Yes," Heph said, and remembered that he actually did have a job, and should be heading to Olympus to do it. He shifted his weight.

"Would you say that you're trustworthy?" Aphrodite asked.

"I work in network security," Heph said. "I have to be."

"And you're Mellie's little brother," Aphrodite said, and lowered her voice even further. "I made it up."

"What?"

"I made up the person I'm seeing. But now I need to see someone for real—well, no, I can fake-date someone, but they have to be a real person, and they have to come to a movie premiere with me in three weeks. And you're a real person. And you need a date to Aoide's wedding."

"I don't understand what's happening," Heph said honestly.

Aphrodite grinned at him. "Would you like to go out with me? For four weeks? We'll go to my premiere and your sister's wedding, and then we'll break up."

For a moment, Heph considered it. If he showed up with a date, he'd be buying himself non-interference time until this time next year. But then there was the other part of the deal with his sisters, the part he actually needed to focus on...

"What were you thinking that would involve?" he asked.

"I hadn't thought about it," Aphrodite admitted. "Maybe... Let's see, my schedule's pretty good at the moment, so maybe two dates a week where the paps can get their photos? Plus the premiere—that'd be a three-night trip to LA."

"I'm sorry," Heph said, with real regret. "My contract at Olympus is ending soon, and I need to hustle to find new clients. I can't spare that kind of time." The casual mention of the press didn't sound too good either, but he didn't want to say so to someone who spent so much time in the public eye. He was an ugly man who used mobility aids; he didn't want to know what the internet would say about him dating one of the most beautiful women in the world, even if it wasn't real. Especially if it wasn't real.

"Oh, okay," Aphrodite said, also looking regretful. Then her eyes lit up again. "Wait. What if I could *be* your new client?"

"What?"

"I'll pay you a hundred grand to go out with me for four weeks," Aphrodite declared. "What do you say?"

"I—" Heph said, and his lungs were empty and his head spun. "I don't think I can... I need to go."

Aphrodite said something, he wasn't sure what, but his wheels were already moving, out of Minerva's double-wide doors and to the elevator, down ten floors and out to the lobby.

He sat there for a few moments staring at a rubber tree in a pot.

Had Aphrodite Urania really offered him money to date her?

And had he really said *no*?

***

Aphrodite watched the elevator doors close on Heph and sighed. It had been such a *neat* solution. "Mellie's little brother who's already proved he's a good guy" was a much better bet than "some rando from an agency," but if she didn't find someone soon, she was going to have to call Thea and admit she needed help from a Hollywood beard. Maybe there was someone on the agency books who still had a normal job. Harrison Ford had been a carpenter, right?

"Tell me you did not just solicit someone in my boss's waiting room," Hecate said from behind her.

Aphrodite swiveled back. "Maybe? I mean, I didn't solicit him for sex." She thought for a moment and added, "And even if I had, sex work is legal, right?"

"It's more about the appropriateness of the venue." Hecate's hands were on her narrow hips, but she seemed more amused than annoyed. "Aphrodite, do you ever think before you do things?"

"Pretty much never," Aphrodite said cheerfully, and pushed herself up out of the plush couch. Minerva Eule did not stint on the luxuries. "It's worked out okay, so far."

"That's just luck," Hecate grumbled, but she opened Minerva's office door and ushered her in.

Aphrodite took the chair Minerva indicated, sat up straight, and tucked her hair behind her ears. She wasn't nervous very often, but the lawyer made her feel like she was back in middle school, being asked to read out loud in front of the class.

Also, rumor had it that Minerva was Hera's BFF, which was why she'd taken on a divorce case in the middle of her busy corporate law schedule. And that meant she had no reason to be nice to Aphrodite.

Minerva wasn't mean, exactly, but there wasn't a lot of evident sympathy as she got Aphrodite to talk through her affair with Zeus Kronion. That particular fling had taken place nine years ago, and lasted only a couple of months, but it was still somehow messing with her life.

Maybe thinking things through before she did them was worth a shot.

"And how old were you when the sexual aspect of the affair began?" Minerva said.

Aphrodite swallowed. "Seventeen."

"So you'd reached the age of consent."

"Yeah. Just. Like two days before."

Minerva put her pen down and unthawed a degree or two. "Do you think he was waiting for that?"

Aphrodite shrugged, trying to pretend indifference. "Maybe. Yeah. But... I mean, he did wait. I didn't work for him. I said yes. Nothing he did was illegal." She picked at a cuticle, then forced her fingers still again before she ruined her manicure. She'd felt so flattered. For two months, she'd felt so special.

"That has turned out to be a common thread," Minerva said.

Aphrodite's throat tightened with shame. "There were other girls? Other girls that young?"

"No, not that," Minerva said hastily. "As far as we've been able to determine, most of Zeus's affairs have been with women older than you were. But he's certainly been careful to take advantage of circumstances where the power dynamic unquestionably favors him, but is not outright illegal." She grimaced. "Now, unethical, yes. I think we could certainly say unethical."

"We sure could," Aphrodite agreed. She wrapped her arms around her stomach, and then forcibly exhaled. "I just... I didn't tell anyone. For years. My dad knew, because he caught us, and of course Zeus knew, and his driver, but it was only a few years ago that I started talking about it in therapy. And then I told other women, if I thought they needed the warning, but before that..."

"Were you afraid of him?"

"No. I was afraid of her, at first. Or what I thought was her." She gestured vaguely at the email printouts in front of Minerva. "I thought she'd sent those. I thought she meant it, that if I told anyone, she'd ruin my life."

"To clarify," Minerva said, back to crisp lawyer mode. "By 'her' and 'she,' you are referring to my client, Hera Kronion?"

"Yeah."

"And now you believe that Zeus Kronion did in fact threaten you, in the false persona of his wife."

"Yeah."

"And you didn't discuss these emails with anyone at the time because of that threat?"

"Yeah," Aphrodite said for a third time, her voice very small. "And because I kind of thought I deserved what she said. I mean, I did sleep with a married man. I knew he was married. I chose to do it anyway."

There was a long pause on the other side of the table. Aphrodite looked up, and saw that Minerva Eule was looking at her steadily. When Aphrodite made eye contact, Minerva reached forward and turned off her vocal recorder.

"Ms. Urania, this is perhaps not my place to say," she said quietly. "But you did not deserve this." She tapped the emails with the tips of her polished fingernails, a disdainful gesture that made Aphrodite feel a bit better.

"You sound like my therapist," Aphrodite said.

"Your therapist is smart. But from where I'm sitting, here's the situation: You broke no promises, and Zeus most assuredly did. Furthermore, while I do not wish to deny your agency, or the agency of the girl you were, the choices you made were only available to you as a result of Zeus's actions. His choices. If he, a thirty-year-old man, had not chased a young woman just over half his age, you would not have had an opportunity to have sex with him. He pursued the affair. He chose to cheat on his wife. He did it again and again, and then, when Hera divorced him the first time, he promised to change."

"And didn't," Aphrodite said.

"And didn't," Minerva agreed. "He lied to my friend. He betrayed her trust, he endangered her health, and he limited her ability to make fully informed choices. Frankly, I hate his guts and I hope he dies." She smiled, a sharp, predatory smile. "But I'll settle for taking half of everything he owns, and wrestling his precious company out of his hands."

"Holy shit," Aphrodite said, staring at her. "That's so fucking hot. Are you seeing anyone?"

"No, and I don't wish to," Minerva said, but a smile played around her lips. "Thank you for the compliment." She cleared her throat and turned the recorder back on. "Now, Ms. Urania, let's return to the timing of the affair..."

Thirty minutes later, Aphrodite left Minerva's office with a new respect for lawyers. Hecate was in her own office, bent over her computer, but she looked up when Aphrodite lingered ostentatiously outside the door, and beckoned her in. "So?"

"So I have a crush on your boss."

"Welcome to the very large and completely hopeless club," Hecate said. "But I meant, how are you feeling?"

Aphrodite thought about it. "Kind of tired. And weird, in my brain. Like I'm trying to hold two realities at the same time."

Hecate clicked something on her laptop and pushed away from her desk. "It's a little early for an existential crisis, but I can take a coffee break now, if you like? I have to add, only if you promise not to ask out the barista."

"How cute is the barista?" Aphrodite asked. "But no, that's okay. I'm gonna go home and chill."

Hecate gave her a considering look, but said only: "Okay. Call me if you need anything."

Aphrodite called her driver from the elevator. "Lina? Can you pick me up in five?"

"I'm parked outside now," Lina said. "You can walk straight to me. Heads up, there's some cameras here."

"Roger that," Aphrodite said, and did a quick check of her appearance in the elevator's polished door. Hair: good. Make-up: good. Outfit: great. Body: rocking. She squared her shoulders, tightened her core, and did the modified version of her catwalk strut through the lobby.

Even looking straight ahead, she could feel the people turning to look her way. By the time she hit the doors and exited to the flash of bulbs, she'd pulled energy from her reserves, and was her best, shining self.

"No time for questions today!" she called, scattering a few smiles to particularly familiar faces. It wasn't anything close to the whole pack, but she spotted a few haphazardly parked motorbikes, a sure sign of paps hurrying to a juicy story. Unfortunately, she was pretty sure what the story was.

"Aphrodite! What are you doing here?

"Is this about Zeus Kronion's divorce?"

Damn. Well, they'd have heard about that eventually.

"Is it true you had an affair with Zeus?" someone else tried. Aphrodite kept her smile serene and sailed past as if she hadn't heard. Lina was already out of the car, holding the door for her. Just a few steps more.

"Where's your secret partner?" someone else shouted. "Why isn't he supporting you?"

Aphrodite stopped, a foot away from the car.

This was a mistake. Now there was blood in the water. The photographers pressed in.

"Did he not know about the Zeus affair?"

"Did he dump you?"

"Whoa, whoa, guys!" Aphrodite said, holding up both hands. "No dumping took place."

"So you're still with the mystery man?"

Aphrodite waggled a finger. "Des, I never said it was a man."

More flash-bulbs. More questions. Honestly, how many times did you have to come out to people before they believed you?

"So why aren't they here?"

"Because sometimes people have to work," Aphrodite said, with a bit of snap to it. She widened her smile. "Just like you guys!" She stepped into the car, ignoring the increased volume, and Lina slammed the door shut before heading around to her own side.

"Whew," Lina said, starting the engine. "They haven't been that bad for a while."

"Sex sells," Aphrodite said. She'd dropped the smile, safe behind the tinted glass. "Secret sex sells even more."

"Mm," Lina said. "You want me to call Gorgon Security, get them to put someone on call?"

"I don't know," Aphrodite said.

Lina's eyes met hers for a brief moment in the rearview mirror. "I think I'd feel better if I wasn't on the hook as solo press escort, next time you go somewhere."

Aphrodite was pretty sure that Lina wasn't actually worried about dealing with the press. She was trying to make it look like Aphrodite would be getting security for Lina, not herself, because she knew how much Aphrodite hated feeling weak and defenseless.

"Ugh," Aphrodite said, and slumped further into the cushy leather. "Yeah, okay."

Lina flashed her a grateful smile. "Any luck finding someone to be your fake date?"

Aphrodite sighed. "No. I thought I was onto a good thing for a minute, but he said no."

"He what?" Lina said. "What an idiot."

"He's actually really smart, I think," Aphrodite said. "Probably too smart for me."

"No such thing," Lina said positively, and Aphrodite beamed at her. Was *Lina* seeing anyone? No, Aphrodite couldn't date her staff, even for pretend.

Maybe asking a cute barista wouldn't be a bad idea after all. She made a mental note to call Hecate later.

***

When Heph finally made it to the office set aside for him at Olympus, there was a visitor waiting for him.

"Oh no," he said, which was an impolite way to greet anyone, but Mark Hermes, Head of Human Resources, didn't seem offended.

Instead, he ran his hand over his shiny brown head and grimaced. "Yes," he said. "I'm afraid so."

Heph left his chair inside the door, and transferred to his stable office chair, which had been made to his specific requirements when he was the Olympus golden whiz-kid. Maybe they'd let him keep the chair when they booted him out the door.

"I was expecting it," he admitted. "All right, I guess you'd better do the formal part."

Mark nodded. "Heph, thank you for your superlative work on this latest contract," he said, his British accent making the compliment seem somehow more genuine. "Unfortunately, Olympus Publishing is not currently in a position to renew your contract for the next financial quarter." He wrinkled his nose. "I was told to add, 'or the foreseeable future,' but no one's making a lot of predictions these days. We can barely see past next week."

"Wow," Heph said dryly. "I wonder who told you to add that."

Mark spread his hands in an innocent gesture, but he was also rolling his eyes upwards. Yeah, it was Zeus.

Heph settled back into the sturdy padding and thought for a second. In a way, it was a compliment that Mark was here himself. HR chiefs didn't usually lower themselves to address contractors, even expensive and well-respected ones. "So, four more weeks."

"Yes," Mark said, looking as if he were biting something back. "There was a suggestion that perhaps you would prefer to resign now, with the promise that we wouldn't invoke the penalty?"

"No," Heph said. "If he wants to get rid of me early, he can fire me himself, and pony up with the cancellation fee."

Mark nodded. "I assume you'll look for other clients?"

"Well, yeah," Heph said. "I like being able to eat."

"I'll be happy to stand as a reference," Mark said. "Of course, everyone in the IT department can speak to your technical expertise, but sometimes HR likes to hear from HR."

"Sure," Heph said, and after a moment, "Thanks." Mark was sticking his neck out, and he did appreciate it, but… "Look, is there any truth to the rumors that Hera's planning to take over?"

Mark winced. "I'm afraid I can't comment on that."

"But she gets half of Zeus's shares, right?"

"I'm not partial to the exact terms of the prenuptial agreement," Mark began, but gave up when Heph squinted at him. "Speaking only for myself, and not in any official capacity… That's what I heard too."

"Huh," Heph said. He didn't know Hera Kronion well, but she might want him back. At the very least, she might not block him.

"And she owes you one," Mark said encouragingly. "For uncovering all that seedy business."

"No," Heph said. "That was just doing my job. Hades owed me for it, and he paid the invoice." He was thinking about another woman who'd said she owed him a favor, of the card he'd tucked away in his beside drawer set. "Can I take the chair?"

"Um?" Mark said.

Heph gestured at the chair he was sitting in. "When I leave, can I take the chair? It's not like anyone else can use it."

Mark smiled. "Officially, Olympus property remains Olympus property, regardless of its utility within the company. Unofficially... I'll help you load it into the car." He held out his hand.

Heph took it and shook, firmly. "Right," he said awkwardly. "I'd better get to work."

Six hours later, Heph was done for the day. His hip had started to go past the usual constant discomfort into the tingly shocks that meant he needed to get home. He climbed into the elevator coming down from the top floor without taking any note of who else was in there.

When two people got off at the 25th floor, he was left with the sole other occupant.

At that point, he noticed.

Zeus Kronion was staring at the elevator buttons, his jaw tight.

Oh. Of course.

The top floor was Zeus's office, home of the nasty scene Hephaestus had interrupted two months ago.

Heph eyed Zeus's clenched fists warily and kept his mouth shut. He wasn't afraid of Zeus Kronion, but there wasn't any point in antagonizing him. Besides, he couldn't think of anything to say.

The elevator went down and down. On three occasions it stopped, and the doors chimed open, only for the people on the other side to realize Zeus was in there and back away.

This was awkward, but the silent treatment wasn't actually a problem for Heph, and the stares of the appalled Olympus employees were almost funny by the third stop. He was still glad when the doors opened on the ground floor. "Excuse me," he muttered. Zeus was standing right in the middle of the doorway.

Zeus didn't move.

"Excuse me," Heph said, louder.

"You could have just kept your nose out of my business," Zeus said, his voice tight. He still wasn't looking at Heph.

"Yeah, okay," Heph said. He shifted his hands on his wheel handles and moved forward. Zeus could get out of his way, or collect a chair to the back of the knees.

Zeus took a step to the side and glared at him. It was a look of such icy contempt that Heph felt his world view shift. He wasn't just an annoyance to Zeus, he realized. Zeus really hated him.

"Good luck finding your next contract," Zeus said, and walked out.

Oh, *shit*.

He'd thought Zeus just wanted him gone. That kind of made sense, in a twisted way. No one would want to be constantly reminded of their worst moment by seeing the person who had witnessed it, even if all of it was the consequences of his own damn stupid choices. But no, Zeus wanted him *punished*. If the CEO and Board Chair of Olympus Publishing had told his business buddies that Heph Smith was a bad bet, that could make things much harder for him.

Heph went home in a thoughtful mood, and pulled the thank you card out of his bedside drawer.

The card was thick card stock, the kind people used for wedding announcements or fancy invitations. Under Aphrodite's handwritten message to him was some typeset text: a phone number, and the legend, "Call, don't text."

Heph blew out a breath. Text was great. Text was something you could think carefully about, working out the right phrases, carefully reading responses a couple of times to make sure you had the nuance right. Talking to someone out loud required quick social responses and a certain amount of charm, neither of which he could reliably produce. But if someone said call, they meant call. He dialed the number before he could think about it any further.

"Hello," said a woman's crisp voice. It wasn't Aphrodite.

"Oh," Heph said. "I think I have the wrong number. Sorry."

"Who were you trying to reach?"

"Um. Aphrodite Urania?"

"And you are?"

"Heph Smith."

"Aha," the woman said, and if her voice wasn't any warmer, there was at least a note of interest in her voice. "Please hold."

Heph smacked himself in the head in time to the beat of the tinkly hold music. Of course Aphrodite hadn't given him her personal phone number. She was beyond famous. He was some guy from IT. He'd probably have to explain himself to a higher-level assistant before he could get through to her, if that even happened.

Heph imagined himself saying "I'd like to agree to fake-date your boss" to some amused underling, and nearly hung up on the spot.

"Heph!" Aphrodite's voice said, warm and bubbly and almost too much for the phone. "Hey! What's up?"

"Hey. I'm sorry to interrupt—"

"You're not. Sorry I didn't answer myself, but I was halfway through something, so I asked Thea to get it."

"Thea?"

"My manager. She's the best. So, are you calling for anything in particular?" Did she sound hopeful? Heph decided, for his own piece of mind, that she did.

"Um, I was thinking about the offer you made me this morning..."

"Yes?"

"If the offer's still open, I'd like to accept. If it's open. And if you don't mind." He could almost feel the words coming out of his mouth, the clunky, awkward phrases. "Actually, I just realized you were probably joking. I'm sorry."

"I wasn't joking," Aphrodite said. "This is *great*."

The tight band around Heph's chest eased. "Really?"

"Yes! Oh my gosh, you're a literal life-saver. Well, a figurative life-saver. Figurative is the metaphorical one, right? Thea was just about to call some soap opera actress I've never even met."

She wasn't lying. She wasn't joking. And despite clearly having other options, she actually seemed to want to go out with him.

Well, to feign going out with him.

"So, my premiere is in three weeks, and your sister's wedding is in four? Two dates a week until then. After that, we can work out how to break up for the press. Grown apart, different interests, our schedules don't match or whatever. That all sound okay?"

"Yes," Heph said, and then: "You, uh, you also mentioned—" He cut off abruptly, aware of his presumption. But the money was why he was doing this. He had to ask.

"Oh, right," Aphrodite said easily. "The hundred grand. Is that still good? I can maybe go up to one twenty—hold on." There was a muffled conversation as the other woman—Thea—said something, her voice sharp. "—Mellie's *brother*, Thea. Hi, Heph, wait just one second." This time, her end of the line went silent, and only the lack of a dial tone was there to reassure him she hadn't just hung up. He scratched his chin, feeling the beard coming in.

"—lo? Heph? Hi?"

"Hi."

"Thea is, like, *insisting* we do a contract with an NDA and stuff. So I'll give you half as a deposit on the signing, and the rest will be placed in escrow until the dissolution of the arrangement. Cool?"

"Of course," Heph said, taken aback. She was going to give him half the money in *advance*? "Um, and a hundred thousand dollars is fine. More than fine, actually. I just need to cover the—"

Aphrodite laughed. It was her real laugh again, that sharp, quick bark. "Heph, I'm buying, let's see, about ten days of your time. Haven't you heard? You shouldn't be getting out of bed for less than ten thousand dollars a day."

Heph smiled, forgetting she couldn't see him. "I thought that only applied to supermodels."

"You're super," Aphrodite promised. "You're super saving my butt."

"Well, do *you* get out of bed for less than ten thousand dollars a day?"

"Depends on what I'm getting out of bed for," Aphrodite said, and her voice had warmed, an arch note running through it. Heph had a sudden vision of Aphrodite in bed, tangled in crisp white sheets, hair mussed and sleepy eyes trained on him.

He shook his head, hard, dismissing the fantasy. "Oh," he said. "Okay."

There was the briefest of pauses, then she resumed, her voice back to normal. "Are you free tomorrow night? If you come over to my place, we could sign the contract and then do our first date."

"Tomorrow?" Heph said.

"Just dinner somewhere," Aphrodite said. "Not super fancy or anything. Oh! Do you have a tuxedo?"

"Yes. So not fancy, but I need a tux?"

"No, for the premiere."

There was a murmur on the other end, and then Aphrodite said, "Thea just reminded me that we'll have lots of time to talk about that. Tomorrow, jeans will be fine."

"Okay."

"Okay, nice talking to you! See you soon!"

"See you," Heph said. "Uh, bye."

Chapter Three

Aphrodite tossed the phone onto the couch beside her and turned to Thea. "See? All sorted!"

Thea was rubbing the spot between her eyebrows again. "Aphrodite, when you asked me to manage you, you didn't mention I'd be risking a damn heart attack every ten minutes."

"Aw," Aphrodite said. "Are you mad at me? I'm sorry. Don't be mad at me."

"You were going to give a man you barely know a hundred grand with no legal protection at all! What was to stop him taking the cash, turning around, and selling the whole story to the press for another pay day?"

"Heph's a good guy, Thea."

Thea lowered her hand from her face and looked at Aphrodite carefully. "You thought Ares was a good guy," she said. Her voice was level and non-judgmental, but Aphrodite still flinched.

"Not exactly," she said, staring at her lap. "I thought he was an okay guy who was really good in bed. I knew he had flaws."

"Well, this Heph might have flaws you don't know about yet," Thea said. "My job is to protect you, hon. Please let me do my job." She looked concerned, which was honestly way worse than mad.

"Okay," Aphrodite said, and touched her arm. "Hey, Thea? You're the best."

"Don't you try your sweet talking," Thea grumbled. "I have to go wrangle a definitely non-standard contract out of your lawyer, and you know how much he hates me."

"Tyr loves you," Aphrodite protested, and then when Thea gave her a skeptical look, "Well, he hates you a lot less than most people. Practically the same thing."

"Oh, good. What an incredible compliment." Thea levered herself off the couch and gathered the papers she'd brought with her. Her business suit was wrinkled, and she'd kicked off her shoes the second she stepped into Aphrodite's apartment, but even in her stocking feet, she was fierce as hell. "You're all clear on the Italy shoot?"

"Yep."

"Where do you want to grab dinner with this guy?"

"Persephone keeps talking about this steakhouse she and Hades go to. The Augean. She says the salad dressing is orgasmic."

"Baby, if we could get orgasmic salad dressing, I'd spend a lot less time on the dating apps. Okay, I'll make it happen." She tapped something on her phone.

"Yay, thank you! Oh, make sure it's wheelchair accessible. If it's not, something else will be fine."

Thea paused mid-tap. "He uses a chair?"

"Yeah," Aphrodite said, and then, off the interested look on Thea's face, "No."

"I mean, if you want to hand the press a story to get them away from the Ares stuff..."

"Not that story," Aphrodite said, putting more firmness into her voice. "We're not doing cutesy inspiring disability stories or pity porn."

"Okay," Thea agreed. "It's tacky, anyway."

"*So* tacky."

"Got it. And I'll arrange for your Gorgon security detail."

Aphrodite scowled.

"Kid," Thea said, and there was compassion in her face. "You need someone with you, okay? You don't see what people say about you online, but I do, and it's nasty right now. That's a red flag to the unhinged element. We're gonna be safe, and not sorry."

"Ugh, fine," Aphrodite said.

"Great." Thea padded over to the door and slipped her stilettos back on. "Enjoy your game."

Aphrodite snuggled back into the velvet depths of her couch, picked up her controller, and unmuted her TV.

The tinkling rhythm of *The Binding*'s wait music was instantly calming, soothing away all thoughts of gross people on the internet and the necessary evils of security. She flicked through her character options and gave her avatar a tricorne hat with a huge peacock feather, a symbol that she'd Ascended at least once.

The Binding was a massively popular multi-player battle royale. In the lore of the game, adventurers were magically gathered by the Architect, a cheery, good-natured wizard, who needed to find the best heroes to save the Weaving, the vast network of worlds that made up the universe. The best way to find those heroes, according to Archie, was to put 66 players in a pocket universe and have them beat the crap out of each other with various low-tech weapons, spells, and computer controlled mobs of enemies. Every two minutes, the pocket universe contracted, and players outside the dimensional walls were swept away by the Vortex. Those who remained were forced closer and closer, until a final showdown was inevitable.

The Binding was Aphrodite's happy place, and she could carry it with her anywhere. She preferred to play the console version, but she could play from her gaming laptop in hotels around the world. As long as she didn't join the voice chat, she was totally anonymous. No one knew who she was, what she was wearing, or if she was having a bad hair day. Aphrodite could play—had played—*The Binding* in ball gowns, her pajamas, a sweatshirt with spaghetti stains down the front, and completely nude.

And none of the other players gave a damn.

What the other players cared about was where they could find the best loot, how many kills they could rack up, and, most crucially, how long they could survive in the battle royale arena that was the deceptively pastoral setting. Everyone was striving to show themselves worthy of Archie's attention, but only one player won each round. Only one player got to Ascend.

And when Aphrodite played, much of the time, that player was her.

XxOceanGirlxX was one of the best. She didn't stream her matches live or compete professionally, but when she showed up in a game, any serious player recognized the name. It was an excellence that had everything to do with Aphrodite's quick reflexes and great memory, and it had absolutely nothing to do with what she looked like.

Aphrodite grinned at the sparkling reminder flag in the top corner of the screen. In two weeks, the new Chapter would drop, and she couldn't wait. The publicity material and the recent novelization were hinting at a darker turn to the game as the Darkstar Covenant began infiltrating the

Weaving and perverting the Architect's pocket dimensions to their own corrupt purposes.

She clicked "Ready to Ascend," and was transported to the Waiting Glade, her avatar's feather waving jauntily in the breeze. A minute later, she was dropping out of the transporter vortex to the hotly-contested territory of Dragonspire Outpost.

It took four seconds for her to drop two dragonlings with a pikestaff and jump off the cliff's edge at the exact point that let her land on the hidden ledge below. Her avatar raced through the tunnels under the Tower of Mirrors, through the labyrinth she'd memorized months ago. There were always good pickings in the dungeons, if you were fast enough.

***

"Heph?"

The voice called him out of his dreams.

Heph opened his eyes, grabbed for his phone on the nightstand and squinted at the time. "Narnie?" he called back, his voice cracked on the word, rusty from sleep.

"Yep. I'm just dropping off some soup."

Heph ran a quick body scan, decided getting up wouldn't be an issue, and carefully rolled to his side, then up to a seated position. He reached for his crutches, and headed out to the kitchen, where Narnie had stuck her head into his open refrigerator.

"Why am I getting soup?" he asked. "Before 8 a.m." In fact, it was much later than he'd usually be up. For some reason, he'd had trouble getting to sleep last night.

Narnie stood up and closed the fridge. There were shiny purple marks beneath her eyes, the sure sign of an all-nighter.

"I was thinking about cell cultures," she said intently. "Do you know about 3D cell cultures?"

Heph had always been more of a mathematician than a biologist, but he knew the basics. "You mean growing cells on a scaffold, instead of flat in a dish?"

"Yes, except actually some people are doing it scaffold-free, now. So last night, I was thinking, what if we could use low-adhesion plates to solve the problem we've been having with the uterine epithelial cells? Anyway, it was late and I couldn't sleep, so while I thought about it, I made soup." She waved at the fridge. "You're welcome."

"Thanks," Heph said. "Is there a reason you're not keeping it?"

"I made a lot of soup," Narnie admitted. "Leo was like, honey, there isn't enough room in the freezer for all this, and I thought I could probably get it in there, but that wasn't what he was actually saying, you know?"

"I know," Heph said, remembering the results of the Great Cupcake Overnighter a year ago. Everyone had tried their best to get through the dainty piles, but the end result had been the Great Ant Infestation.

"Anyway, you're getting some, Aoide and Sara-Beth are getting some, and the rest is going to the local shelter." Narnie gave him a significant look. "You've got enough for two. Why don't you ask Deborah at my lab to help you eat it?"

"Narnie," Heph said, with heavy patience, "I'm sure that Deborah at your lab is cool, but do you seriously think she'd be impressed by a stranger asking her to this place to eat soup his sister made?"

Narnie looked around. Heph's place was a small one-story bungalow. He kept it neat, because he was tidy by nature and it helped to have space for maneuvering his crutches, and on low-mobility days, his chair. His furniture was comfortable and sturdy, and his bookshelves were neatly organized and kept dusted.

But the furniture was also more shabby than shabby-chic. His framed wall-art paid homage to moments of glory in past role-playing campaigns and there was a series of portraits that portrayed Star Trek captains in the style of 18th century admirals. His house shouted "nerd!" It also shouted "bachelor."

"She does really like Star Trek," Narnie said.

"Oh."

"Give me some credit," Narnie said. "I wouldn't set you up with someone who was wrong for you. But you might be right about the soup-as-a-first-date thing."

Heph shrugged. "As it happens, I have a date tonight."

It was a mistake. Narnie's eyes sharpened immediately. "With who?"

"With whom," Heph said, and started beating a tactical retreat towards his bedroom. "Don't worry about it."

Narnie followed him, pulling out her phone. "What's her name? I'll google her."

"Absolutely not."

"You've got to research people, Heph! There are a lot of weirdos on the internet. You can't just trust anyone you meet on the apps."

"Narnie, I know much more than you do about the weirdos on the internet. And I didn't meet her on a dating app."

"Someone at work?"

"Kind of," Heph hedged. Narnie had followed him to his bedroom. "Well, I'm running late. Bye, Narnie." He retreated further into his ensuite bathroom, shut the door in her face and turned the shower on.

"I'll find out!" she yelled through the door.

"Eventually, yes, you will!" he yelled back. "I'm getting naked now! Goodbye!"

There was an exaggerated sigh on the other side of the door, no doubt accompanied by an equally dramatic eyeroll, and then he heard his front door slam.

Heph exhaled, and sat on the bench he'd installed to peel off the shirt and pajama pants he'd slept in. He transferred to his shower seat and tested the water temperature, before adjusting the spray and leaning back against the wall.

Until he knew what was in that contract, he couldn't tell his sisters anything.

Of course, once they found out he was dating Aphrodite Urania, they were going to want him to tell them *everything*.

***

Once again, Heph was at work too late to avoid the crowds, but at least there weren't any awkward encounters in the Olympus elevators.

He settled into his office chair and brought up the to-do list. Quite a few items were missing. There was nothing in the work messaging service to explain the lack; just a request from the Head of IT to call him as soon as he came in.

Call was in bold.

Heph frowned and picked up his desk phone.

"Cleon? Heph here. Where are my bullet points?"

"I'm on my way."

Heph replaced the phone in its cradle slowly. Cleon didn't do phone calls, and he didn't come to people's offices. He'd worked his way to the top from a lowly in-house help desk position, and after he'd guided panicking users through right-click, no, the other-right-click ten thousand times, it was no wonder that he stuck to messaging and email.

Cleon was short, with brown skin and thinning, closely curled hair cut in a flat-top. He checked the hallway before he came in, and then closed the door behind him.

"Okay," Heph said. "What's going on?"

"We've taken a few things off your list," Cleon said, trying to look innocent. It was not a good try. "We thought you could use the extra time."

Heph frowned. "But I'm still working the hours I'm contracted for. I told Mark Hermes I wouldn't be leaving."

"Right, yes," Cleon said, his tone conspiratorial. "But I talked to some of the guys—and Maria—and we decided that you should have your best opportunity to find new opportunities. In case you don't get, uh..."

"The opportunity?" Heph suggested.

"The chance," Cleon said firmly. "Anyway, we rescheduled a few nice-to-haves and Maria's been wanting to try new security protocols for a while, so she's happy. We'll tell Payroll you worked the days you were supposed to, and if you maybe made some calls on your personal phone or worked on your resume on a laptop you brought from home, who would know, eh?" He winked at Heph.

"You've heard that Zeus has told people not to hire me," Heph said. "How did you hear that?"

"I kind of deduced it," Cleon admitted. "When he told me that if anyone called me as a reference for you, I should refer them on to him."

Heph leaned back in his chair and opened his eyes wide, staring at the dingy grey ceiling. "Shit."

"I mean, of course, before I do that I'll be telling them all about how good you are, but..."

"But he's Zeus Kronion." Hermes's offer to be another reference made more sense now.

"Yeah," Cleon said. "I mean, it'll all blow over eventually. But we thought you deserved more than that, so..."

"That's really nice," Heph said gruffly. "But I've actually got something short term lined up that should give me some time to figure out my next move."

"Oh?" Cleon perked up. "That's great! What is it?"

"Confidential, sorry," Heph said. Cleon, unlike Heph's sisters, would be able to take that without question.

Indeed, Cleon didn't press him further. "Congrats," he said sincerely. "I'm glad. This crap shouldn't be happening to you, you know? You did the right thing. You shouldn't be punished for it."

Heph shrugged uncomfortably. "It was just a job."

"It was brave," Cleon said. His voice was unusually firm, and he nodded sharply when Heph looked at him. "A lot of people think they'd do the right thing, but when it comes down to it, they cave. You didn't. I admire that." He wrinkled his nose, looking embarrassed. "But since you already have a contract lined up, maybe you could take back some of those bullet points? Not Maria's, though, if you don't mind, because she really wanted those..."

"I'm on it," Heph said, and turned back to his screens.

***

Heph's bad leg was behaving well today, and he took a painkiller when he got home to try and make sure it stayed that way. Normally, he played it safe with evening events and used his chair, but he was going to unfamiliar places, and he wasn't sure how accessible Aphrodite's home was, nor what the restaurant would be like. He'd forgotten to bring it up on the phone, too flustered by what had seemed, for a brief moment, like flirtation.

It was probably all in his head, but it had felt exhilarating.

He got into his newest pair of jeans, and dug out a polo shirt, remembering at the last second to throw his tux into a tote bag. The polo shirt was tight in the shoulders, and he frowned. If he didn't buy new clothes soon, Mellie would probably insist on taking him shopping.

Aphrodite's manager had texted him the address; an uptown apartment building that even he had heard of. But the closest he'd ever been to the Pantheon was hearing about a few parties that Mellie had gone to in her model days.

There was a doorman (actually a doorwoman, with sleek black hair and a dapper overcoat), and a concierge in a suit, who said "Of course, Mr. Smith" when Heph gave his name. They were both much better dressed than he was, and Heph really hoped Aphrodite had meant it about the jeans.

The concierge put down the phone and said, "Ms. Urania is ready for you, Mr. Smith," and Heph moved over to the opulent elevator.

The walls were lined with tasteful, silver-rimmed mirrors. Violin music was playing. It even *smelled* good, like flowers and cupcakes, without being sickly sweet.

He got out at the penthouse floor, which had a small, marble-floored lobby, and two unmarked doors.

Heph checked the manager's text again. It just said "Penthouse, The Pantheon."

He shrugged uncomfortably and knocked on the door to the left.

A small, Asian woman with silver hair and a deeply lined face opened the door and looked a polite inquiry.

"Um," Heph said. "I'm looking for Aphrodite?"

"She's not here," the woman said, eyeing him appreciatively. "But you can come in and wait for her, if you like."

Heph nodded, and moved forward a step before he heard the sound of the door opening behind him.

"Vega!" Aphrodite's unmistakable voice said. "Stop trying to steal my date!"

Heph stepped back and turned. Aphrodite was also wearing jeans—long, expertly frayed jeans with an inset glittery flare flopping around her bare feet as she strode forward. She was wearing something even more glittery on top, some kind of gold halter neck that was more beaded fringe than concealing fabric. Her toned midriff flashed through the strings of beads, and her bared shoulders were an architectural dream of perfect design. She laid a light, but possessive hand on his upper arm and leaned in.

Heph had three older sisters. Even discounting Mellie's modeling friends, who made money based on the delicacy of their bone structure and their ability to make even the ugliest clothes look good, he'd spent a lot of time being introduced to attractive women. He'd honestly thought himself immune to beauty.

Aphrodite craned over his shoulder, mock-glaring at the elderly woman. Her hair fell forward and brushed the side of his face, and the warm scent of rose and cinnamon baffled his senses.

The elderly woman grinned. "If you're going to deliver handsome boys right to my door, dear, you have to take your chances."

"You've been happily and monogamously married for fifty years," Aphrodite said. "You invited me to your Golden Anniversary."

"And you didn't come," Vega said, her eyes twinkling. "This is my revenge." She winked at Heph.

"I was in Sydney!" Aphrodite said.

"Calm down, dear. Anyone can see that this young man only has eyes for you." She smiled up at Heph again. "But do let me know if you change your mind and want a woman with more experience."

"Um," Heph said.

"You're a menace," Aphrodite informed her. "Heph, my place is this way." She took her hand away, which felt like a loss, even though she was just giving him room to move. "How was your day?"

"Normal," Heph said, then added. "My sister Narnie brought me soup."

"Aw, that's nice!" Aphrodite said, pushing her door open for him. "Is she a good cook?"

"Yeah, she just cooks too—"

He stopped dead. Aphrodite's door had opened into a small, white-walled entrance nook, but once he'd walked around the corner, the room had hit him in in the face.

It was a huge living room, warmly lit and very, very pink.

"Oh, right," Aphrodite said. "Welcome to my little palace." She swept her hand generally around the room.

"Palace" felt right. Despite his initial impression, not everything in the room was pink. The walls were, and the carpet, which sank slightly under his feet, but there were plenty of gold and crimson accents in the furnishings once he'd let his eyes adjust. The focal point was a huge, deep red tufted couch that looked soft enough to embrace the most tired bones in comfort. It was set with fluffy pink cushions, and an enormous dark pink throw was piled in the middle, where Aphrodite had evidently thrown it before she got up to fetch him.

Sitting in a chair beside the couch was a short, round Black woman in a navy business suit, who nodded at Heph and pulled a leather folder out. Aphrodite bounced back into her seat and tucked her long legs up under her.

Heph hesitantly walked over to a gold wooden chair, upholstered in pink brocade. It looked sturdy enough to hold his weight, and the seat was high enough that he wouldn't struggle out of it. He held his crutches loosely in one hand. "I'm Heph," he said, directly to the businesswoman. "Nice to meet you."

It was pointless, because she was obviously Thea, Aphrodite's manager, but a brief conversation on the phone wasn't an introduction, and his moms had spent a lot of time trying to drill some good manners into him.

"Thea Jones," the businesswoman said. She reached out with the leather folder, hesitated a moment when she realized Heph wouldn't be easily able to get up and grab it, and brought it to him instead. "The places to sign are marked with flags."

"But you should read it first," Aphrodite said. "In case there are any issues."

Heph had no intention of signing a contract he hadn't read, but he appreciated Aphrodite saying it. Thea Jones resumed her seat on the couch. Aphrodite played with the fringe of her top. He could sense them both looking at him as he went through the pages.

"You can take your time," Aphrodite said anxiously.

"I read fast," Heph said, and then realized that it sounded like a rebuff. "I mean, thanks, but it's okay. I'm not rushing."

He'd signed enough contracts that the terminology wasn't entirely unfamiliar, even if the content was unusual. Both he and Aphrodite were "enjoined to maintain the appearance of a romantic relationship in public," which appearance "could include but was not constrained to" a dizzying list of gestures, including hand-holding, pet names, kissing, and something referred to as "a copulatory gaze."

Heph decided not to query that one, especially as any physical contact had to be consented to in advance by both parties.

The non-disclosure agreement was the heftiest part of the contract, specifying total secrecy about the contract's existence "except to those persons already informed of the circumstances of the Agreement."

Heph looked up. "Who are the persons already informed?" he asked. "I haven't told anyone about this."

"Good," Thea said, and then cast a disapproving look at Aphrodite.

"I told my friends Persephone and Hecate," she admitted. "And my driver Lina knows, and my publicist Sienna, because they have to. But no one else."

"And both of Aphrodite's friends have agreed to a voluntary NDA," Thea said smoothly. "So you're protected there."

Aphrodite rolled her eyes slightly. "Plus they'd never tell."

Heph nodded. He liked what he'd seen of Persephone Erinyes, and if she and Aphrodite both trusted this Hecate, she was probably all right too. "Okay. I just don't need this getting back to my sisters."

"Absolutely not," Aphrodite said.

Thea coughed. "And of course, should *you* leak the story, to the press, or to any other interested parties, we will pursue legal remedy with extreme prejudice."

"Thea means she'll sue your pants off," Aphrodite said cheerfully. "I'm not worried, though. You seem solid to me."

Heph flushed, and moved to the next page, which noted that either party could cancel the arrangement at any point, but that the penalties for cancellation were different. If Aphrodite canceled before the wedding, she had to pay him the remainder of his fee. If Heph canceled, he was liable for paying back the fifty thousand dollar deposit. That all seemed fair.

The Dates of Work clauses specifically included the three days in L.A. for the premiere and the night before Aoide's wedding; other dates would be decided "by mutual agreement between the parties" but were to be "no less than two occasions a week" for the three weeks leading up the premiere.

He blinked at one clause, and flipped back a few pages, just to make sure. But he was right.

"There's no definite end date to the contract," he said.

Thea frowned, and came to look over his shoulder. Heph pointed at the relevant passage. "Contract to be dissolved with no penalty by mutual agreement."

"Oh, damn it, Tyr," Thea said. "Folks, it looks like we need an amendment. I'm sorry I didn't catch that."

"That's okay," Aphrodite said. "Only, does it mean we can't do the date tonight?"

"I'll get it sorted first thing tomorrow," Thea promised.

"But Heph already came up tonight," Aphrodite protested. "And I'm going to Malta tomorrow and I'm not back until Saturday, so that's the last chance for our second date this week. Can't we just mutually agree to end it after Aoide's wedding?"

Thea looked torn.

"That works for me," Heph said. He already regretted the nitpick. The contract didn't prevent them finishing the arrangement then; it just didn't specify that they *had* to part ways on that date.

Thea had evidently come to the same conclusion. "All right, then," she said briskly. "Sign at the marked points, please, Mr. Smith." She handed him a sleek and deadly looking silver pen.

Aphrodite had already signed on the flagged lines. Her signature was more like printing than handwriting, a slightly-run together *Aphrodite Urania*. He peered closer. Each "I" was topped with a tiny, careful heart.

Heph signed and initialed and dated, page by page, and that was it. At lunch on Sunday, his sisters had challenged him to find a new contract and a date to Aoide's wedding. It was now Tuesday, and he'd done both.

Sure, it was a fake relationship and much more in line with the letter of their agreement than its spirit, but it was done. Maybe his sisters could actually keep their side of the bargain, and finally acknowledge that he was an adult who could look after himself without interference.

He felt a little dizzy, and it wasn't entirely Aphrodite's perfume.

"Right," Thea said, and handed Heph his copy of the contract, which he shoved into his messenger bag. "File that somewhere safe. Aphrodite, your copy will be lodged with Tyr." She tugged the edges of her blazer straight and cracked her back. "And now, I'm going home. Enjoy your date."

"Bye, Thea!"

"Um, it was nice to meet—" Heph said, but the door clicked shut. He looked at Aphrodite. "I don't think she likes me."

"She doesn't *not* like you," Aphrodite said, leaning forward eagerly. "She's just super protective. And really smart."

"I got that part," he said.

"Like you," Aphrodite added. "You're really smart, right?"

"Well," Heph said. "Um."

"Come on, you graduated MIT at eighteen! You hacked those emails!"

Heph decided that now was not the time to discuss the difference between hacking and forensic analysis. "Smart is kind of a subjective value judgment," he said instead.

Aphrodite nodded. "Like beauty," she said, and spread her arms. "Totally subjective. But I'm still gonna say I'm beautiful. And you should say you're smart."

"Um."

"Go on!" Aphrodite said. "Say, 'I'm Heph and I'm smart.'"

She was so ridiculously enthusiastic, and so charming with it. "That sounds like I'm introducing myself at a support meeting."

"I'm the only one here," Aphrodite said, spreading her arms and leaning back. "I won't tell anyone. Pleeaaaase?" The beads parted and fell to either side, giving him an unobstructed view of her smooth stomach and delicate waist.

"Okay," he mumbled. "I'm Heph, and I'm smart."

Aphrodite clapped her hands together and bounced to her feet. "Yay! Okay, I'm gonna grab shoes and a jacket and we can go. I'll be two seconds. Feel free to look around." She dashed out of the room, beads clacking together as she moved.

Heph took a deep breath and shook his head. He'd known he'd be out of his depth, but he had to keep paddling anyway.

Whatever it took, he had to keep his head above water.

***

Aphrodite put on the Balmain gold spike heels, took them off, replaced them with the peony rose Louboutins and then moved on to the jackets closet. She styled herself, and had ever since she'd dropped her modelling agency and hired Thea instead, but it did take a while sometimes.

Besides, she was just a teeny bit nervous. She'd had to push to make him say it, but Heph *was* really smart. He did cool things with computers at his real job, and while her job was a lot harder than most people knew, it was still a matter of fantasy. Glitter and illusion were what kept fashion magic moving.

What if he thought she was shallow? What if he thought she was dumb? She knew she wasn't either, but she also wasn't sure she knew how to talk to a real person.

"Hey, now," she told the face in the mirror, pulling out the negative thoughts before they had time to root. "You do too."

After all, she talked to Hecate and Persephone all the time! There was no need to be nervous! She and Heph would find something they had in common, and they could talk about that.

She pulled on a distressed denim crop jacket, which was perfect *first time*, and pulled her shoulders back. Her boobs bounced a little with the motion, and she bounced again, watching the jiggle with approval. She was giving seventies queen. She was giving fresh girl next door with a touch of fierce. "Go get him," she whispered into the mirror, and blew herself a kiss.

When she came back to the living room, she discovered that Heph had taken her instructions literally. He was looking around her space, leaning on one crutch as he peered at the bookshelf filled with her candlestick collection.

"I'm kind of a maximalist," she said breezily.

"And you really like pink," Heph said without looking at her.

"Yeah," Aphrodite said, immediately on the defensive. Ares had described her place as "like a Care Bear got drunk and vomited glitter everywhere" and had avoided spending the night as much as he could. She'd had to go to his apartment, which was brutalist architecture and mid-century furniture, all brown leather and wooden lines. Not a touch of color or a hint of texture in the whole place.

"I like it," Heph said. "It's unapologetic." He turned around and looked at her properly, and stayed looking at her.

Aphrodite, who was still processing "unapologetic," took that as an enthusiastic thumbs-up for her outfit.

"Well, I'm under-dressed," he said ruefully.

"You're normcore!" Aphrodite said. "It's perfect! Like, not too much, like, not khakis and polo, no, thank you, but jeans and short-sleeves can be major, especially when you're rocking those biceps." The messenger bag slung over his torso wasn't so major; sturdy, utilitarian denim, but scuffed and weathered, and not in a fashion way.

Heph looked aggrieved. It wasn't cool to tell people they were cute when they were angry, but Heph was adorable when he was grumpy—his nose wrinkled up and his heavy eyebrows came down, and he looked like a disgruntled teddy bear. "I haven't worn this shirt for a while," he mumbled, and slipped a finger under a sleeve cuff, giving it a futile tug out. "I didn't realize it would be this tight."

"It's very hot," Aphrodite assured him, and watched his cheeks stain red with some interest.

"One question," he said. He nodded towards the couch. "Is that blanket as soft as it looks?"

"Even softer," Aphrodite said. She scooped up the warm pile of lush fabric and carried it over to him, rubbing her cheek against it on the way. It was made out of some kind of synthetic that was probably super bad for the environment, but no matter how bad her mood was, the second she snuggled into that blanket, she felt better about everything. She held it out for him. "See?"

Heph's mouth fell open as he tentatively stroked the blanket. "Wow."

"Right?"

"I didn't know things could *be* that soft."

"I have another one for my bed," Aphrodite told him. "I got it made into a weighted blanket, and it's the most amazing thing ever. Instant comfort, instant sleep."

Heph's eyes snagged on hers. This close, she could see that his eyes weren't just deep brown. There were flecks of amber in the depths, and a ring of gold at the edge of the irises. She was suddenly very aware that they were alone in her apartment, that it had been six months of self-discovery and her sex toy collection, but no action with another person, no one else's hands in her hair, or nipples under her fingers, or mouth on her pussy.

What would it be like, if Heph spread her out naked on this blanket, if she writhed between the contrast of soft torment beneath her and his rough hands on her skin?

Hot, she was pretty sure. It would be super, super hot.

"We should probably get going?" Heph said hesitantly, and Aphrodite felt her own cheeks flush.

"Right! Absolutely!" she said, and gave herself a mental shake.

She'd been practically telepathically violating the poor guy with her uncontrollable sex thoughts. She'd been like one second away from kissing him right then, and that would have made their whole working relationship super awkward, and *this* was why she was supposed to be trying that whole look before you leap thing.

She had to save the kissing for the paps! That was the entire point of the whole arrangement!

Aphrodite opened the door for Heph, absent-mindedly enjoyed the way the muscles in his back moved as he set off down the hall, and hoped that the paparazzi would be out in force tonight.

Chapter Four

The restaurant had a ramp as well as steps. Heph glanced at Aphrodite who noticed him looking, and said immediately, "I didn't know if you always used a chair."

"Oh, right," Heph said. "You've never seen me with crutches before now."

Their bodyguard—Aphrodite had a *bodyguard*, a large and stony-faced woman with curly dark hair—opened the wide door, glanced around the restaurant, and then nodded at Aphrodite.

"Show time," Aphrodite whispered, partly to him, but he thought mostly to herself, and stepped forward. Heph, caught off-guard, was swept up beside her.

Aphrodite stopped in the doorway, letting the light from the last hour of daylight limn her body, so that she was outlined in gold. The metallic beads hanging from her top shifted and glimmered, refracting the light around her as she paused, just briefly, and stood in contrapposto pose, hip cocked, one arm by her side, the other hand lightly and briefly on Heph's shoulder, a butterfly touch.

She did it so naturally that it barely seemed intentional, but everyone in the restaurant was caught as surely as if she'd summoned a spotlight.

They stopped whatever they were doing and looked at her. Looked at them.

Aphrodite's hand lifted from his shoulder, and she moved forward, smiling at the hostess and giving her the name Thea had booked the table under. The pause in the restaurant's flow was over, the voices perhaps just a little more animated as everyone at the tables pretended they hadn't been staring and turned in on themselves, chatting with lowered voices but obvious intensity.

Heph followed Aphrodite to the table, trying to wrap his head around it. She'd done that on purpose, with an awareness of her space and her body that seemed almost supernatural. Why did he think he could *do* this? She'd met him twice before today. On the first time, she'd actually injured him. On the second, she'd offered him a hundred grand without flinching. And now, on their third meeting, they were on a *date*.

He was on a *date* with Aphrodite Urania.

A flushing waitress took their drink orders and brought them menus, and Heph stared at his for a while without seeing it. Aphrodite had hers open too, but she wasn't really looking at it either; he caught her glancing at him over the top twice, and on the third time noticed that she was looking a little panicked.

As she should, he realized, because she was sitting across from a man she barely knew, and he'd made absolutely no attempt at conversation. She'd done all the work so far, and even if it was for money and reputation, he should be doing better than this. He wasn't naturally charming, but he'd been on dates before. They involved *talking*.

"So, what's happening in Malta tomorrow?" he asked, keeping his voice low enough that the other diners would only see that they were talking.

Aphrodite's face lightened, and she put her menu beside her plate, leaning in. "It's an editorial shoot for *Luxe Italia*. I'm looking forward to it, because Penny Laconia is the stylist, and she's a lot of fun."

"Oh, I know Penny," Heph said. He'd never been to the famed Olympus Wardrobe, which was notoriously bursting with racks of expensive glamor, but he'd met the woman in charge. "She invited me to join her role-playing group once, but I couldn't make the time."

"Like...acting?" Aphrodite asked. "Or a role-playing video game?"

"No, table-top," Heph said. This was hopelessly nerdy, but at least it was talking. And Aphrodite didn't look disgusted or bored. She looked curious, and she at least knew what an RPG was. "Like... Have you heard of Dungeons and Dragons?"

"Oh! Sure."

"Well, like that, then, though I don't think her group uses that system. You kind of improvise a story and maybe roll dice and act on the results."

"So it is like acting? But no script."

"Yeah, kind of."

"Well, that sounds fun," Aphrodite said, and sounded as if she meant it. "Do you do that often?"

"Not much, these days," he said, and she asked another question, and he told her about his table-top role-playing group at MIT, who had been remarkably tolerant about letting a 15-year-old join them, and then the waitress was back, and Heph realized with a start that he'd put the menu aside, and they'd been happily chatting, just as if this was a real first date.

"What do you recommend?" Aphrodite asked the waitress, while Heph frantically scanned the menu.

"The Thrinacian Tri-Tip is very popular," the waitress said.

"I'll have that, with a green salad, dressing on the side. *Lots* of dressing on the side, please." She smiled at the waitress as if they were sharing a joke, and the waitress smiled back.

"And you?" she asked Heph.

"Um, same," Heph said. "Mashed potatoes on the side."

Aphrodite glanced at her bodyguard, who was standing discreetly to one side, placidly ignoring the occasional curious look from another diner, and whispered something else to the waitress. The waitress nodded, and took off, clearly totally entranced.

"What was that?" Heph asked.

"Medea won't eat while she's on duty, but it's too mean to put someone in a room that smells like this and then not feed them, don't you think? I ordered a third meal to go. The kitchen will make it while we eat dessert, and package it to go with us."

"Oh," Heph said. "That's kind."

Aphrodite shrugged, looking uncomfortable, and brought up the topic of Malta again. They kept the conversation shallow until the food came, talking a little about her work and a little about his, and then they could talk about the food, which was uniformly delicious. It was awkward, but no more than it was awkward talking to anyone he didn't know well. He'd definitely had much more painfully boring small talk conversations.

The problem wasn't that he couldn't talk to her; the problem was that she was who she was—and he was who he was. Which was nice enough in his own way, probably, but it was so obviously a bizarre mismatch that he couldn't think anyone would believe it.

"Heads-up," Aphrodite said. They'd been seated at the back of the restaurant, but she had a clear view of the front window, and she'd been looking over his shoulder now and then while they ate. "Paps are here."

"Do we need to do something?" he asked her, keeping his voice down. He'd better work for his money, after all. "I can't hold hands while I'm walking, but maybe across the table?"

"Good idea," Aphrodite said. She smiled and leaned in, as if she were telling him a delicious secret, and he reached out to her, the gesture a little jerky, and she placed both of her hands in his without hesitation.

Her fingers were cool and long and rested lightly on his palms. He was instantly aware that her skin was soft and smooth and his was rough.

"Sorry," he said, trying to make a joke out of it. "Forgot to moisturize today."

"I like it," Aphrodite said, and something flickered in her eyes. Her fingers tightened around his, and she stroked her thumb into his palm.

The touch sparked through him, charging directly to his cock.

"We'll eat dessert," Aphrodite said, her smile deepening as if she knew exactly what he was thinking, and liked it. "Maybe I'll feed it to you. Then we'll go out the back door, to make it look like we're trying. Guaranteed some of the paps will be there. I'll say 'no comment' a few times, and tomorrow it'll all be, Aphrodite's Mystery Man, Unmasked at Last. Is all of that cool?"

"Yes," Heph said. The room was full of people, but they'd all disappeared as he looked at her, so dizzy he couldn't think.

"Maybe we should kiss," she added, her eyes burning into his. "Should we?"

He let himself imagine it for a moment, think about her mouth opening for him, about her body held against his. The tip of her tongue flickered across her bottom lip as she stared at him, waiting for a response, and she was acting, of course, and she was doing a much better job of it than he was, but until he could get a better grip on himself it would be too dangerous. It would be too much.

"No, thank you," he said. "Er...not yet."

Aphrodite, for a very brief moment, looked—not surprised, which might have made sense—but hurt. Then she nodded, and slid her hands slowly from his. He missed the touch at once. "You're right," she said. "That would look too staged."

Heph nodded, as if that was what he'd meant. Then he thought about what the pictures of them kissing would actually look like, with her beautiful and graceful, and him awkward and obviously stunned, and nodded more fervently.

"How was everything?" the waitress asked, appearing again like a magic trick.

"Amazing," Aphrodite said. "My friend Persephone raves about this salad dressing, and I thought she had to be exaggerating, but nope!"

"Oh, you know Persephone!" the waitress exclaimed. "We love her and Hades around here. Although she does keep threatening to leave him and marry the saucier."

"Oh my gosh, it'll never happen," Aphrodite said. "Those two are so gone for each other, it's not even funny."

The waitress laughed, and then clearly remembered she was talking to a mega-star and had to take a second to recover her composure. Heph could sympathize with the sensation. "Um, so...desserts?"

"Not for me," Aphrodite said. "Heph?"

"What's good?"

"Most people go for the chocolate cheesecake, but there's a creme brulee trio that'll blow your mind," the waitress said, and Heph nodded, and paid for his acquiescence ten minutes later, when Aphrodite not only insisted on feeding him some, but unapologetically ate most of the lemon and Earl Grey infused creme brulees herself.

"We'll order two next time," she promised, when he pointed out that she was a filthy dessert thief, and he was reminded that there was going to be a *next time*. There were going to be *five* more next times, plus two long events, and he'd better get his head around the possibility of kissing really fast.

When dessert was done, Aphrodite asked if she could go out the back door, and they got escorted through the busy kitchen by the restaurant manager. Heph concentrated on moving smoothly through the space, calling "behind, behind," as he passed people's backs. He took a breath in the clear space by the cold store, and caught the manager's look of inquiry.

"My mom owns a restaurant," he explained. "Nomi Smith-Waters."

"You're *Nomi*'s kid?" the manager asked, looking more starstruck than he had by Aphrodite, and Aphrodite didn't even act like that was bizarre, she just grinned at him, picked up the box with Medea's meal and asked her to open the door for them.

There were two photographers at the very end of the back alley, right where the restaurant property met the public street. Paps did occasionally break the rules, Aphrodite had explained, but most of them didn't want to risk either the law or the threat of being completely cut off from all leaks and concessions a celebrity might grant them. So these two were loitering at the edge of private property, and took their pictures as Heph and Aphrodite walked towards them.

"Who's your date, Aphrodite?" one asked, his bomber jacket sliding off his skinny shoulders.

"No comment, Derek," Aphrodite said sweetly.

"Is this your mystery man?" the other photographer asked. "Hey, mystery man, what's your name?"

"No comment," Heph said. He was trying for Aphrodite's pleasant firmness, but of course it came out surly. His crutch tip hit a rough spot and he took more weight on his bad leg to compensate for the instability.

His hip warned him, with a sharp stab of pain, that he was pushing it.

"Move back," the bodyguard said, nearly the first words he'd heard from her all night. "Move back, move back, please."

Aphrodite's car slid into the narrow alley, and her driver jumped out to open the door for them. Aphrodite slid in first, and the photographers pressed closer, and then gave up to concentrate on Heph.

"What are the crutches for, buddy?"

"You injured?"

"Been fucking Aphrodite long? Get hurt keeping up with her?"

The last question was an obvious provocation, a way to get some kind of reaction out of him. He'd been warned, but he still looked up and glared instinctively, and the photographer scented blood.

"She good, buddy?" he said, his voice dripping with oily insinuation, and then Heph was in the car, and the bodyguard bundled the crutches in after him and slammed the door, just as the photographers clustered around the restaurant's *front* door realized their miscalculation and came baying around the corner.

"Sorry," he said, when he'd got his breath back, and they'd started driving. "You told me not to react."

"Alexander's one of the worst," she said. "You did great." Her eyes snagged on the place where he was kneading his hip, trying to ease some of the tightness out. "Are you okay?"

"I'm fine," Heph said, still his automatic response after years of trying to work through the messages of self-hate the world had tried to implant in his brain, years of trying to acknowledge what his body needed and honoring that. "No, sorry. I mean, it's not too bad, but I'm not fine. I pushed it tonight. Could you pass me my bag?"

She gave him the messenger bag he'd left in the car, and a chilled bottle of water from the compartment in the middle console to wash down his painkillers, and he tried to relax against the seat, imagining the pills dissolving into his blood and soothing his inflamed muscles and irritated nerves. It was all psychosomatic at this point; the medicine wouldn't actually start to work for another twenty minutes or so. But even the visualization helped, sometimes.

"Hey, so, you don't have to tell me anything," Aphrodite said, after a moment, sounding actually shy, "but is there stuff I should know about—" she gestured at his legs.

"—my disability?" Heph asked. "It's okay, you can say it." He thought for a second. She didn't need his whole origin story, but... "Mostly it's mobility stuff. I'll need longer to get places than you might think. I can't move fast just because I want to, and if I'm using my chair I need to think about steps and door widths." He shrugged. "Long walks on the beach are right out."

"I totally hate sand anyway," Aphrodite said. "Swimsuit shoots are the *worst.*"

"I'll take your word for it," Heph said, instead of finishing the *Star Wars* quote that automatically came to mind whenever someone mentioned sand. "Um, the other thing is that I have medication for my normal pain levels, and more serious meds for more serious pain. I'm good at working within my limits, but if I do need to take the stronger painkillers, I'll be pretty loopy for a while. Probably not date-ready."

"Gotcha," Aphrodite said. "Just call me if you need to cancel."

Heph nodded, and leaned his head back against the seat. "You're back by Saturday? What do you want to do?"

"Surprise me," Aphrodite said, and then, when he blinked at her. "Oh, did you think I'd be coming up with all the dates? That's not fair."

"Huh," Heph said. "You're right. I'll think of something."

***

He had wanted to kiss her.

Aphrodite was absolutely positive of that. They'd had that eye contact, her hands clasped in his, and she had *seen* it, his pupils dilating, a heat in his eyes that matched the heat racing in her blood.

Contrary to popular belief, Aphrodite wasn't constantly surrounded by people who wanted her. Fashion was full of gay men and straight women, for one thing, and for another, being *beautiful* wasn't the same as being *attractive*. She wasn't actually everyone's type. She was just the type everyone was told they *should* want: tall, skinny, white (or at least white-passing—she wasn't a hundred percent certain on that one), with big eyes, symmetrical features, smooth skin, and long, loose hair. She worked hard to fit those beauty standards, because that was where the money was, but she'd be the first to tell people that the standards themselves were dumb.

She *had* told people that, actually, in quite a few interviews, but it didn't seem like they wanted to hear it.

But she knew what desire was, and what it looked like when someone wanted her, and Heph definitely did. And anyone could see he was also a little shy and embarrassed about it, so she'd made the first move, and he'd said *no*.

No, even worse: *no, thank you*.

That was going to be a problem, partly because Aphrodite needed the press to "catch" them canoodling somewhere to make the story stick and keep the publicity alive for the movie, but *mostly* because "kissing Heph" had jumped right to the top of her to-do list.

Aphrodite padded through her apartment, picking things up and putting them down again while she thought, but this was definitely not a one-woman problem. She needed to talk this out.

It was late, but Hecate was a night owl, and also very good at putting her phone on silent mode when she didn't want to be disturbed.

Sure enough, she answered after the dial tone had sounded twice. "Hey. What's up?"

"Is it illegal to sleep with someone you're paying to date you?" Aphrodite asked.

"That's prostitution," Hecate said promptly. "Which is legal here, yes. If you ask them and they say no thanks, you've maybe committed workplace sexual harassment, but since you're operating under a private contract, not subject to—we are talking about Heph Smith, right?"

"Yes. He's yummy."

"I didn't get a good look at him in the office." There was a brief pause. "Although I'm checking out the socials now, and the pics from tonight are already up. Yeah. I can see it. The shoulders, right?"

"And his eyes."

"Can't make out his eyes here. He's kind of squinting, murder-style. But that's a jacked dude."

Aphrodite resisted the urge to ask Hecate to forward the photos. She'd long ago stopped paying attention to what people said about her online. Thea told her anything she actually needed to know, and the rest was just noise.

"So?" she prompted.

"So what?"

"So can I sleep with him?"

There was a distinct choking noise on the other end, and then Hecate said, "I thought you were *joking*."

"Ummm."

"Do not have sex with Heph Smith," Hecate said, just a shade away from an order. "You're bored and horny and you're in a weird contractual relationship you do *not* want to come out in court if anything shady goes down."

Aphrodite thought about Ares's smug glee if he found out she'd had to pay someone to date her, and grimaced. "I get it."

"Seriously, Aphrodite!"

"Seriously, Hecate, I get it, for real. I'll be good." Even when it was way more fun to be bad. "What about when the contract's done?"

Another pause. "Okay. Yes. When the contract is concluded satisfactorily for all parties, you two can smash your good bits together to your heart's content. But *wait*."

"Ugh," Aphrodite said. "Waiting. *Patience.*"

"Practice," Hecate said, a trace of her cat-like smile in her voice. "It's good for you. If you need a distraction, play your game, or get out your vibrator, whatever you need. But don't have sex with him. And introduce him to Persephone and me."

"Persephone's already met him. Technically, you've already met him."

"But he wasn't going out with you then," Hecate said. "Persephone believes the best of everybody, and I love that about her, but my asshole radar is top-notch. If he pings it, I'll let you know."

"Sure, that makes sense," Aphrodite said, feeling more cheerful. Even if she had to *wait*, she could get Hecate's impressions of him, and that meant she could gossip. Gossip wasn't as good as sex, but if she couldn't *have* sex, it would be good enough.

She thought of Heph's hands, the moment when they'd tightened on hers, and she'd felt just a hint of the power of his grip, a little rough and very warm. Then she said goodnight to Hecate, took off all her clothes, and sprawled on top of her soft, soft blanket, her vibrator buzzing between her legs as she gasped and writhed, loving it, but wanting more, more.

It was going to be a long four weeks.

***

Heph had finally gotten himself into work on time, which for most other people was way too early. The yawning security guard waved him through, and he got to walk through the empty hallways of Olympus without having to watch out for hidden obstacles, or move around people, or watch them check themselves so they didn't race past him.

He and Aphrodite had moved together well yesterday. She *had* walked more slowly, of course, but there hadn't been a hint of hesitation or impatience. She'd just done it naturally, matching her pace to his as easily as she'd thrown herself into a pose in the doorway.

How had she done that?

Hm. As long as he got all his contracted work done, he could do what he wanted with his schedule, and he wasn't feeling overly ambitious about doing his best work for Olympus. He logged in, activated the VPN the IT team used when they wanted to spoof access from other countries, opened an incognito window, and started browsing "what do models do."

Ninety minutes later, he closed the window and erased his browsing history, with a new respect for models in general and Aphrodite in particular.

He'd resolutely kept away from recent news and social media, because Aphrodite had warned him not to look at anything anyone wrote about them, but he'd watched runway walk compilation videos—a thing he'd been completely unaware existed until this morning—and Best Of yearly fashion retrospectives, and been stunned all over again by her innate grace. Walking in time beside him hadn't been a fluke; it was her *job* to adjust her gait and pace on demand, and she was acknowledged as one of the best in the business.

Then he'd read a couple of articles about Aphrodite, the kind that went beyond asking her about her love life and beauty routine and instead delved into her history and work. Behind the flippant air and clever soundbites he got the clear picture of a driven, ambitious woman who'd climbed to the top of her industry—and hadn't stepped on anyone else to do it. One of the article authors had clearly tried to find someone who'd say something bad about Aphrodite Urania, but the closest he'd got was a mild complaint that she never texted anyone.

Mellie had once described her old job in self-deprecating terms as "stand still and look pretty," but there was clearly a lot more to it than that.

The building was starting to liven up as people drifted in. Maria dropped by, handing out some apple muffins her girlfriend had made, and loitered in his office afterwards.

"Good muffins," he said.

"You can keep the rest," she said.

Heph paused, mid-reach for another one, and withdrew his hand. "Okay. What's going on?"

"You know how I was going to host a *The Binding* expansion drop party at our place?"

"Yes," Heph said cautiously. He wasn't as into competitive gaming as many of his friends. He preferred story-based open world style games instead. But everyone and their dog had played at least a few rounds of *The Binding*, and he was looking forward to the new map. And to the pseudo-LAN party; watching other people play was almost more entertaining than playing himself.

"Well, Jo and I mixed up our dates. Her parents are coming to stay that weekend."

"So you have to cancel?" Heph said, trying to keep the disappointment out of his voice. Maria was looking upset enough—she didn't need him making her feel bad. "It's okay, Maria, that stuff happens. You don't have to bring me apology muffins."

Maria straightened out of her habitual slouch. "Actually, they're bribe muffins," she said.

"Bribing me to do wh—oh, no."

"Heph, please? Your house has plenty of space. You could easily fit six in the living room. I'll do all the organizing, I promise. You won't have to do that part."

"No, I'd just have to host a party," Heph said. A party he couldn't leave whenever he wanted, because he was *living* at the *venue*. "Maria, surely someone else can…" he let the words trail off. She was already shaking her head—because of course she'd checked with the others. And of course they all had tiny homes, or unsympathetic roommates, or, in Greg's case, had no chance of cleaning up in time. He was the last resort.

"That's okay," Maria said, slouching again. "I knew you were a long shot."

She didn't say it with any bitterness or accusation, but she looked so sad, and that was somehow *worse*. She was his closest work buddy, and she'd taken on a lot of his to-do list to free him up for the job search. It was an unnecessary gesture, because of his deal with Aphrodite, but Maria hadn't known that he had another contract lined up at the time. She'd just done it, because he was her friend, and she thought he needed help.

"Oh, hell," Heph said, the words coming out before he could stop them. "I'll do it."

Maria's eyes went wide. "For real?"

"Yes." He sighed. "But I hope you're serious about organizing, because I hate that stuff. I can give you the space and grab some snacks before-hand, and that's it."

"Dude, I'm on it," Maria promised. "I have a spreadsheet and a mailing list, we are *solid*."

"Okay," Heph said. "Get out of my office. Leave the muffins."

He ate another one while he documented the code he'd written last week, brushing the crumbs off his desk as he worked. There were more people in the halls now, and a growing hubbub in the usually quiet tech offices. Cleon had passed by his door several times, hovering in an awkward way, but when Heph had waved him in he'd shaken his head and backed off.

When Mark Hermes knocked on his door, Heph was almost glad for the interruption. It was hard to focus, when people kept drifting past his door.

"Got some paperwork for you," Mark said. He was giving Heph a strange look, part-puzzled, part-wary.

Heph read through it; a sales document that transferred ownership of his office chair to him instead of Olympus, for the princely sum of one dollar.

"Thanks," he said, and then paused. "You're not going to get in trouble for this?"

Mark waved that aside. "Only if Finance flags it, and Odysseus has assured me they won't. No one in Finance wants to do Zeus any favors."

Heph grunted. "Politics."

"Politics that are unfairly causing you some difficulty," Mark said, his accent sharpening to reveal his aristocratic Oxbridge roots. He held out his hand. "One dollar, please."

Heph fished through his bag and scrounged up some loose change.

Mark tapped on his phone for a second, and emailed him a receipt. "There. All nice and legal." He got up, then hesitated, tapping his fingers restlessly against his thigh.

"Something else?" Heph asked.

"Are you really dating Aphrodite Urania?" Mark blurted.

Heph leaned back while he considered his response. Short and simple seemed best. "Yes," he said. "How did you know?"

"It's all over social media. But how did you—but *how*?"

"We met at the Olympus party last year. Then again during... All this stuff." He pointed upstairs.

"And you asked her out?" Mark looked awed.

"She's a real person," Heph said, unaccountably annoyed. "She's not a statue or an idol or something. My sister's known her for years."

"Oh, of course, Mellie used to model," Mark said, his stance relaxing. "I suppose you're used to it. Asking her out wouldn't seem so strange to you."

"Why should it seem strange?" Heph asked.

Mark hesitated, obviously trying to find a graceful way to phrase "because she's a gorgeous celebrity and you're an ugly nerd."

Heph watched him fumble with some grim schadenfreude, then remembered that Mark had arranged to get him the office chair. Even if it had just been an excuse to get the gossip, he probably owed the guy one.

"As it happens, she asked me," he said, and while Mark sputtered about *that*, he added: "Honestly, it's pretty new. I'm not sure if it'll go anywhere, but we're both having fun. I wish the press would stay out of our business." And that rang alarmingly true to his own ears, for a relationship that only existed for the sake of the press.

"I thought she said she'd been seeing the mystery man for a while," Mark said, and Heph cursed himself, because of *course* Mark kept up with celebrity news, even if Heph didn't. He really needed to watch this press conference before he accidentally jammed his foot so far down his throat a crowbar couldn't get it out.

"Well, pretty new by my standards," he said weakly. "I was with Grace for three years, you know, and then Callie for two…"

"Ah, that's right, you're a long-term man," Mark said, sitting back down. "Whereas, apart from that whole Ares off-again-on-again, she's more notori—*known* for flings."

"Well, maybe I'm a fling," Heph said, and shrugged, trying to make it look nonchalant. "I guess it's about time I had one."

"But do you see long-term potential?" Mark pressed.

Heph eyed him uneasily. The obvious answer was "of course not," but he didn't want to give it for some reason. He hadn't meant to re-open the conversation at all, much less get drawn into a cozy chat with the most notorious gossip in the building.

To be fair, if you asked Mark to keep a secret, he'd never let it slip. But any new Olympus relationship was juicy news, and this one was clearly very juicy indeed.

Actually, there was a thought. "We're both Olympus contractors," Heph said. "Are there any HR problems?"

"Hm? No, no worries there. Independent contractors aren't bound by the workplace relationships policy."

"Oh, good," Heph said, and waited.

Mark blinked.

Heph kept waiting. He was just about to try a mildly inquiring look, and maybe ask if Mark was having any trouble with his computer, when Mark said, "Well!" and got back up. "Nice talking with you, Heph. Enjoy the chair."

"Thanks," Heph said, and watched him leave.

Apparently emboldened, Cleon poked his head through the door immediately afterwards, a nervous smile spreading across his face. "Aren't you the dark horse?" he began.

"I'm not talking about it, Cleon," Heph said, and turned back to his screen.

***

Aphrodite lifted the heavy brocade hem of her gown clear of the sand (the *worst*) and surveyed the beach. "What about that rock?" she asked, tilting her head towards a craggy shelf jutting out of the beach.

"Sure you can climb it?" Penny asked. The Olympus Wardrobe Head was a sturdy, brown-skinned woman in her late 30s with an impeccable eye and encyclopedic fashion knowledge. There was no one Aphrodite preferred to dress her for a shoot.

"Not in the heels, but if you don't mind a barefoot shot, sure."

"Let me check," Penny said, and walked over to the photographer and the editor from the Italian office, who apparently thought she outranked Penny, because Penny was merely a wardrobe girl, while *she* was a junior fashion editor at *Luxe Italia*.

She was probably going to learn exactly how wrong she was about that very soon.

Not Aphrodite's problem, though. Her problem was trying to inject some excitement into this shoot, because despite Penny's killer sense of style, it was threatening to become just another boring beach spread. So far, she'd been asked to lie back on her elbows, roll onto her stomach, stare thoughtfully out towards the ocean, and a dozen other cliche poses.

Sure, the clothes were great, but everything else was boring, boring, boring.

Penny came back. Behind her, the junior editor was looking stunned, her big eyes fixed on Penny's back. "That's a go on the rock," she said, crouching by Aphrodite's feet. "Let me get these shoes."

Aphrodite put one hand on her shoulder and balanced on one leg, then the other, while Penny deftly unbuckled the delicate straps. Modeling was so weird sometimes, when she thought about it. How many other jobs involved people literally dressing you?

Aphrodite tucked as much of the skirt fabric as she could gather under one arm, and used the other hand to aid her climb, her long toes gripping the surface. It was tricky, but not impossible, and she reached the top of the rock platform undamaged. More importantly, the dress wasn't damaged either. She let the heavy material fall and swished experimentally. Yes, this worked.

"Okay!" the photographer yelled from the beach, but his voice was thin, carried away by the wind whipping through her hair. Aphrodite cupped her hand over her ear, shrugged fatalistically, and started posing.

The photographer shouted a few more instructions, but gave up quickly when she ignored him. He took shots as she moved through a few stances, extending her limbs at sharp angles and trying out the space. She imagined the bronze fabric as armor and herself a shieldmaiden, bound to protect her homeland against the brutal invaders from across the sea. Okay, now she was a brave sacrifice to some hideous beast, offering herself to save her people. She went up on her tiptoes and raised her arms above her head, crossed at the wrist. Core tensed, strong through the neck and chest, soft in the hands and fingers. Angry, scared, but yielding. The wind gusted again, blowing the skirt hard against her legs, so that it was tight against the front of her body and billowed behind, yards and yards of fabric blooming like an exotic flower over the sea spray, and her body the delicate stem that kept it upright.

That was the shot. She knew it in her bones. But her bones had been wrong before, so she kept moving, adopting another half-dozen poses, while the wind picked up speed and the tide rolled in.

The photographer signaled a pause and lowered his camera, and Penny came closer, wading into the water in her sensible flip flops. "Are you okay?" she called up. "We're losing the light, but we can get a few more shots today."

"I'm good!" Aphrodite said, and turned a pirouette to demonstrate it, extending one leg high and straight behind her as she came to rest.

"Crap, yes, do that again," Penny said, and scrambled back out of shot as the photographer changed lenses and started frantically snapping. Aphrodite tried a couple more ballet moves, but the long skirt wasn't really right for them, and she went back to more athletic poses, with another leg extension thrown in for kicks.

The wind gusted again, much stronger this time, and the skirt yanked her backwards. Penny shouted, but Aphrodite dropped her body weight instinctively, settling into a crouch and turning to present less surface area to the wind. It tugged again, then settled.

Aphrodite inhaled, then let out a breathless laugh. Her feet had bruised against the rock, and she had a scrape on one palm where she'd flung her hand down for balance, but she felt really *good*.

Penny wasn't laughing. "Okay, come down," she said, her hands raised to help, and Aphrodite clambered down from the rock, letting the dress splash into the water. They didn't need it to stay clean now. The water was up to her knees, and she waded back to shore with adrenaline still zinging through her body.

The junior editor came running with a puffer coat, but Aphrodite fended her off. "Just a quick selfie," she said, retrieving her phone and snapping a few shots.

The junior editor said something in Italian, looking nervous, and Penny nodded. "Isabella wants to remind you that you can't post anything from the shoot online."

"This is just for a friend," Aphrodite assured her, and took one last picture, this one of her scraped hand, held dramatically splayed above her soaked hems. She sent it to Heph, and then allowed herself to be put in the puffer jacket and hustled towards the RV in the parking lot. That section of beach had been closed down for the shoot, but the parking lot was still half-full of locals and tourists alike.

Her phone rang while she was changing.

"Hey!" she said.

"Hi," Heph's gravelly voice said. "Are you okay?"

"Oh yeah, I'm fine. Just wanted to give you a backstage look at my glamorous life."

He rumbled a laugh. "What were you doing?"

"Climbing a rock in a thirty-thousand-dollar dress."

"So, regular work stuff," Heph said, and his voice was so wry that she burst into laughter and felt warm all over.

Someone knocked on the RV door. "Looks like I've got to get going. See you Saturday?"

"Wouldn't miss it," Heph said, and sure, she was paying him, but he sounded like he meant it.

Aphrodite opened the door for Penny, who had acquired a first aid kid and a determined expression. "Well, you look happy," Penny said.

Aphrodite was aware that her smile was more goofy than glamorous, but she figured that would sell it better. "I was talking to my boyfriend."

"That explains it." Penny brandished a saline spray bottle. "Now, show me where it hurts."

Later, after a very good dinner, Aphrodite was deciding between a dutiful early start on her beauty sleep or just *one* round of *The Binding* on her laptop, when her phone rang again.

It wasn't a number from her contacts list.

But she didn't give her number out to many people, and it might be someone who hadn't migrated over from her previous phone.

"Hello?" she said.

"Hello, gorgeous," her ex said huskily. "Glad you picked up."

Mystery solved. "I didn't know it was you," Aphrodite said. "If I did, I wouldn't have answered."

"Aw. That's too bad. I was hoping you'd had time to cool down."

Aphrodite frowned.

Ares' voice was, unfortunately, the first thing she'd fallen for. He'd moved around so many European football clubs that he'd picked up a kind of pan-European accent, and whatever he was saying, his voice absolutely dripped with sex. He could make "Please pass the salt" sound like an invitation to take off her panties and ride him at the breakfast table.

Which, to be fair, had actually happened.

"What do you want, Ares?" she asked.

He chuckled, a noise that had always stirred heat low in her belly. Irritatingly, it still had the same effect. "I want to know if you're naked."

"Nope, we're not doing this," Aphrodite said, and hung up. "Hey, Google? Set to Do Not Disturb."

She opened her laptop. She'd *definitely* earned a round—or two!—of stabbing some imaginary monsters.

Chapter Five

Mellie called Heph mid-afternoon, right as he was getting ready to leave Olympus.

"So, you and Aphrodite," she said.

"Mellie, I'm going home."

"You can spare me five minutes."

"So you can tell me it's a bad idea and she's obviously out of my league?"

"What? Of course not." Mellie sounded genuinely surprised, which was unexpectedly flattering. "She's a peach. If I'd had the chance, I'd have tried to set you two up years ago."

"Well, why didn't you?" Heph demanded.

"Because I didn't get the chance. And then it didn't seem like a good match after all. Models work weird hours, and you like stability and routine. Callie and Grace were both strict nine-to-five girls."

"Oh."

"And then there's that whole on-off *thing* she's got going on with Ares Irontosser."

"Had going on," Heph corrected.

"Mm," Mellie said. "I'm just saying. Don't get too deep."

Heph rolled his eyes. It was probably safe, since she couldn't see him. "I don't think there's much danger of that."

"Good to know. Okay, well, I just called to tell you to revise your website."

"Okay," Heph said, and then: "Why?"

"Because you have a massive publicity coup on your hands," Mellie said, too patiently to convey actual patience with his cluelessness. "As soon as you were identified—"

"I was identified?" Heph said. "By name? I didn't give them my name."

"Heph, it's been nearly 18 hours since they got your face on camera, *of course* they have your name. And every party reporter and fashion flack in the country—and probably a lot overseas—are looking you up right now. Have you even checked your email?"

"Not my personal email," Heph said defensively. "I've been at work."

Mellie sighed, a heavy sound that carried the weight of her disappointment in his inaction. "Well, do that. And update your website; let people know you're available for work."

"I don't think anyone hiring in IT will be looking at the fashion news," Heph said dubiously.

"You'd be surprised," Mellie said. "But you're being talked about everywhere as 'Heph Smith of Vulcan Consulting', and that's brand recognition right there. Capitalize on it, Heph! In every industry, people are much more likely to reach out with job offers to people they've heard of, and right now, they're hearing of you."

"Okay," Heph said, too unnerved to argue.

"Good," Mellie said. "And if this turns into a long-term thing, I can recommend some good publicists who might have room for you on the books."

She hung up, before Heph could even frame a response at the idea of hiring a publicist.

He took the bus home, before the after-school rush limited the available seats, and checked his Vulcan Consulting email inbox on the way.

He had nearly fifty emails from people who wanted interviews or comments or simply just confirmation that he was the Heph Smith seen with Aphrodite Urania last night. Another two came in while he watched, and he tapped out a hasty message to Thea Jones.

She called him two seconds later. "Forward them to me," she said. "I'll get Aphrodite's publicist on it. Well, her publicist's assistant, anyway. Is your home address available anywhere?"

"No," Heph said. Working in IT security made you paranoid very quickly, given the enthusiasm of some sections of the internet for doxxing. He'd scrubbed any record of his address from public access a long time ago. Vulcan Consulting had a post office box, and his website only listed an email address for contact purposes; he gave his phone number to clients only after they'd signed a contract.

"I didn't realize the story would be quite this big," Thea admitted. "Must be a slow news week."

"Thanks?" Heph said.

She laughed, the first time he'd heard her express any sense of humor. "You'll be fine, kid. This is all a great sign. Welcome to the big leagues."

Narnie called while Heph was writing a brief update to his site.

"Hey," she said.

"Hi," Heph replied. "How does this sound? 'I am currently finishing a long-term contract, and will be available for inquiries from potential new clients by June 6th. Serious inquiries only.'"

"Sounds good to me, but pass it through Mellie. *So*, this is the girl you had a date with?"

"Who's 'this?'"

"Ha ha ha." There was a clattering sound from the other side of the line. Narnie shared Heph's appreciation for the satisfying clack of a mechanical keyboard. "Ew, gross, some people are awful."

"Is that observation connected to anything?"

"Just some of the stuff people are saying online. Trolls, you know."

"I don't know," Heph said. "I haven't looked."

"Good, you definitely shouldn't. Oh, this fucking asshole." There was another clatter of typing, and Heph straightened.

"Narnie?"

"Hm?"

"Are you feeding the trolls?"

"What, like I can't defend my little brother from dipshits?"

"Not when I don't want you to," Heph said, putting steel into his voice. "Not when it's just going to cause more drama. Delete it, Narnie."

"Ugh, fine." Another click, somehow sulky. "Done. Anyway, Mellie says you said that this wasn't anything serious, so let me know when it's over and I'll let my friends know you're back on the market."

"You make me sound like a piece of meat."

"And your price is rising, my surly bro," Narnie said cheerfully. "A piece of meat that Aphrodite Urania's taken a bite out of? That's a meal that a lot of ladies will want to devour. You're the dish of the day."

"Your disgusting metaphor is noted," Heph said. "Goodbye, Narnie."

"Bye, Heph. Wait! How was the soup?"

Heph hung up on her and went to his weights bench. After forty minutes of sweating, he smelled like a swamp on a hot day, and his bad hip was giving him some warning signs. He stayed in the shower for longer than usual, letting the hot water ease the strain, and wondering how long he could realistically go without looking at whatever the internet was saying about him.

Aphrodite was coming back on Friday night, and he was on the hook for a Saturday afternoon date. What could they do? What would she like? His previous relationships had involved a lot of movie dates and role-playing games, neither of which seemed suitable for getting press attention. Another meal out was probably the safest option, but it seemed kind of...boring. Ordinary. He could do better than that.

Probably.

He was almost sure.

He dried, dressed, and picked up his phone.

"Hi, Heph!" Aoide said happily. "I was wondering when you'd call."

"I need a favor."

"Of course. But tell me about you and Aphrodite! How long have you been seeing each other?"

Heph paused. Deceiving Mellie and Narnie was one thing, but he really didn't want to lie outright to Aoide. "Well, we met six months ago, right after her breakup. We talked a couple times after that." Literally, a couple of times, as in two, but it was technically accurate. "And then...it just sort of happened."

"Aw, that's cute," Aoide said. "Was it your idea or hers to go public?"

"Hers," he said, on firmer ground.

"Oh? How do you feel about that?"

"It seemed inevitable," Heph said. Again, technically true, but he was pushing it. "But that's the favor I need to ask. Now that we're public, we can go places. I just, uh...can't think of anywhere to go."

Aoide hmmed. "Invite her to the next family lunch."

"Absolutely not," Heph said.

"Worried we'll scare her off?"

"No," Heph conceded. The Smith-Waters clan had been unfailingly polite and even welcoming to his former girlfriends. They just hadn't been...enthusiastic. "But 'hey, meet my moms' isn't exactly great date material. Come on, Aoide, help me out. Mellie and Zion do dinner parties, and Narnie and Leo go hiking, and neither of those are good for me. What do you and Sara-Beth do?"

"Seedy bars with good music," Aoide said promptly. "Cocktails. Go-kart racing. Escape rooms. The zoo, of course."

"Why of course?"

"That was our first date," Aoide said, and he could hear her smiling down the line. "I was on the bus, and there was this gorgeous girl, and she complimented me on my scarf and we started talking. When she said 'this is my stop,' I said 'me too' and she said, 'no way, do you also like going to the zoo by yourself?' and I was so crazy for her after twenty minutes that I said 'no, I only go with you.'"

"And she was impressed by your game?"

"She laughed right in my face, so not so much. But she invited me to come with her anyway, and we were holding hands by the time we got to the pandas, and then we were kissing by the polar bear enclosure, and the rest is history."

"And future," Heph said. "The rest is your future."

There was a sharp inhale on the end of the line, and Aoide's voice came back wobbly. "Every now and then, I remember why you're my favorite brother," she said. "Put that in your wedding speech, would you?"

"Will do," Heph said, making a note. "Okay, you've convinced me. The zoo it is."

"Awesome. New family tradition." There was a murmur on the other end. "Sara-Beth wants to know if Aphrodite looks as good in real life as she does on covers."

"Even better."

"Intriguing, if true," Aoide said. "So. Narnie said that Mellie said that you said you don't think this is the real deal—"

"I don't think I said that."

"What did you say?"

Heph thought. "I don't actually remember."

"Well, is it?"

"I...don't know. It's early."

"Heph, what I need to know is if she's coming to the wedding."

"I invited her," Heph said cautiously. "She said yes."

"Holy shit," Aoide said. There was a loud clatter, and a scream, and then she was back on the line. "Sorry! Sorry, I dropped the phone. Also, Sara-Beth is losing her mind."

There was another shriek in the background. Heph couldn't tell if it was joy or despair. "It's not a big deal," he said.

"You'd better get her to that lunch, Heph," Aoide said. "Gotta go talk my fiancée out of a panic attack. Bye!"

Heph put his phone down slowly. Then he picked it up again, took a deep breath and, much against his better judgment, finally took a look at his social media. Normally, he used his accounts to keep in touch with his college friends. After MIT they'd scattered all over the world, and while they could arrange the occasional RPG session online, in-person meet-ups were tragically rare. He took photos of his food, sometimes, or wrote a quick book review, or commented on politics or the news. Normal stuff. Normal people stuff.

His accounts had thousands of friend requests.

Literally *thousands*.

Most of his accounts had direct messaging locked to people he'd already approved, but someone had found the one that didn't, and his DMs were full. There were interview requests, which by this stage seemed almost reasonable, and a number of messages from total strangers, which did not.

He clicked cautiously on one message from gamewinner092374.

It read, "TAME THAT SLUT, CUCK."

He stared at it, then deleted the message. After a moment's thought, he deleted the account.

Four weeks, he reminded himself. Less than that now. 25 days, and then the world would forget he ever existed.

In the meantime, he had a date to prepare for.

***

Thea had not been enthusiastic about the zoo.

"It's not a public space," she protested. "The paps can't just show up there."

"I'll take a bunch of selfies," Aphrodite told her. "The press will report on those. And there are sure to be people there who'll take pics, too! It'll look more natural."

"You just want to look at pandas," Thea said darkly.

"I really do," Aphrodite admitted. "Do you realize how long it's been since I went to the zoo? The last time I was there was like three years ago, and it was for work. I had to wear a snake, and I didn't see a single panda." She gave Thea her most limpid look. "They had *baby pandas*, Thea."

"Fine," Thea said. "Go look at the toddler pandas. And send me your selfies. I'll draft some copy for Sienna."

The pandas had been adorable. The lizard house had been spectacular. Now she was standing beside Heph in one of the custom-built primate enclosures, watching capuchin monkeys leap gracefully among the trees around them. The enclosure was massive, with lots of full-grown trees, and the pathway for visitors was a wire enclosed tunnel at bough-level. It felt a little as if the humans were the trapped ones, while the monkeys played outside.

It was an illusion, of course. The monkeys were still caged. But Aphrodite hoped it wasn't too tough on them.

"In your expert opinion, are these the most stylish primates?" Heph asked.

Aphrodite laughed. "Well, the brown and white is definitely fashion goals."

"Franciscan friars are fashion goals?"

Aphrodite blinked.

Heph coughed. "It's on the sign," he said, gesturing to the big information board beside her. "Sorry, I thought you'd read it. The first European explorers thought the monkeys looked like an order of friars

who wore brown robes with big white hoods. The order of Minor Ca-
puchins."

"Oh! So that's where the name comes from?" Aphrodite turned to
regard the information board. The text wasn't much use to her, but she
spotted the line drawing of a monk's robes. "Well, religion and fashion
are close relatives, you know. Sometimes they fight each other, and sometimes they're very cozy, but there's always a connection."

"Sounds like my sisters," Heph said. "If you met them all separately,
you'd never think they were part of a family. I mean, they're not biolog-
ically related. They all look different, and they're really different people,
too. But when you put them together, the connection's undeniable."

"And you?"

"What do you mean?"

"When people see the four of you together, is the connection there?"
She regretted the question immediately. It was way too personal for
someone she was paying to date her. She'd been lulled by the sunny
afternoon and the darting monkeys into a false sense of intimacy.

It *was* false intimacy, she reminded herself. It just *felt* real.

But Heph didn't look offended. He was frowning, but not in an angry
way—he was just thinking deeply. "I guess so," he said slowly. "We sort
of...move round each other. Like electrons in an atom."

"I can handle discussion of religion and fashion," Aphrodite said
pertly. "But I draw the line at physics."

Heph laughed. "Fair enough."

"I shouldn't have asked that, though," she admitted. "Sorry.

Heph grinned at her. "What were you going to do if I said no, I feel
no connection to my sisters?"

"Um, point over your shoulder, run away, and avoid you for the rest of my life."

"That seems reasonable."

"I thought so. Oh, look! That one has a baby!"

The capuchin female eyed her, but the baby clinging to her back rubbed its face in its mother's fur. Aphrodite grabbed her phone and crouched beside Heph's chair, angling the shot so that the monkeys were framed in the gap between their heads. "Smile!" she said, and Heph's eyes cut towards her as she took the shot.

His lips hadn't moved. But the smile was in his eyes.

"Cute!" Aphrodite said, inspecting the shot. The press would love that picture.

Her thumb hovered over the screen, and she saved it to her private album. Not the one she was sharing with Thea.

Surely she was allowed one picture, just for herself.

Just one thing, all her own.

***

Heph wasn't sure if he was supposed to be taking pictures too. He didn't really do much with his public-facing social media, and he was even less inclined to do anything with all the weird comments he was getting lately. But when he asked, Aphrodite just shook her head.

"Only if you want to!" she said, scanning the lion enclosure. The big cats were sleeping on golden brown rocks nearly the same color as their fur. Not really an exciting prospect, Heph thought, and he wasn't surprised when she kept moving. That suited him. The zoo's well-kept paths weren't any impediment to his chair, and he was enjoying the exercise.

And the company.

"I looked you up online," Aphrodite said idly. "Well, Thea did. She said you don't use social media very much."

"I do discussion servers and forums," Heph said. "Kind of have to, in my field. But I don't do a lot of public outreach."

"Did you look me up?" Aphrodite asked curiously. "I don't want to bore you by telling you stuff you already know."

"I don't think you could ever be boring," Heph said. "But okay. Why don't you tell me something most people don't know about you? Not, like a deep, dark secret," he added hastily. "I just meant, something about the real you."

Aphrodite hesitated for a moment, long enough that he worried he was pressuring her into revealing something important after all. Or maybe it was just that when so much of your life was on public display, remembering something that people didn't know about you was much harder.

"I'm really good at video games," she said.

Heph laughed.

It was out of surprise at the answer and relief that he hadn't pushed her into a distressing revelation, but he instantly realized he'd made a mistake. Aphrodite went bright red, and her eyes glittered.

"Wow, okay," she said, her back stiff.

"I'm not laughing at you!" Heph said. "I'm sorry, I'm an asshole, but I wasn't—I just didn't expect that."

"Uh-huh, because girls can't be good at video games."

"Girls regularly smoke my ass at video games," Heph said. "My friend Maria is about three bad work days away from going pro with *The Binding*. I was just...you didn't say anything for a minute, and I was thinking, oh no, I've asked her to tell me something, and she's going to tell me about the time she covered up a murder. I honestly wasn't laughing at you, or the idea of you being a gamer."

"I'll cover up your murder," Aphrodite muttered, but her heart clearly wasn't in it. "What's your friend Maria's user name?"

"For *The Binding*? I don't know for sure, but she usually uses Baked-Puppy."

Aphrodite laughed. "BakedPuppy?"

"Private joke, I think. What's yours?"

"Hm," Aphrodite said. "I might tell you later." She gave him a slanted look, something sparking in her eyes. "If you're good."

Heph tilted his head to one side, responding to the tease in her voice. "What if I'm bad?"

Aphrodite stepped into him, lips curved in that deadly smile. "Then just wait till I get you home," she purred.

The air between them was electric. She was standing very close to him, so close that one more step would bring her in arm's reach. He could pull her down to straddle him, feel the smooth skin of her arms shiver under his fingertips, taste the plushness of her lips...

"Drop party on Friday," he blurted.

Aphrodite hesitated. Was he crazy, or had she been right on the verge of taking that step? "Um, what?"

"For *The Binding*'s new map. I'm hosting a drop party at my place on Friday night. Well, Maria was going to be hosting it, but her girlfriend's parents are in town, so I'm doing it. My friends are pretty cool—well, they're nerds, but they're not incels—and I'm sure they won't be weird about--"

"Heph."

"Yeah?"

"You're babbling."

"I know," he admitted. "I realized while I was saying it that I was inviting you to hang out at my house with a bunch of people you don't know. There won't be any photographers. It's not really the deal we made."

"Right," Aphrodite said. "Although... Actually, the contract didn't specify the dates had to be in public." She tapped her lips in thought. "And we're supposed to be having a normal romance, right, with things normal people do? Like meeting each other's friends." She nodded to herself and started walking again. "I could take a couple of selfies with you in the background and get Thea to upload them to Instagram. Hashtag couplegoals."

"You don't run your own Insta? I mean, not that you have to."

"I used to. But it was like ninety percent of people being really cool and nice, and eight percent of people trying to start drama, and two percent of people being super creepy and gross. And the two percent got to me after a while. So no, I'll do content for my brands and stuff, but it all goes through Thea."

Heph remembered the one DM he'd opened and winced. What other nasty turds were lingering in his accounts? He resolved to go on a blocking spree that evening.

"I've been stalked a few times," Aphrodite added. "It was... I hate it. This one guy called Daniel Clark sent all these letters to my publicist.

It's actually pretty sad. He has this delusion disorder where he genuinely thinks I'm in love with him, and that I'm sending him messages."

"Messages?"

"Yeah. He thought that when I blew a kiss in a perfume commercial, it was meant for him. If I wore feathers on the runway, it meant I wanted to be free to go to him." She grimaced. "He called me his little caged bird. He had this plan, for letting us escape together. The police didn't really do anything. They said it was just a sad man writing fan mail, but to call them if it escalated."

"They did *nothing*?"

"Well, they said they'd talk to him. Warn him that he needed to stop. Next thing, I get a letter at home, forgiving me for what my PR team must have made me do." She shuddered. "And that's how I learned he knew where I lived. The police got serious then."

"That's awful," Heph said. "I don't know what to say. That's so terrible, I can't even imagine." Their pace had slowed to a crawl. Instinctively, he reached out and caught Aphrodite's hand as it swung beside him. She stopped walking altogether and turned towards him, swallowing hard.

"I have a permanent restraining order against him, and I haven't heard anything since. But the worst thing is that I had to move." She sounded miserable, and Heph squeezed her hand, his own throat aching with sympathy. "I had a place near Ida Park that I really loved, but it wasn't secure. He scared me out of my home, Heph."

"Oh, sweetheart," Heph said, the endearment falling out of his lips without passing through his brain. "I'm so sorry."

Aphrodite bit her lip and clasped his hand in both of hers for a moment before she let go. Heph watched her pull herself together, recovering her vitality as he watched. "Anyway, I'd love to come to your party! Want to go see the giraffes?"

"Hell, yeah," Heph said, trying to match her cheerfulness. "I love megafauna."

"Everybody loves them big," Aphrodite said, but it was a half-hearted attempt at innuendo, and the quick look she gave him was almost shy. "And after the giraffes, could we go back to the pandas?"

"You bet."

Twenty minutes later, while they were watching the pandas tumble lazily over each other, and pretending not to see the teenage girls taking shots of them on their camera phones, Heph said, "Um, sorry about calling you sweetheart."

"Don't be," Aphrodite said, staring straight ahead. "I liked it."

***

"The zoo," Persephone said thoughtfully. "That's kind of cute."

"You know what's really cute? These pictures," Hecate said. She was scrolling through her phone, thumb flicking quickly. "Heph and Aphrodite holding hands. Heph and Aphrodite looking at pandas. Heph and Aphrodite doing sex eyes. That one's less cute, more flaming hot, but you know what I mean."

Aphrodite handed Hecate a slice of cheesecake and took her phone in exchange. The last picture Hecate had mentioned showed them facing each other, Aphrodite standing so close to Heph that she was nearly touching his knees. Even in the fuzzy phone camera shot, they were making intense eye contact.

Just wait till I get you home, she'd said.

But she hadn't got him home. She'd gotten into his car, and he'd gotten into his, and they'd left without even a kiss on the cheek.

"Oh, sweetheart. I'm so sorry."

Ares had called her pet names. "Babe," "gorgeous," "hot stuff," and a few terms in French and Italian that had been guaranteed panty-droppers, at least when he growled them with that hot look in his eyes. She couldn't remember him ever calling her "sweetheart," not once.

She couldn't remember him saying "sorry" very much, either.

"I didn't realize Dessert with the Dames was an excuse for you to steal my phone," Hecate protested, and Aphrodite gave it back, sinking down into the sofa beside her and taking a forkful of her own cheesecake. Mmm, vanilla.

"This is so good," Persephone said. "I wonder if I can get Hades to expand his cooking into baked goods."

If Aphrodite were having dessert with some of her model friends, they'd all have to talk about how *bad* they were being and how long they'd have to spend training to "work off" the calories. Eating without *talking* about eating was one of the many benefits of hanging out with Persephone and Hecate.

Aphrodite knew that she wasn't truly as unconcerned as Persephone and Hecate were about what they ate. You couldn't work in an image-conscious industry for ten years without picking up some weird body-and-diet baggage. But she was working on it. She'd told her nutritionist that she wanted to focus on intuitive eating when she wasn't on a pre-show diet, and she'd nearly managed to stop negative food and body talk, at least in front of other people. Small steps were still steps.

And in the meantime, she had cheesecake.

"When do I get to meet Heph?" Hecate asked.

"I have something that can help with that," Persephone said, and pulled two black envelopes out of her bag. "You are both invited to Hera's black-and-white party next Thursday. Just an intimate, casual little gathering for eighty of her closest friends. Sorry about the short notice. I'll let her know you can't make it if you have plans."

"Are you kidding?" Hecate said, snatching the envelope from Persephone. "I'd skip either one of your funerals to go to one of Hera Kronion's parties."

"Morbid, but understandable," Persephone said, and shook the other envelope at Aphrodite.

Aphrodite eyed it dubiously. "Does she *know* she's inviting me?"

"Of course. Haven't you been to any of her parties? I know I've seen Olympus models there."

"Sure. But that was before she knew I'd slept with her husband."

"She doesn't blame you for that," Persephone said, and when Aphrodite scrunched up her face, she looked unusually stern. "Seriously. Stop blaming yourself. Bring Heph as your plus one. And Hecate can bring her secret sweetie."

"Nice try, but not a chance," Hecate said. "I can't possibly be distracted with a date. I need my keenest perception to scope out Heph's intentions. And his shoulders." Aphrodite poked her.

"There will be photographers and party reporters for some of the night, so you can get all the press you need," Persephone said. "Hera's doing some PR magic, I think. Look at me, on top of the world, screw my terrible ex, and not in the good way."

"Ah," Aphrodite said. "And if her husband's rumored ex-mistress is there, and they're clearly good with each other, that's even better for avoiding the bitter-and-twisted wife impression."

Persephone frowned. "I guess. I hadn't thought about it."

Aphrodite was absolutely certain that *Hera* had thought about it. The invitation was a signal. Declining it would also be a signal, and one she didn't want to send. "I'm free Thursday. I'll be there."

"Trying not to bang Heph in the bathroom," Hecate said cheerfully.

"You and Heph are having sex?" Persephone asked.

"No," Aphrodite said, glaring at Hecate.

"But she wants to be! Hence sex eyes."

Persephone hesitated. "Is that a good idea?"

"No," Aphrodite said, and sighed. "I'm being sensible."

"Amazing," Persephone said, her eyes twinkling. "Who would have thought?"

"Am I teaching you two how to play Mario Kart or what?" Aphrodite demanded, reaching for her TV remote.

The other two took the subject change happily enough, but a couple of hours later, Persephone lingered for a few minutes after Hecate had left.

"Hey," she said quietly. "I support your right to get your freak on with whoever you choose, obviously—but please don't break Heph's heart if you do. He might have saved my life, back in Zeus's office."

Aphrodite stared at her. "I didn't know it was that bad."

"It was pretty fucking bad," Persephone said. "I didn't really process it at the time, or for a long time after. But Zeus had already locked me in that closet. When Hades got me out, Zeus hurt him, and then hit me. I stabbed his arm with his stupid letter opener, and he let Hades go, but

I saw his face. He was so angry, Aphrodite. He didn't care what he did."
She shuddered. "If he'd taken the letter opener off me, or even just hit me
again, too hard, in the wrong place... Yeah. I don't know. I'm probably
exaggerating."

Aphrodite wrapped both arms around her and squeezed, hard. "But
what if you're not?" she said.

"Yeah," Persephone said. She hugged Aphrodite back and then let go,
dabbing at her eyes. "That's one of the what ifs. The other one is what
if Heph hadn't been there? But he was. And he said something to Zeus,
and it made Zeus realize that he had an audience. That there would be
consequences. So he stopped."

"So what you're telling me," Aphrodite said slowly, "is that I am
dating an actual, real-life hero, who is also smart and kind and knows
interesting facts about capuchin monkeys, and I am *not* allowed to have
sex with him?"

"Wow," Persephone said. "Your life is really hard."

"It's the worst," Aphrodite agreed, and hugged her again. "Love you."

"Love you too. See you Thursday!"

Aphrodite waved at her as the elevator doors closed.

The other penthouse suite door opened, and Vega Zhang stood
framed in it. "Come here," she said.

There was obviously no possibility of denial. Aphrodite went.

Vega put a finger on her lips and eyed Aphrodite up and down.
Aphrodite shifted, suddenly wishing that she weren't wearing sweatpants. Sure, they were *Versace* sweatpants, but she was face to face with
Vega Zhang, who had run the Olympus Wardrobe and high-key transformed the world of fashion. It was hard not to feel under-dressed in
front of her.

"Are you invited to Hera Kronion's black-and-white party?"

"Yes, Vega."

"Good. Bring me your clothing choices at 4 p.m. on Thursday afternoon. I will style you."

Aphrodite sucked in a breath. "*Yes*, Vega. Thank you!"

Vega waved that off. "You will need to impress your young man," she said, and grinned impishly. "Or I'll steal him from you."

"I believe you," Aphrodite said fervently. "He's definitely worth stealing."

Chapter Six

The email subject line read "Serious Inquiry."

It was from the IT department at Titan Publishing, the only real rival to Olympus's magazine publishing empire. Heph scanned the query, nodding to himself. It wasn't a huge contract, but if he could secure it, he might be able to parlay the work into further opportunities. And the noncompete clause from his time as a full-time Olympus employee had expired by now.

"I'd be happy to discuss this further," he wrote, and clicked send. A point for Mellie, he guessed.

The rest of his inbox was just crap: journalists and trolls. He clicked out of the tab and Googled "black and white party."

Aphrodite had forwarded him a picture of the invitation, which was a black card with gold, swoopy lettering, inviting Aphrodite Urania and Guest to the event. From the embossed lettering, he was guessing this was a fancy party, but how fancy did he have to dress?

Forty minutes of browsing the history of Truman Capote's Black and White Ball and a number of Pinterest boards on throwing your own black and white party left him no wiser

He could call Aphrodite, but she was working. He could text Thea, but she was also working, and besides, she might laugh at him. Vaguely wondering why he was so sure that Aphrodite wouldn't laugh at him, he picked up the phone and called the only other person he was sure would know.

"Mellie Smith-Freeman."

"Hi, Mellie. Can I ask your advice about something?"

"Sure," Mellie said, sounding both surprised and pleased.

"I've been invited to a black and white party on Thursday night. I did some research, but I'm not sure what I should be wearing."

"Black and white evening? Black tie for you," Mellie said.

"I can't just wear a suit? I have a suit."

"Is it black?"

"It's dark blue. Isn't that close enough?"

"No. The black and white thing isn't a suggestion. Wear your tuxedo."

"Oh, shit. I took that to Aphrodite's place."

"Why?"

"I..." Well, she'd see it in the news. Better to tell her now. "I'm her date to the premiere of *A Light in Dark Places*. I think her manager wanted to make sure I wasn't going to show up in cargo shorts."

Mellie took a deep breath. "Okay," she said. "I don't know whether I'm more proud that my little brother is going to be walking a premiere red carpet, or more horrified that he plans to do it in a tuxedo he bought for my wedding *four years ago*. But it'll do for the black and white. Does it still fit?"

Heph shifted his shoulders uncomfortably. He'd gotten more into weights since Mellie's wedding, and he was remembering the polo shirt that had pinched his biceps. Aphrodite had approved, but maybe the rules were different for a fitted jacket. "I'm not sure. Maybe not. I didn't try it on."

"You didn't—Okay. One second." There was some muffled murmuring. "I can call in some favors and move my schedule around. Can you meet me at the Olympus Wardrobe department on Wednesday?"

Heph mentally flicked through his schedule. "Yes, any time after noon. But Mellie, please don't feel that you have to do this. I can just go buy a tux and get it altered." Even though he wouldn't know what he was doing, and would have to deal with the curious stares of the sales staff, and struggle in and out of the damn thing while the tailor watched...

"Sure, if that's what you want to do," Mellie said. "But I truly don't mind. Do you want me to help?"

Heph exhaled. "That would be great."

"Then that's what I'll do," Mellie said, with that same note of surprised pleasure. "See you Wednesday."

***

"Hi, Lina!" Aphrodite said, climbing into her car on Monday morning. "Guess what? Vega Zhang is going to make me look pretty!"

Lina, who was secretly a fashion junkie, was suitably impressed with the news that the best stylist in the world was coming out of retirement on Aphrodite's behalf. The bodyguard today was Medea, and she seemed less impressed. Or she could have been ecstatic. With Medea, it was always unnervingly hard to tell.

The gig this morning was shooting some perfume ad work for Hesperides, a luxury goods company that Aphrodite was a brand ambassador for, in an old warehouse by the docks. Aphrodite wasn't sure what about a run-down warehouse said "aspirational designer perfume," but she'd

118

given up questioning such things. She chatted with the hair and makeup team while they dolled her up, and then the advertising stylist helped her into a tight, apple green cut-out dress. It was actually more cut-out than fabric, but it did have one absolutely enormous puff sleeve. Aphrodite poked it a couple of times, grinning as the stiff fabric sprang back into place.

"Okay," the shoot director said, as she sashayed onto set. He was Simon, one name, and a relatively big deal. She hadn't worked with him before, but he had a reputation as a perfectionist who turned out great copy. "Great to have you with us, Aphrodite. Do you want to go through these lines before we start?"

"Lines? I thought this was a static photo shoot?"

"We're hoping to get some video too," Simon said. "I called your agent this morning."

"My manager," Aphrodite corrected, looking over her shoulder. "I don't book through an agency. Thea's on a plane right now, actually."

"My assistant also texted you."

Aphrodite's stomach tightened. "Oh, texting," she said, letting out a little careless laugh. "I don't really do that, you know?"

"No problem," Simon said, his voice cooling a little. "We've got the sides right here." He picked up a few pieces of paper, stapled together, and held them out to her.

Aphrodite could feel sweat prickling at the small of her back. "Um," she said. "I'd really prefer to talk this over with Thea. My schedule today might not allow for it? I can do the photos, though, no problem."

"We're set up for film first." He gestured at one of the stools. "You can have a few minutes to read through the lines while I finalize lighting. It won't blow out the shoot time, I promise."

Aphrodite walked to the appointed stool, feeling like a mechanical wind-up doll. She stared at the pages. Okay, it wasn't a *lot* of writing. Maybe she could manage it. She steadied the paper against her knees, and tried to stop the letters from swimming around. The first word was her name in capital letters. No problem.

The first word after that started with *wh*. *When. When I. When I feel down, what drings*—no, that should be *brings—me up is—*

"Whenever you're ready, Aphrodite," Simon called.

"Just a minute!" she called back, without looking up. If she looked away, she'd lose her place. *What brings me up is the memem—mem-ber—memory—of—*

"Aphrodite," Medea said quietly. "Is there a problem?"

Aphrodite looked up. The light was changing. The production crew were no longer milling about, but waiting by their positions.

Yes, there was a problem. There were too many words, and not enough time.

Aphrodite mentally flicked through her choices. She could ask Medea to read the script to her. Thea did that for her, whenever she had lines to memorize. There was nothing wrong with her memory—she could usually hear something once or twice, and repeat it word perfect. But she didn't know Medea that well.

She could take a photo and send it to Persephone and Hecate, and hope that one of them would get it in time to react, but chances were low. Her dad would definitely still be asleep. Heph... Heph was an early riser.

But he was also really *smart*. What would he think if he knew she couldn't even read a page of writing without asking for help? He wouldn't be mean about it. That wasn't his style. He'd just know. He'd know she couldn't do it.

And if she didn't stop this fast, so would everyone else in this warehouse, and, shortly afterwards, the entire world.

Aphrodite stood up.

"Great," Simon said. "So, you'll stand over here as the chandelier swings behind you, and then—"

"No," Aphrodite said.

"Excuse me?"

"Until the filming is cleared with my manager, I won't be doing it." She looked at the production crew, who'd all fallen silent. "I apologize for all the work you've put in," she said, and then looked back at the director. "Do we go ahead with the magazine photos?"

He stared at her for a long moment, his jaw working. He obviously wanted to yell at her. If it had been even five years earlier, he probably would have gone ahead.

But now she was *the* Aphrodite. She didn't want people to think she was a diva, or difficult to work with, but she could live with it if they did. She waited, hip cocked and eyebrow raised, and watched Simon swallow exactly what he wanted to say to her.

"Yes," he said, in a voice heavy with irony. "I guess we do." He turned to his silent crew and started issuing orders, and the set sprang into action, shuffling light shields around and moving cables.

Aphrodite gave Simon a few minutes to calm down, and then crossed the warehouse floor, putting herself at his disposal. He had her clamber onto the chandelier and pretend she was swinging, made her turn in circles until she was dizzy, and then had her go down on hands and knees, crawling towards the camera "like a sexy tiger."

From the looks the crew were exchanging, Aphrodite was pretty sure this wasn't what the brief had discussed, and that she was being punished for daring to cross him. Unfortunately for this dude's ego, none of this was even in the top twenty weirdest things she'd been asked to do at a shoot. Over the course of her career, she'd been draped with snakes, told to balance in a shallow paddling pool on one leg ("like a sexy flamingo"), and had been suspended in a gilded cage over a large cauldron. She'd done shoots dressed entirely in glitter and feathers. She'd swung on a trapeze. She'd hung upside down from a jungle gym ("like a sexy monkey") while actual children, distraught at the co-option of their play space, had wailed in the background.

Crawling on a dirty warehouse floor in a bodycon dress and making faces as if she were roaring (sexily) was comparatively nothing. Although she did feel sorry for whoever would have to dry-clean the dress afterwards.

After the long shots, they brought out the perfume bottle, which was apple green, but not apple shaped. Instead, it was a kind of narrow pyramid.

"Right," Simon said, as her makeup was touched up and her hair rearranged. "For these close ups, we want you to be really into the bottle. Hold it, caress it, lick it—"

Aphrodite eyed the bottle dubiously. "Lick it?"

"Is there a problem?" he said sharply.

It wasn't worth fighting about. "No problem, but can I get an anti-bacterial wipe on that first? Gotta be careful if I'm putting that in my mouth."

"That's not what I heard from Zeus Kronion," Simon said.

The make-up artist gasped.

The director could have tried to pass it off as a joke, but there wasn't the trace of a smile in his face, and he didn't wink or laugh. He was standing close to her, right in her space, and his eyes traveled with insulting slowness up her body, deliberately lingering on her breasts.

Then, without making eye contact, he looked away.

"Okay. We're done," Aphrodite said.

He made eye contact *then*, staring straight at her. "You're refusing to carry on with the shoot? The part you agreed to in writing?"

"Yep."

Simon rolled his eyes, looking smug. "That would be a breach of contract." He said the next words slowly, as if she were too stupid to comprehend: "You won't be paid."

"I don't give a fuck," Aphrodite said cheerfully. "You just tried to make me feel shitty, and you did it in a totally unacceptable way." She stood up. She was already taller than him, but in the spike heels, she loomed. "Let me be real clear about this. I could have sucked every dick in this room—except yours, obviously, because I would never—and it still wouldn't be okay for you to say a damn thing about it. This is sexual harassment in the workplace."

The man's face went puce. "It was just a—"

"I'm going straight from here to the company offices, where I am going to explain to Arethusa Hesperides that of course I don't *want* to file suit against her company for the gross misconduct of one guy, but if I don't have an immediate assurance of safe working conditions I'm totally gonna do it. Those conditions include your immediate dismissal."

"Ms. Urania, I only—"

"Nope! We're done." She leveled a finger at him. "You fucked with the wrong bitch." She strode past him, towards the door. He put a hand out as if to stop her, but Medea was suddenly between them, calmly saying "please step back, sir," and he fell back, looking confused, and a little bit lost, as if a kitten had yawned, and revealed itself to be a saber tooth tiger.

Aphrodite didn't feel sorry for him. If he'd try that shit on her, she had absolutely no doubt he'd done something similar to other women who crossed him. Most of them wouldn't have had her money or connections. If this was the first time he'd ever faced consequences for being an asshole, she was going to make them good and strong.

Lina wasn't ready for them, of course, and Aphrodite let Medea make the call to her. The car would be parked around here somewhere, and Lina was probably halfway through one of the fantasy novels she chewed through like candy. Aphrodite had always wondered what that would be like. She sometimes listened to audiobooks on long plane rides, but that took hours. Lina could get through two or three books on a slow work day.

The director's assistant came out after a few seconds, looking relieved to see them still there. "Ms. Urania, Simon would like to sincerely apologize for his ill-considered remarks—"

Aphrodite snorted. "He can't even make the apology himself?"

The woman winced. "He's been under a lot of pressure lately."

"I'm sure he has."

"Would you consider perhaps—"

"No," Aphrodite said, as gently as she could. "I told him what I'm going to do. I'm going to do it." She looked at the woman. "I realize that this affects you too. I'm sorry about that. But he was way out of line, and I won't let it go."

"Please," the woman said. "Please just come back and talk to him. He knows he fucked up. He's really sorry. It'll never happen again."

"Heads up," Medea said quietly, and Aphrodite tore her gaze away from the assistant's face and spotted the photojournalist bearing down on them.

"Hey, Derek," she said affably, and made a gesture with her hand that directed the assistant back inside the warehouse. Derek probably already had pictures of their interaction, but at least she could spare the woman from being interrogated. The woman wavered for a second, then took off.

"Hey, Aphrodite," Derek said, his eyes fixed on the woman disappearing back into the building. "What did you do to that girl?"

"Oh, you know me," Aphrodite said pleasantly, a nothing phrase that wasn't as immediately incriminating as "no comment."

"She looked like she was going to cry."

"Did you have a question?" Aphrodite asked. "For me?"

It was an offer, and Derek's eyes gleamed as he recognized it. He could try and pursue this lead, and she'd stonewall him, and maybe be less inclined to cooperate later. Or he could take the opportunity to get her on the record for something else, and take a real story back to his editor. And he might also earn one of the most precious resources of a celebrity reporter—a favor.

"Well, since you mention it," he said, and grabbed his phone. "Have you heard what Ares said on *SportStorm* last night?"

"Derek, I don't even know what *SportStorm* is."

"It's the most popular general sports podcast in the English-speaking world."

"Okay?" Aphrodite said. Medea had stiffened, almost imperceptibly, so this wasn't going to be good, but she was already committed. "You go ahead and tell me what he said."

"Quote from Ares," Derek said, obviously reading off a transcript. "'I knew she'd never be able to replace me, but I didn't know she'd downgrade that far. The guy looks like that? He works with computers? Honestly, it's unbelievable.'"

Aphrodite's fists clenched.

"And then he and the presenter both laugh," Derek added helpfully. "The presenter says that Mr. Smith has to have some fine qualities, because you're known for your good taste, and then Ares says 'Not this time. She's obviously slumming it. Honestly, I wouldn't be surprised if he was paying her.'"

"That son of a bitch," Aphrodite snarled.

Derek looked delighted.

"Heph's many fine qualities include not being a *total asshole*," Aphrodite said. "The insinuation that he's paying me is insulting *and* stupid, because Ares knows I don't need the money. I've bailed *him* out more than once. Remember the gourmet steak food trucks? Fast Fine Dining? What a joke!"

"The car's here, ma'am," Medea said.

Aphrodite registered the warning for what it was, but she was far too mad. She leaned over Derek, speaking directly into his phone, and the microphone she knew was recording her. "Heph Smith is smart, sexy, talented, and fun. He's a real man, with a real job, and he is in *every way* an upgrade on Ares Irontosser. And you can quote me on that."

"Oh, I will," Derek said, his eyes round behind his glasses. "*Thank you, Aphrodite.*"

***

The phone call came when Aphrodite was leaving Hesperides, being driven back to her apartment.

"It's Thea, Aphrodite."

"Hi, Thea! How's your mom?"

"My mom is fine, thank you," Thea said. She sounded as if the courtesies were being forced out of her at gunpoint. "She sends her love and says thank you for the scarf. Now, listen—"

"I've got some good news," Aphrodite said quickly.

There was a pause. "All right," Thea said. "Start with that, then."

"Vega Zhang wants to style me for Hera's black-and-white party on Thursday!"

"That is good news," Thea conceded. "I'll have my assistant start calling pieces in and get the tailor on stand-by."

"Cool," Aphrodite said. She was aware that she sounded a little defiant, but she couldn't help it. Thea would probably have made better choices. Thea wouldn't have jumped right into a situation feet-first, but then, Thea hadn't been in Aphrodite's place.

"Right," Thea said, after another pause. "Was that the full extent of the good news?"

"Ummm…"

"Because the second I took my phone off flight mode, I started getting notifications. I was sitting in business class watching the pings come in. I think my seatmate thought someone must have died. Would you like to guess who they might be from?"

"Simon was being an asshole, Thea."

"I believe you," Thea said. "I've got three voicemails from him, and he gets louder and more aggressive in each one. I've got two from his assistant—one is pleading for forgiveness, and with the other I can't even make out what she's saying between her sobs and his yelling in the background. I've got a notification from a make-up artist I don't even know, who says he heard every word and would be happy to testify if need be, and incidentally do you have any need for an on-call makeup artist? I've got texts from your lawyer that just say CALL ME in capital letters, and right when I was trying to figure out what to do about all of this, I get a call from Arethusa Hesperides. This, if you're interested, was all before I got off the plane."

"Do you seriously think I should have stayed there?" Aphrodite demanded. "After what he said to me?"

"Hell, no," Thea said. "Walking out was absolutely the right move."

Aphrodite settled back. "Okay, then."

"The problem is that instead of taking ten seconds to think about what you were going to do next, you told him you were going to get him fired in front of two dozen people. And then you actually went and got him fired. Do you have any idea how that's going to play out in the press? Any idea of how pissed Arethusa is about this kind of publicity?"

"She agreed with me right away!"

"Again, whether you were in the right isn't the issue. If you'd talked to her *privately* after the shoot—or got me to talk to her—the story would be that she'd terminated the employment of someone who sexually harassed a contractor, no room for abuse in the workplace, Hesperides stands with women et cetera, et cetera. Now, there's a competing story where Aphrodite Urania can't take a joke, so she bullied a CEO into firing a guy who made an off-color remark. You look like a brat and a diva, and she looks like a pushover who caved."

"The people who are going to believe that story were always going to believe it," Aphrodite said. "No matter what I did."

"True," Thea said reluctantly. "But you didn't have to make it easy for them. Anyway, I talked to Arethusa, who fortunately *does* agree with your stance, but isn't your biggest fan right now. I got her calmed down, and was like, whew, handled that. And then guess what happens?"

Aphrodite kept quiet. Thea was going to be a lot happier once she'd got it all out.

"I get to my car, and my assistant says, sorry, Thea, it turns out Aphrodite gave an interview to Derek Cooper and it's all over the internet. There's a *voice recording.*"

"Yeah, about that…"

"That. You were going to stay classy, remember? Ares could run his mouth as much as he likes, but you were staying dignified and unmovable. 'Oh, did he say that? It's sad that he feels that way.' It was working! But then he makes some comment about you not finding anyone, and you make up this whole secret *real* relationship you've been having, which we then have to cover for by creating a *fake* relationship. Ares reacts to *that* by slamming the guy on some meathead podcast and you, apparently, completely lose your mind."

"He had no right to say any of that! Heph's not paying me to date him!"

"No," Thea said. "You're paying *him*. And after this interview, if that ever comes out, you're going to be dragged through the gutter press for months. As it is, we might have to extend the timetable on this thing. We can't stage a strategic withdrawal from the relationship with you defending his honor to the entire world." She sighed again. "At least no one's going to doubt that you mean it. You sound like you're head over heels for the poor guy."

Aphrodite fidgeted. "Mm."

"I'm going to talk to him before the tabloids find him. And what are you going to say when they find *you*?"

"No comment."

"*Exactly*," Thea said, and hung up.

***

"Morning, Heph," Thea said, at 2 p.m. on Wednesday afternoon. After Aphrodite's impromptu interview, she'd taken to checking in with him twice a day.

"It's afternoon," Heph said.

"Hell, is it?" Thea groaned.

"So it's still a slow news week?"

"Nope." Thea was quiet for a moment. "Sorry, kid, but I think you *are* the news now. There are separate fan camps online. #TeamIrontosser and #TeamSmith. All the self-described alpha males are going insane that a soyboy beta cuck has bagged their dream girl and every kid who thinks she's a moon-cursing empath is calling you a perfect cinnamon roll without flaw. It's chaos."

"I think I understood most of that," Heph said. "At least, from context."

"I am going to control this story," Thea promised him. "I've got a plan."

Heph thought about that for a second. "You realize that's terrifying, right?"

Thea laughed. "I'm the terror you want on your side, kid. Don't go online, pass every interview request on to me or Sienna, and what do you say when someone ambushes you on the street?"

"No comment."

"See, that's why I like you," Thea said, and hung up.

Maria was hanging in his door. "*Have* you seen what's happening online?" she asked.

"No," Heph said, which was only a little bit of a lie. Of course he couldn't stay entirely offline. His job demanded otherwise. He *had* to check his email inbox. Fortunately, he'd written a few macros and refined the filters, and now everything with curse words, or trigger words like "soyboy" or "cuck" went directly to trash, everything that mentioned "interview" or "comment" was forwarded to Sienna, Aphrodite's publicist, and almost everything that was work related actually got to him.

True, at Olympus, Greg's emails had gone to trash a few times because Greg was bad at workplace-appropriate language and had tripped the cursing filter, but once Heph had worked that out and whitelisted him, it worked fine.

That said, Heph had taken the occasional peek at the big social media platforms, out of morbid curiosity. On the whole, he preferred the teenagers who filmed themselves miming along to Aphrodite's voice saying "Heph Smith is smart, sexy, talented and fun" to the people who were analyzing their body language in those fuzzy zoo shots to prove that he had ceded the "dominant relationship position" to her, but even the commentators who were defending him and Aphrodite were unnervingly intense about it.

Especially since it was all pretend.

Especially since he'd listened to Aphrodite saying "He is in *every way* an upgrade" just a little too often, and liked it just a little too much.

Maria snapped her fingers in front of his face. "Hey."

Heph refocused. "Rude."

"Pay attention," she said, and pulled the door closed. "Listen. You and I are security specialists, right?"

"That's what it says on my business cards."

"And these assholes online think they're anonymous, right?"

Heph could see where this was going. If he and Maria really tried, they could probably work out someone's real identity from their social media presence within a day. "We're not doxing anyone, Maria."

"Uh-huh. And why's that?"

"I'm ignoring them. They'll get bored and go away."

Maria shook her head. "No. You're a *symbol* now."

"Literal Nazis can stay quiet, and people forget about them. It'll work."

"Not when the people remembering you *are* the Nazis, Heph." She saw his face, and grimaced. "Yeah. Okay, you haven't seen all of it."

"Eugenics talk," Heph said, his voice level. "And, I'm assuming, a fuckton of racism?" It was a fair assumption. There were a lot of people who were ignorant, or dismissive of people with disabilities, or acting out of unconscious bias, all of which was infuriating and dangerous for people like him. And then there were the people who explicitly thought the world would be better off if he didn't exist in it, because he was Black, or disabled, or both, and they were a threat on another level altogether.

"Maybe I shouldn't have brought it up?" Maria said.

"I knew it would be happening," Heph said. "I didn't necessarily need it brought to my attention."

"Right," Maria said. "I'm sorry."

Heph nodded. "I get the urge to do something," he said wearily. "I don't like the idea of people sitting there talking shit about me, and I *really* don't like what they're saying about Aphrodite. But her people are keeping an eye out for anything legally actionable, and the rest we ignore. It's just words." It felt bad as he said it, and Maria's eyes narrowed.

"Right now, it's just words," she said.

"So, right now, we ignore it."

"Okay," Maria said, drawing out the word. She left without saying anything else. But she looked as if she *wanted* to say more, and Heph remembered Aphrodite looking miserable as she described the stalker who had sent her letters and driven her out of a home she loved.

Those letters had been "just words," too.

Heph felt as if he were moving over uneven ground, but he couldn't figure out how to steady himself. And besides, it was 2 p.m., and Mellie and Penny would be waiting for him in the Wardrobe.

***

Actually, they were waiting in the lobby outside the Wardrobe, talking in low voices. Heph had been using his chair, figuring he needed to conserve his energy, but he'd brought his crutches as well. He was already tense about the prospect of navigating the Wardrobe's tight spaces. He couldn't imagine it going well in his chair.

"Oh, good," Penny said, when she saw him. She gave him one of her assessing stares, that started at his shoes—bespoke, but not in the sense she was used to—and ended at his hair (clipped close, just a breath away from a military buzz cut). There wasn't any condemnation in her eyes; more the appreciation of a woman who had just recognized an interesting challenge.

Mellie smiled at him, and he realized he was glad to see her. She knew a lot more about Aphrodite's world than he did.

"Hi," he said, smiling back.

"We're over here," Penny said, and lead him not to the wide doors of the Wardrobe, but to a smaller door by the elevators. Inside was medium sized room, with a blush pink carpet, a dressing table with a lighted mirror, several full-length mirrors at different angles and a white leather couch. Another door was ajar, showing glimpses of an equally plush bathroom, complete with shower. Lined up against the wall without mirrors were two tightly packed, wheeled racks of jackets, shirts, and pants, all black or white. There was a basket filled with black silky things that he figured were bowties and cummerbunds.

There was plenty of room for him and his chair.

"A Wardrobe secret," Penny said, grinning at him. "This is where we put models and celebrities when they don't want the hoi polloi to see them getting fitted for shoots."

"Are you sure you should be wasting it on me?"

Penny and Mellie both laughed, and Heph couldn't think of a way to explain that he'd been serious. He was an IT scrub who wore dark long-sleeved T-shirts and black or brown pants to the office and jeans at home. He owned three shirts with a collar: white for job interviews, black for funerals, and fancy for weddings. This wasn't the sort of place he was entitled to know about, much less be able to use.

Mellie gestured at the racks. "We're going to grab a coffee and catch up. You try them all on—*all* of them, Heph, no settling for whatever kind of fits—and set aside anything you like for us to look at when we come back."

"I can adjust anything that's too big or too long," Penny added. "So don't let that put you off."

"We'll be back in an hour," Mellie concluded, and they both left, chatting animatedly about the recent Met Gala. The theme had been "Threading the Boards: Fashion and the Stage." Aphrodite had worn a long dress inspired by Ellen Terry's famous Lady Macbeth gown, the one covered in shimmering, iridescent beetle wings. The Met Gala version had "scales" cut from Playbill covers and then covered in resin, so that they shivered and scattered light around her.

Heph knew all of this because one of Aphrodite's fans had put together a thread of her greatest looks, and he'd spent far too much time going through it.

He rummaged around in his messenger bag for painkillers and his water bottle, and went through the racks while he waited for them to kick in. Despite Mellie's warning, he had no intention of trying everything on; that would take much longer than an hour, and be a painful exercise besides. He rejected out of hand anything with sequins or rosettes or embroidery. Those were great for a lot of men, but he doubted very much he had the confidence to pull off anything but plain black. He did waver over one jacket with subtle black-on-black embroidery on the lapels, and finally added it to the try-on pile.

In the end, though, the clear winner was a jacket that was a little looser than most of them, fitting at his shoulders, but with more room in the body. It was made out of some kind of shiny fabric, but the shawl collar was a matte velvet, so soft that he rubbed his face in it, and grinned when the fabric caught on his afternoon stubble. The matching pants didn't quite fit, being too loose at the waist and too long, but Penny had said that would be all right. He didn't bother taking it off, settling back in his chair to look at some bug reports while he waited.

When someone knocked at the door, he said, "Come in," without thinking.

The woman who looked inside had shiny, long hair and impressive heels. She was also a complete stranger. She frowned at him and looked around the room. "Is Penny here?"

"She's in the cafeteria," Heph said, but instead of withdrawing, the woman's eyes fixed on his face.

"Excuse me," the woman said. "Are you Heph Smith?"

"Yes?"

"I'm Xanthe, a senior editor with *Luxe.* It's so nice to meet you!" She came in and proffered her hand.

Heph shook it, not sure what else to do. "Uh, I actually work here," he said. "I was an employee here for five years. I've been a consultant for two."

"Sure, right," Xanthe said, perching on the leather couch. "But now you're..." She paused.

Heph didn't know how she'd intended to end the sentence, but he could make some guesses. Some variation on *important,* or *interesting,* or *famous,* although the last definitely wasn't true. He was just dating someone famous. And this woman, who must regularly work with celebrities and encounter them at runway shows and Olympus parties, had somehow found this thrilling enough to make conversation with him.

"I'm so happy for you and Aphrodite," she said. "It's just, like, so encouraging to see people in love, you know?

"Um, right."

"You looked so cute at the zoo! And I thought it was so sweet that she defended you to that reporter!"

Heph's face must have done something, because Xanthe leaned in sympathetically. "What do you think of Ares, though? Not nice, right?"

"Don't know what you're talking about," Heph said. "I thought it was really cool, being called out for being ugly by a famous sportsman."

"And it was gross of him to say you must be paying her!"

"He wouldn't be saying that if he could see my bank account," Heph said, and then remembered that his bank account currently had fifty grand in it that hadn't been there two weeks ago, courtesy of Aphrodite. "I mean... I'm not a tech billionaire. I'm just a guy."

Xanthe nodded enthusiastically. "So, she's a star and you're just a guy—how did you two meet?"

"Heph has no comment," Penny said from the open door, and as Xanthe straightened up, she suddenly looked much less empathetic, and much more focused.

Oh, shit. That hadn't been idle workplace conversation. It had been an interview.

How could he have been so stupid? She'd introduced herself as a journalist and started asking questions. His understanding of journalism ethics was fuzzy, but he hadn't specified anything as off-the-record. Did that mean she could just quote him? Thea was going to commit bloody murder.

"Hi, Penny," Xanthe said, one professional to another, and nodded at the racks. "So, those don't look entirely like Wardrobe pulls to me. Did you call in some new-season pieces from the designers? Is Heph going somewhere special?"

Penny folded her arms. "Xanthe. Did you want your Bahamas shoot to go smoothly?"

Xanthe's eyes were suddenly cautious. "Yes."

"Then scoot."

"Can't blame a girl for trying," Xanthe said cheerfully, and turned back to Heph. "Don't worry, I'll only use that as background. But if you and Aphrodite want to do a sit-down, I guarantee that we at *Luxe* are *very* interested in your story!"

She waved at Penny and shot out the door, calling a greeting to Mellie as she passed her.

"Heph," Mellie said, looking appalled.

He dropped his head in his hands. "I know," he groaned. "Don't tell me."

He waited for Mellie to say something anyway. She almost had to; he'd presented her with a perfect opportunity to scold him. Instead, when he raised his head, she was looking determinedly at his tuxedo. "I like that," she said, sounding almost surprised. "Good fit for you."

"Mellie, did you want to catch up with Diana?" Penny asked, advancing on Heph with a pincushion and a calculating look.

Mellie recognized the obvious cue. "I'm taking you home," she told Heph, before she left. "Don't go anywhere without me."

"Did you really call designers and ask them for clothes?" Heph asked Penny, as she muttered to herself and pinned up his trouser hems. "Just for me?"

"Yes," she said absently. "I think I'll do a mid-length hem. That'll work sitting or standing."

Heph liked Penny Laconia. She was a practical person who did her job very well, something that was unfortunately more rare than he'd like to believe. On the day he'd started at Olympus, at the ripe age of 18, Mellie had told him to find Penny. "Go to her if you have any problems," she'd said, with absolute confidence. "She'll fix them for you."

Heph hadn't, of course. He couldn't think of anything worse than approaching the Head of Wardrobe, metaphorical cap in hand, saying, "If you please, miss, my sister said you'd help me."

But Mellie had obviously also talked to Penny, because six months *after* he'd started, she'd sat down with him in the cafeteria and introduced herself. Heph had tried to be polite, because Mellie's interfering wasn't a good reason to be rude to this woman. And twenty minutes later, she'd nodded and said it was nice to meet him, and left.

And the next day, Cleon said that Heph's request to start early and leave early and take an earlier lunch hour had been approved.

"I thought you said this wasn't very likely," Heph had said.

Cleon had looked mystified. "I didn't think it would be. HR think that if they approve a flexible schedule for anyone, everyone will start clamoring for them." He shrugged. "But I'm happy for you."

Heph had been both happy and *suspicious.*

"Why are you helping me?" he demanded now. "I know you can't really have the time. Is it just because of Mellie? Or do you feel *sorry* for me?"

Penny sat back on her heels, her head tilted, and regarded him closely. "I don't feel sorry for you," she said. "And truthfully, I like Mellie, and I don't mind doing her a favor, but I'm doing this for you."

Heph blinked at her.

"Because I like you too. You're a good guy. And Hades is one of my best friends, and I heard a little bit about what went on upstairs, and Mark Hermes let slip that you'd been blackballed for it."

She scowled. "Do you think I like knowing that the boss is a creep and liar? I hate it. I hate that just by being here and doing the job that I love, I put money in his pocket. But Odysseus and I have a kid, and we can't afford to quit. Frankly, Olympus can't afford to lose us. So when Zeus gets what's coming to him, and a new CEO takes over, there will be a working Olympus left to support her."

"Her?"

"Or him, or them," Penny said, and winked at him. "Who knows, right? And in the meantime, I style you for Hera's party so that she can show the entire world that she was always the one who brought the style and grace, and he's the dirtbag who did her wrong. There, that hem works. Mellie said your shoes need to be made to measure?"

Heph nodded, and held out his worse leg. His shoes were comfortable, but definitely more practical than elegant. "That one's the twisted foot."

"If your orthotics supplier can give you the specs, I can probably get you something more formal custom-made for the premiere."

Heph hesitated. "That would be good," he said, and added hastily. "But I should pay for them."

Penny pursed her lips. "You'll pay for them at the discount I get."

"Deal," Heph said, and slapped hands with her to seal the bargain.

Mellie took Heph home, to save him the bus trip, and it wasn't until he got out of the car that he realized she hadn't grilled him about his work life or his recent dates with Aphrodite. They'd talked exclusively about what he should expect at the party, with some diverting stories about terrible guests at some of the glitzier events she'd run. The stories had been reassuring. Whatever social faux pas he might commit, he probably wasn't going to throw up in Hera's hot tub.

Weirdly, *not* being interrogated about work had reminded him of the Titan query. The IT Head had promised to get back to him by end of business yesterday, but he hadn't heard anything.

Frowning, he tried the number at the bottom of the email signature.

"Phoebe Delphis speaking."

"Hello, Ms. Delphis. This is Heph Smith of Vulcan Consulting. You asked me to get in touch regarding a network security contract."

The woman's voice, which hadn't been particularly warm, went almost arctic. "I'm sorry, someone from our Human Resources team should have been in touch. We're no longer interested."

"Oh. Well, if other contracts come up, I hope you'll keep Vulcan—"

"No, I don't think so," she said. "Vulcan isn't a suitable match for us. Goodbye, Mr. Smith."

"What?" Heph said, and the phone went dead.

He put it down, frowning. Did Zeus have influence over Titan? If even his enemies weren't interested in hiring Heph, finding work was going to be much tougher than he'd thought.

Chapter Seven

Heph was leaning on his crutches in his front doorway, staring at her.

Aphrodite had been stared at by the best. Normally, her reactions ranged from preening smugness to calm acceptance. For some reason, Heph was making her feel sort of shy. Pleased, but shy.

"Well, what do you think?" she asked, twirling the skirt of her gown just a bit.

"I can't think," Heph said. She could swear his voice was rumbling an octave lower than usual. "I'm too stunned to think. You look incredible."

Aphrodite giggled, and felt a flush rise up her neck. What was wrong with her? "You know, for someone who claims he's not charming, you can definitely give a girl a compliment."

Heph shook his head. His gaze surveyed her dress again, and then returned to her face. "That's not a compliment. I'm literally speechless."

Aphrodite was glad; glad that she'd given into Vega, glad that she'd come to Heph's door herself instead of sending Lina. And she was *very* glad that she'd said yes to the black molded corselet that looked like a smooth piece of futuristic battle armor. It wrapped around her mid-torso in smooth curves, shoving her boobs up, giving her a definite waist, and adding a martial contrast to the rich sheen of the smooth ivory silk.

The dress dropped in heavy pleats to the floor and rose to a wide, high collar that rested on her shoulder points. Only her arms and collarbones were bared.

It was a lot less skin than she usually exposed, with not a hint of cleavage or a glimpse of ankle. No thigh slit, no cut outs, nothing transparent, features that had heavily featured in the gowns the designers she regularly pulled from had sent her. Vega had tossed them all aside, and then produced this gown from a designer Aphrodite had never heard of, but was definitely asking Thea to look up.

"You look good, too," she told Heph, which was very true. Her fingers itched to see if his jacket collar was as soft as it looked. She stepped closer and indulged the urge, pretending to adjust the fit. It *was* soft, and he smelled great too. Not that he smelled bad, normally, but tonight he was wearing some kind of cologne. She inhaled deeply. Cedarwood, she thought, and something kind of herbal. Sage?

"Do I smell that bad?" Heph asked, and she realized that she was standing in his doorway, fully sniffing the poor guy. He sounded amused, not offended, but she still felt her flush deepen.

"No, definitely the opposite!" she said. "Wait, before we go, can I get the tour?"

"If you like," Heph said. "I mean, you're going to see it all tomorrow."

"Oh, sure. But I gotta make sure the facilities are up to standard, you know?"

Heph laughed, and moved backward. She really liked his laugh. It was a kind of steady thunder. Never mocking or mean—just happy.

Heph's house was all on one level. Smaller than hers, and regrettably less pink, but super neat and comfortable looking, the wooden floors burnished. His kitchen looked like a space he actually used, with low counters and polished pans. His living space had a TV that wasn't as flashy as hers, but was still perfectly respectable for console gaming, and his home office had a tower and monitor set-up that she envied. There wasn't any point in her getting a proper gamer desktop or chair set up when she was away so often (and she was still death on her laptop, anyway) but she did have yearnings in that direction. Maybe it wouldn't be *so* frivolous.

"So, does it meet your approval?" Heph said. He sounded a little uncertain.

"Oh, *absolutely,*" she assured him, smiling wide. "I'm very into this set-up."

He grinned.

"You've got a lot of bookshelves."

Heph nodded. "I like paper books. Narnie keeps telling me that e-readers are the future, but I like something I can touch. Feel free to borrow anything you like the look of."

"Oh, that's okay," Aphrodite said. "Um, what else is there?" She scootched past him and down the hall to a random door. Bathroom, where she caught a huge whiff of that cedarwood and sage scent.

Bedroom.

Mistake.

His bed was the only untidy thing in the whole house, rumpled russet covers flung back, slate-gray sheets turned over them. One pillow at the top, dented from his head. Those sheets would feel cool and smooth against her body as he rocked into her from behind. She could bury her head in that pillow and beg for more, harder.

Heph reached past her, his crutch dangling from his wrist as he grabbed the door handle and pulled the door shut. His broad hand passed within a whisper of her breast.

"Sorry," he said gruffly. "I didn't clean up for company." His deep voice seemed to reverberate down her spine, vibrating out from there to touch every part of her body.

She would very much like him to touch some parts of her body, right now.

"That's okay!" she said, and bolted back down the hallway. There was another door through the kitchen that she hadn't noticed before, but she definitely wasn't going to explore now. With her luck, it'd be his special sex dungeon, fitted out with an intriguing display of specialty items, none of which she was allowed to *use*.

This was crazy. This whole fake relationship thing was crazy. She should just tell him she wanted him, that they should cancel the whole deal, skip the party, and get him out of those shiny formal pants.

"I wanted to say thanks, by the way," he said, and she paused, the words crowding in her mouth.

"What for?"

"For the opportunity. Finding new clients has been more difficult than I thought it would be."

"Why?" Aphrodite said, confused. Didn't everybody need IT?

"Zeus blacklisted me," Heph said. "Right now, he's telling everyone who cares to ask—and even those that don't—that hiring me is a great way to piss off the Olympus CEO and board chair. One of my long-term clients canceled today. And a job that looked like a strong possibility mysteriously fell through."

"That son of a *bitch*," Aphrodite snarled.

"I'll be fine," Heph said. It sounded automatic, like he was used to saying that a lot. "But that's why I wanted to say thanks. I've got savings, but your contract is really going to help. With that, if I'm careful, I can go two years without working at all. By then, this will have all died down and I'll be solid again." He grimaced. "Probably."

Right. *Right.* She was paying him, that was how this worked. She couldn't ask him to throw that away for hot sex—even *really* hot sex—and Hecate had been brutally clear that she couldn't have sex with him *while* she was paying him.

Then she realized something, and frowned.

"Everything okay?" Heph asked.

"Sure," Aphrodite said absently. "Let's get going, I think we're fashionably late enough now. Thea will be waiting."

It had occurred to her that Heph might say *no.*

He wanted her. She was never wrong about that. But he might want *more* than hot sex. He might want a real relationship. He might want a *girlfriend.* And if he did, he probably wanted someone stable and smart who knew a lot about interesting things, not some impulsive, pretty girl who couldn't read any of the books on his shelves.

"You took your time," Thea said, as they joined her and Medea in the back seat. Aphrodite's normal town car had been replaced by a hire limo for the evening and Lina had muttered contemptuously about the engine specs all the way out to Heph's place.

"Hi, Thea," Heph said. "Sorry again about that Xanthe thing."

Thea smiled at him. "No problem," she said, with obvious affection. "I've promised her your first exclusive sit-down interview as a couple."

Heph's eyes widened.

"Scheduled for *after* your sister's wedding," Thea continued, her eyes twinkling. "Which, oh dear, you'll have broken up by the time it's meant to happen. In the meantime, she'll be kneecapping every other Olympus journalist in the building to protect her exclusive. I love it when I get the press to do my dirty work for me. So don't apologize. Really, I should be thanking you."

Aphrodite pouted. "How come you're nice to Heph when he makes mistakes, but when I make them, you yell at me?"

Thea bopped her lightly on the nose with the tip of her stylus. "Because Heph doesn't have ten years of experience in the public eye."

Heph frowned. "Aphrodite told a sexist creep to stick it and made sure that everyone knew he was a creep," he rumbled. "I don't think that was a mistake. Maybe if more people followed her example, there'd be a lot fewer creeps."

There was a startled pause, and then Thea said, "I take your point. Let's go over the safe topics to discuss with the party reporters tonight," and started scrolling through her phone.

Aphrodite felt this warm, gooey sensation in her chest. It was the same reaction she'd had the first time Persephone had brought her cookies, or the first time Hecate had told a fan who was whining about her refusal to hug him in a selfie to fuck the fuck off. She *liked* Heph. He'd stuck up for her, even to Thea, and he clearly meant what he said.

He wasn't totally right, of course—most women *couldn't* do what she'd done at that photoshoot and get away with it. If Aphrodite had exposed every creep and misogynist she'd had to deal with over her career, her career would have lasted maybe three months, and the creeps would have kept right on rolling. But now that she *could* do it... Maybe he was right. Maybe she should follow her own example.

He was so *good*.

He *deserved* a proper girlfriend.

And it couldn't be her.

She'd only ever managed one long term relationship, if you could even call what Ares and she had had a relationship. It was more like a succession of fireworks: exciting, brilliant, and powerful, followed by alarm bells and painful burns. She'd come in close and then cut and run. Ares had detailed her failings in numerous fights, and while he was an absolute asshole, he was also right. She wasn't good girlfriend material.

"Don't worry," Heph said. "I won't embarrass you tonight. I'll find a spot in the corner while you dazzle everyone." His tone was light, but she thought he might mean it, too.

"Of course you won't embarrass me," Aphrodite said indignantly. "You could never."

"You were just kind of quiet," he said. "Are you sure everything's okay?"

No! It wasn't okay! Because she wanted him *so bad* and she couldn't have him, because he was going to end up with some safe, serious girl named Belinda or something. And she would have to be *happy* for him, because who wouldn't be happy for Heph?

The car slowed down and pulled to a halt.

"Okay, kids," Thea said. "It's show time. Make Mama proud."

***

Hera had arranged a black carpet leading into the lobby of her apartment building, photographers held back by white velvet ropes on both sides.

Heph's first thought was to wonder what the other people in the building were supposed to do if they wanted to run to the corner store for a quart of milk. Had Hera asked them to use a back entrance? Had they been bribed to stay at home?

Then the cameras went off, the shouting started, and he entirely forgot about Hera's neighbors.

His crutch tips were struggling with the carpet, catching on the deep pile. The noise felt like a solid roar of "Aphrodite! Aphrodite!" She was beside him, her pace effortlessly matching his, turning and waving as she walked. He stopped worrying about trying to keep up and concentrated on moving steadily instead, even if he was slow.

"Heph!" someone called, and he looked up, startled when the light flashed in his face.

"That's Bella," Aphrodite murmured, and Heph recognized the name from Thea's list. Someone who could be trusted to toss them some softball questions. They changed course towards her.

"Amazing dress," Bella enthused. "A few more poses?" The photo-journalist beside her was snapping away as Aphrodite fluidly posed. Bella gestured at him. "And Heph, of course."

"I'm not really someone who can pose," he said, smiling awkwardly to soften it. Thea had advised him to "lean into that self-deprecation thing you do so well," and he still wasn't sure what to think about that.

In a swirl of silk and a cloud of perfume, Aphrodite appeared beside him. "Look just over my shoulder," she said. "Lift your chin a bit? Perfect. That's your angle."

He darted his eyes towards her without moving his head, and caught the grin on her perfectly made-up face.

She stooped slightly and kissed his cheek. The flashbulbs went off all at once.

Her lips were soft, the pressure barely noticeable. She lingered there for a split-second, then withdrew, eyes downcast.

Heph desperately hoped he wasn't blushing, but from the heat in his cheeks, he suspected that was a lost cause.

"Aw," Bella said. "So, you two are still in the honeymoon phase?"

Aphrodite hesitated.

"That's right," Heph said stoutly. He wasn't sure what was wrong, but if Aphrodite was flustered, it was up to him.

"And you've been dating for...?"

"We've been seeing each other casually for a few months," he said, following the script. "We've been officially girlfriend and boyfriend for a few weeks."

"And how did you meet?"

"I do some consultation work for Olympus, and Aphrodite works with them too, so..." Heph shrugged awkwardly. He wanted to limit the outright lies as much as he could. Aphrodite and Thea were obviously humoring him, but neither of them had to face his sisters. The more consistent the story was, the less likely he'd make a mistake for one of them to pounce on. So they were being vague about the timeline and how their "relationship" had started, and letting people assume, as Bella obviously did, that it was a wildly improbable workplace romance.

"We'd better get inside," Aphrodite said brightly. "Nice to talk to you, Bella!"

There were more photos, of course, and more questions. Heph followed Aphrodite's cue and ignored the latter. They moved behind the discreet black screen that had been set up to shield the elevator block, probably so that none of Hera's guests had to suffer the indignity of photographs depicting them waiting for an elevator like the peasant class.

"I'm sorry," Aphrodite said, so low he almost missed it.

"What for?"

"Kissing you. I mean, kissing your cheek. I didn't clear it with you beforehand."

Heph nearly said "It's in the contract" or "That's okay" or something equally awkward and ham-handed, but he remembered the zoo.

"Don't be sorry," he said. "I liked it."

Aphrodite looked at him, her green-blue eyes sharpening with intent. The first few times she'd focused on him like that, he'd been more or less stunned by the incomparable beauty of her face, by the fact that she, Aphrodite Urania, was paying attention to him.

She wasn't any less beautiful now, but he could see her better. He could see the warmth in her eyes, the smile lurking in the corner of her lips. He could see the vulnerability of the apology she'd offered, and her pleasure at his response.

She bent towards him, clearly intent on repeating the kiss, and Heph gestured to stop her. She hesitated.

"It's my turn," Heph said. He reached up and planted his lips on the highest point of her cheekbone. It was a friendly gesture, he told himself, a way to put her back at her ease and show her that he truly hadn't minded.

Her skin was petal-soft under his lips. She smelled like roses and cinnamon.

She gasped, very quietly, but he heard it, and when he pulled back he saw the pink flowering in her cheeks. She pressed her hand to the spot, her eyes soft.

"Thank you," she said quietly.

The elevator doors opened. They walked in, side by side, and were companionably silent all the way up, the quiet air alive with all the things they weren't saying.

***

Two hours later, Heph yearned for that silence. Hera's guests, in a variety of fancy gowns and somber suits, weren't particularly loud or raucous, but there were a lot of them, and for some reason, a lot of them wanted to *talk* to him. He'd understood why the party reporters darting through the penthouse had made a beeline for him and Aphrodite as soon as they'd arrived. They were doing their jobs and chasing the story.

But most of the actual guests were important people. He'd spotted entertainment moguls, charity trust leaders, business men and women—noticeably more women than men—and several legitimate celebrities, like Aphrodite. The mayor was here. His own mother, a mere city councilor, probably hadn't ranked high enough to qualify for the guest list.

The mayor was also visibly struggling to remember why he looked familiar, as Aphrodite praised her work funding after-school literacy programs.

"I'm Heph Smith," he said. "Thetis Smith-Waters's son."

"Ah!" Mayor Summers' face cleared. She was wearing a plain black gown with elegant lines, a row of pearls her only decoration. "Yes, of course. You're the youngest, aren't you?"

"That's me."

"Heph runs Vulcan Consulting, an IT company specializing in net-work security," Aphrodite put in. She'd been saying that, and things like it, all night, and he wasn't sure why. Maybe she needed to emphasize his normal-person qualities for the party reporters.

The mayor's gaze turned thoughtful. "Are you any good?" she asked bluntly.

His mother had been working with this woman for four years, and talked about her often. Here was one person he was sure he could be honest around. "Yes," he said, just as forthright. "I'm one of the best in the business."

"How much do you cost?" she said, and then, at the polite murmur of the man next to her, "all right, yes, I'm being reminded not to talk shop at social events." She nodded at him. "I'll remember you next time, Mr. Smith."

Aphrodite's hand touched his arm, feather-light. She'd been touching him a lot. Nothing intrusive or anything that impeded his movement. Just those light, soft touches, on his arm, on his shoulder, brushing dust away from his velvet collar. If she kept doing it, he was going to have to ask her to stop — not because he didn't like it, but because he liked it way too much.

Each time she laid her hands on him he felt it like sparks on his skin, surging helplessly around his entire nervous system. Why the hell had he kissed her? He'd felt that contact on his lips all night.

"Are you okay?" she whispered. Her breath was warm on his ear.

And that was the other thing.

"My hip isn't doing so great," he admitted.

He should have brought his chair. The thick pile of Hera's many rugs would have been a challenge, and maneuvering through the crowd would have been even more of one, but after two hours of standing beside Aphrodite while she charmed people and posed for pictures with the other guests, he was aching all over. His bad hip had reached the stage of shooting pain up his spine and down his leg in occasional electrical jolts. It was a bad sign, both for his ability to see out the evening, and for the party he was supposed to be hosting himself the next day.

"Can I help?"

Heph was on the verge of saying no. But she was already helping him, with the unexpected boon of that contract. And he was helping her too, wasn't he? He'd done pretty well with the small talk and believable romance stuff tonight. "I've got painkillers with me, but I could use somewhere quiet to sit down while they take effect."

"On it," Aphrodite said instantly, and darted away, graceful as a gazelle in her improbable heels. She returned two minutes later with their hostess.

Hera had opted to ignore her own theme. She was wearing gold.

Even to someone as fashion-blind as Heph, the long gold gown in that sea of black and white was a statement. She would dominate every picture of the event. She was going to be the talk of the society pages. She was proclaiming herself to be someone who didn't have to follow the rules, who broke them with impeccable taste and irreproachable style. A leader. A queen.

And the glitter in her dark eyes said she knew exactly what she was doing.

"I do apologize," she said, right away, and Heph thought she might actually mean it. "I should have considered this in advance." She personally ushered them out of the crowded main space and down the penthouse hallway, moving aside the discreet black velvet rope that tactfully declared this space off limits to guests. Pausing outside one door, she tapped twice, and then opened it.

Heph was right behind her, so he had an excellent view of what happened next. The two people already in the room were springing away from each other, both of them red and flustered.

Persephone Erinyes turned away from the door, adjusting the top of her white gown. Hades Kronion stepped hastily behind a chair.

Heph sympathized. He'd spent a lot of the evening telling his own body to behave. Formal trousers looked good, but there was absolutely no room for error.

"Oh, really," Hera said. "Can't you two keep your hands off each other for half an hour?"

Persephone turned back, restored to decency. "Sorry, Hera," she said, her cheeks bright pink. She glared at Heph—no, over his shoulder, at Aphrodite, who had clapped both hands over her mouth and was shaking violently, her eyes bright with the laughter she was suppressing.

The room was a sort of study, or maybe a library. Bookshelves lined the room, and there was a desk towards the window, a dainty antique gold thing with curving legs that had probably cost more than Heph's house deposit, with a silver laptop positioned in the center. There was a small, tapestried sofa, and a few chairs around a coffee table, one with an ottoman and a neatly folded red and white striped blanket flung over the back.

Heph's hip chose that moment to lock up completely. He hissed involuntarily as the pain gnawed at the joint, strong enough that his vision grayed out at the edges. He leaned on his crutches and his better leg, breathing through the agony.

"Don't grab him," he heard Aphrodite say, all amusement gone from her voice, and then she was right beside him. Not touching him, not trying to interfere, but there if he needed her. "Sofa or chair?"

"Chair," he ground out, panting. The spasm eased a little, the first shock over, and he took the few steps necessary to the chair with the blanket on it. His hip was numb for the moment. He knew that the pain would be back soon, and it was a race between that brief grace period and the need to move slowly, in case he did more damage he couldn't feel.

He sat down, and bent forward to hoist his leg up onto the ottoman with his hands, not trusting his hip to do the lifting. Aphrodite put a glass of water on the table beside him, and he pulled his painkillers out of his pocket. He normally tried to be stingy with the stronger opioids—they made him sleepy and sometimes nauseated—but this time he took the maximum dose.

"I'm okay," he said.

Aphrodite's worried face swam into his field of vision. "Are you sure? I can call Lina. We can leave."

"The worst is over," Heph said, only partly lying. The immediate effects would ease soon, now that he'd taken the pills. The longer-term effects were something to worry about tomorrow. "I'll just sit out the rest of the night in here. It'd look weird if we left now. Let's not ruin Hera's party."

"I appreciate the thought," Hera said. It was impossible to tell whether she was amused, or angry, or insulted.

"Are you sure?" Aphrodite said. She was kneeling in front of him, her dress pooling around her.

Heph groped for her hand and squeezed it. "Yes."

"The reporters will be leaving in an hour or so," Hera said. "If you truly don't mind waiting, Heph…"

"I don't," Heph said and Aphrodite gave him a wobbly smile. There was a tension in her face he didn't recognize. "I'm honestly fine," he told her. "It happens sometimes. I'm used to it." He loosened his grip on her hand, but she didn't pull away. Her fingers stroked his palm, a soothing gesture he wasn't sure she was aware she was making. For a moment, all he wanted to do was lean into her, ask her to rub the back of his neck, let her take care of him.

But he couldn't do it. He already liked her too much. He couldn't ask for more; he couldn't give her so much control over him. If he gave in any further, he'd be totally lost.

"Go get pictures with Hera," he said, as firmly as he dared.

Aphrodite nodded, and rose to her feet in a single graceful movement. Hera was looking at her with approval. "I'll be back when the reporters go," she said, and it was a promise.

As the door closed behind her, Heph let his head sink back against the chair, closed his eyes, and exhaled.

"Do you mind if I stay?" a voice asked tentatively.

Heph opened his eyes to regard Hades. Persephone had evidently left with Hera and Aphrodite. "No, of course not." He knew Hades a little. They'd hung out at Olympus parties before, mostly because two awkward guys could linger together in a corner and look less awkward, without expecting each other to make sparkling conversation.

Hades nodded towards the window, which had the drapes drawn firmly closed. "I'd had about as much as I could take, you see. Hera got me to hide in here once I'd pressed sufficient palms."

Oh, right. They were on the twelfth floor, and Hades had that heights phobia.

"Honestly, it's good not to be the only invalid," Heph said, and Hades smiled in recognition. "Sorry about the interruption," Heph added.

Hades raised his eyebrows. "Please don't get me wrong," he said, "But I was a lot happier to see you the last time you surprised me."

Heph grinned at him. "Hey, I didn't make you grope your girlfriend in the middle of your sister-in-law's party."

"Sister," Hades said. "I'm just going with sister."

"Smart," Heph said. The morphine was starting to kick in. The throbbing in his hip was easing a little, but it would be another half hour before he was truly comfortable. "Sisters are good. Don't tell mine I said that."

Hades smiled. "Has Aphrodite met your family?"

"Oh, Mellie's met her. But not as my girlfriend."

"Persephone and Aphrodite are good friends," Hades said tentatively. "I know we haven't spent as much time together, but perhaps we could have a drink some time?"

"That would be great," Heph said, with a sincerity that surprised him, and only then remembered that this was all fake. Aphrodite wasn't really his girlfriend, and if Hades thought she was, then his own girlfriend was lying to him, and any friendship between them would be on false pretenses. He frowned, trying to look as if he'd just remembered something. "But I'm pretty busy for the next month or so. Can we rain-check?"

"Certainly," Hades said, looking curious.

Heph nodded, and reached for his glass of water.

"Persephone told me about your contractual arrangement," Hades added, and Heph sputtered on his sip, forcing the swallow down before he could spray water all over Hera's furnishings. Hades leaned forward, looking worried, but Heph waved him away.

"She wasn't supposed to do that," Heph said, when he'd recovered enough to speak.

Hades shrugged. "We come as a package deal." He was trying to sound nonchalant, Heph thought, but there was a definite note of smug triumph in his voice.

"So you know Aphrodite and I aren't actually dating," Heph said.

"You could have fooled me."

"We're supposed to fool you," Heph said, exasperated. "That's the whole point."

"Hm," Hades said. "I wonder, have you considered—"

There was a peremptory rap on the door, and then it opened without a pause, as a very large man with shoulder-length blond hair walked in, holding two glasses of amber liquid in one big hand. He was wearing all-white. There were other men there in what Aphrodite had told him was white-tie, but those had been white tuxedos. To Heph's confused eye, this looked like a ship captain's uniform.

"Hey, bro," he was saying, "I heard you were—oh." He stopped and regarded Heph thoughtfully. "We've met, right?"

"Heph Smith."

"Don Kronion. Oh, right, you're the unfriendly genius."

"Please excuse him," Hades said, sighing. "I'd claim that he was raised in a barn, but we grew up in the same house, so..."

Heph shrugged. "It's accurate."

Don pointed at him. "I like this guy." He shook one of the glasses at Hades. The ice cube tinkled against the sides.

"I better not," Hades said. "Anxiety meds."

Don nodded, and offered the glass to Heph.

"I just took a morphine tab."

"Well, now I feel left out," Don complained. For a moment, he looked as if he were contemplating downing the spare drink, but he put it down on a bookshelf instead and sipped his own, while the abandoned glass leaked condensation onto the fine wood.

Hades gave his brother a disapproving look. "Could you get a coaster? We don't want to ruin Hera's furniture."

"Zeus chose the bookshelves," Don said. "He'll probably get them in the separation of assets."

"Oh, in that case," Hades said, and left the glass where it was. "Are you enjoying the party?"

"What's not to enjoy?" Don said, and leered. It seemed to be an automatic expression. "Lots of ladies here tonight, and they appreciate quality when they see it."

"Yes, why are there so many women?" Hades asked. "Hera usually tries to keep the numbers more or less even."

Don swirled the amber liquid in his glass. "She invited a lot of heavy hitters in the entertainment and publishing industries. Most of the men declined. Other engagements."

"But the heavy hitting women came?"

"Almost all of them. And some of these women are the wives of the heavy hitting men, who know that snubbing Hera might turn out to be a bad idea socially, even if they don't think she has the business impact Zeus does. Hera thinks they might be hedging their bets—send your wife to the party, but stay Zeus's golfing buddy yourself."

Hades made a face. "I know some of those men. That's exactly how they think."

Don grinned. "Hera thought they'd think that way too. Tonight isn't *for* them. It's for the ladies." He waved at the doorway. "If you went out there right now, you'd see that all of those wives have been separated out into separate groups. Whatever group they're in has at least one or two of Hera's friends, and you can bet they're hitting every talking point on the briefing. By the end of the evening, those women will be Hera's staunch supporters. Spies and saboteurs, in the homes of Zeus's own allies."

"There was a briefing?" Hades asked.

"Brother, there was a *slideshow*. Hera has never experienced a moment of chill in her entire life, but right now she's scaring the shit out of me." The obvious affection in his voice made a lie out of the words.

"Are the war metaphors hers or yours?"

"Hers, of course." Don nodded at Heph. "Your date agreeing to come was a, quote, major victory."

"I know Zeus is your brother," Heph said hesitantly, "but—"

"Yeah, we hate him," Don said easily. "Don't we, Hades?"

Hades looked torn. "Hate might be a little too strong…"

"Not for me," Don said. The words had the iron finality of a prison door closing.

"I would say, we're currently estranged," Hades said carefully.

"Well, I hate him. He blacklisted me," Heph said, staring at the glass on the bookshelf. He hoped it left a big, ugly water mark. His thoughts were fuzzing a little at the edges as the morphine took a firm grip on his m-receptors and the dopamine flooded his brain. He hoped, in a distant sort of way, that he wouldn't say anything too stupid. "He canceled my contract and now he's trying to make sure I don't get more. I spent six years doing great work for him, and two more ignoring a lot of opportunities so I could have more time for my Olympus contracts, and he's fucked me over. Just like that."

There was a little silence. When he looked up, both brothers were staring at him. They didn't look much alike—Hades had a tall, spare frame, dark hair, and a neatly clipped beard, while Don was basically a blond mountain—but they had identical curious expressions on their face.

"Why didn't you tell me?" Hades asked.

"Why would I?" Heph said blankly.

"Because we've known each other for years? Well, it doesn't matter. I can certainly help you find something."

"I don't need help," Heph snapped. His brain wanted him to be in a good mood, but he couldn't stand pity. "My work is exceptional. Someone will appreciate it, even if Zeus doesn't."

Hades looked startled. "But surely—"

"Man says he doesn't want help," Don said, giving his older brother a complex look. "Leave him alone."

There was a moment of tense silence, then a thunderous crash from down the hall. The muffled noise of the party abruptly stilled.

"That wasn't the kitchen," Hades said, jumping to his feet. "Zeus's office?"

"Hera," Don said, and bolted for the door.

***

"Are you sure Heph shouldn't go home?" Persephone asked, as Hera shut the study door.

Aphrodite shook her head. "If he says he's fine, he means it. He hates it when people fuss." Every instinct told her to go back inside and fuss anyway, as if she could smother the pain with her care. But Heph knew what he was doing, and he'd told her to leave.

And he'd been right to, said a small, nasty voice at the back of her head. What did she know about caring for people? What did she know about anything, except looking pretty and playing dumb games?

Heph didn't need her, and good for him.

She touched her cheek, where she could still feel the ghostly pressure of his kiss. It had been a nice gesture, a good, friendly way to soothe over an awkward moment, and also hot as hell.

So why did it make her want to cry?

"While I have the opportunity," Hera said, "I would like to say that I'm very glad you accepted the invitation for this evening."

Aphrodite flushed. "Oh, sure. Well, I mean... I owe you."

"You owe me *nothing*," Hera said forcefully. "And you are aiding me nonetheless. I want you to know that I am grateful."

It was an effort to meet those dark, hard eyes. Aphrodite managed it, abstractly admiring how someone so small and dainty was nevertheless so absolutely *terrifying*. "I believed terrible things about you," she said baldly. "I told other people you'd threatened and degraded me."

"You had every reason to believe it," Hera said. "Zeus was—is—very clever. Completely ruthless, of course, but a good strategist." She paused. "And I'm aware that my own manner is...not inviting. I imagine it was difficult to consider approaching me in person, either to check the validity of those emails, or to confront me."

Honestly, Aphrodite had never considered it. The false Hera of those emails had threatened to destroy her career before it had barely started.

She hadn't even cleared all her father's debts at that point. She would have done almost anything to avoid going back to the kind of poverty that people like Hera threw charity balls to fundraise for.

Persephone was lingering behind them, her huge blue eyes filled with sympathy.

Aphrodite squeezed her own eyes shut. "I'm sorry I slept with him," she said, hearing her own voice break. "I'm so sorry, Hera."

A small hand rested on her shoulder for a moment. Aphrodite opened her eyes to find Hera standing in front of her, looking solemn. "I understand regret," she said quietly. "I only hope you will not carry it on my behalf."

"Oh," Aphrodite said, and impulsively hugged the shorter woman.

Hera made a stifled sound. At first, her hands lay limply by her sides at first, but then she lifted them and patted Aphrodite's back uncertainly. "You'll smudge your mascara," she said.

"I don't care."

"Yes, but the pictures," Hera said urgently, and Aphrodite laughed and let her go.

They went back to the party and posed together for a few shots: "laughing" over glasses of golden champagne, "chatting" in front of Persephone's spectacular mural. Hera placed herself between Aphrodite and Persephone in all the compositions. That gold dress was going to make everybody else her monochromatic background. It was the bossest of boss moves.

"Where's Hecate?" Aphrodite murmured to Persephone, as Hera smoothly answered a few questions about her taste in artwork. She wasn't one hundred percent certain she wanted Hecate's sharp eye on her at the moment, what with all the confused feelings and neediness Heph was causing, but she hadn't seen her all night.

"Still at the office with Minerva," Persephone whispered back. "Zeus's lawyers delivered his financial disclosure records just before they were ready to leave."

Aphrodite frowned. Surely that had been hours ago?

Bella-the-reporter popped up on her blind side, smiling brightly. "Aphrodite, can I take it that your presence here means the rumors of bad blood between you and Hera have been greatly exaggerated?"

Aphrodite beamed at her. "Hera's amazing," she said. "I've got nothing but respect for her. I was just telling her that she should run for office; I'd vote for her in a second."

"Is she planning to run for office?"

"Oh, it was just, like, a saying, you know?"

"So, these rumors that you had an affair with Zeus in his playboy days..." Bella trailed off. Not, unfortunately, because Aphrodite was giving her the stink-eye, which she definitely was, but because there was a stir in the crowd, a ripple as if a stone had been thrown into a pond. Aphrodite craned, grateful for her height, and caught a glimpse of the two women slicing through the room.

It was Minerva Eule, wearing a grey suit and red shoes, clearly straight from the office and absolutely not in theme. Hecate followed in her wake, hauling a leather satchel that was obviously packed with printouts and manila folders. She *was* wearing black, but that was probably an accident—Hecate always wore black.

Aphrodite didn't need to look at Hera to know something was wrong. Bella spotted it too, as alert as a bloodhound on the scent. In a minute she'd start pointing her nose at a story.

Aphrodite stepped forward. "Minerva, you made it!" she said, her voice floating easily over the hushing crowd. She grabbed the bag from Hecate, who gave her a dubious look, but relinquished it. "Oh my gosh, thank you so much for working late."

Minerva was frowning at her, clearly about to demand what Aphrodite was babbling about.

"Ah, those are the contracts you mentioned, Aphrodite?" Hera said. She got beside Minerva and laid a hand on her forearm. Minerva tilted her head at her, outrage giving way to puzzlement, "Let me show you a place to go over them in peace."

"That's super nice of you," Aphrodite said, tossing her hair back with a giggle. "I know, so silly to bring business to your party."

"Not at all," Hera said, her teeth gleaming. "I understand these things can't wait, and we're all very excited about your new acting ventures. I assume Persephone will be your witness?"

"Um, yes," Persephone said gamely. It wasn't at all convincing, but it didn't matter, because the photos would show Aphrodite with the bulging bag of paperwork, and Minerva on a mission to deliver it to her.

"A new movie role?" Bella said. "Aphrodite, would you mind answering a few—"

"Maybe later," Aphrodite said, gaily hoisting the bag. It was heavy, but she'd walked the Victoria's Secret Fashion Show with 60-pound wings on her back, and that had been while wearing a fantasy bra made from solid gold. The designer had sculpted the gold into two seashells, set with pearls and diamonds. If Aphrodite could make that thing look not only comfortable, but desirable, she could turn this satchel into a cute accessory.

Hera called one of her staff over, and murmured instructions to start clearing out the reporters. It was early, but they couldn't claim they hadn't got their stories tonight. Then she led the parade of women down the hallway, past the study where Heph was holed up, to a larger office at the back of the penthouse.

It was cold in there, all gleaming chrome and glass, the curtains drawn open to reveal the city lights below. Aphrodite didn't need the curl of Hera's lip to tell her that this was Zeus's home office. Former office.

Aphrodite put the heavy bag on the desk and backed away, wondering if she could just get out of there. Maybe go and see if Heph would let her take care of him; maybe see if he'd be willing to take care of her. He could, just, like, hold her hand, or maybe she could curl up beside him and share his warmth. They were almost friends, right? That would be an almost friendly thing they could do.

"How bad is it?" Hera asked.

"He sold half his Olympus shares," Minerva said. "Before you served him with the notice of intent to divorce."

Hera went very still. "He was served the day after I knew he'd cheated."

"Yes. He'd done the sale the day before."

Hera's hands were gripping each other so tightly that Aphrodite was afraid she'd break her fingers. "He probably did it from his office," she said. "The moment after Hades and Persephone left. He *planned* this. He knew that I'd file for divorce if I ever found out he'd cheated again. He knew I'd come for him, and he planned what to do if that happened."

"You get half the money from the sale, though, right?" Aphrodite asked, and Hera looked at her, dark eyes like deep pools.

"Yes," she said. "But I have plenty of money. I want the shares. I want *Olympus*." She cocked her head at Minerva. "Who bought them?"

"A shell company. I have my clerks working on it."

"How much did Zeus sell them for?"

Minerva winced, the first time Aphrodite had ever seen her less than perfectly comfortable. "One dollar."

Hera picked up a heavy glass trophy from a nearby shelf, and without changing expression, hurled it against the wall.

The glass shattered in a thunderous detonation. Aphrodite jumped backwards as hundreds of glittering shards scattered across the study floor.

"I didn't anticipate this," Hera said. Her face was bone white, her lipstick a slash of red in her pale face. "I should have. Every time I think he can't go *lower*..."

"What do you need?" Persephone asked, and Don Kronion burst through the door.

His eyes went immediately to Hera, frozen and furious in the middle of the group of women. He took one step towards her, and stopped the moment she flung up her hand.

"Later," she said, biting off the word. "I have to...this evening has to go *well*. Minerva, what on earth possessed you to come in like that?"

Minerva looked genuinely baffled. "I thought you'd want to learn about this as soon as possible. And in person."

Hera's face softened as she studied her friend's woebegone expression. "Never mind," she said. "Aphrodite, if you truly don't mind maintaining the pretense of a movie contract, I'd appreciate it."

"No problem," Aphrodite said. The initial shock of Zeus's petty vengeance was wearing off, and she was discovering a vast pool of molten rage simmering inside her. This fucking man, all these fucking men, wandering around and screwing up other people's lives, shrugging off the destruction they left in their wake, and so outraged anytime anyone tried to hold them to account, like consequences just didn't *apply* to them. Because so often, they didn't. They got away with things.

Zeus had hurt Hera the most, and the worst, but he'd hurt so many other women too. He'd hurt Persephone. He'd hurt that Semele girl, the one who'd had his *baby*, and kept it quiet because he'd threatened her with Hera. The same bludgeon he'd used on Aphrodite, twisting women against women and walking away scot-free. And when those men got away with it, they just *kept going*, like Ares with his string of model-actress girlfriends all aimed at her, like Simon-the-director who'd made that crack about her sucking dick because she'd dared to defy him.

Well, she'd showed him, at least.

She'd show Zeus too.

"Aphrodite," Hecate said sharply. "What are you thinking?"

"I'm thinking it's time to tell people about who Zeus Kronion really is," she snarled.

Hecate's eyes darted immediately to Hera, and to Minerva, standing beside her.

"My strategy is to take the high road," Hera said crisply. "Vengeful women don't get companies."

"Why not fight dirty?" Aphrodite demanded. "Zeus is!"

Don Kronion nodded fervently, but Hera shook her head. "Zeus *can.*" Her iron self-control cracked for a moment, and Aphrodite saw the fury there. "But if you're willing to talk to the press about Zeus's actions with *you*, Aphrodite..."

"You bet your ass," Aphrodite said staunchly. There was an uncomfortable quiver in her stomach, a reminder of the shame and pain she'd felt as a teenager. But she wasn't that scared kid anymore. She could do this.

"We'll need to craft the story," Hera said thoughtfully

Aphrodite nodded as if a carefully managed narrative had been her intention all along. "I'll give you my manager's number?"

Hera made a graceful gesture of thanks, relaxing from that awful rigidity.

Hecate audibly exhaled in relief, and Aphrodite felt the sting of it. All right, so she really had been going to grab that party reporter and tell her the whole sordid story right there on the spot, but Hecate didn't have to act as if she were a *total* disaster.

"All right," she said, trying not to sound hurt. "Back to it, then?" She stepped around Don, back into the hallway, and found Heph there.

Hades and Heph had evidently chosen to wait outside the crowded room. Heph was leaning heavily on his crutches and visibly sweating, but his eyes were steady on hers, and she saw pride and affection in there.

He'd hauled himself out of a chair and come to her, because he thought she might need him.

"Oh," Aphrodite said, and smiled at him, piercingly aware of the tremor in her lips and in her heart.

Oh no.

Chapter Eight

Heph woke up, and regretted it immediately.

His hip was alternately stabbing and shocking him, unpleasant tingles running up and down his right side. Tentative exploration revealed his bad knee had joined the party, going red and puffy with inflammation and even his better leg was aching, protesting the extra work he'd put it to last night in an effort to spare the worse side.

He wasn't going to be working today. He'd be damn lucky to be up to hosting this party tonight from his chair, if he could host it at all. He lay quietly for a moment, running over the moves he'd need to make in his head. His bed remote control would raise him up so that he could reach the water and painkillers on his bedside table without much difficulty. He'd had the foresight to put an energy bar there last night, so he wouldn't be taking them on an empty stomach, and once the anti-inflammatories and painkillers had kicked in, he could see about getting into his chair.

He'd have to rest as much as possible, to have both the energy and the fortitude to make the party work. And he'd need help to get everything organized beforehand.

For a moment, he contemplated calling Maria and canceling now.

She'd accept it, of course. But she'd be disappointed, and so would their other friends. He would have done it anyway—he'd disappointed people before—except for Aphrodite. She had really wanted to come, to play *The Binding* with regular people in a normal setting, instead of alone in her apartment or the hotel room du jour.

And he wanted that for her.

The worst part was what he was going to have to do to make it happen.

He took the pills, an effort which made him pant and swear. While he waited for them to be effective, he texted Cleon, letting him know he wouldn't be in. Almost everything Heph did for Olympus required him to be on-site, at his secure workstation, so working from home wasn't an option. He'd have to find time later next week to get through the dwindling list of tasks to finish before Olympus officially kicked him out.

No. Shit. He was going to Los Angeles next week. From Wednesday to Friday, he was going to be in a hotel with Aphrodite. Thea had assured him it was a two-bedroom suite with an accessible bathroom, so at least they wouldn't be sharing a bed. But how was he going to spend three days in close proximity to her—breathing her perfume, watching her move, listening to the delighted cackle of her real laugh—without completely losing his mind?

He put it aside to worry about later and made the call he wasn't looking forward to.

"Hey!" Narnie said cheerfully. "Is it finally my turn?"

"What?"

"You asked Aoide for help thinking of dates, and you asked Mellie for help getting dressed."

"For *picking a tuxedo*," Heph said. "Not 'getting dressed.'"

"Whatever. They were both like, guess what, Heph asked me for help! That never happens."

"You three help me all the time. Two weeks ago you showed up with soup at 8 a.m."

"Sure," Narnie said. "But you don't *ask* us. We sort of push our way in."

"Is this self-awareness?" Heph wondered. "Because I swear I've been telling you to stop pushing for years."

"But then you wouldn't get the help!" Narnie said.

"I don't *need*—" Heph started, and then paused. In fact, he did need help. That was why he was calling her in the first place.

"Anyway, Aoide told Mellie and me to stop pushing after Mother's Day, and we've been trying."

"Soup aside."

"Aoide yelled at me for that," Narnie admitted. "Good soup, though, right?"

"Right."

"So, why'd you call?"

Heph huffed out a breath. "Are you still working Sunday to Thursday at the lab?"

"Yep."

"So you have today off?"

"Yep."

"Did you have plans?"

"Gosh, Heph. Why do you ask?"

She was really going to make him say it.

"Narnie," Heph said, and groaned. "I was hoping you could do me a favor."

He could hear the satisfaction in her voice, thick as whipped cream. "Of *course*, Hephapotamous. What do you need?"

***

Aphrodite tugged her red romper suit into place and frowned in her hand mirror. "I'm still not sure about this lip," she said.

"You look great," Lina said loyally.

"Okay. Do I look hot, but approachable, and also warm, powerful, and caregiving?"

Lina furrowed her brow. "That might be a lot to ask of a lipstick."

"That's what I thought," Aphrodite said and sighed. "Okay. Wait for me? If Heph's out or sleeping, I'll leave the package on his step and we can take off again."

"And if he's in?"

Aphrodite grinned at her. "Then you can take off by yourself. And don't wait up."

Lina's eyebrows rose. "Oh?"

"Well, maybe," Aphrodite said. "I don't know! Why is it so hard to fake-date someone? The movies make it look easy."

"They absolutely do not," Lina said, but Aphrodite was already on her feet (her lucky black Balmain spike heel boots, for confidence; she'd been wearing those the first time she got the call from a *big* brand) and hauling the giant gift box out of the back seat with her very own hands.

Either she needed to put some more work into her weight training, or she'd slightly overpacked the damn thing. By the time she reached

174

Heph's door, she was panting a little, and could feel sweat prickling at her upper lip.

She knocked, posed, and waited.

Nothing.

Damn! Oh well, hopefully he'd like the stuff anyway. She put the box down, with a noise that was definitely not a grunt, just as the door swung open.

She straightened up fast, instinctively cocking her hip, finding her angle and smiling brightly at...

... the girl standing in Heph's doorway.

The *hot* girl standing in Heph's doorway, in an aqua green athleisure shorts and hoodie set, the sleeves shoved up to her elbows. The color would have looked awful on almost anyone, but on her it emphasized the hard muscle under her dark brown thighs and picked out the gold and yellow highlights in her lustrous eyes, which were fringed with what looked to be long, dense, and entirely *real* eyelashes. Her hair was a black buzz-cut, displaying a perfectly constructed skull and her high cheekbones and plush lips wouldn't have been out of place on any high fashion cover.

"Hi," Aphrodite said, wondering if she could straight up *murder a guy* for cheating on her when they weren't really going out, or if that was some kind of contract dispute that needed lawyers before she was allowed to take bloody revenge. He wasn't supposed to be auditioning possible Belindas *already.* "I'm Aphrodite."

"I know who you are," the hot girl said, smiling.

Oh, and now she was *laughing?* "Heph's *girlfriend,*" Aphrodite said, the smile dropping from her face as she delivered her best, diamond-hard death-glare. She couldn't beat Hera, or even Hecate, but she hadn't grown up poor and scrappy without knowing how to deliver some serious stink-eye.

"I'm Narnie," the hot girl said, and Aphrodite's whole insides melted with relief.

"Oh, Heph's *sister*!" she said, and then panicked when the girl—Narnie—dropped *her* smile and raised both eyebrows.

"You think my brother's a cheater?" she demanded.

"I hadn't had to think about it before!" Aphrodite said, but now that she *was* thinking, of course Heph wasn't a cheater. "I just showed up to see how he was doing and there was a hot girl in his house before 9 a.m.!" And then she'd insulted that girl, Heph's *sister*, who was obviously standing there figuring out whether to be angry or amused.

Narnie, after a teetering moment that could have gone either way, decided to laugh. "Heph!" she yelled towards the back of the house. "Your girlfriend is here!" She motioned towards Heph's room.

"Don't let him get up," she advised Aphrodite. "He's determined to go ahead with this stupid party, and if he's going to make it at all, he needs to reserve his energy. I'll be in the kitchen." Where she was helping him get ready for the party, of course, because he wasn't feeling well and she was his *sister*.

Aphrodite picked up the gift box and the shreds of her dignity and fled down the hall, towards Heph's faintly startled "What?"

He was half on his back in his tilted bed, dressed in loose grey shorts and a T-shirt with holes in it. Not chic and purposefully distressed holes, just holes, one big enough to show a flash of the brown skin underneath. The clothes were entirely the wrong color for his skin tone, his stubble situation was unfortunate, he was wearing, oh no, *oatmeal bed socks*, and her insides went warm and tight at the sight of him.

Oh, man. She had it bad.

"Hey!" he said, looking *adorably* confused and, now that she looked closer, visibly struggling to focus on her. His pupils were huge and black, and the leg furthest away from her had a big, white patch on the side of the knee.

"You're here," he said, squinting as if he wasn't quite sure he could trust that.

"Sure am," Aphrodite said, and plonked the box down on a handy desk, stretching out her arms in relief.

"I'll get up," Heph decided.

"Your sister says no."

Heph scowled. "'m not scared of m'sister."

"Of course not, but let's be reasonable," Aphrodite said cheerfully. "You're in no condition to take her in a fight, and I can't risk breaking a nail. Premiere's in a week."

"Oh yeah," he said, and scrunched his nose up. "That's gonna be hard."

Aphrodite felt a tug in her chest. He was doing his best with all the media attention, but she knew he wasn't comfortable with it. And he couldn't shrug it off the way she did. He didn't have a Thea or Sienna standing between him and the world. She was the only shield he had, and she wasn't sure she was a great one.

Oh, hell. The interview she'd promised to give about Zeus was probably going to attract even more eyes to Heph.

Well, they were breaking up in two weeks, and that would be that. She'd set him free to find his perfect Belinda, and she'd...keep being her, she guessed. And she was awesome, so she didn't have to feel sad about that, and even if she did it would probably stop after a while.

Probably.

"Why are you here?" Heph asked. He looked as if he were waking up a little more.

"I'm so glad you asked," Aphrodite said, and started pulling things out of the basket.

She might have gone just a *little* overboard, but in her defense, people did keep sending her products they wanted her to try out, and there were goodie bags at a lot of the things she went to, and unless she wanted to ruin her health *and* her diet, she'd never be able to drink all the champagne she was gifted.

Heph probably couldn't drink champagne either right now, but his friends would enjoy it at the party, right? Parties needed champagne.

Heph stared at the rapidly growing pile of facial masks, special serums and fancy candles in some bewilderment. Aphrodite had thrown a couple of her own favorite candle holders in there at the last minute. One was a silver-plated Art Nouveau thing with clean, graceful lines. The other was a pink china monstrosity with coy shepherdesses and pleading goatherds that she'd bought because it was pink and hilariously ugly. Heph's eyes went even wider when she set it on his bedside table.

"I meant to ask," he said, sounding more like himself. "What's the deal with all the candlesticks?"

"Oh, that," Aphrodite said. "I've always liked candles, but I wasn't allowed to burn any in the—in the place I lived as a kid. So when I started making money, and we were living in better places, my dad told me to buy as many candles as I wanted." She grinned. "He probably wouldn't have said that if he knew about Jo Malone. His idea of fancy candles was something from Bath and Bodyworks. But, luckily, I kept making money.

"And then I started buying candlesticks, too. Some of them are antiques, and some are cute, and some just make me laugh." She tapped a coy shepherdess on her upturned nose. "Persephone keeps telling me to get them appraised and maybe loan a couple to some museums."

"Will you?"

"Maybe I'll donate them in my will, but I don't want to hand them out now. I have them because I like them. I like seeing them." And every time she saw them, she knew that she'd never go back to that kind of poverty, the kind where you had three outfits for school and rotated them so that you only wore the same thing twice a week, the kind where you and your father ate cold beans out of a can for dinner because the power was off again. If her career prospects dried up overnight and all of her investments went bad and Thea ran away to Brazil with all the money in her bank accounts, she could always sell her candlesticks.

"You don't—" Heph started, and then he screwed up his face, in the way he did when he was trying to think of a more polite and less blunt way of saying the thing he wanted to say. "You haven't talked about your father much."

"He's the best," Aphrodite said. "He'd like you."

"I wasn't sure if he was still, um...with us."

"He retired to California." The words came out before she could stop them: "Would you like to meet him?"

"Yes," Heph said, clearly without thinking about it at all. Then he stopped and blinked at her. Of course he did. Because the girl you were *fake-dating* didn't take you home to Daddy.

"Great, because I was thinking," Aphrodite said desperately. "Even when this is..." she gestured between the two of them. "When this is done, I want to stay friends. Do you want to be friends?"

"Yes," Heph said.

"Yay! Awesome! Because honestly, you're good company and you make me laugh and I like hanging out with you, even when the cameras aren't there. Especially when the cameras aren't there." She gulped in air, aware that she was red in the face. "So, fantastic, I'll talk to Thea and we'll get time to meet my dad on the premiere trip."

"My mothers are hosting a family lunch tomorrow," Heph said. "My sisters and their partners will be there. Would you like to come?"

"Of *course*," Aphrodite said, because she had just no way of getting out of it. "That would be *amazing*."

She stared at Heph.

Heph stared at her.

"The box!" Aphrodite said, grasping by some instinct at their former topic of conversation. "Two more things."

She reached in and pulled out the messenger bag she'd had made for him. She'd observed his bag closely, and she thought this was similar in proportions. The strap and corners were reinforced with leather, and the black canvas was some kind of technical fabric that she'd been assured was both strong and light. It was sleek, practical, and about eighty times more stylish than his own battered bag.

"I thought you might like something new for the premiere," she said. "But if you want to take your old one, that's totally fine." With a sense of impending doom, she realized she meant it. If Heph showed up with his scuffed bag because he liked it more, she'd be sad he hadn't liked her gift. But she wouldn't care in the least that she was standing beside a man holding that bag, even though it was objectively horrible and the fashion bloggers would have a field day.

Heph's eyes went wide as she handed the bag to him, and he stroked the fabric covetously, then looked inside. "Pockets!" he said.

"The designer said you'd want them. His husband works in IT."

"It's perfect." He placed it on the bed beside him and looked up at her. "I don't even know how to say thank you."

"You're doing just fine," Aphrodite said, delighted. "Last thing!" She had to practically turn herself upside down to get deep enough into the box, but it was absolutely worth it when she came back holding an armful of furry pink blanket and saw Heph's stunned face.

"Your blanket!" Heph said, and began to laugh.

"It's probably too hot for it," Aphrodite said regretfully.

"For this, I'll put the AC on," he assured her, and buried his hands in the fur as she laid it across his lap. "Damn, that's soft."

A timer went off on his phone, and Aphrodite jumped.

"Next dose," Heph explained, reaching for a plastic container on his nightstand. "I'm trying to keep on top of the pain, rather than wait for it to hit me."

"You sure you don't want to cancel tonight?"

Heph grinned at her. "You said you were good at this game. Don't you want to smoke my friends?"

"I mean, definitely, but not if you're hurting. I shouldn't have made you stand so long last night."

"You didn't make me," Heph said. "I chose to do it." He shrugged. "It was a bad choice, but it was mine. I'm thinking for the premiere, I'll do the red carpet on my feet, but take my chair for the after party and any other events. Will that be a pain to arrange?"

"No," Aphrodite said. If it *was* a pain, well, that was why Thea got her fifteen percent. "You can use it for the red carpet, too."

"Nah," Heph said, and smiled at her.

His choice, Aphrodite reminded herself, distracted by the softness of his smile. It had occurred to her that this was the longest time they'd spent together alone. Their "dates" had all been public. All their time unobserved had been snatched before or after dates, in his place or hers.

This time together felt like an unimaginable luxury.

"Do you want to sit down?" Heph said, and patted the bed beside him.

"I won't hurt you?"

"You'd have to lie right on top of me to do that," Heph said, and Aphrodite froze in place, flashing on an image of her doing exactly that, only both of their clothes were missing, and Heph wasn't hurting, he was welcoming her, his smile soft as she sank down on him, his big hands rising to cover her breasts as she started to move...

There was a reddish flush to Heph's cheeks, and Aphrodite wondered what *he* was thinking. Probably better not to ask.

Ugh, why was being sensible so *hard*?

She took off her boots and eased herself onto the bed. Despite the assurance, she was careful not to let her weight lean into him. The fur tickled her bare legs, and she slid them under the blanket.

"Should I be helping Narnie?" she wondered.

"I'm sure she's got it under control," Heph said, and yawned. "Very efficient, my sisters."

"I know how to clean," Aphrodite said. "I'm not completely useless, you know."

"You're not at all useless," Heph said sleepily. "Who told you you were?"

Ares. Aphrodite almost said it, but she didn't want to bring her ex into this moment of grace. And also, he'd made it clear that she was useful for some things: being charming, looking decorative, great sex.

It *had* been really great sex. Honestly, that was the worst thing. Even when she was so mad at him she could barely turn her rage into words, even when she knew he didn't respect her or understand her, even when he'd actually insulted her, right to her face, the sex had been astounding. It might have been good *because* he wasn't good for her, which was some fucked up personal trauma shit she should probably explore with the therapist she hadn't seen in a while, but it had still been undeniably good.

She was hardly the first person in the world to make bad decisions for good dick, but it still kind of sucked that she could be that dumb about it.

Heph mumbled something and snuggled deeper under the blanket.

Well, she wasn't going to inflict her bad decisions on him, anyway. She could walk away from this with her head held high, as long as she didn't hurt him. If she could just keep thinking with her head, and not with regions lower, everything would be fine.

Heph's head fell against her shoulder, which, previous to meeting him, had never been an erogenous zone. Now the contact shocked her into a state of sensual appreciation. Even the part where he was deeply asleep, breathing with his mouth open, and probably about to drool on her was impossibly cute.

"Well, this sucks," Aphrodite whispered.

Okay. Okay, cool. She could sit here and simmer in a heady stew of lust and affection, or she could put some of her frustrated energy to good use, and *maybe* make friends with Narnie so that lunch tomorrow wouldn't be a complete clusterfuck.

She carefully tipped Heph's head onto a pillow, snagged a few of the goodies from his desk, and tiptoed out, armed and ready to charm.

***

He was warm and floating, wrapped in something infinitely soft and immeasurably soothing. A light cinnamon-rose scent teased his senses, and he reached out one arm for the other body that should be there.

The absence of that body made him frown. That wasn't how this dream went. In the dream she turned to him, clothed only in her red-gold hair, rosy nipples standing proud against her tanned skin, and kissed him, her hands sliding down his body to touch—

Heph surfaced out of sleep, slightly confused and really hard.

He could hear voices and laughter from the living room. Narnie was there, he remembered, and—

He woke up the rest of the way. Aphrodite was here. Aphrodite had wrapped him in her incredible blanket, which was not only so soft it would cause sensual override in a seasoned celibate, but smelled like her, and then left him there.

And thank goodness, because his erection was making it damn hard to think, and if he'd woken up next to her, he would have thrown the whole arrangement over his shoulder and asked if he could kiss her for real.

Heph groaned and rolled over, pressing his cock into the mattress in the vain hope that he could convince it to calm down. Only then did he realize that his hip was doing much better. It ached, but the sensation of glass grinding in his joints had lessened to a dull throbbing, and the movement of rolling hadn't sent electric shocks down his leg.

There was a tentative tapping on the door. Aphrodite, he assumed, since Narnie would have just burst through, probably yelling, "Wake up, Hephalump!"

"I'm awake!" he said, only just stopping himself from adding "Don't come in!" as if that wouldn't be a huge hint to his less than chaste state of body and mind.

Aphrodite opened the door partway, poking her head through the gap. Her hair was pulled back in a messy braid, and it fell forward over her shoulder. "How are you feeling?"

"Much better," Heph said, perilously aware that even the sound of her voice was making his cock stir. "I'm going to get up in a minute."

"Oh good, because your guests are arriving in an hour."

Heph blinked. "What? What time is it? How long was I asleep?"

"Most of the day," Aphrodite said cheerfully. "You must have needed it."

Come to think of it, the light in the room had changed, and his bladder was full, and he was suddenly, outrageously hungry.

"Okay," he said. "Okay, wow, I definitely better get up."

"Do you need a hand?" Aphrodite asked.

Heph choked back an image of her giving him her hand and letting him wrap her long fingers around his cock, moving them up and down until she caught his perfect rhythm.

"I'm fine," he said, voice strangled.

Fortunately—unfortunately?—she took him at his word and closed the door again. Heph dragged himself out of bed, and went to take care of the whole situation in the shower. It was hardly the first time he'd jerked off with one of his sisters in the next room, but knowing Aphrodite was there made it so much harder, in more than one sense of the word.

He focused on the purely physical sensations and pushed the fantasy away as he sat on his shower bench and got himself off. Slick lube, good grip, the tightening in his balls as he came, spilling over his fingers with a half-stifled groan.

The fantasy came as he was actually showering. Aphrodite naked in the shower with him. Aphrodite running a washcloth slowly over her body. Aphrodite standing in front of him, water slicking her hair and beading on her skin, clutching his shoulders as he buried his face in her thighs and found the wet heat at her center...

Fuck. He was no better than a horny teenager with a centerfold pinned to his wall, except that teenager had some excuse because of all the rampant hormones. His hormones were supposed to be better-regulated than this.

He cleaned up and got dressed. He had to move cautiously, and it wasn't an entirely pain-free experience, but he'd done all the right things to care for himself, even if the rest had been mostly an accident. Plus, he'd been lucky. There were times where it didn't matter what he did or how careful he was; his body would still object, tearing itself apart in a blind fury of pain. This time, it had worked out.

He wheeled himself out to the living room and his jaw literally dropped.

The gaming parties he'd been to before had ranged from Maria's comfortable, fairy-light festooned apartment with her girlfriend's famed seven bean dip, to shabby dorm room lounges with a couple of franchise pizza boxes discarded on top of the kitchenette microwave, to (only once, thank goodness) a shared house with black mold in the bathroom sink and rats in the walls. Players would set up their systems on flimsy plastic fold-out tables, or use lap desks in a pinch. Competition was fierce for the few comfortable seats, and the fanciest beverage on offer tended to be a grocery store IPA selection box.

His living room furniture had been either removed completely, or shoved against the walls. In the surprisingly large area that gave them, Narnie and Aphrodite had set up what were probably still fold out tables—but these ones had wooden tops, and sturdy-looking chrome legs, a far cry from the wobbly things he was used to. On the tables were Binding-themed plastic cubicle-style dividers, which would give each player the illusion of their own space and prevent anyone from seeing their screen while they were playing. There was a comfortable computer chair for each player, which looked—and smelled—suspiciously new.

And then there was the snack table. Heph didn't know what to say about the snack table. Each dish was labeled with a card in Narnie's fluid handwriting, but his sister sure didn't know what a Lava Energy Boost or Triple Health Scroll were, and the cake in the shape of the Firestorm Tome was a perfect replica of the game's most sought-after bonus spell.

Instead of eating off cardboard plates with paper napkins, his guests were apparently going to be dining from pink china with a rose pattern, with pink and red cloth napkins. Heph, remembering the rosy decor of Aphrodite's apartment, knew exactly where the plates and linen had come from.

The crowning touch was the wooden bar cart parked beside the table. Heph usually used it to store the overflow of his to-be-read pile. Now it was set with crystal champagne flutes, and two demure bottles, each chilling in its own silver bucket of ice.

Narnie and Aphrodite had apparently been very busy. And he'd apparently been very tired, because he had no idea how he'd slept through what must have been some major furniture construction and rearrangement. Aphrodite had even snuck into his room and retrieved her hideous pink china shepherdess candlestick, which now had pride of place on his mantelpiece.

"Is it all right?" Aphrodite asked. "There's more champagne, of course, but it's in the fridge."

"How did you *do* this?" Heph asked.

Aphrodite shrugged. "I got Lina to fetch a few things, and Narnie was able to stay a bit longer than she'd planned."

Narnie had agreed to stay for an hour or two, to make sure his kitchen and bathroom were ready for guests and that there were enough snacks in the house to feed them. She hadn't been supposed to stay *all day*, getting cozy with his fake girlfriend while they transformed his living space. Right now, she was hovering behind Aphrodite, giving him meaningful looks over her shoulder.

"You don't like it," Aphrodite said. "Is it too much? I worried it was too much."

"It's not too much!" Narnie said, and glared at Heph.

"It's going to blow them away," Heph said, with perfect honesty. His friends were *nerds*. Fun nerds, not the living-in-mom's-basement stereotype beloved of media, and some of them had probably gone to classy events before, but he was pretty sure none of them had ever been to a map release party with a champagne bar.

"Are you sure?" Aphrodite surveyed the room uncertainly. "I got hold of your friend Maria, and she said it looked okay, but—"

"She said it looked amazing," Narnie interjected. "Not okay. She said amazing, and then she literally teared up on the phone because she was so sad she was missing out."

"It's incredible," Heph said. "I never imagined my house could look this good."

Aphrodite stopped fidgeting with the hem of her shorts with her long, slim fingers, and the tension he hadn't noticed went out of her shoulders.

"Well, I'm gonna head out," Narnie said. "Heph, walk me to the door."

It wasn't the time to make a joke about his wheels. He obediently went with her, as Aphrodite, eyes narrowed, made adjustments to the snack layout.

"Thanks for helping out," he said, trying not to sound either grudging or suspicious.

"Oh, you're *welcome*," Narnie said. "I learned a *lot*."

"About...throwing a party?"

"No! Well, yes. But about Aphrodite. Heph, you better not screw this up."

Heph rolled his eyes. "But no pressure, right?"

"Are you kidding?" Narnie poked him in the chest. "I am pressuring you, right now! That girl is incredible. She's generous, she's thoughtful, and she's obviously head over heels for you. Do *not* screw this up. I want her at my next birthday party! I want our kids to play together! And I want my brother to be happy, of course," she added, in a clear afterthought.

"I thought you were waiting for her to dump me so I could date Deborah from the lab."

"I was wrong."

Heph deliberately widened his eyes. "Excuse me? Can you say that again? Maybe write it down for me?"

"You're hilarious. No, forget Deborah. You're staying with Aphrodite." She pointed at him, a gesture that was no less threatening for it being accompanied by a brilliant smile. "You're going to be super happy together, and make everyone around you sick with envy. I love that for you!" She waved and took off before he could muster a reply, practically skipping in her fluorescent yellow sneaks.

Heph went back into the house with a deep sense of foreboding.

In addition to the baked goods she'd turned out of her freezer, Narnie had apparently gotten deep into her kitchen vibe while Aphrodite did the party set-up. There was a pan of lasagna in his fridge and a gigantic green salad on the counter, and Aphrodite proved more than willing to share both with him.

"Narnie likes you," he said, after the first pangs of hunger had abated.

Aphrodite licked a smear of tomato sauce from the corner of her lip, an unconscious gesture Heph felt was deeply unfair. "I like her too."

"What did you two talk about?"

"Oh, you know," Aphrodite said, and busied herself pulling her hair out of her braid and finger-combing it into place. "Girl stuff."

"That's not an answer," Heph said suspiciously.

"There may have been baby photos," Aphrodite admitted.

Heph winced. "Please tell me they stopped when I was a baby."

"Oh no. I heard all about your Transformers phase."

In middle school, Heph had worn increasingly elaborate Transformers costumes for three Halloweens in a row. Aoide or one of his moms had always gamely gone with him for trick-or-treating, as he earnestly demonstrated the transformation aspects of his costume to every home on the block. With sound effects.

"I liked the rrrrrrr-clang transformation especially," Aphrodite said, with a thoughtful air.

"Well, now I need to see your childhood Halloween pictures," Heph said. "Fair is fair."

"I don't really have any," Aphrodite said. "You know I grew up poor, right? It's in all my profiles. Rags-to-riches Cinderella stuff."

It probably wasn't the time to discuss just how deep his research had gone. "I think I saw something about that."

"Well, yeah. So, Halloween for me was black cat ears from the dollar store, or some silver foil scrunched up to make alien antennae. Dad couldn't spend money on a real costume, and he sure didn't have the time to make anything." She grinned. "Or the skills, honestly. I love my dad, but he's not crafty." She looked faintly wistful. "And then people started dressing me for Halloween, so I never got the proper homemade costume experience."

"Did Narnie show you the garage?" Heph demanded.

Aphrodite's eyes darted to the other door in his kitchen. "No?"

"Hm. Come on, then." He opened the door and moved down the short ramp.

Aphrodite followed. "It's dark," she said uncertainly.

"The switch is in a weird place," Heph said, and groped around at his current head height until he found it. "Ready?"

"For what?" Aphrodite wondered, but when he threw the switch and the room lit up, he was rewarded by her unrestrained gasp. "Heph! Is this all yours?"

"Yep," Heph said, and surveyed his workshop with pride.

The garage had been useless to him as a car storage facility. Heph *could* drive, and even had a license kicking around somewhere, but it was an often painful and almost always unnecessary effort. He had public transportation and car services when he needed to get somewhere. At a pinch, his chair could fold to fit in most trunks.

And in the garage, he had his workshop.

It was a well-regulated space, with benches at different heights for whether he'd be sitting or standing. Along the right side he'd placed the 3D printers, the robotics components, and the mini laser-cutter. The middle benches were reserved for more traditional tools, including a soldering station and a jigsaw cutter. The left was where he stored his materials in racks of shelves, which included sheets of wood, plastic, metal and foam, spools of wire, and a huge library of paint in a startling array of colors.

Standing in the corner nearest the ramp were a couple of adjustable dress forms and a few polystyrene heads. They were all currently dressed in various pieces he'd made – fantasy armor, molded superhero masks, a Bronze Age helm. Aphrodite immediately gravitated towards the display.

"You made these? Can I touch?"

"Sure."

From a table, she picked up a crooked staff with a green orb on the top. It sputtered into glowing life as her hand touched the sensor embedded in the side. "Heph! This is amazing. How long have you been doing this?"

"I started with cardboard box Transformers," Heph said. "I really got obsessed at MIT, when I figured out how to add the robotics and programming components. I took commissions right after college, and that plus my Olympus salary went to paying down my student loans. I mostly do stuff for friends now."

"Do you go to cons and stuff? Do the cosplay thing?"

"Cons are too crowded. A lot of them work harder on accessibility these days, but there's a point where I just don't want to be around that many people."

"Aha! You're an introvert!"

Heph laughed. "What was your first clue?"

Aphrodite grinned at him without answering, and wandered around the workshop instead, hands tucked carefully behind her back as she asked questions and exclaimed over his creations. Heph watched her, aware of the warmth rising in his chest. He wasn't sure he could stop it.

He wasn't sure he wanted to.

"So," he said, after a few minutes. "What do you want to be for Halloween this year?"

She spun and looked at him, lips parted in delighted surprise, her hair flaring around her. The lights in the workshop caught the movement and reflected off her red-gold curls, so that for a moment she was outlined in light.

Heph didn't let anyone into the shop. It was the one private place he'd kept free from meddling sisters and curious friends, the one place that was just his.

Having Aphrodite there, even invited, should have felt like an intrusion.

He looked at her, glowing in the middle of the place he cherished most, and it felt like the most natural, right thing that had ever happened to him.

"Heph," she said, and there were tears in her eyes. "Heph, that is the nicest—do you mean it? You'll really make something for me?"

"I'll make something incredible for you," Heph said steadily. "You just tell me what you want, and I'll make it happen."

"Oh," Aphrodite said. "Can I think about it?"

"Take all the time you need."

She took a few steps towards him, her face alight with joy, and he felt as if he were caught in a column of sunlight slicing through clouds. Her eyes met his, then dipped lower, to his mouth.

"Heph," she said, her voice a caress.

The doorbell rang, and they both jolted.

"Would you mind getting that?" Heph asked.

"Oh! Sure!" She hesitated, the barest pause, and then was gone, back up the ramp and into the house. He heard her light voice greeting someone at the door, and the excited chatter as his first guests glimpsed the set-up.

He dropped his head into his hands.

Okay. All right. He was falling in love with her.

Well, of course he was. With hindsight, Heph could see that he'd never stood a chance. And if he was right, if those long looks and hesitations meant what he thought they could, there was a possibility she might even reciprocate. At least, on some level.

The problem, as he figured it, was that he couldn't be *sure*.

Narnie, who didn't know about the contract, had said Aphrodite was head over heels for him. Hades, who *did* know about it, had said they looked like a real couple. They weren't right now, but maybe they could be. He had a chance to make all the lies he'd been telling retroactively true, if he was just brave enough to ask her.

Or he could ruin everything—his tenuous financial security, their burgeoning friendship, and her sense of safety—with one question.

She got harassed *all the time.* In the street, at work, all over the internet. Even in her own home, she'd had to deal with the intrusions of a stalker, some man who felt entitled to her because he thought she loved him.

Heph couldn't do it. Even if all the signs were positive, until she said something, he couldn't ask, because the thought of joining the group of men who'd forced their unwelcome attentions on Aphrodite Urania made him feel sick to his stomach.

He turned off the lights and rolled up the ramp to the living room

***

At first, Aphrodite hung around the edges of the party. Heph realized she was doing it deliberately, somehow dimming her radiance so that the others were comfortable chatting with each other as they set up their machines. Heph's own desktop was languishing in his home office. He'd half-intended to play from there, but Narnie and Aphrodite had so adroitly arranged the living space that there was easily room for him. Plus his office was full of the furniture the women had moved in there earlier.

Aphrodite watched over Heph's shoulder as the group registered themselves as a party and hit the log-in screen. Once in the game, it would be every adventurer for themselves, but one of *The Binding*'s most popular features was the ability for people to play with their friends—even if they were also playing *against* their friends.

The log-in screen gave them a two-minute countdown while the rest of the queue filled in, and Heph stretched out his fingers, inspecting the new map. The only landmark they'd kept from the previous map was the Architect's Tower, still dead center. The other points of interest had all been replaced, though they were roughly in the same places. Halfling Hollow had become Castle Stonehelm. Dragonspire Outpost was now Ravensedge.

"They're definitely going dark," Greg said, with some relish.

"That's new," Aphrodite observed, as one of the cute bunnies that usually hopped through the Waiting Glade instead snarled at the screen, revealing sharp fangs tipped with blood.

"You've played *The Binding*?" William Simpson asked. William Park, beside him, looked up sharply.

"Oh, sure, hasn't everyone?" Aphrodite said carelessly. "If only to see what all the talk was about."

Heph watched both Williams write her off as a casual gamer and tensed, but Aphrodite slid him a wink that said she'd been aiming for exactly that. Belinda Lau and Harmony Freeman, the only other women in attendance, exchanged a glance.

"Here we go, here we go," Greg said, bouncing in his seat. The screen blurred around the avatars. The game was on.

Heph did all right in the first couple of games, making it to the top twenty before he was swept away into the Aether. In the previous map, the Aether had been a sort of peaceful lavender-grey mist. Now it was a lightning seared vortex in which he could hear painful groans and creepy whispers. Aphrodite was watching the screen over his shoulder, eyes narrowed in concentration. Her fingers twitched now and then, as if she had the mouse under her fingers. Twice, she gave a sharp intake of breath, and he wondered what opportunity or danger she'd spotted. The third time, he caught a spear through the ribs as Greg stole his items, did a quick victory dance, and vanished into a fog. It wasn't much consolation when a player from outside the group literally cut Greg off at the knees a minute later. The legs spurted realistic looking blood for a few seconds before dissolving into pixel sparkles.

"It's a lot gorier," Aphrodite observed quietly, as both Williams were knocked out, Simpson a split-second after Park. "They did tease that at the end of the novelization, though."

Greg blinked at her. "You read that?"

"Sure. I wanted to know more about the Architect's Study."

Belinda groaned as a horde of NPC goblins pulled her into the Under-Gorge, yanked off her headphones, and pushed away from her spot at the table. "Do you want my station for the next game?" she asked Aphrodite. "My rig's pretty standard, so there won't be any surprises."

"Oh, that's okay," Aphrodite said. "I brought my laptop and downloaded the update this afternoon."

William Simpson snorted, but quietly. Heph had heard his rant on gaming with a laptop rather than a tower twice, and had no desire to hear it again. He did have the satisfaction of seeing his eyes widen when Aphrodite produced not only a high-end gaming-specific laptop, but a SeaSerpentV2 mouse and a PlatinumSeries Apogee Pro TKL keyboard.

"Nice gear," Harmony said.

"Thanks!" Aphrodite said, and meticulously adjusted the settings on Belinda's chair until she was at the perfect height. She logged in, and every other person in the room went silent as XxOceanGirlxX joined the party.

"No fucking way," Greg said.

Aphrodite grinned at him and settled her bright pink headphones over her ears as the log-in screen counted them down. She jumped almost immediately into the Haunted Forest, and Heph dropped with her, unsurprised when her avatar promptly picked up a pitchfork and stabbed his with it. He nudged his chair closer to her, watching her screen over her shoulder,

She never hesitated, never got lost, and never had to backtrack. Every move was quick, confident, and flowed naturally into the next one. Her spatial awareness was uncanny, and she appeared able to instantly grasp the effect and range of the game's new weapons.

From the reactions of the others, XxOceanGirlxX had been a name well known to more serious gamers, and he could see why. Aphrodite was one of the best players he'd ever seen. When she picked off her last opponent with a frankly ridiculous shot from the back of a spiraling dragon and Ascended, the room went silent for a breathless moment.

Then Greg shouted, "Fuck, yeah!" and the group burst into raucous applause.

Aphrodite, flushed with her success, grinned broadly and got to her feet. "More champagne?" she asked brightly. "I think more champagne."

"I thought you hadn't played the new release!" Belinda said.

"I hadn't."

"Then how did you find your way through the Haunted Forest?"

"It's just the old Mirror Maze map reversed and turned 30 degrees," Aphrodite said. "Not very innovative." The part where she'd apparently memorized the Mirror Maze passed unremarked—that was standard hardcore fare—but recognizing the reversal in the moment of play, while she was also dodging dark dryads and leaping over Darkstar Void tentacles was genuinely impressive.

"How'd you get that extra boost on the Celestial Longbow?" Greg demanded, and Aphrodite explained how she'd noticed the coupling effects of new items while she poured wine with a steady hand. After champagne and cake, she settled everyone in for a couple of rounds of coordinated play, where they worked together to eliminate players from outside their group, then passionately betrayed each other in an orgy of blood.

Aphrodite didn't win every time, though she was clearly the best player in the room. Luck still played a part, and strong players were often targets for coordinated efforts. When Harmony and Belinda joined forces and knocked her out early in one free-for-all round, she took a few selfies for her socials, and wandered over to Heph's spot by the snack table.

"You doing okay?" she murmured.

Heph ran a mental body scan. His hip was tingling a bit, the sign that he'd ignored at Hera's place last night. Tonight's celebration was far less draining, but pushing it two nights in a row went past risky to flat stupidity. And... Aphrodite wasn't pushing him. She was just asking. If he said he was fine, she'd go back to running the party.

But he wasn't fine.

"I've got maybe half an hour left in the tank," he said back, under cover of the whoops as William Park escaped a pit-trap and clambered up the side of the Architect's Tower, only to fall to Harmony's invisible caltrop trap.

"Okay, one more round!" Aphrodite said, as the Ascent music played. "Fill your glasses, everyone!"

"It's still early," Greg protested.

"My hip's fucked," Heph said. "I'm kicking you out in thirty minutes so I can take my medicine and lie down."

"Oh, okay," Greg said, and poured another glass. "You know, I don't usually drink wine, but this stuff is nice."

"Highest ranked player doesn't have to do clean-up?" Belinda suggested.

"Highest ranked and Aphrodite," Heph said, and when she made a face at him, he held up his hands. "You spent all day setting up. You don't do clean-up too."

"Yep, that's fair," Belinda said, and proceeded to play the dirtiest game Heph had ever seen, culminating in drawing a mob of NPCs to literally stampede over Greg, Heph, and Aphrodite. Her avatar would have died a moment later, swept away by the Aether, but she Ascended before it could happen.

Smirking, Belinda poured the last of the champagne into two glasses and clinked hers against Aphrodite's. "We're going to chat while they do the dirty work," she said. "I'm dying to hear about how long your Met Gala dress took."

"Oh, it was like a billion fittings," Aphrodite said, and launched into a description of the process. Heph would have liked to hear that himself, but he was apparently on 'telling people what to move and where' duty. William Park had claimed the dishes, and Harmony and Greg were clearing and dismantling tables, so he took William Simpson to his office to grab some of the living room furniture.

"How the hell did you get so lucky?" William demanded.

"Lucky? I was the first out of all of us, nearly every round," Heph said, bemused.

"No, not the game, man. Aphrodite."

"Oh. Well, we're both Olympus contractors, so—"

"I can't believe you're going out with a supermodel who games!" William said. Thanks to the champagne, his voice was probably a little louder than he meant it to be. "That's the dream girl, man!"

"Aphrodite isn't a dream," Heph said sharply. "She's a real person."

"Yeah, but—"

"No but," Heph said. "Modeling is her job, and she's really good at it, but how often have you gone out with someone because of their job?"

William looked thoughtful. "When I was fourteen, I thought the guy at the mall hot dog stand got to take all the hot dogs home."

"So you wanted to date the hot dog guy for the free hot dogs?"

"That, and he was super buff," William said, and briefly went to a happy place. "But yeah, man, I get it. Sorry. She's super nice, actually. And that shot she did in the first game from the Cloud Dragon... Okay, so where do I put these chairs?"

The party broke up in a happy clatter of goodbyes and reminiscence over the evening's highlights. Heph was pretty sure most of them would be going home to play some more, but that was fine; he'd fulfilled his social obligations for at least six months, and his hip had gone past tingling into a definite ache. Belinda hugged Aphrodite before she left, and Greg offered to play with her again, "literally any time, my sleep schedule is imaginary, time zones don't matter."

All in all, Heph thought it had been a huge success. It couldn't have gone better if his actual girlfriend had been meeting his friends for the first time. But he had to treat this like a professional engagement, because until it was over, it was. He turned to Aphrodite, who had lingered behind, and smiled at her.

"Did you get the pictures you needed?" he asked.

"Hm? Oh, yeah. Sienna's going to put them on my socials and tag your friends. Well, Harmony asked to be left out, but the Williams and Belinda were cool with it." She frowned. "Does Greg really not have any social media? Like, *none*?"

"Email and message boards, and that's it. I can give you his forum handle, if you want to read some of his better rants."

"No, that's okay," she said. "We looked like the real deal, tonight, huh?"

"Yes," Heph said. "I think we were pretty convincing."

"I went to the bathroom at the wrong moment," Aphrodite said. "I heard you and William in the study."

"Shit," Heph said. "I'm sorry."

She smiled at him, but it wasn't her practiced beam or the toothy grin she sometimes produced in unguarded moments. This was a small, trembling thing, a quirk of the lips that didn't look entirely happy. "It was sweet of you to defend me. It's nice that you think I'm a real person."

Heph blinked. "Uh. You're welcome?"

"I'm not, though, you know."

"Not what?"

"Not real." She gestured between them. "This is... I started this, because I needed something fake. You're real, but I'm not." She screwed up her nose. "You deserve real."

"Hey," Heph said, aware that there was something going on, but not sure what it was. "You don't—you're real, okay? Everyone loved you tonight, even when you were kicking all our asses. The real you."

She made a small motion with her hand, as if she were brushing it away, and changed the subject. "Don't tell Hera," she said. "But I liked your party better."

"You're the one who made it good," Heph said. "Aphrodite, what's wrong?"

Her eyes were too bright. "Nothing," she said, her breezy voice at odds with her expression. "Probably just a little too much champagne. Oh, look, there's Lina. I'll see you at lunch tomorrow."

"Bye," Heph said, and watched her run down his path to the big black car.

Between his hip, napping all day, and whatever...that...had been, he was pretty sure he wouldn't be sleeping tonight.

Chapter Nine

"Just how many gift boxes are you able to supply at no notice?" Heph murmured into Aphrodite's ear.

She ignored the way his soft breath sent shivers down her neck and made an airy gesture. "Oh, you know. People send me things."

"I don't know," Heph said. "People don't send me designer clothing or bottles of champagne. When I go to conferences, I get drink bottles, or special keyboards, or, weirdly, tickets to sports games."

"Really?"

"Yeah. Lots of tech marketing people are actually former jocks. They're not sure what nerds want. But this could be a good side hustle for you."

"You think?"

"Sure, if the brand ambassadorial stuff doesn't work out. Open a gift shop." He shrugged. "Or you could go the pro gaming route."

"Gaming is for *not* work," Aphrodite said firmly. "Are you saying you think I should retire?"

"I think you should do whatever you want," Heph said. "I'm just outlining more options." He grinned at her, and she felt the now-familiar squeeze in her chest.

That morning, she and Lina had picked him up in a chair-accessible SUV. Heph had given Lina a bag full of books, then gently explained that the car had been designed for powered chairs.

"Mine folds," he said. "It fits in most trunks."

"Do you want a powered one?"

"I don't really need one. I might get a scooter, eventually."

Narnie's baby picture show-and-tell had made it clear that he'd grown up with the injuries. There were lots of pictures of a very small Heph in casts and hospital beds, and Narnie had referred to surgeries in passing, but Aphrodite wasn't sure what had caused the original damage. She hadn't asked if it was going to get worse.

It hadn't been any of her business.

Lina looked up from the bag, her eyes bright with greedy anticipation. "I can borrow all of these?"

"Sure," Heph said. "Just make sure you give them back." He gestured at his house. "You know where I live."

"I've always wanted to read these Zenna Hendersons." Lina grinned at Aphrodite. "Your boyfriend has great taste."

"Um, obviously," Aphrodite had said. "He picked me."

Then she'd realized what she'd said. She kept forgetting that their relationship was fake. Even when she'd met Belinda—one of his friends was actually named Belinda, and she was a total genius babe!—she'd had to work really hard not to try and scare her off or stake out her territory, because even if it *felt* like he could be hers, Heph was forbidden ground.

It had been exhausting, even though (maybe especially because) Belinda was really nice. So she'd tearily confessed to how fake she was, and Heph had just looked...confused. Not, like, confused about why she was bothering to tell him something so obvious, but confused about what she was saying.

He hadn't pushed her to talk about it today, either. Probably he was embarrassed for her, or didn't know what to say. It had all been true, but it was kind of humiliating to remember.

Now, together, they watched his family dig through the gift box she'd put on their outdoor table after an incredible lunch. Aphrodite appreciated the Smith-Waters approach to presents. When she gave stuff to people in the fashion world, they either acted aloof or gushed cliches. Sometimes she felt like they'd act indifferent to a Faberge egg, and sometimes she thought they'd call a half-sucked cough drop from the bottom of her handbag "gorge!" and "fire!"

The Smith-Waterses, on the other hand, had dug into the gift box with genuine enthusiasm, and a distinct lack of gush.

"Ooh!" Narnie said. "Is this a Versace hoodie? It's so ugly. I love it."

"I hoped you would," Aphrodite said. What was fashionably oversized on her was a snug fit on Narnie's more generous frame. Her husband Leo made groping motions in her direction as she zipped it up and posed at him.

Mellie was admiring her new silver Balenciaga earrings in a compact mirror. They were cute, but Aphrodite already had them in gold, so she'd put them in her gift closet a few months ago. Mellie, she seemed to remember, had a thing about earrings.

"This is what I miss about modeling," Mellie said. "Pretty much the only thing I miss, to be honest. The hours were horrible, but the stuff was nice."

"People give you stuff now," her husband Zion protested. "You get invited to catering showcases and bridal fairs all the time."

Mellie smiled fondly at him. "I love that you think cake samples are the same as couture jewelry."

"Hey, last week you brought me a slice of lemon and white chocolate wrapped in a napkin. I can't eat earrings."

"I did include some snacks," Aphrodite put in. Actually, now that she thought about it, bringing snacks to Nomi Waters' house was probably like showing up to an independent designer showcase in head-to-toe Zara. She shot Heph's mother a nervous glance. "Um, can't guarantee they're any good…"

Nomi, apparently psychic, smiled at her. "Don't worry, hon. Marcona almonds are always welcome. Come and sit down with me while my greedy children spoil themselves." She gestured towards an outdoor seating area, shaded by a canopy. "I know you probably need to avoid the sun."

Aphrodite had generously smeared herself with SPF50—sun damage was no model's friend—but she was happy to sit with Nomi, for what she assumed would be a maternal interrogation. She mentally rehearsed the story. She and Heph had recited it over and over for the reporters, but telling his family was different. She hadn't had to lie to anyone important in her life.

She wasn't sure she was ready to lie to the people important in his.

Aoide joined them, which just made things worse, because Aphrodite was nervous to meet her for reasons that had nothing to do with her being Heph's sister.

"*The Drowned Moon* is like my favorite album in the world," she told her.

Aoide smiled politely. "Thank you."

"No, for real," Aphrodite persisted. "When it first came out I put "Willow Dream" on repeat and cried for two hours."

Aoide blinked at her. "Wait. You really like my music?"

"Heph didn't tell you?"

"He doesn't tell us much," Aoide said.

"Hm," Nomi said mildly. "I wonder why."

"Hey, I'm the least interfering one," Aoide protested.

"All three of you made that ridiculous bargain with him," Nomi said. "Take your share of the responsibility, my darling."

"Bargain?" Aphrodite asked.

Aoide shifted uncomfortably. "It was mostly to get Mellie and Narnie off his back," she said, flicking her blonde hair out of her eyes. "We said that if Heph could get a new contract and a date to my wedding within a month, we'd never interfere with him again. Well, unless he asked."

Sara-Beth, Aoide's fiancée, dropped into the seat beside her bride-to-be and kissed her neck. "Are you telling her about the bet?"

"It wasn't a *bet*," Aoide said.

"You gave him a challenge you thought he couldn't meet and offered him something if he succeeded. Same difference."

"But now we have to keep the promise," Aoide said, and she made no attempt to match Sara-Beth's light-heartedness. She looked genuinely concerned. "I mean, Narnie and Mellie do go too far, but Heph doesn't know when to stop and he's too stubborn to let people help him."

"What are you talking about?" Aphrodite said, and lifted her chin when Aoide blinked at her. "He's smart, determined, capable, and he totally asks for help when he needs it. Narnie and I did the party set-up last night, and then Heph and I kicked everyone out before nine o'clock so he could take care of himself.'"

"You did?" Aoide said, sounding taken-aback.

"You did?" Nomi echoed, and then smiled beatifically at Aphrodite.

"*Heph* did," Aphrodite said firmly. "So as far as I can see, you've got nothing to worry about."

"But what if—" Aoide said.

"Come and help me carry dessert out," Nomi said, and when her daughter looked rebellious, she added, "Now," with more than a hint of steel in her voice.

"Yes, chef," Aoide said, and got up. Trailing after her mother, she still looked concerned, but she gave Heph a considering look as she passed him by, then glanced back at Aphrodite.

Heph raised his eyebrows at Aphrodite. She raised her hands in a shrug.

"You handled that pretty well," Sara-Beth said judiciously, and leaned forward, offering her hand. "Welcome to the Smith-Waters Auxiliary Club."

Aphrodite laughed and shook it. "How often do we meet?"

"Quarterly for cocktails, and more often if there's an emergency," Sara-Beth said, and winked at her. "But we've got to stick together. All that love and concern can be a little..."

"Overbearing?"

"I was going to say 'much.' But that too. I don't know about you, but I was raised by the WASPiest of WASPs. Meeting the Smith-Waterses was like an iceberg sailing directly into the sun."

"I was raised by my dad." Aphrodite thought about it. "He did his best. No icebergs. But not always...clear sailing."

"Aphrodite!" Narnie yelled from the table. "Tell Mellie she can't take the Hesperides hair band out of my pile!"

"Tell Narnie she can't take the hair band because she doesn't have *hair*," Mellie retorted, and Aphrodite laughed and got to her feet.

"It was nice to meet you," she told Sara-Beth.

"You too," the other woman replied. "I'm glad you're coming to our wedding. Do you want to do something together after we get back from the honeymoon? I can give you the in-law lowdown."

"I'd love to," Aphrodite said, smiling, and took three steps away before she realized she was lying. It had felt real, so real that she'd believed it. She was so fake that she could be fake even to *herself*.

She stopped, stricken.

Across that colorful, sunny garden, Heph looked up and caught her eye.

Narnie and Mellie were taking pictures of each other with the hair band, argument apparently forgotten as they worked their angles. Nomi was laying a tray of dainty pastries on the smooth wooden table, while Aoide poured ruby-red juice into tall glasses filled with mint sprigs and ice. Leo and Zion were discussing something that involved a lot of big arm gestures and bouts of laughter.

Heph was surrounded by people who loved and liked him, who took his love for them as an accepted truth of the universe, and repaid it with genuine affection, even if they were sometimes pushy about its expression. Aphrodite didn't belong in that picture and she knew it.

But still, he was looking out of the picture, straight at her. As if he could see her, and wanted to bring her inside.

She wanted it too. All she had to do was reach forward and step into the frame.

But then everyone would see she didn't belong there, as awkward and clumsy as a child's drawing tacked to a masterpiece. Not evil, not *bad*.

You wouldn't blame the child in that situation for being a bad artist. You'd just take the drawing off the Rembrandt and put it somewhere else.

Heph's face was changing as she looked at him, going from slightly quizzical to concerned. She caught a flicker of movement coming around the edge of the house, and gladly turned to wave at Lina, who was picking her way down the garden path with an apologetic look for Heph's family and Aphrodite's phone in her hand.

Aphrodite had told her she was available for emergencies only.

"It's not your dad," Lina said quickly, and Aphrodite's heart lurched into action again. "It's Hera Kronion."

"Did you tell her I was busy?"

Lina paused. "Um, I mean… It's Hera Kronion."

Aphrodite took the phone. She kind of wanted to be annoyed at Lina, but, to be honest, she probably would have done the same thing. "Hello?"

"Hello," Hera's crisp voice said. "I apologize for calling on the weekend, but I've been offered an opportunity, and I wanted to extend it to you."

"What opportunity?"

"An interview with Gaia," Hera said. Even her measured tones couldn't conceal her excitement. "Well, I say that I've been offered the interview, but it's really both of us. She wants to talk to both of us. A full episode."

"Holy shit," Aphrodite said. Gaia—only one name necessary— was probably the most influential woman in the world, and her talk show, with its thoughtful, candid interviews, had been a global success for twenty-five years. She'd spoken to celebrities and politicians, authors and philanthropists, artists and entrepreneurs. Gaia had made no-names stars and brought down a corrupt governor. "Gaia. Seriously?"

"Yes," Hera said. "I have a friend who made a suggestion, and she was interested enough to call me. She's always been good at exposing corporate corruption and abuse. You remember the Scylla interview?"

"Yes! Totally destroyed Circe Cosmetics." Aphrodite walked a little further from the garden party, onto the lush lawn, between two enormous rosebushes. "So this is...what? Betrayed wife and ex-way-too-young mistress?"

"Yes. But less about that narrative, I think. I hope. More about powerful men getting away with what they want, whenever they want, unless women stick together."

"Okay," Aphrodite said. "Yeah. That tracks." She paused. "Did you tell her about Semele?"

"No," Hera said. "How did you—Ah. Persephone. Well, Semele has made it very clear that she doesn't wish to be a part of the story. She is concerned for her son's welfare, and I can't say I think she's wrong." There was a note of pain in her voice, so well-concealed that Aphrodite wondered if she even knew it was there herself. "So far, Zeus has not tried to exercise any paternal rights over Dio, and I suspect it's not likely to occur to him. Unless, of course, Dio is brought up in another context."

"Right," Aphrodite said. "So let's not do that." Heph had followed her as far as his chair would allow, lingering at the edge of the paved area. Out of earshot, but there if she needed him.

"Aphrodite," Hera said, and her voice was very serious. "Do consider carefully. I know we discussed an interview at my party, but I was thinking a print interview, or perhaps a well-vetted TV appearance. But this is Gaia. I hope she'll be sympathetic, but I know she'll be thorough. And everyone will see it, or at least pretend they have. If you say yes, people who have never heard of you, or me, or Zeus, or even Olympus, will be discussing your past and passing judgment."

"There are already rumors about me and Zeus," Aphrodite said. "It's come up at work, even."

"They could remain rumors, if you never confirm them."

"What if he tells?" Aphrodite asked. "What if someone else does? It isn't secret, exactly—it's just been quiet. I'd rather be loud." She grinned. "We have a chance to one-shot him, then scoop the loot."

There was a startled pause, then, "I don't quite understand the metaphor."

"Video games."

"Oh, yes," Hera said, politely baffled. "But please understand. Zeus can be very generous to the people he likes, and extremely vindictive towards those he doesn't, even if that involves cutting off his nose to spite his face. And you book a lot of work through Olympus titles."

In the warm garden, Aphrodite felt a chill. "You think he'd blacklist me."

"I would say it's a strong possibility."

"But if *you* get Olympus..."

"Well, I wouldn't want to be seen doing anyone any favors," Hera said demurely. "But you *are* very good."

"Thank you," Aphrodite said absently, and tried to think it through. All right, so for the foreseeable future, she could kiss direct Olympus work goodbye. Olympus might also say no to advertising that featured her, or even refuse to cover shows she walked in. That was less likely, but possible. But there were other magazines, there was the movie stuff, she could lean more into the personal branding Thea wanted her to try...and she had her savings and investments.

She glanced at Lina, who was hovering by Heph. Aphrodite Urania wasn't a one-woman operation. Did she have the right to gamble with Lina's job, too? Wait, no, that was the wrong kind of thinking. Lina was capable and awesome; if Aphrodite got struck by lightning tomorrow, Lina would get a new job by the end of the week. Though, hopefully, only after attending Aphrodite's funeral and tearfully declaring her the best boss she'd ever have.

"Aphrodite?" Hera said, with a hint of unease.

"I was thinking," Aphrodite said. "Yes. Let's do it."

"Very well, then," Hera said, and if Aphrodite hadn't been listening for it, she wouldn't have caught the tiny, relieved exhale of held breath.

"When are we talking about, though?" Aphrodite continued. "I've got this movie premiere coming up, and Heph's sister is getting married. I have time in between, but after that my schedule gets pretty tight."

"Ah, yes. She gave me several possibilities for dates."

And that, of course, made it clear just how interested Gaia was in this story. Most people cleared their schedules for her, not the other way around. After a moment, Hera named a date that fell exactly between the premiere and wedding. "Will that work?"

"Yep," Aphrodite said. For someone else, she might have pretended to check a calendar or diary. But Thea had gone through the schedule with her only three days ago, and her memory was excellent. And she didn't mind if Hera knew it.

"Then I'll have my people send yours the necessary releases. Gaia's team will expedite research and start publicity for the episode. You'll likely receive questions about the matter at the premiere, but she's expecting an exclusive."

"Perfect excuse to tell them I can't answer," Aphrodite said cheerfully. She winked at Heph, who had relaxed a little, though he was still keeping an eye on her.

"Thank you," Hera said, after another one of those tiny pauses. "I very much appreciate your willingness to assist in this matter." The words were stilted and formal, but the sentiment was clearly sincere.

Aphrodite realized, right then, that she liked Hera. Hera wasn't the cold, vengeful demon she'd dreaded for ten years—she was dignified and intense and also *super* awkward. "Hey," Aphrodite said, infusing her voice with warmth. "You're *welcome*, girlfriend."

"Oh," Hera said, sounding taken aback. "Well, goodbye."

She hung up and Aphrodite grinned, sauntering back to Heph.

"You look pleased with yourself," he said, and she *was*, so pleased that she bent down and smacked him on the lips, an impulsive, friendly smooch.

Damn her impulses. She pulled away, too quickly to make the gesture seem casual.

"Sorry," Aphrodite muttered, and then handed her phone to Lina, who looked as if she'd bit back a catcall with considerable effort. "I'm going to help nail Zeus to the wall and yank Olympus right out of his slimy hands," she told Heph. "And Hera doesn't know it yet, but we're totally going to be friends."

His eyes had dilated with shock, and maybe something else. "Glad to hear it," he said, and his voice was rough, with a dark note that made her spine tingle pleasantly.

"But Zeus might take it out on you," she realized, which took some of the fun out of the moment. "What happens if he fires you now?"

Heph shook his head. "He won't. There's only two weeks left in the contract. If he fires me now, he pays a big contract cancellation penalty that's way more than the rest of my fee."

She scrunched up her nose. "But if he does, then it doesn't look good for you, right?"

"Is whatever you're going to do important?"

"Yes."

"Then don't worry about me," Heph said firmly. "Go ahead and do it." After a moment he added. "I'm dying to know what it is, of course."

"I'll tell you soon," Aphrodite promised, and fell into step beside him as they moved back to his loving, boisterous, *large* family. "But first, dessert. And then I'm calling Thea. This is definitely something she needs to know first."

***

"Hi, Aphrodite," Heph said, adjusting the mic against his cheek.

"Thea just called me," she said, sounding both tense and excited. "Gaia teased the interview on *Tuesdays with Tim* this morning."

"How do you feel?"

"I don't know! Scared? Excited? Anyway, I was thinking, I'm going to need to be in LA for that anyway and flying back and forth is such a pain in the ass. Do you want to stay another couple nights?"

He should say no. He should say that Aoide needed him to do wedding prep and that he'd have to fly back the day after the premiere, with or without her.

"Let me think about it?" he said.

"Okay."

"I might need to work." He'd come in on Sunday and put in a full day, and left very late yesterday. He'd stuck to his chair both days. Even with regular breaks to stretch and eat, he could feel his already low energy reserves ebbing. But he didn't want to leave the IT department in the lurch.

Zeus, yes.

Olympus, no.

"Okay, let me know! See you tonight!" Aphrodite's voice was almost too light. She was keeping something back.

Which was fine. She was his employer. Even if he'd hoped, after the party at his place, after the way his family had embraced her, that she might want to be more than that.

But their date tonight had been Aphrodite's choice, and she'd opted for a restaurant date like their first: a public event, with paparazzi instead of selfies. She was kind and empathetic. If she'd picked up on his feelings and wanted to signal that she didn't reciprocate after all, this would be one way to do it.

But then, why had she asked him to stay another couple of nights with her in Los Angeles? Was she deliberately sending mixed signals?

"Or she needs a friend," he muttered. "You jackass." If he was going to do a terrifying and important interview, he'd definitely want support close by. Maybe she hadn't recognized his feelings at all. Maybe she'd taken his stated desire to be friends at face value and was just asking him to be there for her.

In a friendly, non-sexual, definitely non-romantic way.

Heph smacked himself in the forehead, hard, and got back to work.

Or, at least, he tried. A pop-up on his screen informed him that his password was incorrect.

He tried again, typing more slowly to make sure he was entering it correctly.

Nope.

His desk phone rang, and he glared at it suspiciously.

"Hello, Heph?" Mark Hermes's voice said. He sounded unusually grave. "Do you have a moment?"

"Okay," Heph said, glancing at the computer that wouldn't accept his password. "Go ahead."

"Mr. Kronion has instructed me to action the early cancellation clause in your contract."

"Right," Heph said, after a moment. "He's a vindictive piece of shit, isn't he?"

There was a brief pause on the other end of the line. "I've been instructed to inform you that you have thirty minutes to leave the building," Hermes said carefully.

Heph frowned. There wasn't the telltale echo of speakerphone, but...

"Is he there with you right now? Listening to you fire me?"

"Yes," Hermes said. "Thirty minutes precisely. Please see Odysseus in the Finance department to receive your early cancellation payout."

"I had a week and a half to go. All this is going to do is fuck his IT department. Doesn't he give a crap about anyone who works for him?"

"No," Hermes said. "Mmm-hmm. That's correct. Twenty-nine minutes, now."

"Got it," Heph said, and hung up. Twenty-nine minutes to get down to Finance on the eighth floor and collect his early cancellation payout. In the fucking lunch hour, when the halls would be full. That wasn't enough time to formally hand over his responsibilities, or tell someone about the code he'd been working on that morning, or say goodbye to the people he'd worked with for eight years.

What a vicious asshole Zeus Kronion was. Before, Heph hadn't regretted breaking up the fight between Zeus and Hades, because it was the right thing to do. Now he was actively glad he'd had some part in Zeus's downfall. And if he could do anything else to make that fall as painful and unpleasant as possible, he was definitely going to do it.

He cleared his desk, ruthlessly emptying everything he liked and used into his messenger bag without any attempt to organize it. His limited edition *The Stars are Falling* mug, the one Grace had got him for his birthday, was in the floor kitchenette. On the way back from retrieving it, he poked his head into Cleon's office.

One look at the Head of IT was enough to tell him who'd been given the order to lock him out of the system.

"Heph," Cleon said, looking about ten years older than he was. "I'm so sorry."

"I'm going to make about five times what I would have this week from the early cancellation payout," Heph said gruffly. "Don't be sorry. Listen, Maria knows what she's doing, but if there are any problems, just call me, okay?"

"But we can't pay you," Cleon said.

"It's not a job. It's a favor to a friend."

Cleon held his eye for a moment, then nodded. "All right," he said, and came forward to shake Heph's hand. "But only if we get really stuck."

Heph got to the elevator without having to talk to anyone else, and spent the downwards journey going through every curse word he knew, including the ones he could remember from his college German elective. Since that was the only course he'd ever done less than well on, he ended up muttering "scheisse, scheisse, scheisse," until he felt silly and stopped.

It was weird, going to a Finance department on the eighth floor instead of in the basement, a Finance department without Hades Kronion in charge. The Acting Head of Finance was Odysseus Turner, who was standing in his office doorway, watching Heph approach. Odysseus was short, wiry, and disturbingly perceptive. Heph nodded at him when he got closer, and got a considering look in return.

A woman with her hair in pigtails handed Odysseus a sheaf of paper.

"Thank you, Cherry," Odysseus said, and gestured Heph over to his desk, closing the door behind them. "Sign at the marked places, please."

Heph did as he was told, and shoved the paper back. Eight years of his working life, done. "When do I get my check? End of the month?"

"Today," Odysseus said. "And one more thing." He held out another, single piece of paper.

Heph glanced at it, then looked more closely. It was a hand-written list of companies, some asterisked with names beside them. "What's this?"

Odysseus looked smug. "A little something Hades asked me to put together. These are all companies with reasons to dislike Olympus in general or Zeus in particular. The marked names are the people to talk to."

"I don't need this."

"Of course not, but it couldn't hurt, could it?"

Heph resisted the urge to crumple the offending sheet in his fist, and instead laid it carefully back on the desk. "No," he said through gritted teeth. "Thank you. I don't want people thinking I need help. Is that everything?"

Odysseus leaned back in his office chair. "So," he said slowly. "Hades told me that Persephone told him about this contract you have with Aphrodite."

"Why the hell did I even sign an NDA?" Heph demanded. "If everyone's going to gossip about this, I might as well tell my family and watch the whole thing blow up. Doesn't anyone realize that if this gets out Aphrodite's going to have to deal with even more crap from the press and her asshole of an ex?"

"*I* realized it," Odysseus said. "I told Hades to keep his mouth shut from here on out. And I haven't told anyone, not even my wife, and I know damn well she can keep a secret."

Penny probably *would* keep the secret, but if she didn't, or even hinted, she was a direct line to Mellie, and then Aoide and Narnie, and then Heph was screwed. He shivered at the crisis averted. "Thanks," he said gruffly.

"Of course, the bigger problem is that you're in love with her," Odysseus said.

It was so sharp and fast that Heph knew his face had shown the truth before he had the tiniest hope of covering it up. "Why are you like this?" he asked, staring at Odysseus.

"Misspent youth," Odysseus said, unruffled.

"You haven't even talked to me since this all started!"

"Nope. But Penny and Hades did, and they both talk to me. Also, I can read body language in pictures much better than some sad incel online."

"You better keep that a secret too," Heph warned him.

Odysseus held up his hand. "My word of honor on it. But she likes you, you like her... Why don't you just ask her out?"

"Because I can't," Heph said, though he noted the easy assurance of the "she likes you." "I'm working for her, and she gets harassed all the time. I'm not going to add to that."

"If you want my advice..."

"I don't," Heph said.

"Ah. My apologies." Odysseus paused. "Have you ever met Penny's cousin Helen?"

Heph narrowed his eyes. "I don't think so. Maybe?"

"Oh, you'd remember. She's maybe the most beautiful woman I've ever seen."

Heph arched an eyebrow.

"Yes," Odysseus said. "Including Aphrodite. Helen is considerably less confident, but a similar problem might apply, which is that decent people, aware that she must be approached all the time, tend to avoid approaching her and adding to that burden. So the only men—and it's nearly always men—who do try to pursue her are assholes."

"Oh, shit."

"Yep. It's been happening since she was twelve. Fortunately, the women of her family are no fools." He smiled, his eyes softening. "Penny can be fierce when she's riled, and say what you will about Ness, but she's a fighter."

Heph had encountered Ness Laconia, who worked in the copy writing department, on several occasions. "Fighter" was probably the most positive spin you could put on her.

"Anyway," Odysseus said. "Helen was defended, so this didn't happen. But I could see how if she wasn't, she might get into the habit of thinking that assholes were the only ones interested. She might have grown up thinking that good people didn't want her. That she didn't *deserve* them."

Heph frowned. Zeus and Ares were both assholes. Who had Aphrodite dated in between? There'd been a liaison with that actress who'd later been convicted of enticing people into joining a cult, the much older Broadway star who'd boasted about bagging Aphrodite after two dates, the singer who'd recently been exposed for bullying her staff...

Okay. Damn.

"So, assuming that asking her out doesn't *make* me an asshole, which is a pretty big assumption... You think I should ask her out so that she knows good people are interested?"

"Well, there's a problem there too," Odysseus said. "Helen was all set to marry the first nice guy who asked her."

"How did that work out?"

"Just fine for Helen," Odysseus said cheerfully. "The man she left at the altar, not so much." He tapped the list Heph had rejected. "If you do want advice, I've got some."

Heph sighed. "Go ahead."

"Use this list. Find a job. Then tear up the contract, give her money back, and *ask her*. If she says no, well, you have your answer. If she says yes, you have a while to work out if she means it." He shoved the sheet of paper across the desk.

After a moment, Heph took it.

"I'd offer you a whiskey to celebrate your dramatic departure," Odysseus said. "But I know you're not much of a drinker."

"Also, it's just after noon," Heph pointed out.

"Also that," Odysseus agreed, and got up. "I hope to see you again soon, Heph."

"You too," Heph said, and grasped the proffered hand. As last encounters at Olympus went, this hadn't been a bad one.

***

Heph got home, dumped his messenger bag on the kitchen table, and made himself put a call into the first name on the list. The head of IT at Hyperion Industries was vague about possible upcoming contracts, but did ask Heph to send his resume. Heph did, put the list on his fridge door where he'd see it every morning, and went straight to his workshop.

What he needed was some good, solid work with his hands. Something fiddly and technical that would require all his attention, with nothing spare leftover to worry about his job or his love life. Or lack of it.

He hadn't done much in the workshop for a few weeks. Summer and con season were both well under way now, and he liked to get the majority of the work done early. In winter, people were around to get fitted, and he had plenty of time to make adjustments and fine tune details.

However, Greg was going to a con in Australia in November, and he'd requested a costume from *The Binding* for the occasion. It was called the

Centurion, because you could only buy the skin once you'd Ascended one hundred times.

Heph had pointed out that historical centurions had been called that because they commanded a hundred legionnaires, not because they did something a hundred times.

Greg had pointed out that he didn't give a shit.

Heph had thoughtfully added that a centurion's cohort had been reduced to eighty even before the Imperial era, so they should really be called octarions.

Greg had told him that if he didn't want to make the fucking costume he should just say so, and did he want this money for materials or not?

Heph had stopped picking at the historical accuracy of the costume or the name after that, not because there wasn't a lot to pick at, but because Greg was getting that weird tremor beside his eye, and that was usually the point it stopped being fun for both of them. And a hundred Ascensions was certainly something to celebrate. He didn't wonder that Greg wanted to advertise it.

How many times had Aphrodite Ascended? He'd watched XxOcean-GirlxX win four times in one evening. Even with the advantage of group play, it was impressive.

No. No, he wasn't thinking about Aphrodite right now.

Heph opened the design notes and reference pictures on his laptop and determinedly considered the project.

The costume itself wouldn't be too difficult. It was a breastplate, greaves, shoulder plates, and a segmented arm-guard, all of which he'd mold out of high-density foam and spray-paint to match the colors on Greg's avatar. Greg could supply his own clothes to go underneath, which was just as well. Heph could sew if he needed to, but he preferred hardware. The accessories were more interesting.

On his avatar, Greg had swapped out the standard close-fitting helmet for a more exclusive (and much more expensive) faceplate in the shape of a shark's gaping maw. He'd accompanied that by also equipping the net of the Master of the Deep, a limited-edition item that had only been available to purchase during a special event. The net was formed out of thin golden wires draped around the torso, tying in a complicated knot at shoulder and waist.

Honestly, Greg had probably spent twice as much on his virtual character than this costume was going to cost, even if Heph charged him for the labor.

He'd need to check his mold of Greg before he started the armor, and the faceplate was going to require some tricky design, so the net it was. Heph found his industrial-sized coil of 14 gauge aluminum wire, carried it over to one of his prep tables, and started methodically measuring and cutting lengths.

Three hours later, he had a pleasant burn in his shoulders, a less pleasant scrape across his knuckles where his needle-nose pliers had skidded at an unlucky moment, and fully half of a knotted wire net. It was still the dull gray of the original wire, since he'd finish the whole thing before he painted it, but he'd made a solid start.

He hefted it, and frowned. Solid was the word. For something that was mostly holes, this was going to be a significant weight. Well, draped over Greg's torso it shouldn't be too much, and the wire was going to look a lot closer to the video game version than even metallic-painted string would. Still, maybe he'd reduce the proposed length a little bit.

Even better than the progress he'd made had been the effect of the activity on his fevered brain. He thought he could get through the date tonight and even three days in Los Angeles without losing his cool.

And in the meantime, he'd be doing his damn best to find a job.

***

Heph opted for his crutches for the date. He was sure now that Aphrodite would never pick a place he couldn't get to in the chair, whether or not he happened to be using it that day, but he wanted to start working the muscles again. The rest had done his hip good; it didn't even twinge as he swung out the door and into the car he'd called.

The driver, a skinny white guy, kept looking at him in the back mirror.

"Is there a problem?" Heph asked.

"No, man," the driver said, then, eagerly, "Are you really going out with Aphrodite Urania?"

Oh, good. His very first man-on-the-street recognition moment. Thea had coached him for this. He was supposed to do short answers, polite, but not giving much away. "Yes."

"What's she like?"

"Generous," Heph said. "And really funny."

"I saw the pictures from your drop party. Does she for real play *The Binding*, or was that some gamer girl bullshit?"

Heph gave him a blank look. "Why would anyone pretend to play a game?"

The driver looked equally blank. "For... I dunno, man. Street cred?"

"You think Aphrodite Urania needs street cred?"

"Maybe she was trying to impress you."

"Well, she's the best player I've ever seen," Heph said. "She could go pro if she wanted. So, yeah. I was impressed."

"Huh," the guy said, and lapsed into silence. Heph was thankful he stayed quiet all the way there.

The doorman buzzed him through the security door and he took the elevator up to Aphrodite's penthouse, going over the brief conversation in his head. He'd been polite. Mostly. He gave the driver five stars and a generous tip, because that was polite too, and pushed the buzzer.

There was a long pause, then the door swung open. Thea was blocking the doorway, looking more ferocious than usual. "Sorry, date's cancelled," she said.

"What?" Heph said, and craned around her towards the figure on the couch, who was tucked into a tight ball, her head buried in her knees. "Why?"

Aphrodite lifted her face and stared at him.

She was crying.

And Heph was moving before he could think about it. Thea was getting out of his way, looking startled by whatever was in his face, and every muscle he had was geared towards getting him to Aphrodite at top speed without reserving any energy for later. He didn't stop until he was beside her on the couch, his arms locked around her as she sank into his embrace and buried her shining head in his shoulder.

"What's wrong?" he said, stroking her back. There was a brittle tension in her spine that he didn't like.

She pulled back and laughed, a poor attempt at her usual melodic tone.

"I'm sorry," she said. "I totally forgot about the date."

"Who cares? I don't care. What's happened?"

Wordlessly, she pointed at the table where there was a small pink giftbox. The lid was open, and on a bed of red velvet was a single downy feather.

"The feather?" Heph said, puzzled. Was it some kind of fashion jewelry? It looked like an ordinary fluffy white feather. Was he missing some important symbolism? Was this an elaborate dis-invitation from a glamorous event?

And then he remembered a sunny afternoon at the zoo, and looked up sharply. "Is this from that guy? The stalker who called you his caged bird?"

"I think so," Aphrodite said. Her skin was still glowing, but she was far too pale, with a sallow tinge to her cheeks. "He didn't sign it. There's no note. I didn't know he was even back in the city." Her voice rose in pitch. "Aren't they supposed to let me know if he's back?"

Heph reached out and she grabbed his hand.

"Right," Thea said, breezily efficient. "I'll pack you a few things for a hotel tonight, then you're off to L.A. while the police check this out. Don't worry about a thing, okay?" She looked at Aphrodite. "I'm booking you something with great room service and a masseuse," she said. "And someone from Gorgon will be on the door."

Aphrodite nodded, a small, curbed motion that had none of her usual exuberance, and Heph couldn't stand it.

"Or you could stay with me," he said. "No room service, but I can do a neck and shoulder rub."

"Yes," Aphrodite said immediately, and then she turned to Thea. "Can I?"

Her manager was frowning. Heph caught her sidelong glance at their linked hands, but didn't let go. He wasn't sure he even could; Aphrodite had a tight grip on him.

"How's your security?" Thea asked.

"I've got cameras and an alarm system. And Aphrodite's bodyguard is welcome to come too."

Thea frowned. "I'm not sure..."

"I want to stay with Heph," Aphrodite said.

"Then that's what's gonna happen, baby," Thea said. Heph caught the endearment, and looked at her more closely. Thea's face was relaxed, but her fingers were trembling just a little as she called Gorgon Security.

She was worried, and trying not to show Aphrodite that she was worried.

"Maybe a hotel would be more secure," he told Aphrodite. "I can stay there with you, if that helps?"

"Someone will recognize me," she said. "Someone always does. And if they tell... No one will see me at your place."

"No," Heph said, and looked around the room. "Okay. How many candlesticks do you want to bring?"

Chapter Ten

Aphrodite nearly burst into tears all over again.

"What?" Heph said, looking a little panicked.

"Nothing," she said, and sniffed back a truly gross amount of snot. "I'm just... You knew I'd like to bring some candlesticks."

"You can bring them all," Heph said. "And your pink blanket, and as many face masks as you need. We'll rent a truck if we need to."

"Slow down there, kid," Thea said. "Aphrodite, let's go get the essentials, hm?"

Aphrodite let go of Heph's hand with some reluctance. He was just so *solid*. She'd been so scared, and Thea had tried to make her feel better, but it wasn't until Heph's arms had gone around her that she'd actually felt *safe*.

"I was going to figure out the styling for LA tomorrow morning," she confessed, as she followed Thea to the bedroom and the walk-in closet beyond.

"I'll do that, hon. You stay with Heph and go straight to the airport. I'll get your bags packed and travel with them." She gave Aphrodite a stern look, probably just in case Aphrodite thought she was getting soft. "I'll be flying first class, of course. And we need to have the talk about you getting a personal assistant again."

"Right now?"

"No, we're going to have another talk right now." Thea pointed to a stool with a fluffy white sheepskin seat.

Aphrodite sat.

"So, I thought this fake relationship idea was crazy, but Sienna gave me the social media stats yesterday and your brand recognition has gone through the roof. You're reaching entirely new markets. That gamer thing is huge. Did you know video games are a bigger industry than movies, TV, and music combined?"

"Sure. Everyone knows that."

"Maybe *gamers* know that," Thea said. "I didn't know. And I also wish you'd told me just how good you are, because damn, girl. You've repositioned yourself as the thinking geek's dream, and there are a lot of thinking geeks."

Aphrodite scowled. She hadn't *repositioned* herself. She'd just *been* herself.

"We've got a lot of brand and sponsorship offers coming in, with big numbers attached. Sienna told me that these people love that you're with Heph. That makes you attainable and non-threatening. So I'm thinking, we keep this up after the wedding, and run this fake relationship road as far as it can take us."

"No," Aphrodite said, without thinking about it.

"Oh? You don't like Heph? That's okay. We can set you up with another cute geek."

"No!" Aphrodite said. She jumped to her feet with the force of her denial, and then caught the gleam in Thea's eyes. "Thea!"

Thea pointed at her. "I knew it. You've gone and lost your head for this man."

Aphrodite slumped back into her seat. "Please don't tell me off for making dumb choices, Thea. I can't take it tonight."

"Heph is not a dumb choice," Thea said. "But he is your *employee,* at least right now. Just hold it together for ten days. Then you can jump his bones."

"I can't," Aphrodite moaned. "He's too *good*. I'll *ruin* him."

Thea cocked her head. "Well, that's some nonsense," she said firmly. After a moment she added, "Did you want to...talk about it?" Her voice was unusually tentative. Comforting heart-to-hearts weren't really Thea's deal, so it meant something that she was willing to make the effort.

But Aphrodite still couldn't conceive of unleashing all of her confusion and crazy on her manager. She held up her hands. "No, I'm sorry. I'm just being silly. It's been a rough night."

"Of course," Thea said, looking relieved. "Well, let's get you out of here. Gorgon should be ready by now."

Gorgon Security was more than ready. Medea was in the living room, interrogating Heph about his home security measures, which apparently included an alarm system and cameras on both doors. Aphrodite was impressed, but Medea probably wouldn't have been happy unless Heph also had a secure concrete bunker and a wall-mounted turret with a rocket launcher.

"Who has access to your keys?" Medea asked.

"My sisters, my moms."

"All of them?"

"I have a chronic pain condition that restricts or prevents movement sometimes," Heph said. He was visibly trying to stay polite. "If I need help, I might not be able to get up and let people in."

Aphrodite sat beside him. Without consciously thinking about it, her hand stole towards his, and he caught her, warm and strong. "The Smith-Waters family aren't stalking me," she said. "Medea, come on. The man promised me a shoulder rub."

Medea's face didn't move. "It's not a secure location."

"Okay," Aphrodite said. "I still want to go. So let's go."

Medea's jaw flexed in a movement Aphrodite easily interpreted as "save me from my clients who won't save themselves," but ten minutes later they were out the door, and twenty minutes after that Aphrodite was installed in Heph's house, as he ceremoniously unpacked her candlesticks and gave them to her to put on every flat surface.

"You get my bed," he told her, and she nearly let go of her pink china shepherdess candlestick. She tightened her grip and placed it safely on the mantelpiece instead.

"But where will you sleep?" she asked, fighting not to sound flirtatious.

"Couch folds out," Heph said, gruffly enough that she knew he wasn't going to give in if she tried to swap. "What do you want for dinner?"

"What have you got?" Aphrodite asked.

Heph frowned, and lowered himself into his chair. "Well, let's see," he said, and Aphrodite followed him to the kitchen to watch his big hands deftly prepare a quick beef and vegetable stir-fry. She'd noticed at the party that his kitchen counters were lower than in most places, but it wasn't until she watched him expertly wheeling around the space, pulling oils and spices out of knee-high drawers, and briskly stirring the contents of the wok on the low cooktop that she realized how much the kitchen had been adjusted to suit someone in a chair.

"I really like your kitchen," she said.

Heph glanced at her. "Thanks. This place was originally owned by a couple. One of them used a chair, so the bathroom was already accessible when I bought it, but her husband did all the cooking, so I had to get the kitchen rebuilt myself."

"I guess if you're Nomi Waters's kid, you need a kitchen."

"Oh, Narnie's the only real cook. Mellie and I know the basics, and Aoide's never been that interested. Do you cook?"

"Not really," she confessed. "I can like, steam veggies and add chopped chicken. But I have a delivery service that provides me a macronutrient diet already portioned out, so mostly I eat that, or eat out."

"What did you eat when you were a kid?"

"Whatever was cheap and easy. My dad's specialty was ramen with frozen vegetables, chicken nuggets on the side."

Heph looked wistful. "That sounds nice. We ate a lot of experiments and restaurant leftovers that needed to be used up."

"I feel so bad for you," Aphrodite said. "Facing a Michelin-star dining experience every night. It must have been horrible."

Heph laughed. "Oh, *now* I know we were spoiled. But when I was a kid, I would have killed for some chicken nuggets and ketchup instead of yesterday's seared tuna with a citrus yuzu reduction. Can you get those bowls?"

Aphrodite fetched the bowls from the indicated drawer and handed them to Heph one at a time while he dished up. Her mouth was watering.

"Should I get a bowl for Medea?" Heph wondered. "Where is she, anyway?"

"In the car outside, and she won't want you to bring her a serving. Heph, I'm so sorry! I invite you out for dinner, and here you are cooking for me."

"It's fine," he said. "Actually, better than fine. No cameras here."

They sat on the couch, eating from their laps, in a cozy silence. Normally, Aphrodite would try to fill silences, bringing energy and sparkle into a conversation. But Heph wasn't demanding that from her. And after the stress of the previous hours, this small, comfortable moment was exactly what she needed.

She put her plate on the coffee table, burped discreetly, and stretched. "Thea wants me to hire a personal assistant," she said.

"I wondered why you didn't have one," Heph said. "I thought most celebrities did."

Aphrodite shrugged. "Lina and Thea do most of what a PA would do. I pay them more for the extra responsibilities," she added defensively. "I don't, like, exploit them."

Heph nodded.

If he'd pushed, if he'd wanted to know more about *why* she didn't have a PA, she would have diverted the conversation to dinner, or asked if he wanted to play something. But he just accepted it. Aphrodite took a deep breath.

"Also," she said, "I can't read. A PA would figure that out pretty fast."

Heph looked at her, his eyes widening slightly. "Oh," he said, and then, as things clearly began to slide into place in that big, beautiful brain she liked so much, "*Oh.*"

"I mean, I *can*," she added hastily. "Like, if it's not too complicated, and I have enough time, I can work it out. But the kind of reading most people do, like just look at something and understand it, I can't do that." She waved at his bookshelves. "And I definitely can't do *that.*"

Heph looked hesitant. "You said you'd read *The Binding* novelization."

"Audiobook. But if I'm reading with my eyes, the letters start to slide around. I can't keep them in my head for long enough to make sense of them. Which is super weird, because otherwise my memory is really good, but I guess that's just how my brain works."

"Is it dyslexia?"

"I don't exactly have a formal diagnosis, but yeah, probably."

"But wasn't it picked up at school? Didn't anyone try to help you?"

"Heph, I was *poor*. I went to underfunded public schools with over-worked teachers. They tried their best, but I wasn't the only kid in my classes who couldn't really read. It was pretty obvious I wasn't going to go to college or do anything that involved a lot of book learning, and the teachers put more effort into the kids who were." She shrugged. "I figured I'd be waitressing. Maybe dancing. I could move pretty well, even though I was too tall and didn't have any curves. And then that talent scout spotted me at the mall, and suddenly being a tall, skinny girl with no curves was a good thing."

"You have curves," Heph said. "They're just subtle."

"Thank you for noticing."

"Well, I wouldn't want them to go unappreciated." He looked at her steadily. "But this is a secret?"

"Well. Kinda. Yeah." She wrinkled her nose. "I know I shouldn't be like...ashamed, or whatever. But at first my dad was like, don't tell people, they'll try to cheat you. And then, people have so many shitty ideas about models, you know? Like they already think we're dumb. They used to say it to my face. Now they do it behind my back, but I don't want to give them any extra ammunition. And..." she waved at the bookshelves again. "It's hard sometimes, and I can't do some things, but I get by, you know? I don't see why it has to be anyone's business but mine."

"This may shock you," Heph said solemnly, "but I do know something about how difficult it is to move through a world that wasn't made for you."

Aphrodite widened her eyes at him. "No way!"

"It's true." He hesitated a moment. "I'm honored that you told me. Maybe it doesn't need saying, but I won't be telling anyone else."

She grinned at him. "Do *you* want to be my PA?"

"Don't PAs have to be good with people? I wouldn't last a day."

"Well, in that case, I think you'd better give me that shoulder rub," Aphrodite said. "You lured me here with it."

"Now I'm worried I've talked myself up too much," Heph complained, but when she got up and settled on the floor by his feet, facing away from him, he made space between his knees for her.

"Okay," he said, almost to himself, and then his hands came down on her shoulders, his thumbs resting lightly on the base of her neck. "Let me know if I'm pushing too hard."

"I can take it," Aphrodite told him, only half-meaning the innuendo. Just the touch was already a comfort. Even if he turned out to be a shitty masseur of the "rub a little and declare it over" school, this was still a good deal for her.

Heph, it turned out, was not a shitty masseur.

It made sense that someone who had to be so aware of his own body would know what to do with hers. His hands were strong, but his fingers probed delicately at the knots in her shoulders, and her breathing deepened as he gently eased away the tension she hadn't even known she was carrying.

"This okay?" he said, after a while. His hands kept moving, carefully kneading her muscles in slow, sure strokes.

"Feels good," she said, aware that her voice was sliding into a slurred mumble, and not really caring about it. All she wanted was for him to keep touching her, to keep soothing her with his big hands and his kind heart. Her hair had fallen either side of her face, a soft curtain between herself and the world. Her only connection to reality was those magical hands.

"More pressure?"

"Sure," she said.

He pushed harder, and she groaned, a low note that vibrated in her throat, as he worked the muscles again. His fingers stroked up her neck, and then pressed firmly in and up at the base of her skull.

It didn't hurt, exactly, but her eyes flew open and she gasped.

"Trigger points," Heph said, sounding a little bit smug. He released the pressure after a minute and Aphrodite gasped again as the blood flowed back. She'd been lulled and drowsy, but she was wide awake now.

And hot. And tingling all over. Heph's hands were on her shoulders, but he might as well have slipped them between her thighs.

She was flexible and strong and she'd done yoga five days a week for nearly ten years. She rose smoothly from the floor and pivoted, knowing that the motion set her hair flaring around her, knowing that her skin was flushed and her eyes hooded. She moistened her parted lips with the tip of her tongue, and watched Heph's eyes track the motion.

She moved slow, giving him time to react, to pull away or say stop if he was going to, but he didn't. He stayed still as she climbed on top of him, sliding her knees on either side of his waist. She was supporting most of her own weight, but she dipped down enough to make contact. Enough to know without looking that he was hard for her.

His arms went around her then, huge and strong, and she nearly purred with the comfort of it.

"Hey," she said.

"Hey," Heph replied.

They were going to kiss. She could feel the sweet anticipation stretch between them, like taffy about to snap. She gave into the gravitational pull and leaned in, her lips hovering just above his. "Is this okay?" she whispered.

Heph's eyes were huge and dark. "Yes," he said, in that bass rumble, and that was it, she just had to taste him.

His lips were velvet soft, parting almost immediately, and she slipped her tongue inside with practiced skill, taking her time, letting the hunger rise and burn within her. His hands settled on her back again, but this time he wasn't polite, and he wasn't interested in easing her pain. He stroked firmly down her back and grabbed her ass. She moaned, and he used the grip to pull her more snugly against him. She could feel his cock, pressing firmly against the seam of her jeans, and she wriggled a little, catching his groan with her lips and swallowing it down.

This wasn't fair, and she knew it, but she wanted him so bad, and he wanted her too. She could *feel* him wanting her. Thea and Hecate's warnings about employer ethics didn't mean anything when her insides were liquid honey, and Persephone's request that she not break Heph's heart was a distant memory dissolving, and the only thing left to rely on was her own sense of right and wrong.

Aphrodite Urania summoned up the barest remnants of her shredding self-control and pulled away.

It was maybe the hardest thing she'd ever done. He was magnetic, that was the problem, there were actual magnets in his skin that were attracting her fingertips, so that even as she moved backwards she was reaching for him, and he caught her hand in his, tugging her to sit on the couch beside him.

But he didn't pull her any closer than that. He'd recognized her hesitation. Her heart ached, because he was so perceptive and so kind, and she was trying to find the best way to phrase, "I'm sorry, I didn't mean it" when she *wasn't* sorry, and she *had* meant it.

He smiled at her and the words stuck behind her teeth.

"I was going to wait until I got another job," he said. "But screw it. Aphrodite, I'm voiding our contract."

She stared at him, feeling the sting of the rejection almost before she could comprehend it. "What? Why?"

He lifted her hand to his lips and kissed her knuckles, and she nearly melted on the spot.

"So I can ask you out," Heph said. "For real. Do you want to be my girlfriend?"

***

Aphrodite hesitated just a moment too long, and Heph felt his guts clench, delight turning to horror.

"Oh shit," he said, and let her go. "I'm so sorry."

"No, no," Aphrodite said, and cupped his face in her hands. "Please don't be sorry."

He searched her face. She'd got a message from her *stalker* that evening. He'd brought her to his home and promised her safety, and then...

Well, then *she'd* kissed him. That part, he was sure of. Kissed him, and climbed on top of him, and made eager little noises as he'd grabbed her ass and pulled her close. And he'd been so sure, sure enough that he was ready to take the risk of ruining something good so that he could grasp at everything better.

"Um, should we just laugh it off and forget I said anything?" he asked.

Aphrodite was frowning, a tiny wrinkle between her eyebrows. Her long fingers were curling behind his ears, delicately stroking the soft skin there. He wasn't sure she even knew she was doing it, but his ears were extremely happy about the attention.

"I don't want to forget," she said. "I really like you, Heph."

"I like you too," he told her. "Um. Just in case that wasn't obvious."

"Never hurts to get a verbal reminder," she assured him, but that little frown was still there. "I think the answer's yes?"

"Sounding a bit uncertain there," Heph observed. He tried to make a little more distance between them again, and she let him go this time. "Look, I realize my timing is awful. You've got your premiere, and I'm supposed to be there. Contract or not, that's still happening. If you want to say no, I promise, I won't throw a fit about it. I'll walk the red carpet with you and say everything we need to say to the press."

"I don't *want* to say no," she said, making definite eye contact. No, he wasn't imagining the heat and affection in her eyes. "I want to say yes. But, I mean, the truth is that I'm not good at this. Relationships, I mean. Dating. Especially with someone like you."

"Someone like me?"

"Someone *good*," Aphrodite said, and made a helpless little motion with her hand.

Score one for Odysseus, Heph registered dizzily, still buzzing with the affirmation of *I want to say yes.* "Well, if it helps, I'm great at relationships," he said, hoping to lighten the mood. "I can actually supply references. My exes still send me birthday cards."

Aphrodite pointed at him. "Right! Yes! That's the problem!"

"Okay, I'm lost again," he told her. "You like me, you *want* to date me, but you're not sure you know how?"

She opened her mouth, looked thoughtful, and closed it again. "I guess?" she said at last.

"Would you, um, be willing to learn? Sorry! That was patronizing." He buried his face in his hands, only a little theatrically, and when he looked up again she was grinning at him, looking marginally more relaxed.

"How about a free trial?" she suggested.

"Like a game pass? One month try before you buy?"

"Yes! And then if either of us wants to cancel, no harm, no foul."

"Well, that actually is how relationships work," Heph said carefully. "If at any point one of us wanted to walk away, that would be that."

"Of course, sure, but if we have the free trial, we could be nice to each other about it, right? Because we're just trying it out. How does that sound?"

It sounded...awful, actually. Like she was leaving herself an escape route, when he was desperate for some certainty. But he believed her when she said she liked him, and she was willing to give a relationship a try, and at least they'd dispensed with the damn contract.

He had some suspicions why someone as generous and loving as Aphrodite thought she was bad at relationships, and he kind of wanted to go and find Ares Irontosser and punch him in the face.

Except Ares Irontosser was a professional soccer player who would promptly kick the shit out of him, so perhaps he'd better reign in that impulse.

"Okay," he said. "Free trial."

She snuggled in against him then, her arm going around his shoulder. He wrapped his arm around her waist and leaned in for the sideways embrace.

"Sorry," she mumbled.

"What for?"

"I totally killed the mood," she said repentantly.

"Maybe just as well," he said. "Big day tomorrow. And you're not wrong to want to take things slow if you're not sure."

"The problem is that I also want to take them *fast*," Aphrodite said.

Heph would have been very interested in exploring that idea in more detail, but at that point Aphrodite yawned widely.

"All right," he said, knowing that he'd possibly curse himself forever. "Bed for you."

Aphrodite perked up.

"Alone," Heph added. "I need to sleep too."

"We could *just* sleep," Aphrodite said demurely.

"And if we get into bed together, you think that'll happen?"

"No," Aphrodite said, and pouted at him, biting her lip. It was incredibly sexy, but the effect was somewhat ruined when she yawned again. "Okay! Okay, I'm going to take a shower, and then I'm going to bed. Good night, Heph."

She padded down the hall, and Heph very determinedly did not follow her, because if he caught even one glimpse of her tucked up into his bed, much less in the shower, he was damn sure he wasn't going to be able to resist her. And he needed to, if only to prove to himself that he could.

So he focused on cleaning up after dinner, stacking the dishwasher and handwashing the wok and his knives. Then he checked his fridge for things that wouldn't last through the trip to LA and threw a few things in the garbage, making a mental note to ask Narnie or Mellie to put his trash out while he was away. Then he got out of his chair and scrubbed his sink, paying special attention to the nooks and crannies around the faucets.

None of it actually helped. He was still hyperaware of his hallway, and the rooms down it.

Bathroom.

Bedroom.

But the kitchen chores had at least given him something to do while he waited for Aphrodite to stop running the shower and get safely into bed. He hadn't shown her where he kept the extra pillows, but she was a competent adult who could find them herself or ask him if she couldn't. There was absolutely no reason to knock and ask if she needed anything, like an extra towel for her hair, or another blanket, or an orgasm.

He sprayed the benches and wiped them down. For the second time, but it never hurt to be food safe.

Aphrodite's phone was sitting where she'd left it, on the corner of the bench. As he went to move it out of the way, it lit up and vibrated. No ringtone; she'd obviously left it on silent. And it was flashing just a number, not a name from her contacts list.

Heph looked down the hallway, not sure whether to be delighted or horrified at having an excuse to talk to her.

There was no light coming out from under his bedroom door.

Ah.

Well, whoever it was could leave a message. Or it could be someone from the police, calling with important information, and he shouldn't let it go to voicemail...

He picked up the phone, which was in a clear sparkly pink case and flashed him a background pic of Aphrodite licking the tip of Persephone's nose, for reasons that were probably very important to their friendship.

"Hello?" he said cautiously.

"Who's this?" a male voice demanded.. "Why are you answering Aphrodite's phone?"

Heph couldn't place the accent. It sounded most like a mix of Scottish and Italian. But his hackles rose at the demand, and at the tone. Was this her stalker? He wondered if he should go to the door and signal Medea.

"Who may I say is calling?" he asked instead. Maybe if it *was* the stalker, they could get something more actionable, something that the police would actually do something about.

"Ares Irontosser," the voice said. "Who the fuck are you?"

Ah. Not Thea, and not the stalker. Just the jerk who had made Aphrodite think she couldn't do relationships. "This is Heph Smith."

"Oh, the *boyfriend*," Ares said, his voice laced with contempt. "Right. Put Aphrodite on."

"She's sleeping," Heph said. He didn't make any attempt to conceal his dislike. "Can I help you?"

A snort. "Fuck, no. Wait. Yeah. Give her a message for me. Tell her I'll be seeing her soon. Got it?"

"Sure," Heph said, and hung up. What an *asshole*.

***

"You do realize that I've now been ruined for anything but first class?" Heph said.

Aphrodite grinned at him. "Isn't it the *best*?"

"I had no idea plane travel could be anything but horrible," he said. "And uncomfortable, and humiliating. I'm a big, Black man with metallic mobility aids—do you know how many times I've been pulled aside for a 'random' search?"

Aphrodite grimaced. "A lot?"

"A *lot*," Heph said. They were sitting in the back of the town car provided by the studio, heading towards her dad's place in Newport Beach. No Lina, unfortunately, but Thea had checked the driver's credentials, and she was Gorgon approved.

Aphrodite was holding Heph's hand. She was finding it pretty difficult to *stop* holding his hand.

The prospect of going to sleep the night before had seemed impossible, if it wasn't that every bone and muscle had demanded she lie down and stop moving. Her head had been spinning, but her body had yanked her into Heph's crisp, clean sheets in the room that smelled faintly of cedarwood and sage and dropped her into sleep as if she'd fallen off a cliff. She hadn't woken until Heph had knocked on the door the next morning to let her know they were heading to the airport in twenty minutes.

Heph, her *boyfriend*.

Her boyfriend on a free trial basis, she reminded herself.

She was delighted, and hopeful, and totally terrified.

Maybe, if *one* of the people in a relationship was stable and secure and good at this, it didn't matter if the other one was a relationship trainwreck? If she was an emotional dumpster fire, Heph was like...an emotional marine park. But a good one, not the kind that kept killer whales in tiny tanks until they got floppy fins and turned murderous.

"What are you thinking about?" Heph asked.

"Aquariums," Aphrodite said.

"Do you want to visit one?"

"What? No. Want to make out?"

Heph made a startled noise which Aphrodite thought meant 'there's a driver up front and I'm about to meet your dad, so not right at this very moment.' "Yes," he said after a second, his voice roughening in that way she liked. "At the hotel."

"Deal," she said.

"I want to do more than make out," he said. "Actually."

"Oh, me too," Aphrodite said. "Pretty sure the fancy suites give us condoms, but maybe we need to stop on the way."

"I've got it covered."

"Ba-dum-tiss," Aphrodite said, and got to experience the hitherto unexpected delight of watching Heph giggle so hard he couldn't speak.

He sobered up before they got to her dad's place. Aphrodite had bought her dad his own condo in Newport Beach as part of the retirement package she'd made him take when he stopped being her manager. Making sure that he'd never have to worry about money again, even if her career turned into a pile of flaming pig snot, had been the first thing she'd made Thea and her lawyer Tyr work on together, to their mutual dismay.

"This is amazing," Heph said, as they pulled up outside the sunny, yellow-painted home. It had uninterrupted ocean views, and huge picture windows ready to take advantage of them. Aphrodite spotted her dad peering through one of the windows and sprang out of the car to wave wildly at him.

For once, she abandoned Heph to move at his own pace, as she sprinted up the path and through the unlocked door. Cyrus Urania met her in the hallway, his wiry arms still wrapping around her with surprising strength. He smelled of Old Bay and the pine-and-lavender cologne he'd always used on special occasions. Add tobacco, and it was the scent of her childhood. And even without the cigarettes he'd given up ten years ago, it would always be the smell of home.

"Now, don't crush me," he said, and pushed her back, his hands still gripping her upper arms as he peered down at her. Aphrodite was taller than most people, but at six foot three her dad had her beat.

He used that height with intent, as Heph hesitated in the sunlit doorway.

"Daddy, this is Heph," she said, and couldn't help smiling at his obvious nervousness.

"Is it, now?" Cyrus said. "Well, come on in, son, what're you waiting for?"

"The invitation, sir," Heph said, and swung through the door.

"Hmph," Cyrus said, and added to Aphrodite, not at all quietly, "Well, he's got better manners than the last one."

"See if I bring any more home," Aphrodite muttered, and followed him to the kitchen, where Cyrus sat them at the breakfast bar and produced a selection of snacks. She grinned at the display. It was roughly half local deli treats, including the organic vegan cashew cheese Cyrus had introduced to her on her last visit. The other half was varieties of beef jerky, Cyrus's foolproof snob detector snack.

Ares had taken the tiniest bite of jerky when Cyrus urged it on him, and then claimed his training diet wouldn't allow him to eat more.

Heph reached straight for the honey chipotle.

Under the guise of casual conversation, Cyrus proceeded to put Heph through a battery of questions about himself, his job, and his people. He looked mildly interested when he learned that Heph and his sisters had been adopted.

"Do you know your birth mom? What's her story?"

"You don't have to answer that," Aphrodite interjected.

"I don't mind," Heph said, and then bent a stern eye on her father. He'd been incredibly polite through the interrogation, and Aphrodite had been waiting for the pushback. "And if I did mind, I'm sure your dad wouldn't press."

Cyrus cackled, patently unoffended. "Well?"

"She lives in a different city, but I've met her," Heph said. "She came to my graduation, and we catch up by phone sometimes. When she had me, she was young, and she'd made some mistakes. She wasn't in a good place to be a parent, but I think..." He paused, obviously picking his words with care. "I love my family, and I wouldn't swap them. But I think, in general, it would be better if people got the support they needed to be parents, instead of it being a thing where we say, well, either you can do it by yourself, or you can't, and if you can't, you give that baby up or we'll take it away."

"Some women just aren't meant to be mothers," Cyrus said, with the scowl he reserved for Aphrodite's mom.

"Shanice is," Heph said. "She's got two kids now, and she's a great mom." He shrugged. "Like I said, things worked out well for me. I'm just saying that I wish they hadn't had to."

"That's fair," Cyrus said. His eyes rested on Aphrodite. "Pretty sure we've all got some things we wish hadn't had to happen. And your sisters?"

Heph's jaw tightened. "You'd have to ask them," he replied, his voice level, and absolutely final.

Cyrus nodded. "So, son, tell me, what put you in that chair?"

Aphrodite choked on her drink. "Dad!" she sputtered.

"It's a few things," Heph said, looking unfazed. "I had a clubfoot when I was born, twisted all the way around, and my bones were a lot more fragile than most kids when I was younger. I've got hip dysplasia in both hips, worse on this side." He nodded towards his bad leg. "This leg's about an inch shorter, which doesn't help. The wear and tear means I've got arthritis and some nerve damage."

"It hurt much?"

"Sometimes. Sometimes a lot."

"They can treat that stuff nowadays, can't they? Half the women in this town have got new hips."

"There are treatments that help, sure," Heph said. "I've had a few surgeries and I'll probably have more. But there's no permanent fix, if that's what you're asking." He placed a light emphasis on *fix*, as if he were putting quote marks around it.

"Then how are you gonna look after my little girl?" Cyrus demanded.

"Dad, *stop*," Aphrodite said. She'd forgotten—the one and only time she'd brought Ares to meet Cyrus, he'd been asked the same question. Ares had been on what passed for his best behavior, so instead of getting outraged, he'd talked about his earnings, about his brand campaigns and his future profit projections. Cyrus had listened, and snorted, and told Aphrodite he wasn't worth her time.

And he'd been right, at least about Ares, but she didn't want him saying that about *Heph*.

"I'm not gonna take care of her," Heph said, and took a long sip of his iced tea.

"Is that so?" Cyrus said, his eyes narrowing to icy blue slits.

"Yes, sir. You raised a woman who can take care of herself. If I tried to take over, she'd kick my ass."

Cyrus leaned back and roared with laughter. "Yes, she would!" he gurgled. "That's my girl!"

"I am so sorry," Aphrodite said, reaching across the breakfast bar to swipe at her dad's head. "This is why I *never bring my friends home.*"

"You can keep bringing this one," Cyrus said. "And I want to meet those two girls you keep talking about, especially the artist." He waved at his kitchen wall, lovingly emblazoned with a decal of a tropical sunset, presumably because the sunsets outside the window weren't spectacular enough. I think I need some new art. Have you met this Persephone, Heph? She any good?"

Heph replied with a generous critique of Persephone's muralistic talents, and Aphrodite subsided, satisfied for now. Cyrus had gone from "son" to "Heph" very casually, but she wasn't fooled. That was a sign of respect he didn't give just anyone.

Cyrus hadn't been the perfect parent. But he'd done his best, always. He'd been in his late 40s when he'd married her mother because she was pregnant. And then Dione had run off just months after giving birth, leaving Cyrus literally holding the baby.

Aphrodite was pretty sure her mother was dead.

She'd tried to find out for sure. Not for herself—she'd never known any parent but Cyrus, and didn't want to—but she knew the mystery still bugged him sometimes. She'd wanted to present him with the truth, if she could find it. But every private investigator had told her the same thing—her mother's trail was impossible to follow through the mess of name changes, under-the-table jobs, and petty crimes. Dione Urania had just disappeared. And if she hadn't brought herself to Aphrodite's notice when her daughter's face and body were earning her millions, she either wanted to stay hidden, or she wasn't in a condition to want anything anymore.

"You still with us?" Heph asked quietly, and she started, realizing that the bantering conversation had stopped. He and her dad were both looking at her. They were very different men—Cyrus tall, skinny, and white, Heph wide, strong, and Black—but their faces had the same expression of mild concern.

For some reason, that yanked at her heartstrings in a way nothing else had. She sucked in a breath, then summoned a smile that clearly fooled neither of them. "I was just thinking that we need to get going," she said, ignoring the tight squeeze in her chest. "Heph, would you mind waiting outside for a moment?"

"She's gonna scold me," Cyrus said, winking hugely at Heph. "For being a nosy old asshole."

"Damn right I am," Aphrodite said.

Heph laughed. "Nice to meet you, sir," he said, and offered his hand.

Her dad shook it firmly. "You can call me Cyrus."

From Heph's widening eyes, he knew exactly how much of a concession that was, but he left the two of them alone without further comment.

"All right," Cyrus said. "Let me have it."

"You were super rude!" Aphrodite said. "It wasn't okay to ask about his birth mom, or his body!"

"He didn't mind."

"And what if he had?" Aphrodite demanded. "I wanted him to like you, Dad!"

"Huh," Cyrus said. "And here I thought you wanted me to like him."

Aphrodite stopped short. "That too," she said weakly, startled by the distinction. No, she hadn't worried about Ares liking her father, because she'd known he never would. In fact, she'd braced herself before their one disastrous meeting, knowing that she'd have to deal with Ares's complaints afterwards.

But she'd wanted Heph to like her dad, to see the loving heart beneath the rough exterior.

"Well, I do like him," Cyrus said, his tone more conciliatory.

"You should."

"I'm sorry that I was a little tough on him."

"Hm," Aphrodite said, not totally convinced.

"You can tell him so," Cyrus added, in what he clearly thought was a magnanimous gesture. "He's still not good enough for you, though."

Aphrodite rolled her eyes. "Uh-huh. And should I be asking about *your* love life?"

"Oh, that's going fine these days," Cyrus said, undaunted. "Lot of rich widows around here, looking for a bit of rough trade."

"Dad!"

"You'd be surprised what a woman can get up to with a replacement hip," Cyrus said, and patted her hand when she groaned. "What else did you want to tell me? The thing you don't want to say?"

Aphrodite grimaced. There was never any point in trying to keep things from her father. "I'm going to be doing an interview on Gaia's show next week," she said.

Cyrus whistled. "About your movie?"

Aphrodite dropped her gaze to her hands. "No. About the affair I had with Zeus Kronion."

When she dared to look up, Cyrus's face had gone very still. "Now, why would you be bringing up that old business?"

"Because it's important," Aphrodite said. Her throat was tight. "Because he kept doing things like that, long after you stopped him doing it to me. And if someone doesn't stop him for good, he'll just keep going."

Cyrus picked up the cashew cheese and opened the fridge to put it inside. "I don't see that stopping him is your job," he said, his back to her. "It seems to me like you don't need to have anything else to do with that man. You've got a good life. Money. A career."

"It's because of that career that it's got to be me," Aphrodite said. "People listen to me, Dad."

"Doesn't mean they'll believe you." Cyrus walked back to the breakfast bar and hoisted himself onto his stool.

"No," Aphrodite admitted. "But they won't be able to pretend they didn't hear. The other women he's done this to… They don't have my voice. It's me and Hera, his ex-wife. We're going on the show together. People won't be able to ignore us."

"That so."

"Yes." She waited.

"So what you're telling me," Cyrus said, "is that you're gonna go on TV and tell the whole world that I was a crappy father."

"Dad. No."

"Can't really blame you. A good father would have noticed. A good father would have stopped it before it happened."

"It's not about you, Dad!" Her voice was too loud. She took a deep breath and tried again. "It's about me, and Hera, and what we need. It's about making something right out of everything Zeus did wrong."

"Are there gonna be reporters outside my door again?"

"Maybe," Aphrodite said. "Probably, yes."

"Then it's a little bit about me, isn't it? Letting my teenage daughter meet with this grown man, letting him put his hands on her, pimping her out for the money she was making..." Cyrus's eyes were unfocused, looking past her. "I tried my best after your mom left, but I knew I'd let you down somehow."

Aphrodite put her hand on her father's arm. "Dad," she said, not unkindly. "Stop. I've told you before, these feelings, these ideas you have about this—it's not up to me to hear them. You should talk them over with a professional."

She said that last without expecting a positive response—Cyrus had been supportive of her own forays into therapy, but dismissive of the idea for himself—but this time he nodded.

"I might think about that," he said.

"Really?" Aphrodite blurted. "I mean, Dad, that's great! What made you change your mind?"

"Eloise two doors down goes to a shrink every second Tuesday," he said.

"Oh?" Aphrodite said cautiously.

"And she's still a little crazy. But I bet she'd be even crazier without it. Maybe I'll give it a shot." He winked at her. "Besides, a little crazy can be sexy."

"Is Eloise the one who likes the leopard print blouses?"

"That's her." Cyrus was quiet a moment. "I hear what you're saying, Aphrodite. About Zeus hurting other girls. I still don't know that it's up to you to stop him, but I know that's something you get to decide."

"That's right," Aphrodite said, and then smiled at him. "Besides, Dad, at least one thing is your fault. You raised me to be a fighter. Acting on my heart, leaping before I look—"

"Don't mean you have to jump off a cliff," Cyrus grumbled, but he took her hand in his and squeezed. "You'd better go find that man of yours."

"Yeah, old ladies love him," Aphrodite said. "I don't want to have to go up against Eloise. I bet she fights dirty."

"She bites," Cyrus agreed, his eyes gleaming.

"Aaaaand that's my cue," Aphrodite said, swinging off her stool. "Bye, Dad. I love you. Don't talk to any reporters, even if they're cute."

"I know the drill," he said, and pecked her on the cheek. "I love you, baby. Knock 'em dead."

"Always do, Daddy," Aphrodite said, and went outside to find Heph, yet to be approached by elderly cougars. He was leaning on his crutches, looking out over the sea.

He hadn't seen her yet, and she paused, using the moment to take him in.

Aphrodite both loved and distrusted beauty. She'd always been drawn to beautiful images, clothes, and objects. But she also knew how much of it was an illusion. Not necessarily wrong, or deceptive. But if you changed the lighting, changed the color scheme, slapped on some product, angled your head this way instead of that... So much of beauty depended on your perspective.

Heph was wearing a maroon t-shirt made out of a soft knit material and the distressed jeans he'd worn on their first date. His shoulders swelled under the shirt, his biceps pressing against the tight cuffs. Aphrodite was pretty sure he wasn't beautiful to himself—he'd said a few dismissive things in that direction. But he was beautiful to her, and had been ever since she'd met him, tumbling into his lap at that ill-fated Olympus winter party when she'd broken up with Ares.

Or maybe it wasn't ill-fated. Persephone and Hades had begun their relationship at that party. She'd met Heph for the first time.

Maybe they'd all been exactly where they were meant to be.

Heph had his hand raised against the sun, squinting out over the waves. If she was looking at his eyes right now, she'd see the gold gleaming in them.

He was hers. Her boyfriend, who was kind and smart and made beautiful things with his clever hands.

It should have made her happy.

And it did. It really did. She liked him and she wanted him, and she was pretty sure she was falling in love with him, and knowing he felt the same way filled her with joy.

But underneath, still, the queasy certainty that she didn't know what she was doing and was going to screw it all up.

He turned, alerted by some sense of her presence, and smiled, which went a long way towards making the queasy feeling go away.

"Hey," he said. "Do you want to head to the hotel now?" His grin curved wickedly, and she knew that he was imagining what they'd discussed doing in that hotel.

All uncertainty fled. This part, Aphrodite was very sure of.

"I absolutely do," she said, her voice deliberately husky, and exaggerated the sway of her hips as she sauntered towards the car.

Chapter Eleven

When Aphrodite had said "hotel suite," Heph had been expecting a little living room with two tiny bedrooms. He knew Aphrodite and Thea well enough now to know that neither of them would have forgotten he needed turning space for his chair and an accessible bathroom, but he'd stayed in accessible hotel rooms before, and they were still pretty small.

Aphrodite had booked a bunch of rooms and had the hotel staff open the connecting doors. Furniture had been shifted, new furnishings brought in, and the combined space had been turned into a huge living area, with two connected bedrooms, each with their own walk-in closets and ensuite bathrooms. Heph's bathroom even had an accessible tub, something that he'd wanted for a long time, but hadn't been able to justify spending on.

Aphrodite praised the concierge, tipped her extravagantly, and closed the main door behind her.

Then she turned, grinned at Heph, and took her top off.

His mouth went dry.

She wore no bra. Her breasts were small and round, and they bounced slightly as she posed, back arched, nipples thrust proudly towards him.

He'd seen those breasts in a dozen photoshoots, but the rose-tipped reality of them was literally breath-taking.

"Where do you want me?" she asked, and the purring invitation in her voice was underscored by the heat in her eyes.

Heph lowered himself onto the wide, high-backed couch and leaned his crutches against the end. "Why don't you bring yourself over here?" he growled, and watched Aphrodite shiver. Her nipples tightened as she sauntered towards him, breasts bouncing with every step.

Heph held up his hand as she stood in front of him, then hooked his fingers into the waistband of her pants, tugging her closer.

"This okay?" he said, his hands wide and greedy against the slight curve of her hips. "How rough do you like it?"

Aphrodite's tongue darted out, the pink tip moistening her bottom lip. "I can do rough," she said softly. "Or gentle. Or anything you like."

Heph nodded, and unzipped her fly. He thrust one hand inside, and cupped her sex, squeezing. He increased the pressure until she gasped, let go, and squeezed again, smiling as her eyelids fluttered closed. Her panties were flimsy, silky things, already slick under his fingers. He hooked them aside and slid two fingers up and inside her.

Aphrodite gasped again, and her eyes flew open.

"That's good?" Heph said. "You want more?"

"Please," she managed.

He added a third finger, marveling at the soft, slick heat of her, at the little sighs and gasps she let out. He'd been with women who waxed and trimmed, but Aphrodite was completely bare. Another requirement of the job that demanded so much from her. But maybe she liked this part.

She was looking down at him, her eyes round and pupils dark, as his hand moved against her skin

"I need more," she said.

"You'll get it," Heph said, and slid his hand out of her pants.

"Hey!" Aphrodite whined, and he grinned up at her.

Then he tugged her pants and panties down together in one firm gesture and yanked her towards him.

Specifically, towards his face.

"Holy shit," Aphrodite whispered, and then he was grabbing her ass with both hands, holding her in place while he delved into her with tongue and lips and just a touch of teeth, stroking her clit with long, fast swipes of his tongue. He wasn't trying to be polite or restrained; he wanted to devour her, to eat at her until she fell apart.

Dimly, he felt her hands braced on his shoulders, heard the sounds she was making, but his focus was on the quivers in her muscles, the involuntary jerks and spasms, the motions that made her press forward and jump back.

"More, more, inside me," she was saying, and then one of her hands was grabbing frantically at one of his, trying to pry the fingers off her ass, and he realized what she wanted.

"I got you," he rumbled, and she shivered again as his voice reverberated against her flesh. He thrust his fingers inside her again, while his tongue went back to work on her clit, and she shrieked, a sound of abandonment and delight as his hand moved between her thighs. He felt them tighten, the muscles going hard as her breath came in gasps, and then she clenched around his fingers, and came and came and came, babbling something that might have been his name.

She fell forward against him, and he pulled back in time to catch her.

"Aphrodite?" he said.

Her hair had fallen over her face, and she was still shaking. Not with orgasm, now.

She was crying.

***

"Aphrodite?" she heard Heph say. "Whoa, honey, look at me, okay? Sweetheart, what's wrong?"

Aphrodite blinked hard, and realized that she was blinking away tears. Heph had rolled her onto her back on the couch and was leaning on one elbow above her, looking worried.

Aphrodite stared up at him. "That was..." she said, and ran out of words. She snaked a hand around his neck and did a stomach crunch to raise her mouth to his, pouring everything she couldn't say into the kiss.

Heph kissed her back, with devouring intensity. She could taste herself on his lips, salt and musk.

"You had me worried for a minute," he said. "But everything's okay?"

"I went to *space*," she said, still stunned by how hard she'd come, so hard that she'd been shocked right out of her body for a moment. "What the fuck, Heph? Nice boys shouldn't be able to eat pussy like that!"

"I'm a nerd," he said. "I research and experiment."

"Feel free to experiment some more," she told him, and then, when he grinned and made as if to dip his head again, she caught his chin and kissed him. "Okay, but can we fuck? Because I really want to fuck."

Heph caught his breath, and then lowered himself carefully onto one side. "That sounds nice," he said demurely.

263

Aphrodite wriggled around and kissed him again, sliding her hands up under his shirt and touching every inch of him. With his willing assistance and some laughter-inducing fumbling, she got him laid bare to her eager eyes.

His big brown chest was covered in tight curls, and she rubbed her cheek against him like a cat. The bulky muscle of his arms and chest and shoulders was even better than her very detailed dreams, and she skated her fingers along the skin, grinning when he shivered. His cock was long and thick and beautiful, lying along the crease of his hip.

"Anything I need to know?" she asked, gesturing at his hips. There was some scarring there and along the long bones of the thighs, paler marks against his skin.

"Some positions don't work for very long," he said. He was so straightforward and honest, and it was absurdly sexy. "Missionary isn't my favorite."

"What works?" Aphrodite asked, and grinned as his eyes darkened.

"Find me a condom, and I'll show you," he growled.

She scooped up her jeans from the floor and pulled a condom out of the back pocket with a flourish. "Ta-daa!"

Heph went to grab for it and she held it out of reach. "Oh, no, sir," she said, letting the heat back into her eyes. "Allow me."

She slid the condom onto his cock, taking advantage of the moment to cup his balls in her other hand, lightly tickling the sensitive skin. He caught her wrist and tugged her up and onto him, and she kissed him again, lazily sliding her thigh between his legs.

"Turn over," he told her, and she obeyed, arching back against him as he arranged her body, facing away from his, both of them on their sides, her knees curled up. He kissed the back of her neck, and guided himself into her from behind.

"Ohhh," Aphrodite said, her eyelids fluttering closed as he moved. There was no frenzied thrusting. Just a gradual in-and-out as he used his strength to hold her nearly immobile against him, whispering in her ear a detailed description of all the things he wanted to do with her, how badly he wanted her.

She heard his breathing catch and shift and pushed back harder against him, using her own hip motion to increase the pace, until he stiffened and gasped, his grip slackening as he came.

Aphrodite relaxed into the warm circle of his arms, blissfully calm. She drifted for a while, lulled by Heph's steady breathing against her neck, and the comfort of his embrace. When his fingers started a gentle exploration of her breasts, she hummed and wriggled around to face him again.

"Hey," she whispered, and kissed him.

"Was that the whole sentence?" he wondered.

"Yep."

"Cool," he said, and returned the kiss. It started gentle, but soon they were panting, open-mouthed, limbs tangling around each other.

The rap on the door was an unwelcome surprise.

"Aphrodite!" Thea called.

"We're busy!" she yelled back, while Heph sputtered a laugh, resting his forehead against her collarbone.

"Get unbusy!" Thea said, undeterred. "You've got a red carpet to get ready for. I'm coming back in five minutes, and I'm walking straight in."

Aphrodite sighed. "She's right," she said, with extreme reluctance.

"Seriously?" Heph said. "It's only, what, 2 p.m.?"

"Oh, shit," Aphrodite said, and rolled off the couch. "Then we're already running late."

***

If Heph thought Hera's black and white party had prepared him for what the premiere would be like, he'd been wrong.

Aphrodite's preparation had taken several intense hours in their hotel suite as her skin was prepped, her manicure redone, her hair styled, her makeup airbrushed on and finally, ceremoniously, her shimmering golden gown lowered over her shining head by three attendants, all of them visibly holding their breaths as the glittering folds settled around her legs. Aphrodite threw several poses, frowning thoughtfully in the enormous mirror that had been brought in for the occasion, the hotel's mirror being deemed insufficient for their purposes.

"Do I need another stitch or two in the waist?" she asked.

Sienna, her publicist, took several shots on her phone and frowned. "Maybe." She showed the screen to Aphrodite. "What do you think?"

Heph had talked to Sienna a few times on the phone, and had formed a hazy vision of her as a tiny blonde dynamo in a pink power suit, an image that had cemented itself when Aphrodite mentioned she'd been a cheerleader. In person, Sienna was actually a broad, solid woman with light brown skin and loose black curls. She'd been a base for cheerleading pyramids, not the tiny flyer he'd been imagining.

He had got the power suit right. Sienna was wearing a matching skirt and blazer in a pink so radiant it almost outshone Aphrodite's metallics, though she'd apparently change into black before the premiere.

Aphrodite scrolled through the pictures and frowned. "I don't know... I think it's showing up as a little loose on the bodice."

This started a twenty minute discussion, eventually decided in favor of the stitches. A seamstress, evidently on call, came in, smiled briefly at Heph's confusion, flashed a needle over the fabric twice, and left again, to actual applause.

It could have been laughable—all these people, getting one person into a fancy dress—but Heph didn't feel the need to laugh. They were treating this process as if it were vitally important because it was. Because what Aphrodite wore and how she wore it would have real impact on the movie's success, her future career, and even how well her interview with Gaia next week might turn out.

Meanwhile, Heph himself had been thoroughly buffed and polished. His stubble had been artistically shaped and his hair cut by another stylist Thea had booked just for him. The tuxedo Penny Laconia had arranged fit perfectly, in a way that made him uncomfortably aware of how long he'd been ignoring the increasingly bad sizing of his own wardrobe.

"I think I need to go clothes shopping," he muttered.

"I'll take you any time," the stylist said, eyeing him up. "Want me to queer eye you, baby?"

"Hands off, Bertrand," Aphrodite called from the other side of the living room, where she was being spritzed with perfume in mathematically precise increments. "Mine's the only queer eye that gets to see this guy naked."

Heph felt the blood rush to his cheeks as he remembered just how naked they'd been a few hours ago.

Bertrand grinned at him. "Just kidding, hon." Before Heph could stop him, he knelt down to wipe a buffing cloth over Heph's already highly polished patent-leather shoes. From the casual way he did it, it was an everyday action for him, something completely normal. When Heph looked at Aphrodite, she was getting strapped into her own shoes, Sienna's strong fingers making quick work of the thin buckles.

And then, in a rush of movement and quiet phone calls and last minute make-up checks, they were riding with Sienna and Thea in a limousine that drove a couple of miles and joined the queues outside the legendary Regency Village Theater.

The red carpet was a blur of flashlights, eager cheers from the public crowding the security barriers on the other side of the street, and way, way more people bustling about than Heph would have believed from what the cameras caught.

It seemed as if every guest had their own entourage, plus the studio personnel, plus the adroit workers from the location events staff. They were all wearing black, talking urgently into headsets and walkie-talkies, carrying all the objects a celebrity couldn't wear or carry but might need inside, and pointing the stars under their care in various directions for poses and brief interviews. Aphrodite's two-person crew was actually restrained.

"Dana!" Aphrodite called, and the small, silver-haired woman talking animatedly to an interviewer further down the gauntlet turned around and spotted both of them.

In all of the discussion of the movie and the premiere, Heph had somehow missed that he was going to be actually meeting Dana Sellen, who'd starred in three pivotal science-fiction series and been the focus of his teenage fantasies.

"Aphrodite!" she called back. "And this is Heph? Hello!"

Later, the pictures would show him grinning like an idiot as he shook Dana Sellen's hand. Dana pulled the two of them into her orbit as they completed the rest of the press gauntlet, and sure, they were mugging for the cameras, but he thought there was real respect and affection in the way the women hugged, then posed for pictures together.

The theater itself was comparatively quiet. Thea got Heph to his seat near the front, then vanished. Dana made a speech, the producer made a speech, the cast posed on stage for one last set of group shots, and then Aphrodite rejoined him as the lights began to dim and people reluctantly looked away from their phones.

Heph realized he was sitting beside Juan Lopez, who was sitting beside Marjorie Qu, and had to take a deep breath against the rising panic of knowing he *wasn't meant to be here*. Not amongst all these bright and beautiful people, who were genuine celebrities.

Aphrodite seemed calm about it.

Because she was one of them, Heph thought, blinking hard. And she wanted him there. So maybe he did belong, even if it seemed completely ridiculous.

He settled back against the plush velvet chair, and watched.

After ten minutes, he knew he'd be able to make nice chit-chat at the afterparty.

After twenty minutes, he knew it was a genuinely good movie.

There were flaws; some heavy-handed dialogue and more than a few moments where the computer-generated imagery was too bland for his practiced eye. The cinematography wasn't anything special, and the soundtrack leaned too heavily on zesty pop hits and swooping strings. *A Light in Dark Places* probably wouldn't be getting Best Picture nominations.

But for a first-time director, Dana's vision was clear and her control of the story strong. And her character's chemistry with Marjorie's was undeniable, as the two ex-partners—in both senses of the word—teamed up for one last shot at saving the world.

"Ooh," Aphrodite squeaked beside him, as the battered superheroes hesitantly entered a shiny, futuristic laboratory. They walked into a gigantic room where the curved far wall was made up entirely of screens showing mayhem and catastrophe across the globe—more dubious CGI, but Heph only noted it in the back of his mind. In front of the screens was an enormous high-backed chair, the occupant only a shadow.

Ominous violins ratcheted up the tension as the heroes approached.

"Remember," Beacon muttered to her partner, summoning flames to her hands. "She's dangerous."

"Doctor Greenblade?" Mistress Midnight asked tentatively.

The chair swung around, and the lighting in the room immediately switched from doom and gloom to a wash of sunrise pink and gold.

"Hiiiii!" Aphrodite's Greenblade caroled, bouncing out of her fur-lined chair to hug both nervous heroes to her chest. She was wearing plain black slacks and a light pink t shirt under a white lab coat—definitely the plainest outfit Heph had ever seen her in. The movie had stopped short of the hair bun and glasses cliche, but she'd clearly been dressed down for the role.

But regardless of her costume, Aphrodite's undeniable charisma just poured off the screen. Greenblade rattled through greetings and whisked the heroes through a speedy tour of her secret lab, and Heph felt the audience responding. When she delivered a pithy one-liner with a wink, the crowd laughed.

Under the sound, Heph heard Aphrodite's tiny sigh of relief. He reached out, wrapping one arm around her shoulders, and she snuggled into him.

Greenblade's role in the narrative was important, but small. Even so, the final edit had kept most of what Aphrodite had described to him of the filming, and it was easy to see why. The camera loved her. When Beacon and Mistress Midnight limped out of the starship rubble, to be greeted by their anxious former sidekick and their ragtag crew of former allies and enemies, Aphrodite's vivid face particularly caught the eye in the crowd shot.

Or maybe he'd just been looking for her.

Still, Heph decided, no matter how alluring and vibrant the screen version was, the real woman was better.

When the credits rolled, there was a standing ovation. Heph, caught by surprise, got up a little late, but applauded with enthusiasm. Juan, grinning widely, leaned into him and half-said, half-shouted, "It's mandatory."

"What?" Heph asked.

"The ovation. It's expected at these things. It doesn't mean they actually liked it."

"I liked it," Heph said. "You were great."

Juan's eyes flashed gratitude and a hint of suspicion, and Heph realized that this Hollywood star was nervous. That Dana, on Aphrodite's other side was worried, and even Marjorie Qu, who already had an Academy Award, was looking at him, the normal person, for his reaction. "I mean it," he said.

"You can trust Heph," Aphrodite said, to Juan. "He's always honest."

Juan's smile widened, and Heph sat down with relief as the crowd finally subsided.

The afterparty was held in a nearby hotel ballroom, and involved a series of "candid" shots, tiny snacks that no one seemed to eat, and drinks they held but rarely drank. There were other celebrities there too, some Heph recognized and many he didn't.

Heph sat in his chair, which Sienna had produced for him at the hotel, and sipped half a glass of champagne while Aphrodite chatted with people she knew, and a few who introduced themselves to her. She introduced him to the costume designer before she left to work the room. Heph was halfway through an interesting discussion of the armor Greenblade had designed for Marjorie's Beacon to wear in the climactic battle when Aphrodite reappeared beside him.

"We've got to go," she said.

"Okay," Heph said, partly relieved. He'd liked talking to Kimiko, but they'd been at this thing for a while.

"Now," Aphrodite added, and the tension in his voice made him look closer. She was staring across the room, at a big, wide-shouldered man who stood out among the slender Hollywood people, heading straight towards them with an arrogant set to his celebrated jawline.

Ares Irontosser, in the flesh.

"Fuck, he's seen us," Aphrodite said.

And the press had seen him too, narrowing in on the forthcoming greeting

"Oh shit," Heph said, his stomach sinking. "Aphrodite, I forgot to tell you—"

"Aphrodite, baby!" Ares said, and stepped familiarly close to Aphrodite.

Her hands went up with graceful ease, resting on his shoulders so that he couldn't get the tight embrace he'd been aiming for, and she artlessly turned her face at the last minute, so that his kiss landed firmly on her cheek.

Heph's entire being was consumed with the desire to run Ares down for assuming he could touch her, but he had to abstractly admire the smoothness with which she turned a possessive power move into a friendly greeting between people who were no longer close. The cameras flashed, and Ares's smile was a little less triumphant as he turned to Heph.

"And this must be the famous non-famous Heph," Ares said. He leaned down, exaggerating how far he had to lower himself to reach Heph's level, and held his hand out. "Good to meet you, man."

Heph couldn't bring himself to smile, even with the flashes going off in his face. He hoped he was projecting an air of polite disinterestedness, but suspected he looked like a scowling bulldog as he shook Ares's hand.

He wasn't surprised that Ares tightened his grip immediately, attempting to grind the bones of his palm even as he smiled into Heph's eyes. It was exactly the move he'd expect, even if Ares hadn't personally disliked him. He was just that sort of guy.

Ares apparently didn't have anything close to the same insight. He hadn't expected to be anticipated, much less resisted. He hadn't expected the hard muscle of Heph's hand, nor the strength of his forearms. Ares had unbalanced himself to make Heph look smaller and more vulnerable; Heph, grounded in his chair, with a much lower center of gravity, used that leverage to tug Ares further in and deliver a heavy clap on the shoulder with his other hand that he sincerely hoped would leave a bruise.

"Good to meet you too," he said.

Ares's eyes flashed pure murder, and he tried to pull away. Heph held his hand just long enough to indicate that he could keep him there if he wanted, and then let go. Ares actually stumbled.

Heph's satisfaction was short-lived.

Aphrodite, clearly still playing for the cameras, said, "I didn't know you'd be at this thing! What a nice surprise."

"A surprise?" Ares said. "Didn't Heph pass on my message?"

"Message?" Aphrodite repeated, and her eyes fastened on Heph's, with a question he couldn't satisfactorily answer.

He hadn't known the bastard had literally meant he'd see her soon. He hadn't known that the message had been anything other than a taunt, Ares lashing out at the woman who'd dumped him and her new, vastly inferior partner.

But Heph hadn't passed the message on. And now Aphrodite was being ambushed in front of the cameras.

"Of course!" she said. "I, like, totally forgot!"

The reporters probably didn't hear the false note. But Heph did, and he saw that Ares had understood too.

"Oh, sure," Ares said casually. "He probably wrote it down for you, yeah?"

Aphrodite flinched. It was barely visible; more of a micro-expression than a reaction. But Ares's smile broadened, and Heph was suddenly frozen with rage. Ares was standing there, casually holding Aphrodite's secret illiteracy over her head like a weight he could drop on her at any moment.

Like he could crush her with it.

And as intense as Heph's fury was, he was guilty too. He'd opened the door for this to happen.

"Hey, Ares," he began, with no idea of what he was going to say next, and then Thea appeared, like a guardian angel.

Or the Angel of Death. The photographers weren't looking her way, but Heph caught the glare she directed at Ares, and wondered that he didn't spontaneously combust.

"I'm so sorry to break this up," she murmured, voice deferential, while her eyes promised dire torments, "but Marjorie and Dana were hoping they could get a few more group photos..."

"Oh, for sure," Aphrodite said, and gave Ares the most gracious of smiles. Her hand rested on Heph's shoulder for a moment; the perfect display of unity for the cameras.

He was imagining it, of course; he couldn't really feel the temperature of her hand through the layers of tux jacket and shirt. But he thought he felt a chill.

***

"Aphrodite, I'm so sorry," Heph said, the moment they were out of earshot.

He meant it, she was pretty sure. His brown eyes were worried, and she'd watched every emotion pass through them during that brief, horrible encounter. The shock, then the realization of his mistake, then the rage, then the guilt. Heph couldn't lie, not even with his face.

Fortunately, she could. She was really, really good at it.

"I think we sold it," she said lightly.

"I should have told you he called."

"When was that?"

"Last night. You'd just gone to bed, and I didn't want to disturb you, but I thought that if it was something about the stalker case—"

"Right, right. Makes sense." They were making hasty progress through the ballroom, and she spotted a balcony, through a half-ajar curtain. She turned to Thea. "Do Dana and Marjorie really want me?"

"Yes," Thea said. "But they can wait, if you need a minute."

"Just a breath of fresh air," Aphrodite said, and took a few steps in that direction. She only needed a few moments, to reset and calm down.

She waited for Heph to call her back. To demand that she listen to his apology. To shout at her, and make her shout back, until they turned a small mistake into a gigantic drama. Her shoulders were already going up as she waited for the call, her blood heating as she figured out what she was going to say first.

She realized, with a sickening jolt, that she was waiting for him to act like Ares.

Had she been lying to herself, all this time? Had she actually *enjoyed* the fights and the drama? Did some sick part of herself need them?

But Heph wouldn't do that. He'd been so unable to pretend to fall for her that he'd had to go ahead and do it for real.

His follow up to an honest mistake was an honest apology, and that was so much harder than defensiveness and drama, because it demanded honesty from *her*, and she couldn't give it. She wasn't sure it was there to give.

She'd been right to fear a relationship with Heph. She'd sucked him right in, and now she was going to drown him, with her pettiness and her deceit.

Breathe. Breathe. She just needed to get to the balcony and breathe, and get herself back together.

Two steps from the curtain, the reporter caught her.

"Aphrodite, quick question," she said, and Aphrodite recognized her. She'd been at the press conference that had started this entire disaster, the blonde with the perky ponytail who had asked if she was worried Ares was moving on forever.

The reporter's hair was down now, but her eyes were still huge and falsely sympathetic as she leaned in. "Great movie!" she said.

"Thanks. What was the question?"

"Sources have told me that you have a learning disability," the reporter said. "Frankly, they told me that you're illiterate."

Aphrodite felt the floor drop away beneath her. Only years of training and experience could have kept her on her feet right then, but she did it, stayed upright and poised. "What the hell?" she said blankly. "What sources?"

"Oh, I can't say," the reporter said, but her eyes darted across the room.

"Right," Aphrodite said. "Well, I can't tell you how to do your job, but you might not want to listen to every 'source' with a grudge."

The reporter laughed, but her eyes glittered, sharp as a blade. "Is there any truth to the statement?"

"Excuse me?" Aphrodite said, letting her tone frost over. Thea was heading towards her, Heph in her wake. She only had to fend this woman off for a few more seconds.

"Can you read?" the woman asked. Her voice was clear, and the question fell into one of those weird silences that came over gatherings every now and then. This was no longer a private conversation.

Aphrodite stared at her. She couldn't fend her off with a no com-ment—that would be as good as an admission. And she couldn't admit it, because... Well, because everyone would know exactly who she was then. A dumb, pretty, poor girl who'd somehow lucked out and made it big.

So she assumed an expression of rueful annoyance, looked the reporter straight in the eye, and lied.

"Um, of course?" she said, and laughed dismissively. "Everyone can read!"

She turned away, from the reporter's disappointed expression, from Heph's shocked face, and escaped onto the balcony.

***

For Aphrodite, the party was pretty much over after that. She watched herself smile and hug her co-stars. She cheered when Dana cracked open a bottle of champagne as the first reviews were released. She danced with Juan and with Marjorie when the music started, and no matter how much she smiled, she didn't feel any of it. She was a robot following her program, not a single deviation from the code.

And then she spotted Heph, waiting quietly in the corner, and couldn't pretend any longer.

"Hey, baby," she said, sauntering over to him. "Want to get out of here?"

Heph smiled. It was harder to tell in the dim light, but she thought it didn't reach his eyes. "Yes, please," he said.

They were quiet in the car and in the elevator. Heph excused himself to shower and change, and when he came out of the bathroom in his PJs, Aphrodite was waiting for him, wearing a sleep tank and shorts set, and sitting cross-legged in the middle of the bed.

Heph stopped, looking uncertain, and she realized what she'd done. He had returned to his chair, and she'd picked the one spot he couldn't easily get to from it. He could reach her, but it would take some effort and cost some dignity. He couldn't just reach out and touch her.

Aphrodite hugged her knees to her chest and braced herself.

"You didn't like that I told that reporter I could read," she said.

"You got ambushed at a party," Heph said. "It's hard to make decisions in the moment."

"But you think I should have told her the truth."

Heph looked at her steadily. "I think you get to decide who knows that," he said.

And she could see that he meant it. He really did think that it was up to her. But she could also see that he was disappointed.

"You're mad at me," she said. "You think that I should speak up. Let people know dyslexia can be part of anyone's life, even if they're rich and famous. Be an inspiration to little girls who are struggling. Show them they can be a success."

"Um. I think that last part is all you," Heph said cautiously. "I hadn't thought about it that hard, though, for the record, I think you'd be a great role model. I... Look, it's absolutely your choice. But I've been working all my life not to be ashamed of my disabilities. When you can straight up deny yours—deny that they could even exist—it doesn't feel great."

"I'm going to keep doing that," she said abruptly.

"Keep concealing your reading issues? As I said, that's your—"

"No. Lying. I'm going to lie a lot, pretty much every day. The whole time we're together, I'll be lying."

Heph looked baffled. "I know your job depends on maintaining an appearance," he began.

"I'll lie to you," Aphrodite said, and watched that hit home. "I won't mean to, not at first. It'll just be easier, so I'll do it, and you'll believe me. And then I'll do it again, and I'll be waiting for you to catch me, but you won't, and then you will, and then you'll break up with me, and I'll deserve it."

"This isn't—"

"So I'm breaking up with you," Aphrodite said, and felt the first tears fall, gigantic drops that splattered hotly against her bare legs. "I'm breaking up with you now, because I don't want to hurt you."

Heph sat very, very still. "Too late," he said at last.

The tears just would not *stop*. She scraped them away from her cheeks with impatient hands. "I'm sorry," she said. "I just think this is the best decision."

"Okay," Heph said.

That felt like a stab to the heart. But she went on, because she had to, and she had to try to be as fair as she could. "About the contract."

"What about it?" Heph asked. "We dissolved it. You're either coming to my sister's wedding as my girlfriend, or you're not coming. So you're not coming." He said it with stiff finality, and Aphrodite realized that losing him meant losing the Smith-Waters clan too. She'd never trade in-jokes with Mellie again, or eat Narnie's soup, or marvel at Heph's family with Aoide's fiancée.

"If you want," she managed. "But about the money. You earned it. You should keep it."

Heph's jaw set. "No."

"Heph, please. Please, just take it. You did everything right. You took all the risks. It's me who can't *do* this. Not for real."

"Why not?"

"Because *I'm* not real," Aphrodite said. "I tried to tell you! I'm shallow and stupid. I couldn't even make it work with Ares, and he only wanted the fake me! But you're a good person. So good that I fooled you into wanting to be with me, when I'm fake all the way through."

"You are not shallow," Heph said. "You are not fake, and you are not stupid. You didn't fool me about anything. And I love you."

Aphrodite shot backwards, away from the words and the stark honesty of the way he said them. "You can't!" she said. "I can't even fucking *read*."

"So what?" Heph demanded. "You think I can't mean it, because you have a *disability*? What the fuck, Aphrodite! What do you think of me?" He gestured at himself; his body, his chair. "Do I mean less to you because of this?"

"No! Of course not!"

"Then I don't *get* it," Heph said, and his frustration was so palpable that all Aphrodite wanted to do was lie again, and tell him that she hadn't meant it, that she was taking it back, that of course they could be together and she wouldn't let him down.

Instead, she stared at his face, his wonderful, beloved face, and was lost for words.

"But I don't have to get it," Heph said heavily. "You want to break up. So we're broken up."

"Can we be—"

"No," Heph said, flinging a hand up. "Don't ask me that right now." He took a deep breath. "Okay. This is what's going to happen next. I'm going to call Thea, tell her what's happened, and ask to be flown home, tonight or early tomorrow."

Aphrodite nodded.

"I won't be talking to the press. Whatever story you two want to put together is fine, but I don't want to be a part of it." He went back into the bathroom and emerged with his pants laid over his knees. He fished around in there and pulled out his key-chain, then separated out one of the keys.

"This is for picking up your stuff that's still at my house," he said quietly. "I'll get one of my sisters to give me her spare."

Aphrodite nodded again. She was afraid of what noises might come out if she tried to speak.

"I'd appreciate it if you send Lina to pick the things up. I'd like to say goodbye."

"Okay," Aphrodite said. She had to force the word out through the tangle of barbed wire lodged in her throat, but she managed it, and was distantly proud of that.

"Okay," Heph said, and awkwardly tossed the key in her direction. Aphrodite caught it, and resisted the urge to hug the cold metal object to her heart. From Heph's hand to hers. It was probably the closest they'd ever come to touching again.

Heph wheeled towards the connecting door, and hesitated on the threshold. "Just for the record," he said quietly, without looking at her. "I'm so angry and heartbroken right now that I can barely think."

"Of course you are," Aphrodite said. "It's my fault. I'm so—"

"But I don't have any regrets," Heph said, cutting in, and now he did look at her. His deep brown eyes were filled with pain. "Not one. If I knew it would end like this, I'd do it all again." He looked at her, frozen in the middle of the huge, white bed, shook his head, and left.

Aphrodite clutched the key in her hand so hard that the edges cut, and buried her first wails in her pillow.

Chapter Twelve

Narnie picked Heph up at the airport the next morning. She didn't ask why he'd come back early and alone.

Heph had texted Aoide to let her know Aphrodite wouldn't be attending the wedding, and that had no doubt made the rounds even before he got on the plane. Thea, her voice very gentle, had promised to send his luggage and his chair to his house to meet him there. Heph had thanked her for everything, repeated that he wouldn't be talking to the press, and hung up.

"So..." Narnie said, as she parked outside his place.

"Please don't," Heph said.

"Well, just let me know if I need to beat her up."

Heph snorted. "No."

"Okay." Narnie peered over his shoulder. "What's that?"

Heph looked. There was an enormous box standing in front of his door.

For a moment, his heart leapt. Maybe Aphrodite had changed her mind. Maybe she'd sent him the biggest gift box of all time as an apology. He slid out of Narnie's stupidly enormous truck and made his way towards it.

But the card taped to the front was from Mark Hermes. "Enjoy!" it read.

Heph slumped. "It's my chair from work," he said dully. "I guess it was delivered while I was away."

"That's... nice?" Narnie said. "Help me out here, Heph. You're scaring me. You weren't like this when things ended with your other girlfriends."

"With them, I knew things were over before they ended," Heph said tightly. "This was a surprise."

"Are you *sure* I shouldn't beat her up?"

"I thought you liked her."

"I do," Narnie said. "But you're my Heph. I'd beat up a thousand supermodel ex-girlfriends if it would make you feel better."

"It wouldn't," Heph said, and watched as she opened the door for him and wrestled the chair inside. Knowing Narnie had his back *did* make him feel better, even if he couldn't condone her proposed actions. He sat on the couch and thought, with no enthusiasm, about all the things he should be doing. Unpacking. Laundry. Finding another job.

"I'm putting a six-pack in the fridge," Narnie called from the kitchen.

"Why?" Heph called back, and she came into the living room to regard him.

"Because the first time Leo and I broke up I shotgunned eight beers in a row."

Heph eyed her.

"I'm not saying you should do that," Narnie said. "I'm just saying that the misery the next morning really took my mind off my broken heart."

"You and Leo have been together for nearly ten years."

"I'm also saying that," Narnie said, and slid him a hopeful look.

"No," Heph said. "We're not getting back together so you can braid her hair and trade hoodies."

"Aw," Narnie said. "Do you want me to stay? Help you drink those beers?"

"No," Heph said, and closed his eyes for a moment. The last time Narnie had been in his house, Aphrodite had been there too.

When he opened his eyes, Narnie was looking at him with real concern.

He tried to smile. "I'll be fine," he told her.

Aphrodite was wrong about him.

He wasn't always honest.

***

"Aphrodite," Thea said again.

Aphrodite curled herself tighter under the covers. "Go away," she mumbled.

"You said you were coming in here to get dressed," Thea said. "That was an hour ago."

"I'm dressed," Aphrodite said, and heaved one arm out of the giant white bed to prove it.

"Great," Thea said wryly. "You're wearing Issey Miyake in bed. I know they're all about the origami effect, but I'm not sure the shirt's meant to have that many creases."

"The interview isn't until tomorrow. I don't have to do anything today."

"You're supposed to be meeting Hera for lunch and a final strategy session. Then you've got a meeting with studio execs, and a couple of interviews Sienna would like you to fit in. And Dana Sellen wants to know if you're available for dinner. She has a new film project you might be interested in."

Aphrodite flopped her exposed arm in a gesture too sulky to be a wave. "Can't you move that stuff around?"

There was a brief pause. "No," Thea said, and her voice was inflexible. "I've been moving things around for two days. This is where they have moved to. You need to get up."

"I'm too sad," Aphrodite said.

"Then you shouldn't have broken up with someone who made you happy," Thea said, and when Aphrodite sat up, outraged, she thrust a phone at her. "Here. You've got a call you have to take. Or I quit."

Aphrodite scowled at her, but took the phone. "Hello?"

"Get out of bed," Hecate ordered.

"Why can't you be more like Persephone? She's much nicer."

"You don't need nice. You need a bitch, and that bitch is me. Get up and do your job, Aphrodite."

Aphrodite flung the covers back and surged out of bed. "Fine," she said. "I'm doing it. Is that all?"

Thea nodded in satisfaction and left.

"No," Hecate said. "I also want to know why, after weeks of telling us how sexy and kind and amazing Heph is, you went out with him for a grand total of one day before dumping his ass. I got the 'Heph tore up the contract and asked me out and I said yes!' voicemail, and then the 'you guys seriously Heph is so good in bed I came so hard I cried' voicemail, and finally the 'I had to break up with Heph for his own good because I'm a terrible person' voicemail, all within 24 hours. It was a journey."

Aphrodite sat down again. "But I had to. I told Persephone all about it yesterday. Didn't she tell you?"

"Yes. She called me and relayed most of your drunken babbling, which is why I have taken the morning off my very important job and am calling you now," Hecate said. "She said you weren't making a lot of sense, but she got the bizarre impression that you think you're fake."

Aphrodite steeled herself. "I am."

"Uh-huh," Hecate said, not sounding impressed. "And what makes you think that?"

"I lie all the time. My whole life is just pretending."

"You're a *model*," Hecate said. "And now you're an actress. Well done, by the way. Have you even bothered to look at the reviews?"

Despite herself, Aphrodite felt a faint stirring of hope. "No. Thea tried to tell me about them yesterday, but I was..."

"Wallowing?" Hecate asked. "Here, let me quote. 'Urania brings an appealing warmth to her small role.' 'Aphrodite Urania provides a welcome moment of genuine levity.' 'Urania is clearly playing a version of herself, but has a grounded presence well beyond the usual model/actress cameo.'"

"Oh," Aphrodite said.

"Genuine," Hecate repeated meaningfully. "Appealing. Grounded."

"That just means I'm good at fooling them."

"Let's try this, then: Aphrodite, you are the most generous person I have ever met. And before you say it, it's not because you're rich. Hades and Hera and Minerva all have money, and none of them give like you do. You see what people need and you give it to them. That's one real thing, okay?"

"Okay," Aphrodite conceded.

"Second, you made friends with Persephone."

"Oh, like that's hard."

"It is, actually," Hecate said. "Persephone is sweet and warm and loving, and she should have a ton of close friends, but she doesn't, because her mother is a demon from hell. So even though she's friendly to everybody, she keeps part of herself locked away and protected. She eventually opened up to me, and then to Hades. You took one look at her, decided you were going to be friends, and plowed right through her walls. You couldn't have done that if you were fake. You'd be too concerned with keeping your own walls up."

"Hm," Aphrodite said. She was flicking through possible tops hung in her wardrobe, because unfortunately, Thea had been right, and this Miyake wasn't going to make it.

"You better be listening to me," Hecate said. "This is some of my top-level analysis. I should be charging you billable minutes."

"I'm listening," Aphrodite said. "I just don't know if I can believe you. I *feel* fake." She held a turquoise blouse under her chin and nodded at herself in the mirror.

"Girl, have you never heard of Impostor Syndrome?" Hecate demanded. "We all feel fake! Hasn't your therapist ever brought this up?"

"Sometimes," Aphrodite said reluctantly.

"And I bet you ran away from it. You're not fake, Aphrodite. You're scared that you're *real*. And you're scared the real you isn't enough."

Aphrodite sat down in the middle of the wardrobe with a thump that jarred her bones, turquoise silk crushed in her fist. "Hot damn," she whispered.

"Exactly," Hecate said. Her voice had shifted, less steely and more sympathetic. "And believe me, I understand the feeling. Being yourself is fucking terrifying. But you're enough, okay? You're enough for me and Persephone and your dad, and your team, and everyone else in your bizarre, spectacular life."

"Oh," Aphrodite said. She was crying again, but this wasn't the same painful sobs wrenched out of her body. This felt like something deep inside her was melting, and leaking out of her eyes. She mopped at her face with the blouse. "And I could have been enough for Heph. That's what you're telling me?"

"Maybe," Hecate said. "I'm not in your heart. I don't know for sure. Maybe you needed to break up with him."

"Then why have I been crying for two days?" Aphrodite demanded.

"Well, that's kind of my point," Hecate said patiently.

"Oh, shit. What do I do?"

"Do you want to get Heph back?"

"Yes."

"Why?"

"Because I love him. Because...because he loves me." It was harder to say the second sentence, and much harder to believe it. But she'd seen it. And he'd said it. And Heph didn't lie. "He loves me," she said again, her voice stronger. "We can make it work. I'll be brave, this time. I won't run away."

Hecate exhaled. "Okay. Well, call him."

Aphrodite nodded, forgetting Hecate couldn't see her. Then she paused. "Actually, I might have another idea."

"You literally *just* said you were going to be brave," Hecate said.

"Yep," Aphrodite said, her brain clicking through the possibilities. "I am. I'm going to be really brave. Okay, I love you, gotta go!"

"What are—" Hecate began, but Aphrodite hung up and bounced to her feet.

"Thea!" she called, stripping off her Miyake and grabbing another top at random. "Can you get me in touch with Gaia's people before the Hera lunch, please?"

***

On Wednesday, Heph was using his self-imposed lunch break to write his best man's speech when his phone alarm went off.

He was relieved, because writing about the wonders of true love and deep commitment was the last thing he wanted to be doing right now, and puzzled, because as far as he knew he hadn't set any alarms for the day. Working from home for his few remaining clients wasn't the kind of commitment that needed alarms, and he didn't need reminders to keep working through the list of job leads Odysseus had given him.

But when he glanced at the screen, Heph realized he'd actually set the alarm last week.

APHRODITE'S INTERVIEW, the notification read.

Heph stabbed the off button on the alarm, put his phone down, wrote a sentence, erased a sentence, wrote two more sentences, erased a paragraph, and finally gave in to the inevitable.

He used his TV almost exclusively for streaming, and by the time he figured out how to get an actual broadcast, the interview had evidently been going for a while. The camera was focused on Hera Kronion, her face very still as she described Zeus's history of infidelity.

"But you forgave him," Gaia said, her beautiful, dark face solemn. "You divorced him, and then you remarried."

"Yes," Hera said. Even underneath the TV makeup, she looked pale. "He promised me he'd changed, and I believed him."

"Do you believe people can change?"

"I do," Hera said. "And I believe in second chances." She looked faintly startled, as if she'd surprised herself, then nodded at Gaia. "But in this case... He did cheat on me again. And I'm not sure I believe in third chances."

"You've chosen to protect the privacy of the young woman involved in that most recent infidelity," Gaia said. "Which I find very admirable, by the way, so we're not going to snoop." She waved her finger at her studio audience, who chuckled obligingly. A quick cross to the crowd showed them absolutely rapt.

"But one of the women he had an affair with in that earlier period was you, Aphrodite," Gaia continued, and the camera refocused, a mid-shot of Aphrodite, sitting comfortably beside Hera.

She was wearing a pink blazer over a cream tank top and slacks, a perfect complement to Hera's muted grey ensemble. More somber than her usual clothing choices, but not so conservative that she'd be suspected of dressing for the part. Heph resigned himself to the fact that even his brief association with Aphrodite had taught him more about fashion than Mellie had managed in twenty-six years, and listened closely, his heart pounding in his chest.

"Was that a question, Gaia?" she asked pertly, and Gaia laughed, surprised into genuine amusement.

"I mean, the answer is yes," Aphrodite continued. "Zeus and I had a brief affair nearly nine years ago."

"And how old were you at the time?" Gaia asked delicately.

Aphrodite didn't flinch. "I was seventeen years old," she said. "Seventeen and two days, actually."

Gaia paused for a moment, while her audience muttered amongst themselves. "And did that come out of nowhere?" she asked.

Aphrodite blew out a breath. "At the time, I was... No. It didn't come out of nowhere. He'd been flirting with me for a few months. Showing up to some of my shoots for Olympus titles. Talking to me at parties. And I was flattered. He was important, and I was just starting to be noticed. I flirted back."

"Was he grooming you?"

"You'd have to ask him about his motives," Aphrodite said. "All I can say is that when he first kissed me, I wasn't surprised."

"But your affair was consensual?"

"Yes," Aphrodite said. "I consented." The camera caught her turn towards the woman sitting beside her, the convulsive motion as Hera caught her hand and held it. "I'm so sorry," she said to Hera, and the room was still, as if it were just the two of them.

Hera looked back at her, eyes steady. "You don't need to apologize to me," she said, and while the words were stiff, her voice was soft. "I mean that. I'll always mean it."

"Okay, but I'll always be sorry," Aphrodite said, on a laugh that had a hint of tears in it, and the audience laughed with her.

"How long did the affair continue?" Gaia asked.

"A few months. And then my dad found out—he was still my manager at the time—and he was furious. Not at me. At Zeus. It stopped then."

"Who broke it off?"

Aphrodite paused, her face arrested. "I've never thought about that before. I'm not sure either of us did, officially. I think it was just so obvious that we wouldn't continue. At least, it was obvious to me. Zeus called a few times, and I didn't answer."

Hera's eyebrows went up.

"You ghosted him?" Gaia asked.

Aphrodite blinked. "I guess I did."

"And then you received the emails, signed by Hera," Gaia said. "Can you tell us about that, please?"

Heph's pulse raced unpleasantly as Aphrodite went through the content of the emails, her voice ragged as she repeated some of the nastier comments.

"That must have hurt to read," Gaia said quietly.

"Yes," Aphrodite said. "Although 'read' isn't quite the right word. I have low literacy and probable dyslexia, so I use a text-to-speech program to listen to my emails. They were read out loud to me, by this nice lady robot voice."

It took Heph a second to realize what she'd said. She'd done it so easily, so lightly, as if she weren't ashamed, as if this was just another fact about her. She was Aphrodite Urania, she was six feet tall, she was the brand ambassador for Hesperides, and she was functionally illiterate.

Neither Hera nor Gaia looked surprised at the revelation.

"Did that lessen the impact, do you think?" Gaia asked.

"No," Aphrodite said. "I have a really good memory for the spoken word." She gestured at the camera. "I wasn't reading off the autocue, before. I was remembering what those emails said. That's the problem. I can't forget."

Gaia cut to commercial.

Heph pushed himself away from the TV and to the kitchen sink, splashing cold water over his face and wrists as if he could wash away the heat that was flushing his entire body. He hadn't thought about how Aphrodite must have first processed those emails. When he'd first looked at them, he'd imagined her reading them the same way he had, and even when he'd known that she wouldn't, he hadn't adjusted his mental image. That was careless.

What had it been like, to have an uncaring robot voice tell her those things, for her to lock away in her brilliant memory?

And what did it mean, that she'd decided to be honest about the illiteracy she'd kept secret for so long? And it was a decision, not a spur-of-the-moment impulse. She'd talked it over with Gaia and Hera beforehand.

Obviously, telling the truth meant something to her. But did it mean anything to them?

Did it mean there could *be* a them?

He rolled back to the TV where Hera was explaining that she had never sent the emails, that they hadn't come from an account she knew about, and that until a few months ago, she hadn't even known that Aphrodite and Zeus had had an affair at all.

"So how did this come out?" Gaia asked.

"I can't speak to the whole process," Hera said, which Heph figured was code for "my lawyer warned me not to talk about it." "But in the course of another investigation, the emails sent to Aphrodite came to light, and were found to have been sent from Olympus Inc. From Zeus's office."

"Who found that information?"

"Heph," Aphrodite said. "He called me before he checked it out, because he wanted to be sure that he had my permission. I mean, you can imagine how unusual that is for me. My privacy has been invaded over and over, since I was sixteen years old. But he checked. I thought that was so sweet."

"This is Heph Smith, your boyfriend," Gaia said, obviously clarifying for the audience. Again, neither she nor Hera looked surprised by the direction Aphrodite was taking the interview. Heph began to have some suspicions. "Was that how you met?"

"I'd met him before then," Aphrodite said, ignoring the boyfriend part. "Well, 'met' might be the wrong word. I literally tripped over him. It was an amazing first impression, I'm sure. But that he asked for permission to go searching—that he cared—that really caught my attention."

Aphrodite was looking directly into the camera. "Heph cares," she said again. "He cares about the truth. And he finds out what's really there, and you finally have no choice but to believe him. That's why I love him."

Heph was literally breathless for a moment. He had to concentrate on expelling air and inhaling again. For a single, horrible, moment, he sympathized with Aphrodite's stalker. How would it feel, to genuinely believe that Aphrodite was sending him messages of love? How could he do anything but respond?

But Heph wasn't delusional, and he definitely wasn't a stalker. He hadn't imagined that message. She'd said it live on national television, straight to camera.

His phone lit up again. A call from Mellie.

Heph hit decline.

Four texts from Narnie arrived next. The first said WTF!!! The second was a row of exclamation marks. The third was an image of a cinnamon roll in a pink heart frame, and the last was a GIF of two women with rivers of rainbow tears pouring out of their eyes.

Aoide also texted him. It was a single question mark.

Heph was pretty sure he knew the answer.

***

"You were amazing," Aphrodite said, the second they were off the set and away from the cameras.

"You too," Hera said. She was twisting around, trying to unhook her microphone set from her grey shift dress. A tech came over to help. "Thank you," she said.

"You too." The tech's eyes were wide. "That was really good. Like... Really, really good."

"Oh," Hera said. "Thank you?"

The tech scurried away, and Hera looked confused. "I didn't think airing my dirty laundry in public was that impressive."

It was such an old-fashioned phrase to say that Aphrodite just had to hug her, so she did. Hera was still stiff, but Aphrodite had snuck in a hug when they met today, and another just before they went on stage, so she was loosening up a bit. One day, Hera would hug *her*, and then she'd know they were friends.

Gaia strolled up beside them. "Jay is new," she said, looking fondly after the tech. "They've probably never seen a movement start before."

"A movement?" Aphrodite said, startled in her turn.

"Well, a new moment in a very old movement," Gaia said. Her eyes were luminous and deep, and Aphrodite remembered that she'd just turned sixty. In her time, the host had seen a lot of unscrupulous people exposed—and many more getting away with it. "It was good work. And very good TV, of course."

Thea was heading towards Aphrodite, a phone in each hand and a gleam in her eye. "People are in, Aphrodite. We're getting calls for follow-ups, future film opportunities—Dana's going to be very happy she got in first—and the head of social marketing at Cyclone wants to talk to you."

Aphrodite raised her eyebrows. Cyclone was the company that made *The Binding*. "I definitely want to talk to them."

"I thought you would," Thea said, sounding smug. "And I have offers too. If you're serious about getting a personal assistant, I can add some more clients."

"Why don't you set up your own agency?" Aphrodite asked. "I can invest the seed capital."

Thea stared at her.

With some real satisfaction in rendering her speechless, Aphrodite took her own phone out of Thea's limp hand. "I'm going back to the dressing room," she said. "Got to make a call."

And she fully intended to.

But Heph called her first.

"Hi," he said, and after four whole days of not hearing his voice, her knees actually weakened at the sound.

"Hi," she said breathlessly, and hoped she didn't sound like an idiot. Wait, no, that was negative self-talk, and she was supposed to be avoiding that.

"I watched the interview. You were great."

"Thank you. How are you?"

"I'm fine," he said automatically. Then he paused. "Actually, I'm not fine. I miss you."

Aphrodite closed her eyes and leaned back against her dressing room door, weak with relief. "I miss you, too," she said. "So much. Heph, I'm so sorry. I fucked up. Can you forgive me?"

"Yes," he said immediately. "And I'm sorry that I didn't take your concerns seriously before. I can't just expect you to show up with no baggage. That's not realistic."

"Baggage, I've got," Aphrodite said. "Want to help me unpack it?"

He laughed, that soft, bass rumble that reverberated down her body. "I think you've got to do most of that yourself. But I'll help you find one of those carts to haul it around."

"Are we getting back together?" Aphrodite asked. "It sounds like we might be! But I want to make sure, is that what's happening?"

"If you want," Heph said hesitantly. "If you want to take it slow, that's fine."

"No. I'm in. For real this time." She considered it. "I can't promise I won't get scared again. But I'll be scared *with* you, okay? I won't run away. Heph?"

"Yes?"

"Will you be my boyfriend?"

"Yes," he said, and his voice broke on the word. "When are you coming home? When can I see you?"

"I'm going to the airport from the studio. I'll be back this afternoon. Can I go straight to your place?"

"I can't believe I'm saying this, but I've got a meeting this afternoon. I'm confirming a consultancy package. It literally just came up."

"That's great! Heph, that's fantastic news."

"But I might not be there when you arrive."

"That's okay," Aphrodite said. "I have a key." She was clutching it now. The key he'd given her to collect her things would open the door back to him. "I'll be waiting for you. I promise."

***

Heph couldn't stop grinning as he left Hesperides.

What had been described to him as "a consultancy opportunity" in the email had turned out to be a huge, long-term contract that would easily replace his Olympus income, and then some. He'd probably have to hire someone himself, at least part-time, in order to keep the smaller clients happy and keep more clients coming in. He wasn't going to make the mistake of counting on one big job again.

So he had a contract—a genuine one—and he would have a real date to Aoide's wedding, who was heading to his house from the airport right now.

And that meant his sisters couldn't get away with pushing him around anymore. Strangely, the thought made him more amused than relieved.

It was going to be a lot easier to ask for help when it wasn't shoved at him, unwanted. Maybe he could even offer *them* something.

He ordered a car, and his phone rang while he was waiting. "Maria!" he said. "I was just thinking of you. Listen, are you able to take on some part-time—"

"Heph, shut up and listen," she said. Her voice was deadly serious. He could hear the clatter of her keyboard and the buzz of servers in the background. His former colleague was probably at Olympus right now, calling him on her headset.

His stomach plummeted. "Oh, shit," he said. "Has Zeus done something?"

"Him?" She sounded genuinely startled. "No. Heph, you've been doxxed. Some asshole has posted your address on a forum."

"What?"

"Are you at home right now?"

"No," Heph said.

Maria exhaled with relief. "Okay. Good. There's a lot of nasty shit on this forum, a lot of gross incel resentment about you and Aphrodite. Now they're talking about telling the police you're a terrorist and sending SWAT teams to your house, that kind of thing. I set up a throwaway account to monitor it a while ago, but I think some of the chat has moved into private groups, and that means they might actually do something."

"I'm not home," Heph said, a fist clutching around his heart. "But Aphrodite was headed there."

There was a brief pause. "Call her," Maria said calmly. "Call her now."

"Can you call the police while I do?" he said.

Maria's voice went tight. "Heph... You *want* me to send the police to your home?"

"I know the risks," he said, "The cops aren't my buddies. But Aphrodite has a stalker who's recently resurfaced."

"Shit," Maria said.

A car pulled up beside Heph. The driver looked vaguely familiar.

"He sent stuff to her address. Tell the cops that, tell them there's an open case on him. Maybe they can help her." He swung backwards into the car and yanked his crutches in after him.

"*Shit,*" Maria said. "Any chance I can convince you to stay away?"

Heph laughed without humor. "Would you, if it were Jo?"

"No," Maria said. "Oh, fuck. Please stay safe, Heph." She hung up without further conversation, and Heph immediately hit the contacts list for Aphrodite's number.

"Hey, man," said the driver. "Nice to see you again."

Aphrodite wasn't picking up. "Again?" he said. "Can you go faster?"

"I dropped you off at your moms' for Mother's Day." He laughed. "Didn't know you were famous, then."

"I'm not. My girlfriend is." This time he waited through Aphrodite's cheery voicemail message. "Aphrodite, it's Heph. Don't go to my place, and if you're there now, leave. Your stalker might have my address." He hung up and tried her number again.

"Oh, shit," said the driver, and the car shot forward.

Heph sat in the backseat and tried to think. Thea's phone went to voicemail. Lina picked up.

"Heph!" she said. "I saw the interview! Wasn't she great?"

Heph outlined the situation in a few words. "Did you drop Aphrodite off?" he demanded. "Is Medea or someone else there with her?"

"Oh, fuck," Lina said, her voice shaky. "No, she told me not to pick her up at the airport. She said she wanted to meet you by herself. As herself."

"No security?" Heph asked, his stomach dropping.

"I'll call Gorgon right now and send them there," Lina said, and Heph hung up and tried Aphrodite again.

No response.

The driver pulled up outside Heph's house and hit the brakes. "I'll wait for you," he promised.

Heph nodded. Stealth wasn't really his strongest point, so he didn't even try. He did leave one of his crutches in the car, relying solely on the one for his worse leg. It reduced his mobility, but meant he had one hand entirely free. The door didn't show any signs of forced entry, though he wasn't sure what he should be looking for.

He turned his key and pushed the door open, just a crack. "Hello?" he called.

No reply.

"Aphrodite?" Heph called, and pushed the door open wider. "Are you here?"

She wasn't here. She was fine. Her flight had probably hit a scheduling problem and she was circling the city above him with her phone in airplane mode. The chance that the stalker would see his address on those forums, that he'd come here at all, was ludicrously small.

What Heph needed to do was close the door and leave before the cops arrived, because that could also be dangerous.

Knowing all of that, with the odds running through his head, he still stepped inside.

The first thing he saw was the pink cardigan discarded on his couch, which hadn't been there when he left.

The second thing he saw was the broken kitchen window. He hurtled forward, his heart in his throat, suddenly convinced he'd see Aphrodite lying behind his kitchen island in a pool of her own blood.

She wasn't there.

But was there was a man crouched behind the island, rising to his feet as Heph rounded the corner, one of Heph's sharp kitchen knives clutched in his skinny hand.

Heph stopped.

The man looked at him. He was older than Heph had thought he'd be, in perhaps his mid-forties. White, scrawny, thinning hair, wearing nondescript jeans and a plaid flannel over a white undershirt. Despite the knife gleaming in his fist, he didn't look angry. In fact, when he finally spoke, he sounded very reasonable.

"Hello," he said. "Listen, okay? You've got to stay away from my little bird."

Chapter Thirteen

Aphrodite crouched at the top of the ramp in the dark garage, her heart hammering. It had been just luck that she'd been in here, setting up Heph's surprise. She'd heard the window break and peeked out the connecting door to the kitchen in time to see the man climb in, feet first.

She'd never seen him in person, but she'd seen the mugshot, and she caught a glimpse of part of his face as he landed, and that was enough for her to identify the intruder.

It was Daniel Clark, and he'd come for her at last.

She'd ducked back into the garage and closed the door, some impulse making her hide silently and smoothly when all she wanted to do was scream and run. But quiet had been the best move after all. He'd rattled the handle and moved on when he found it locked, while she leaned against the other side of the door, both hands pressed over her mouth.

She could hear him walking around the house, sometimes humming, sometimes mumbling words and phrases. If she hadn't been so terrified, she could have pitied him. The delusion wasn't his fault. He hadn't chosen to believe she loved him. It was a torture devised by the brain that had turned on him.

But all her empathy had fled with her fear.

She'd turned the lights off as soon as she'd hidden, and now she closed her eyes as well, pulling up her mental image of the garage. She could manually open the big door from the inside, but it would make a lot of noise—she'd have to get there quietly, then get out as quickly as she could before she caught Daniel's attention.

She didn't know if he was armed, if he could shoot at her as she ran. But she had to get to safety. And she had to warn Heph. He'd be coming home any minute.

The map in her head was clear. She crept through the space as easily as her avatar would run through passages in *The Binding*, her bare feet silent on the concrete floor. Bless Heph for his organization and cleanliness. He'd left nice, wide aisles for his chair around the workspaces, and she didn't have to worry about clutter underfoot to give her away. She placed her hand on the lever that would manually open the garage door and cautiously pushed down, testing the movement.

It moved as if it had been oiled, which it probably had. She took a deep breath, rehearsing the action in her head. Shove down, push the door up and out, run like hell, and call for help as soon as she was safe.

Then she heard the voices.

Heph, calling her name.

Daniel Clark, responding.

Oh no. Oh no.

Aphrodite raced noiselessly through the garage, away from safety and back to the door that separated her from Heph.

On the way, she remembered something from her mental map, and scooped it up. Not much of a weapon, maybe, but it was better than nothing. And Heph had nothing.

Just her.

***

"You're Daniel, right? Aphrodite's not here," Heph said. It took an act of will not to look at the discarded cardigan. He could smell roses. Wherever Aphrodite was hiding, he hoped she'd stay there. Should he tell the man the police were on their way? Would that scare him off or anger him into violent action?

"Oh, I know," Daniel Clark said. "I came here to talk to you. You've got to stop pretending to date her."

"What?" Heph said.

"It's just confusing the situation," Daniel said, his voice patient.

He was a few steps away from Heph, the knife waving back and forth as he gestured. If he lunged, Heph might be able to dodge, and then tackle him. On the ground, Heph should have the advantage.

But that knife gave him extra reach as well as a weapon. If Heph couldn't get out of the way in time... He tried shifting his weight back, wincing as his hip yelled at him. Daniel watched him.

"Sorry, I'm confused too," he said. "Can you please explain?"

Daniel huffed a sigh. "Look, I understand why she has to pretend to be with those flashy people. The star-types." He grimaced. "That's just how Hollywood is. Her PR team is making her do it."

"Right," Heph said. He backed off a few halting steps. "I get how that could work."

Daniel followed, but the distance between them stayed the same. He didn't want to get close to Heph, either. "But you... You're just a guy.

That's dangerous. If she pretends to go out with you, anyone could think they have a chance with her."

"I see what you mean," Heph said. A few more steps, backing up past the living room wall and the mantelpiece.

"They don't, of course, because she loves me," Daniel said. He looked wistful, and the tip of the knife dipped lower. "When it's safe, we can be together. But until then, it's just not right. You can't make her go on TV and say that she loves you." His eyes narrowed, and he pointed the knife at Heph, the first direct threat. "That's not okay."

"I get it," Heph said. "That was the PR team, actually."

"Okay," Daniel said slowly, his eyes scanning Heph. "It was their idea?"

"Totally."

"I think you're lying to me," Daniel decided. "I'm not stupid, you know. I know the truth. I worked out the messages!"

"I understand," Heph said, but he didn't sound convincing, even to himself. "I'm sorry, man."

Daniel had stopped paying attention. He was staring at the cardigan on Heph's couch. "She's here," he said, and then his eyes, and the knife, swung back towards Heph. "You're keeping her here! Where is she? Let her out!" His voice rose to a shriek. "Let her out!"

The door to the garage burst open.

"I'm right here," Aphrodite said, outlined in the frame.

Even in the adrenaline-rush terror of the moment, Heph couldn't help noticing that she was nearly nude.

A tiny wisp of sea-green chiffon was wrapped around her hips. A matching bra did almost nothing to conceal her breasts. Her shimmering hair glowed in the late afternoon light, moving in soft waves as her hands reached up and out.

Towards Daniel.

He reached back, the knife falling from his loose hand, Heph entirely forgotten.

And the golden net Aphrodite had tossed hit him in the chest.

It was heavy, Heph knew. She must have thrown it with all her strength. And it gave him exactly the moment he needed.

Daniel grunted in pain.

Heph grabbed the pink ceramic candlestick off the mantelpiece and swung it as Daniel staggered back towards him. The candlestick shattered against the side of the man's head, and he crumpled.

Aphrodite, her lips skinned back from her teeth, catapulted forward and landed on top of the fallen man. One bare foot lashed out, shoving the fallen knife further away. Heph added his own weight to the pile, and peered at Daniel's face.

"He's not dead," he said, with relief. There was blood on the side of Daniel's head where the ceramic shards had cut, but his eyelids were fluttering, and there was air rushing in and out of his lips.

"I don't care," Aphrodite snarled. "He could have hurt you!"

"Or you," Heph said, and clutched her to him. It was kind of awkward, embracing your girlfriend while you were both sitting on top of the man you'd just rendered nearly unconscious, but it was also the only possible thing he could do. "This may be a dumb question, but why—"

"I was going to seduce you in your workshop," Aphrodite explained.

"Oh, okay," Heph said. "Yes, that definitely would have worked. Sorry about your candlestick."

"Well, it was one of my favorites," Aphrodite told him. Her eyes were moving anxiously over him. "But it died heroically. By the way, I love you."

"I love you too," Heph said. "Do you think these are the weirdest possible circumstances for us to say that to each other?"

"Aw, give it some time," Aphrodite said. "I bet we can do weirder."

***

"Were you wearing lingerie when the cops came in?" Persephone asked. She'd come straight to the police station from painting a mural, and was covered in specks of half-dried paint, which she'd managed to smear over Aphrodite during some prolonged hugging. Aphrodite didn't mind.

"No, Medea from Gorgon had arrived before then, and she tied Daniel up with those zip-tie things. So I went and got my clothes back on." She leaned against Persephone's comfortable body. "Thank you for coming."

"Of course! I left a message for Hecate too, but I think she had a date with her mysterious lover."

Hades came back from the reception desk, where he'd been speaking to the officer on duty. "He can't give me an ETA. Would it help if I got my lawyer down here too?"

"I don't know," Aphrodite said doubtfully. "My lawyer, Tyr, he went in to talk with Heph an hour ago. The police didn't *arrest* him. They said that they just wanted him to answer a few questions, and Heph said that in that case he'd like legal counsel, so I called—I've told you this already, haven't I?"

Persephone put her hand on Aphrodite's jiggling knee. "You can tell us again, if you need to," she said calmly. "You can tell us all night."

"Well, I hope it won't take all night," Aphrodite said. "They *did* arrest Daniel Clark though, so that's good."

She'd told them that too. And cried all over Persephone, and she couldn't stop moving around. Tyr had gotten her out of her interview really fast, so why was Heph's taking so long? These plastic chairs were uncomfortable, and the vending machine coffee she kept drinking was super gross.

Tyr came through the door that led to the back part of the station, and Aphrodite sprang to her feet.

"He's coming," Tyr told her. "No charges."

"Oh," Aphrodite said, and fell back into her chair. "Oh, *thank* you."

Tyr shrugged. "Clark was an intruder in your boyfriend's home, that knife had Clark's prints on it, and he has a history of stalking you, including a recent incident that was logged with police." He scowled. "I had a word with them about how long it took them to get there."

He was saying something else, but Aphrodite couldn't hear him, because behind him, Heph was maneuvering his chair through the tight doorway, coming to a halt in front of her.

"Hey," he said, and held out his hands.

"Hey," she said, and held on tight. She could feel the tremble in his hands. He was paler around the lips, and there was a careful tension in the way he was sitting. "Did you take your meds?"

He shook his head. "Wanted a clear head. I'll take them now. Uh, the police told me my place is a crime scene, and that I can't go back right now. Can I crash at yours?"

"Of course!" She led the way through the station door, which meant she had a very good view of Hecate hurrying towards them, wearing a black sequined tube top and slinky black pants. Behind her lingered a tall person with a pixie cut, who wasn't looking sure of their welcome.

"Oh, good, you're both out," Hecate said, the intent expression on her face giving way to relief. "Thank goodness." She bent over and caught her breath, then hugged Aphrodite hard.

Aphrodite caught the scent of peaches and a whiff of something alcoholic. "Did you interrupt your date for me?" she asked.

"Um, of course? I was going to use my scary lawyer powers."

"Do those work when you're drunk?"

"I'm tipsy at best. We'd barely got to the club before I got Persephone's message." She spotted Persephone, staring past both of them at the person loitering behind Hecate. "Uh-oh."

"Is that Terry?" Persephone demanded, grinning widely. "Is your date Terry?"

"Oooh," Aphrodite said, and looked at Hecate's date with new interest. Terry gave her a stiff little wave.

"Can we focus on Aphrodite and Heph right now?" Hecate said.

"Oh, our problems are all old news," Aphrodite said. "You dating Terry, that's new and juicy."

Persephone actually bounced. "This is so great! Get over here!" She waved at Terry, who smiled at her and sauntered closer.

"There's no *this*," Hecate muttered.

Heph's hand tugged on hers, and she leaned down.

"Who's Terry?" he whispered.

"An Olympus intern," Aphrodite whispered back. "They're friends with Persephone. And apparently friends-with-benefits with Hecate."

"But it's been weeks! Why wouldn't either of you tell me?" Persephone was saying. "Did you think I'd be mad? You two are great together."

"Because I knew you'd act like this! And we're not *together*," Hecate said.

Her voice was probably a little louder than she wanted. Aphrodite straightened in time to catch the look that flashed across Terry's face.

"Right," they said. "Well… It look like everything's fine here, so I think I'll be heading home. Bye, Hecate."

"I didn't mean you had to—" Hecate said, but she said it to Terry's back.

Persephone was looking chastened, and Hecate was looking pained and normally Aphrodite would want to do something about both of those things.

But not this time. Even more than she wanted to help her friends, she needed to get Heph back home, where he could take his pills and they could finally be safe together.

For real.

"Okay, thanks for coming, bye!" she said, and pulled out her phone. "Lina? Can you please bring the car around?"

"Paps," Heph said, on a resigned note.

Aphrodite spotted Derek across the street, and rolled her eyes at him. He gave her a thumbs up and crossed towards them.

"Got a friend at the station, Derek?" she asked, putting her phone back in her purse.

"I'm a friendly guy," Derek said. "What were you in for? Drunk and disorderly?"

"No comment."

"Any reason why Heph was spotted flying back separately from LA?"

"No comment."

"Aphrodite, you've got to give me something," he complained.

Aphrodite looked him up and down. "You know, I really don't," she said. "Come on, Heph. Let's go home."

***

Heph woke up with a naked woman drooling on his shoulder.

This was unusual enough that he had to adjust to the situation. He wasn't in his own home, but in a big, soft bed. The light filtering through the curtains was rosy, pink-tinted by the color of the drapes and the walls. His body, also naked, was half-covered in a light pink sheet, and a fuzzy blanket was crumpled over his feet.

It was the blanket that brought him back to himself. Last night, once the painkillers had kicked in, Aphrodite had stripped and laid herself on that blanket, demonstrating in some detail how and where she liked to be touched, while Heph added some helpful suggestions of his own. His spirit was willing, but the flesh wasn't having it. He'd enjoyed the observations, though, and had resolved to put them into action as soon as possible.

"Hm?" Aphrodite murmured against him. She coughed, sputtered on her own drool, coughed again, and lifted her head to stare at him with bleary eyes. For a second, she looked totally confused, and then awareness and joy both flooded over her face. "Heph!"

"Hello."

314

"This is really happening," she marveled, and moved to kiss him, then hesitated. "Hold on, I need to brush my teeth."

She rolled off the bed, and he heard water running and the sounds of vigorous scrubbing. He tested his own breath with some huffing into a cupped hand, and then, satisfied, rolled over to find the other thing Aphrodite had showed him last night. When she came back to bed, all minty fresh, he was casually slicking up the pink silicon dildo with lube.

Aphrodite's eyes narrowed with intent. "Well, hey there," she said.

"I was just thinking," Heph said. "If you didn't mind."

She pretended to think about it. "I believe I can fit it into my busy schedule," she said, and crawled up the bed. She sprawled back onto her elbows, just within reach, and crooked one knee up. "But I might need to make a few adjustments."

"I'd be happy to help with that," Heph said, and gently opened her folds with his lube-slick fingers. Aphrodite sighed as he stroked around her clit in tightening circles, exactly the way she'd showed him last night.

"Please, Heph," she said.

"Please what?"

"Put it in me. Please."

"Are you ready?" he asked, and she made a frustrated whine in the back of her throat he took as a no, so he slid a couple of fingers inside and crooked them, pressing up.

"Oh," Aphrodite said, her eyes opening wide. "Yup. There we go."

He pressed a little more firmly, feeling her inner walls contract and relax around his fingers. When his fingers could move easily, he pulled his hand free, and before she could complain, eased the dildo in.

Aphrodite whimpered, her eyes locked on his as he pushed it in, inch by slow inch. "More," she whispered.

"I've got you," he said. "You just take your time, baby."

His own cock was throbbing, and he moved the dildo the way he wanted to move, firm thrusts and steadily increasing rhythm, until Aphrodite took matters into her own hands and reached for her clit. He pressed the dildo inside and held it while she brought herself to orgasm, shaking violently. Her eyes glazed over, and she took a few deep breaths before she laughed, and rolled up onto her knees, bouncing the mattress a little underneath them.

"How's your hip?" she asked.

"Not ready for vigorous activity," he admitted, with considerable regret.

"Aw, poor man," Aphrodite said, her voice sweet. "Why don't you lie back and let me take care of it?" She knelt beside him, her focus on his cock making her intentions very clear.

Heph lay back among the pillows and watched her gather up her hair in a loose fist at the back of her head. "You hold this for me," she instructed, replacing her hand with his. "And I'll concentrate on making you feel better." She looked at him sternly. "And don't you dare move your hips." Then she dipped down to take him in her mouth, her tongue swirling greedily around the head of his cock.

Afterwards, when the endorphins from the orgasm had cleared out a lot of the residual ache and his painkillers had done the rest, and Aphrodite had brushed her teeth for the second time, she snuggled into him. "Are you sure you want to be my boyfriend?" she asked. "I can be very needy and demanding."

"Demand away," Heph said, and kissed the tip of her nose. "Are you sure you want to be my girlfriend? It's hard to take me places, and I'm no good at talking to the press."

"You don't need to," Aphrodite said. "Actually, I'm going to do a lot less talking to the press myself. Thea says I am now famous enough to be private. Which means I'm more in demand when I *do* choose to talk."

"That's a thing?" Heph asked. "Huh. I guess that's a thing."

She nodded, and wriggled even closer. "So," she said. "Am I still invited to your sister's wedding?"

***

"Do I look okay?" Heph muttered.

Aphrodite adjusted his bow-tie, kissed his cheek, and wiped her lipstick smudge off. "You look amazing."

He smiled at her, then went back to sorting through his note cards. "I'm going to screw this up."

Aphrodite shrugged. "Well, if you do, everyone here loves you, so it won't matter."

"You're supposed to say that I'll be incredible," Heph complained. "World's most spectacular best man speech, gold medal, fame and fortune." He looked at her. "What if I claim a headache and put you in as my replacement? You'd do a much better job, and you know the speech better than I do."

This was probably true. Heph had been rewriting and practicing his speech over the last few days, and Aphrodite had ended up memorizing several versions of it. The problem was that Heph talking about true love and joyful union was a total turn on, and they ended most of the practice sessions in bed. They'd been making up for all the lost time they'd squandered on that stupid contract.

They also had to get a lot of loving in, because they were both going to be very busy, very soon. Heph was starting his Hesperides contract on Monday, and Aphrodite had a lot of press appearances lined up—since *A Light in Dark Places* was looking more and more like a sleeper hit, the studio had belatedly decided to put more effort into promoting it, and the Gaia interview had put Aphrodite at the top of their bankable talent list.

And after *that* she had a super secret voice acting gig lined up with Cyclone, who were absolutely delighted that supermodel Aphrodite Urania was so good at their game. Their next patch was going to include an apprentice to the Architect, the Ascendant, who would guide players to the secrets behind *The Binding*.

She would guide them with Aphrodite's voice.

Narnie dropped into the chair beside her, fanning herself with the menu. "How're you holding up?" she asked, and then, not waiting for the answer: "So, Mellie and I were talking. Since we're not allowed to bug Heph about his career and love life anymore, are we allowed to bug you?"

"I mean, sure, but both of those are going great," Aphrodite said. "I don't think you'll have much to work with."

"Well, what are you bad at?" Narnie said, and then her dark skin got even darker. "Oh shit. I didn't mean—"

Aphrodite laughed. "It's okay, Narnie. Thea's finding me a tutor who specializes in adult literacy learning." Now that the secret was out, there was no reason not to try. She'd probably never be an especially fluent reader, but maybe she could work up to texting. It would be kind of nice to able to join a group chat.

But Narnie so obviously wanted to include her in the family circle, and she did know a lot of things Aphrodite didn't. She considered it. "Can you teach me how to cook?"

Heph looked up from his notecards, his face alarmed.

"*Yes*," Narnie said. "*Absolutely.* I'll call you next week." She bounced to her feet and hustled away.

"I don't know if your kitchen will survive Narnie," Heph said. "Do you even own a frying pan?"

"Hush, you," Aphrodite said, poking him. "Or I won't let you eat any of the results."

He caught her hand and kissed it. Well, it was definitely the right place for PDA. At the center of the main table, Sara-Beth and Aoide were alternating kisses with loving stares into each other's eyes, as deliriously happy as they were overwhelmed by the heightened emotions of the day. Heph's moms were dancing, wrapped in each other's arms, and even Sara-Beth's WASP-y parents had unbent enough to hold hands.

None of them were doing it for an audience, real or imagined. It was for themselves and each other. Aphrodite thought about that for a second, as the song finished and the mistress of ceremonies announced that it was time for the speeches.

"Okay," Heph said, breathing deep. "Here we go."

"Remember," Aphrodite said. "If you get scared, just imagine everyone in their underwear."

"My entire family is here," Heph pointed out.

"Good point. Imagine me in my underwear."

Heph's eyes locked on hers, and she felt the heat tingle under her skin. "That's definitely inspiring," he rumbled. "Luckily, I don't have to imagine."

He released his wheelchair brake and made his way up to the main stage, where the MC handed him the microphone.

"Hi," he said. "I'm Heph Smith, Aoide's brother."

Aphrodite whooped a cheer, prompting laughter and scattered applause.

"Love," Heph said, without looking at his cards. "It's weird, and mysterious, and often inexplicable." His eyes caught Aphrodite's. "But it's real. And these two have found it."

Aphrodite smiled.

So had they.

Hera Takes Charge

D ear Ms Rheczack,

Thank you for informing the Olympus Publishing, Inc. Human Resources department of your name change from Hera Kronion to Hera Rheczack.

We appreciate the notification, and will make sure that all future correspondence is correctly named, whether in your role as stockholder, or in any other role you may take up at Olympus Publishing.

~~Congrats on dumping Zeus!~~
~~We're all rooting for you to be CEO.~~
~~I hear the other brother is free?~~

I would like to take this opportunity to personally wish you the best of luck in your future endeavors.

Yours sincerely,
Mark Hermes
Head of Human Resources

Hera has divorced Zeus for the second and final time. Now she has her eyes on the prize; taking over from him as CEO of Olympus Publishing.

Don, Zeus's brother, has his eye on Hera. After twenty years of yearning, is love finally in the plan?

Buy *Hera Takes Charge*!

About the Author

Kate Healey lives in New Zealand and writes spicy contemporary rom-coms with a mythic twist. Karen Healey, who looks suspiciously similar, lives in New Zealand and writes fantasy romance, science fiction and young adult fiction. They both drink a lot of coffee.

Find more about Karen at http://karenhealey.com and sign up for her newsletter at http://thathealeygirl.com . You'll get the first news on new books, weird research rabbitholes, and occasional freebies!

Also by Kate Healey

Olympus Inc. Series:

Penelope Pops the Question (a newsletter freebie, available when you sign up at http://thathealeygirl.com!)

Persephone in Bloom

Aphrodite Unbound

Hera Takes Charge

Ask Cassandra

As Karen Healey:

Movie Magic Series:

"Jingle Spells" (a newsletter freebie, available when you sign up at http://thathealeygirl.com)

Bespoke & Bespelled

Savory & Supernatural

The Hidden Histories Series (with Robyn Fleming):

The Empress of Timbra

The Spymaster's Apprentice

Young Adult:

Guardian of the Dead

The Shattering

When We Wake

While We Run

Acknowledgements

My thanks, as always, to my most excellent BFF and editor Robyn Fleming, and to Alison Cooley for her stunning cover work. I am indebted to Shawn O'Hara for inventing *The Binding*, and to Jameson York for his IT support. Rue Dickey was my sensitivity reader for Heph, and his comments were both encouraging and insightful – all remaining errors or missteps are mine.

I'm so grateful for the support of my lovely colleagues in Romancelandia, Stephanie Burgis, Tansy Rayner Roberts, Courtney Clark Michaels and A.J. Lancaster, who are all wonderful writers and even better people. Thank you to the friends and family members who cheered me on, bought me desserts, asked me if maybe I needed a break, and, in the case of my mother, reorganized my kitchen while I finished the manuscript. Special, special thank yous to Kristen, who loves Aphrodite as much as I do.

This book is dedicated to my sister, Gina Healey. Arohanui.